'A thrilling chase-cum-travelogue ... depicted Antarctic wonderland ... an in a short punchy novel'

'It is or ... ate ... nov ... – and ... 's best books' SFX

'A chase thriller set in late 21st-century Antarctica that combines elements of Jack London, J.G. Ballard and William Gibson. A significant contribution to writing about the anthropocene'   *Economist*

'McAuley is a nature poet of imaginary lands'   *Locus*

'A haunting and engaging piece of science fiction that is every bit as good a piece of writing as the best literary fiction'
Popular Science

'Cli-fi transcendent. An exquisite human story set on an undiscovered continent of our near future. *Austral* may be McAuley's best yet. And the best near-future novel yet written. Paul McAuley has quickened science fiction. The future has changed'   Stephen Baxter,
author of *The Massacre of Mankind*

'The excitement of a new country appearing right here on Earth, a real possibility that is quite fascinating in itself, is doubled down here by way of a thrilling kidnap-and-rescue plot that ranges across this beautiful new landscape, showing how we will soon be not only terraforming Earth, but finding new ways to take care of each other. It's a vivid example of science fiction at its best'   Kim Stanley Robinson,
author of *Red Mars*

'Oh boy, it's a good one. A cracking setup; great writing; great pacing; a genuinely fresh narrative voice, and for once

– hooray! – a male author writing a complex, first-person female narrator who is neither a broflake's wet-dream, nor a wooden stereotype. Austral is big, strong, powerful, and yet with real vulnerabilities; a flawed and relatable heroine with agency, feelings and spirit. And to cap it all, Austral is fat - genetically edited to be fat in a way that enhances her strength and endurance, and in the context of her race, is only ever mentioned as a positive. Hallelujah. It can be done'

Joanne Harris,
author of *The Gospel of Loki*

'Bleakly beautiful, *Austral* is both a finely-honed character study and a powerful evocation of landscape and change, delivered with icy clarity. This is the kind of fiction we will need as the Anthropocene takes hold'

Alastair Reynolds,
author of *Revelation Space*

'A beautifully worked tale of post-environment collapse Antarctica, and a genetically-tweaked cold-adapted woman's attempt to escape. As ever McAuley writes superbly: his prose is always elegant without being showy, expressive and clear without ever being pedestrian. And he's capable of gorgeous descriptive vividness. Plus: rounded characterisation and a tremendous command of tension and pace . . . There's some-thing deceptively simple about *Austral*: you read it quickly, and it lives in your head for a long time after'

Adam Roberts,
author of *The Real-Town Murders*

'*Austral* offers a damning perspective on the society that renders her and other huskies outcasts, people to be feared and scorned. She's resourceful with a wry sense of humour and dominated by a will to liberate herself from the society that spurns her'
SciFi Now

Also by Paul McAuley from Gollancz:

400 Billion Stars
Cowboy Angels
Eternal Light
Fairyland
Pasquale's Angel
Red Dust
The Quiet War
Gardens of the Sun
In the Mouth of the Whale
Evening's Empires
Something Coming Through
Into Everywhere

AUSTRAL

PAUL McAULEY

This edition first published in Great Britain in 2018 by Gollancz

First published in Great Britain in 2017 by Gollancz
an imprint of the Orion Publishing Group Ltd
Carmelite House, 50 Victoria Embankment
London EC4Y 0DZ

An Hachette UK Company

3 5 7 9 10 8 6 4

A CIP catalogue record for this book is
available from the British Library.

ISBN 978 1 473 21732 4

Printed and bound by Clays Ltd, Elcograf S.p.A.

www.unlikelyworld.co.uk
www.gollancz.co.uk

To Georgina McAuley
1966–2017

How many miseries our father caused!
And is there one of them that does not fall
On us while yet we live?

Sophocles, Antigone

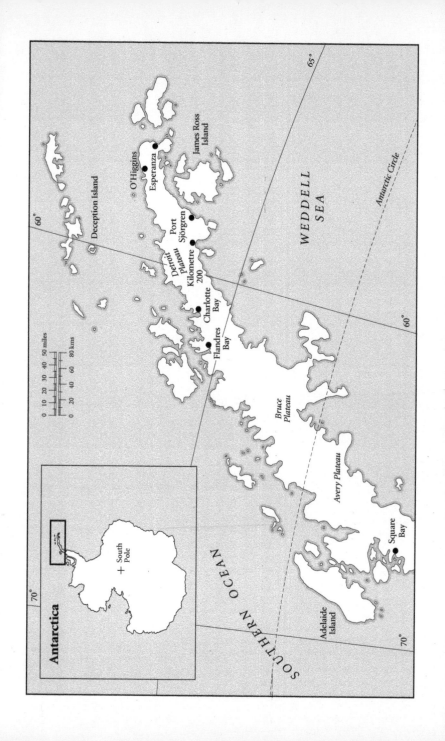

1

My birth was a political act. Conceived in a laboratory dish by direct injection of a sperm into an egg, I was customised by a suite of targeted genes, grown inside a smart little chamber to a ball of about a hundred cells, and on the fifth day transferred to my mother's uterus. I drew my first breath among the snows of the south, spent much of my childhood in exile on a volcanic island and most of the rest working in the farm stacks of a state orphanage. I've been a convict, a corrections officer and consort to a criminal, I committed the so-called kidnapping of the century, but first and foremost I'm a husky. An edited person. Something more than human, according to Mama and the other free ecopoets. A victim of discrimination and intersectional inequality, according to do-gooders trying to make excuses on my behalf. A remorseless monster driven by greed and an unreasoning lust for revenge, according to the news feeds which sucked my story to the bare marrow.

Truth is, the truth is way more complicated than the public record. I don't mean to justify what I did. I broke plenty of laws and made some questionable choices, no doubt about that. But I wasn't any kind of criminal mastermind and all I ever wanted was to claim a small portion of what was rightfully mine – just enough to pay for passage to my idea of heaven. The rest is blast and mudslinging by hypocrites and holy rollers who've never, ever had to question who they are or wonder about the shape of their lives, how they wound up in a dead end so early.

So this is my own account of what happened and why, as true as I can tell it. It's your story, too. The story of how you came to be. How I tried to save you. And it's the story of our family and the story of the peninsula, wound around each other like the rose and the briar in Kamilah Toomy's fairy tale. As for what started all the fuss – frankly? It was an accident. Two lives crossing at the wrong moment. I didn't plan on getting involved in kidnap and political scandal. At the time, I was trying to escape from a completely different kind of trouble.

This was at Kilometre 200, one of the work camps on the Trans-Antarctica Railway, the big post-independence project to link the cities at the northern end of the peninsula with settlements along the east coast and the mines in the Eternity Range and the Pensacola Mountains. The camp's long gone, but if you care to look it up you'll find it was south of Shortcut Col, close to the first of the three bowstring bridges that span the delta of the Eliason River. That's where I was working, one of the corrections officers, when Alberto Toomy invited himself to the official opening of those bridges and my life went all to smash.

First I heard about that, I was playing a game of basketball with my home girls. Two on two on a half-court marked out in chalk in a corner of the parking lot behind the staff quarters, the hoop and backboard bolted to the pole of a floodlight. Late April, the autumnal equinox a month past. Seven in the evening and already dark. A small snowfall blowing in from the sea, slanting through the floodlight's glare and beginning to dust the asphalt. Drones were carving random loops in the black air above the cons' barracks, hounds were dreaming machine dreams of old chases and take-downs in their lightless kennels, and off in the distance a train howled long and lonesome as it hauled construction materials towards the railhead at Kilometre 260, where some of our cons had already gone, where all of us in the camp would be moving after the engineering works around the bridges had been signed off.

We'd just finished our shift, another day driving our strings to complete pretty-work ahead of the ribbon-cutting ceremony, and were blowing off steam before dinner. Paz and me v. Lola and Sage. The four of us dressed in shorts, tank-tops and sneakers, making a lot of noise. The cold didn't bother us. We were made for the cold. After warming up with jump shots before getting down to it, first to score twenty-one, no referee to call out fouls, we were sweating like racehorses.

Paz noticed that I was hanging back instead of barging in like I usually did, all shoulder checks and sharp elbows. In a brief time-out, while Sage trotted off to retrieve the ball from a far corner of the parking lot, she asked me if I was OK.

'Never better,' I said.

'Really?'

'Really.'

'Because you're looking kind of pinched.'

Paz Sandoval was thirty-four, almost exactly ten years older than me. Smart, strong, doggedly independent. She spent two hours each and every day pressing iron in the gym, took exactly zero shit from anyone. A few days before, a newb CO had made a remark to his newb pals as we'd brushed past them on the way to the canteen. Some dumb joke about mistaking us for men. Nothing we hadn't heard a hundred times before. If it wasn't that, it was our size, or whether our mothers had been seals or walruses. Not to mention the name-calling. Chanks. Buffarillos. Whelephants. Yetis. Shit I'd been hearing just about all my life. Yetis? It isn't as if we have a pelt, like bears do. Paz didn't have any hair at all. Part of her bodybuilding thing, like the protein shakes she drank at breakfast. She shaved her scalp every morning, too, oiled it so it shone dark as mahogany. Anyway, she grabbed that newb by the front of his shirt and pinned him against the wall and held him there, the soles of his polished black boots kicking a metre off the ground, until he apologised. You could straighten out newbs if you caught them early, she told us afterwards, but if you let them get away with any kind of shit they'd assume you'd given them permission to be assholes for the rest of their life.

It was Paz who'd brought the four of us together in our first days at Kilometre 200, back when we were living in trailers while the cons finished building the camp. The only husky COs on the roster, we'd bonded over a bottle of vodka flavoured with chilli and fish oil, which Paz claimed was the customary drink of the husky nation. When Sage said that she'd never heard of it before, Paz told her that we were the newest kids on the block, we made up our traditions as we went along. She flaunted her difference, said that mundanes mistrusted us because they were afraid, and they had plenty to be afraid about. We were made for the south, could survive where they couldn't, and one day we'd take it from them. Meanwhile, she said, we had to look out for each other because no one else would, and we all swore an oath she worked up on the spot, and sealed it with a toast.

The point being, I looked up to Paz, I knew she'd always have my back, but lately I'd been keeping secrets from her, and from Sage and Lola too. Which was why, when she said I was looking kind of pinched, I felt a freezing caution, wondering if she had guessed what I was incubating, or knew about Keever's plans.

I told her that something I'd eaten had disagreed with me, which was what I'd told my sergeant after she'd heard me barfing in the john the day before, and she said that she wasn't surprised, what with the health food kick I'd been on lately.

'Seaweed crackers and boiled rice might do for mundanes, kiddo, but people like us need real fuel.'

'I reckon Stral's on a diet,' Lola said. She was a big blonde girl with a healthy glow in her cheeks, sharp blue eyes, and a jones for every kind of gossip and rumour. 'Reckon her boyfriend's been complaining that she's too heavy for him.'

After I'd hooked up with Keever Bishop, Paz had told me that I was a damn fool, not because he was a con and I was a CO, that wasn't uncommon in the camps, but because of who he was and what he could do. She was right to be concerned, but at the time I was too flattered and excited by Keever's attention to see that. Lola, though, was just plain jealous, and never missed a chance to let me know.

'He likes me just the way I am,' I told her. 'Likes something to hold on to. You though, he'd need a saddle.'

'And you know I'd give him the ride of his life,' Lola said. 'But don't worry, as far as him and me are concerned, it's strictly business.'

It was, too, as I'd soon find out. But I shouldn't get ahead of the story.

4

'Look at you two,' Paz said. 'Standing up to each other like bulldogs in the yard, waiting to see who'll back down first.'

'Save that shit for after the game,' Sage said, bouncing the ball as she walked back to us. 'Are we playing or are we playing?'

Paz took the ball out, immediately passed it to me, and Lola was waving her hands in my face, ragging me with the trash talk she was so good at. I faked left and went right, and the space in front of the hoop was clear. I took one bounce and three strides and lofted the ball. I remember it clearly because of what came after. That lovely moment when you're in the air and the ball is rising towards the hoop. When everything is suspended. When anything is possible.

My feet slapped asphalt, the ball rattled the rim and bounced back, and Sage, small and quick and dark, stole it for two easy points. We were setting up again, Paz telling me she was going to whiz up one of her special shakes to give me back my edge, when Vincente Opazo walked up out of the shadows and said that I was wanted over at the block.

'You can wait one minute,' Lola said, 'while we take two more points and the game.'

'He wants a word,' Vincente said, looking at me.

Paz walked up to him, bouncing the ball slowly and deliberately. 'Are you trying to give us orders, Vincente?'

'Hey, don't shoot the messenger,' Vincente said. He was your basic shlubby mundane, blue down jacket zipped tight against the cold, fists balled in his pockets, his watch cap pulled over his ears. Paz overtopped him by thirty centimetres and outclassed him in every way.

'If you were anything like a real CO,' she said, still bouncing the ball, 'you'd be policing a string instead of running errands for King Con.'

Vincente did his best to ignore that, telling me, 'He said right away.'

'I better go,' I said.

'You aren't even going to ask why?' Lola said.

'Vincente won't know. He's just an errand boy,' Paz said, and caught the ball on the rebound and threw it over her shoulder.

It smacked into the backboard with a sound like a pistol shot. 'You want to run along, Stral, it's your call.'

'I guess it is,' I said, and told Lola and Sage that I'd beat their asses tomorrow.

As we headed across the parking lot towards the south gate, Vincente swore he didn't know what was up or why I was wanted, only that it was urgent. 'It's probably nothing. You know how Keever is.'

'Better than you.'

I wanted to believe that this wasn't anything – after all, this was hardly the first time Keever had sent someone to collect me. But I was already strung tight, what with the little secret I was incubating and there being just four days to go before everything kicked off, and this imperial summons had cranked up my anxiety by several notches. I hadn't seen Keever for a couple of days, ever since one of his lawyers turned up on the wrong side of midnight and he'd told me to get dressed and leave so he could have a private one-on-one with her, and I was certain that he wanted more than just a word with me, was afraid that he'd found out about my secret. That he'd found out about you.

Like every other con at that hour Keever was locked down in his block, but he wasn't in one of the dorms with the chumps, carnals and choros, the rows of bunk beds and oppressive heat and glaring lights, the restless clamour and rank odour, that prison smell you can never get used to. No, Keever had commandeered the infirmary cell of Block #3 for his own personal use, and that was where Vincente Opazo took me, the two of us passing through the gate in the perimeter wire and the block's sally port without any of the guards questioning where I was going or why I was out of uniform. And before we get any further, yes, Keever is Keever Bishop. Your father. I'll get to how we met soon enough. Meanwhile, picture him sitting on his bed (a steel-framed cot like the one I had in my room in the staff quarters, no bunk for him), bare-chested in gym shorts, talking with his numbers man, Mike Mike.

Keever Bishop. Mr Snow. White hair cropped in a flat-top, narrow sideburns angling along his jaw line. Skin so pale it had

6

a blue tint, no tattoos or mods, the zipper of a scar low on his belly where someone had shanked him ten years ago, back when he was still hustling on the street. He'd never had it fixed. Flaunted it like a trophy. Otherwise, he was fastidious about his appearance. He had to wear jeans and a denim shirt like the rest of the cons, but his gear was fresh each and every day, starched and ironed, and his work boots were spit-shined. His room was painted white, walls and floor and ceiling, and he kept it obsessively neat. He made his own bed, too. Hospital corners. I admired that stark simplicity, that precision. The discipline of it. And I liked to listen to him talk about his apartment – the one the government had tried to confiscate, claiming that he'd bought it with the proceeds of criminal activities, a move that had failed because, like the rest of his assets, it was owned by an offshore trust. It was fifty floors up in one of the towers in the best part of Esperanza, with views across the city to the Antarctic Sound. Five bedrooms, a hangar-sized living room with a media pit and live walls, tropical plants in a balcony greenhouse, the whole bit. I'd decided that when I got my own apartment in the Wheel I would have a greenhouse too, even though New Zealand was so lush plants grew anywhere and everywhere.

I didn't love Keever Bishop. Let's be clear about that. He was using me and I was using him. No, love didn't come into it, but I definitely admired and respected him. He knew what he wanted and knew what he had to do to get it, and he was only slightly inconvenienced by being in jail. He had a sinecure in the maintenance depot, off the line and out of the weather, keeping tabs on his various interests on the outside and running his muling business – most of the drugs, vapes, patches, candy, fones, porn and what else went through him. He kept the COs sweet with kickbacks, slipped them a little extra on their kids' birthdays, and didn't complain whenever the camp commandant, in a feeble attempt to assert her authority, ordered them to turn over his room.

'I can do more business while I'm in here than if I was on the outside,' Keever told me more than once. 'There aren't any distractions, I don't have to deal with every little thing, I can concentrate on taking it to the next level. It isn't about making money any more. It's about figuring out how to best use the money I already have.'

He didn't need to dismiss Vincente – the man had already made himself scarce – and he didn't ask me to sit down either. Leaning back on the bed and giving me a sleepy-eyed stare, saying, 'Looking good in that kit, Austral. Nice glow on you.'

He always called me by my full name. Never Stral, like most everyone else.

'I was playing basketball,' I said, like he didn't already know. I was numb with anticipation. Keever was smiling, though as usual you had to look hard to be sure, and it could have meant anything.

He said, 'I have some news that might be of interest.'

I realised with a stab of relief was that this wasn't about you, then wondered if it might be something to do with that lawyer who'd arrived in the middle of the night, wondered if Keever had somehow lodged another appeal, even though every avenue for appeal had been exhausted. Or maybe something had gone wrong with his plans, which meant that he wouldn't be leaving any time soon, I'd have to confess before I started showing . . .

'What it is,' Keever said, 'there's going to be a last-minute guest at the ribbon-cutting ceremony. Honourable Deputy Alberto Toomy. I see you didn't know.'

'This is the first I've heard,' I said.

It was also, you can bet, just about the last thing I'd expected. I was wondering if this was some kind of trick, because why would Alberto Toomy want to come all the way out here to take part in what was basically an exercise in government propaganda?

'I thought you might be keeping track of the man,' Keever said. 'Given he's your rich uncle and all.'

'Tell me this isn't one of your weird jokes,' I said, wishing that I'd never told Keever my family history. How one of the honourable deputies in the opposition party happened to be the half-brother of my father, so on.

'It came down the wire an hour ago,' Keever said. 'Honourable Deputy Toomy claims that he has a right to attend, what with him being the Shadow Minister of Justice, and the railway being a project started by his party. Not to mention that his company supplies construction droids and skilled labour. He also claims that the prison service tried to stop him coming. Which isn't true, but it makes a good story. And he wants a tour of the camp. Says that he wants to make sure the state is doing its best to rehabilitate cons through tough love and hard labour.'

'Man's a righteous crusader,' Mike Mike said.

He was a big soft-spoken man with a shaved head and a neat goatee, serving an L note for a double homicide. He managed Keever's business inside the wire, kept every debit and credit locked inside his head, dealt with those who couldn't pay what they owed. I liked him, liked to think that he liked me. We had something in common, anyhow. We both had to keep Keever happy at all times.

'What it comes down to, Alberto wants to remind the world he exists,' Keever said. 'Talking the kind of talk about crime and punishment supporters of his party like to hear. Telling them that the present government is too soft, the work camps are more like holiday resorts, how he'll toughen things up after National Unity wins the next election. The commandant's office is in an uproar, trying to figure out how to deal with it. They can't stop the Honourable Deputy coming, and they know he's out to make trouble. They know he'll be digging around for dirt he can use to cook up a scandal. And that if he doesn't find any he'll just make something up.'

Keever liked to give these little lectures, liked to prove that he knew more about any given topic than anyone else. It was a vital part of his business, one of the ways he overmastered people. Forget alpha male, he'd say. I'm the apex predator. I'm the one gets to suck the marrow from the bones of everyone else.

'Man wants to stir up a serious political shitstorm,' Mike Mike said.

'Although that isn't the only reason he's coming here,' Keever told me. 'It isn't even the real reason. Care to take a guess at what that might be?'

Still trying to process the news, I told him I couldn't even begin.

'The Honourable Deputy and me have some business needs settling,' he said. 'But the trouble he'll cause just by coming here will be useful too.'

'Man's a wild card,' Mike Mike said.

'One that'll divert attention away from me, as long as I play it right,' Keever said. 'And I think you can help me with that, Austral. You claim he's your uncle.'

'My half-uncle. Strictly speaking.'

'And as I recall the two of you have never met.'

That derailed me for a second. As usual, Keever was two steps ahead.

'He's never troubled me,' I said. 'And I've never troubled him. Never needed nor wanted to.'

'And he hasn't reached out to you. Made contact ahead of this visit he's planning.'

'Like I said, this is the first I've heard.'

I could see what was coming, and I knew there wasn't a thing I could do about it.

'That's what I thought. Because if he knew you were working here, you can bet his people would have been all over it. And you can bet I would have heard about something like that. But I haven't, not a peep. So what I'm thinking, his coming here, it's a stroke of luck too good to be true,' Keever said, and patted the bed beside him. 'Sit down. Let me tell you how we're going to make use of it.'

2

I first met Keever Bishop back in Star City, a cluster of broke-down apartment blocks on the west side of Esperanza, home to most of the peninsula's husky community and a lively mix of welfare clients, refugees and former jailbirds. I moved there at age eighteen. Officially an adult, I'd been released from the orphanage and given a fone, a one-room efficiency and a work placement. For the first time in my life I was all on my own, and I thought it was wonderful. I was no longer living in a dorm, was no longer forced to abide by a million stupid rules and pay for my keep by working in farm stacks, could go anywhere I wanted whenever I wanted. An old friend of my grandmother's, Alicia Whangapirita, reached out and offered me a job in some stinky fish-processing plant on the west coast, but I blew her off. I was done with all that business. I believed that I could find my own path in the world.

The work placement was supervisor of an assembly line in a manufactory that turned out pumps and centrifugal filters for greenhouse aquaponics. Eight hours a day in a windowless shed flooded with the dull red light droids found useful for some reason, noise-cancelling headphones clamped over my ears to muffle the industrial screech and clang, ticking off a quota of random quality checks. It was epically dull, no company but the droids, no hope of promotion. I quit after a month and kind of fell into a life of crime.

I'd taken to hanging out in a bar in a corner of my block, and that's where I met Bryan Williams and was introduced to the pickpocketing business. Bryan was a skinny white guy in his early forties, old as dirt as far as I was concerned, and yeah, I know, an obvious father figure. He was kind of nervy when he wasn't working, permanently sucking on a vape, fiddling with the elephant-seal-hair bracelet he wore for good luck, knuckle-rolling an ancient dollar coin, but when he was on the job he was awesomely smooth, enviably cool. A veritable Zen master of what he called the ancient art.

He'd been using another husky girl as a stall, but she'd gotten herself pregnant and I took her place. We sometimes trolled for marks in crowds outside sporting events or concerts, but did most of our work in the underground passages, access points and shopping arcades of CORE, the city under the city. I'd barge into a mark and Bryan would steady them and do his thing, or I'd bellow out that someone had snatched my shit, this big young husky in distress getting everyone's attention, people patting their pockets to check their valuables, Bryan picking a couple of likely targets and moving in. He taught me how to stall someone by asking for directions while he did a walk-by touch to check the goods, how to bump and lift with or without the concealed hand, how to deal with a mark who felt the dip and started squealing. Nighttimes when pickings were slim we'd cruise for sleepers on the subway, snatch their stuff, rip their credit with a bootleg reader, and jump the capsule just before it moved off.

It wasn't ever going to make us rich, but it was steady work and Bryan was good at it. He knew Keever Bishop slightly, and one time we had a drink with him in the bar, although when I told him about it several years later in Kilometre 200 Keever claimed that he didn't remember. He didn't recall taking my hand and giving me a palm reading either, a corny pick-up trick he barely needed to use given his reputation. He said that Bryan and me were the classic odd couple, very sweet to see, and although ours was basically a business relationship, we'd hardly ever slept together. Bryan didn't contradict him and neither did I. I was hypnotised by his tickling touch and his cool unblinking gaze, trying to pretend that I wasn't impressed and failing completely.

Keever had been born and raised in Star City, came back every so often to check on the street trade he still had a piece of, hang out at the bar and a couple of other places he owned, and do good works – dashing credit to people in need, sorting out petty disputes, subsidising a community centre, cleaning up the local park, organising repairs the city wouldn't pay for, so on. Everyone in the bar knew him and knew his history, knew who he'd hurt or buried to get to where he was, and no one ever questioned his right to do as he pleased. He was like a leopard seal lazing in a penguin rookery. Lordly, dangerous, utterly at ease. After toying with Bryan and me for a couple of minutes he was suddenly up and off, glad-handing some old rogue who'd just come in, and Bryan took a long shuddering draw on his vape stick and told me to be careful, the man had a thing for huskies.

We'd had been working together for about a year by then, and Bryan had just gotten into snap, this military nano that tweaked your head, sharpened your reactions. He said that it soothed his nerves and honed his edge, but pretty soon he needed it just to maintain, and most everything he stole was funding his habit. That old sad story. He started to get careless, his carelessness got us arrested, and we both drew hard time because it was an election year and the government was trying to appease voters by acting tough on crime.

I was given six months because it was my first offence, Bryan copped three years and change. When I came out, the Progressive Democrat Union had ousted the National Unity Party, which had run the peninsula since before I was born. There was a lot of talk about new beginnings and letting in sunlight, a fresh chapter in history, so on, but as far as huskies were concerned it was meet the new boss, same as the old boss. We were still being squeezed by travel restrictions and selective labour laws, hassled by police stops and the insults and assaults of the ignorant and prejudiced, were still second-class citizens. Barely human.

Jail had been a shock, a reversion to barracks life and compulsory work, this time in a fish farm, but I buckled down and kept a low profile, and when I was released a friendly CO suggested that I should apply for work in the prison service. There was a training programme for former prisoners, wards of the state and others who had experience of the wrong side of the justice system, and a shortage of husky applicants. Bulling cons was one of the few jobs we were actually encouraged to do, mainly because our kind were over-represented in the prison population.

I soon discovered that ex-con COs were paid half the wages of their straight counterparts and given the worst assignments, but I didn't much care. It was steady work, and I was saving as much of my pay as I could because I wanted to escape the peninsula and find a place where people like me were treated like actual human beings.

By the time Bryan was paroled I was supervising cons in the farm stacks of a work camp on the outskirts of O'Higgins. I saw him just once, found that he was already back on the job and back on the shit. 'Just a little now and then, to keep me sharp,' he said, but I knew that there was no hope for him. He was stabbed to death during some stupid argument with a dealer a couple of months later, about the time I was sent south to Kilometre 200.

This was at the beginning of September, towards the end of winter. Temperatures never much above minus ten degrees Celsius, snowstorms, blank days of sea fret or low cloud, but whenever the weather cleared the views were tremendous. Kilometre 200 was at the edge of a basin that had once been the confluence of three glaciers, and after the ice retreated ecopoets planted forests along the courses of meltwater rivers running towards the Larsen Inlet. There was a range of snow-clad mountain peaks to the north. A curve of cold blue sea to the south and west. It was as clean and wild and empty as the dreams of the first days of settlement, when the peninsula's potential hadn't yet been wrecked by compromise and greed. The kind of country Mama and I had hiked across after our escape.

The camp was still being built when I arrived. My first job was supervising cons stringing wire around the perimeter of their prefab barracks. Contractors handled the trains, track-laying machines, construction droids, industrial printers, so on. Everything else – unloading and distribution of construction material, labour in a quarry and gravel plant at the foot of Holt Nunatak, landscaping the long embankment that curved towards the three bridges over the river delta – was done by convict labour. A good chunk of the peninsula's population was in prison and it went against our pioneer spirit to allow men and women to laze around in cells when they could be doing something useful instead.

I was in charge of one of the strings of cons working on the embankment. We kept them at it in all but the worst weather. There were plenty of injuries, and a lot of frostbite. It wasn't uncommon for a con to be missing a couple of fingers or a toe or three. There were suicides, too, and several cons were killed during escape attempts, even though they were tagged and there was nothing but wilderness all around. One time, a couple of COs captured a con trying to get across the wire, gave him the choice of being shot on the spot or making a run for it. They allowed him a fair head start, took bets on when the hounds would take him down. A shade under fifteen minutes, it turned out.

One death I specially remember happened a month or so after I arrived. After an epic snowstorm that shut down work for a couple of days, my string was one of half a dozen set to digging out construction materials stockpiled at the northern end of the first bridge. I didn't hear the hue and cry until it was almost on me, looked up just as a man in an orange windproof ran past, pursued by a CO. I joined in, chasing the man past a group of cons who'd stopped work to watch the sport, chasing him out onto the bridge. We were closing in on him when a drone surfed in and smacked into his back and knocked him down. The two of us piled on and tried to pin him as he writhed like a landed fish. The other CO reeled back because he'd been kicked in the face, the con wrenched free of his windproof, leaving me holding it by a sleeve, and bounced to his feet and was off and running again, running straight out onto a stringer girder that ended between the second and third truss of the unfinished bridge.

He balanced there, no way forward, forty metres above a channel packed with jagged ice. I was shouting at him to give it up, still holding the damn windproof, when the drone dropped down and lit him up with its spots. He yelled something and jumped, and as he fell the drone riddled him with a burst of taglets.

I balled up the windproof and flung it after him. It blew sideways, settled in a leat of fast-running black water, was swept away under the ice. That's probably what happened to the body, too. A couple of drones spent the rest of the day hunting for it but failed to find anything, the log entry blandly recorded the whole mess as a fatal injury incurred during an escape attempt, the con's meagre possessions were packed up and mailed to his family, and that, as they say, was that.

When I told him the story, Keever said it was how it had to be, in the camps. The authorities couldn't show any weakness because it might encourage a general uprising, like the one at the nickel mine in the Pensacola Mountains. Eighteen COs, three supervisors and more than a hundred cons dead, millions of dollars of damage to equipment and millions more in lost production, the army brought in to suppress the last of it.

'Out here everything is either black or white,' Keever said. 'No half measures. You always know exactly what's what.'

I didn't think that the poor son of a bitch could have known that he'd be denied his chosen manner of dying when he'd made his suicide leap, but although I hadn't been hooked up with Keever for very long I already knew better than to contradict him.

How he'd ended up in jail, he'd been trying to give up the street life, trying to become a respectable businessman, but had been sucked into some kind of crooked cleverness involving tax evasion and the financing of a new football stadium. He claimed to find it amusing that, given all the nasty stuff he'd done to get to the point where he could think about going over to the other side, he'd been sent down for white-collar crime. But then a piece of that nasty stuff caught up with him, and that was why he was planning to escape.

But I'm getting ahead of myself again.

At the first lock-up Keever was sent to, straight jail rather than a work camp, one of his rivals organised a serious attempt to assassinate him. None of the other jails around and about Esperanza and O'Higgins were any safer – Keever had plenty of enemies – so he chose a work camp outside their reach, run by a commandant who'd been appointed by a politician who owed him several favours. Keever didn't ever tell me the name of that politician, but I reckon you can work out who it was.

Anyway, that's why the camp administration let Keever do whatever he wanted, as long as it didn't interfere with construction work. He had his own room. He had his crew – Mike Mike, half a dozen bodyguards and enforcers, a guy who cooked for him so that he didn't have to eat jail chow, so on. And he had his various business interests inside the wire, which he ran more for amusement than profit. The gambling circles, the trade in bootleg liquor, the contraband goods which COs purchased while on leave in Esperanza, O'Higgins or Port Sjörgren, and smuggled through the wire.

I started to work in the contraband biz because I wanted to build up my escape fund as quickly as possible. After Mama and I got away from Deception Island, we'd tried and failed to trek all the way down the spine of the peninsula to the mainland, hoping to find a clandestine community of ecopoets that according to fable and rumour was hidden somewhere in the far south. I thought that I could do better this time around. I dreamed of getting all the way to New Zealand, where edited people had the same rights as everyone else. I dreamed of escaping the ruins of my life and making a fresh start.

I even knew where I wanted to live – this big ring-shaped wind turbine called the Wheel, which stood in the flooded margin of Auckland's Waitematā Harbour, with apartments set one above the other in its revolving outer rim. I had dozens of pictures of it stored in my fone. My favourite, a night shot, showed the Wheel rising above its reflection in black water, the shaped fog of charged water droplets that it used to generate electricity glowing blue and pink in its hub. It looked like the very gateway to Heaven.

Edited people needed permits to travel inside the peninsula, and weren't allowed to travel outside it at all, but I'd heard about a people-smuggling operation working out of Square Bay, and some months back, on leave in Esperanza, I'd met a woman, friend of a friend, who told me how much it would cost, where I should stay when I got to Square Bay, the café where I should hang out so that the smugglers could check me over.

17

That was all I had. You couldn't look up these people anywhere. You couldn't reach out to them. You had to go to their place of business and wait for them to make contact. If they ever did. The fee for transporting me to New Zealand was pretty fucking outrageous, it would have taken five or six years to save that much on nothing but a CO's salary, but I knew that some of the other guards were making out like bandits from Keever Bishop's contraband business, and reckoned that it was worth the risk. So I started muling shit across the wire, and a couple of weeks later Keever sent word that he wanted to meet me.

Like I already said, I was flattered by his attention. Keever told me all kinds of pretty lies about why he'd chosen me to be his baby on the inside, and I chose to believe them. Now, of course, I want to shake some sense into my younger self. Pin her against a wall and give her some straight talk. Tell her that she was being used, tell her that if she was hoping to find stability, someone who could give her chaotic life some shape, she was looking in the wrong place. Not that it would have done any good. She would have told me that she wasn't in love with Keever, no way, but she admired his unshakeable self-belief and liked it when he told her that he loved his big strong girl, liked that he made her feel special. There was no end to my naivety back then.

The sex wasn't all that. Every time reminded me of my first, quickly over with Keever breathing hard in my ear. But as far as he was concerned, sex wasn't really the point. He got off on dominating people who were physically stronger than him. It was part of his apex predator guano. He liked to get into the faces of bull cons, men bigger than me, all muscles and mods, scars and tattoos, and talk trash to them. He paid cons to fight each other, talked about setting up a darknet channel where people could bet on them like horse races.

Sometimes, he'd stand in the door of his room and howl like a demented dog. You didn't know what to say to him when he got like that. When his ice-cold control slipped. Or when, maybe, because everything he did was calculated, he took it off for a moment, like you or I would take off a mask. His control was the mask he wore to hide what he really was.

18

But he could show a sweeter side too. He loved to fuss over my feet, for instance. Loved to massage them, trim and file my nails, smooth away calluses. 'He only does what he does for himself,' Paz warned me, but I didn't care. I liked that he paid attention to me.

And that's how it was until Keever's past caught up with him. This was in February, the end of our short summer. The bridges over the river delta had been completed, the first trains had been run across them, but there was still plenty of work to do. Painting kilometres of steel and ceramic, fixing the decking, installing a signalling and control section, planting the embankments with tough grasses and shrubs to stabilise them, so on. In the middle of all this, with plans for the ribbon-cutting ceremony on Independence Day beginning to be drawn up, news sites reported that the Australian government wanted to extradite Keever on an old murder charge.

It dated from a visit he'd made after a business deal had gone badly wrong, swindling him out of several million dollars. He'd kidnapped, tortured and killed six people in retribution, and now one of his former associates had been arrested and was putting him in the frame in exchange for a plea bargain. The peninsula's new government was happy to agree to the extradition request because of Keever's links with the old regime, he was looking at serious time, maybe even the death penalty, and because the Ministry of Justice was fast-tracking his case he'd quickly run out of options in court. That was why he had cooked up his escape plan, and now he wanted to promote me from a bit part to a major role. He told Mike Mike to put ice under himself for a minute, and when we were alone he pulled my feet into his lap and began to unlace my sneakers.

'When your long-lost uncle comes here, he'll bring journalists with him,' he said. 'That's how the man works. And there'll also be a media crew reporting on the ceremony to big up the government. Putting it out live. So when you do what I want you to do, Honourable Deputy Toomy will have to give you a fair shake.'

'A fair shake about what?'

Keever eased off my right sneaker and dropped it on the floor, started to unlace the left. 'Alberto Toomy is a rising star in the

National Unity Party. Maybe the next president, if the NUP gets back into power. Why not? He's handsome, he's rich, and he has the kind of tragic past that makes a great story. His wife and son having died, so sad, in some kind of skiing accident in the back country.'

'It was in the Eternity Range, five years ago,' I said. 'They were wild skiing and there was an avalanche.'

Sue me and send me to hell, but when I'd heard about that I'd felt a small glow of satisfaction, felt that the world had punished the Toomy family for their arrogance and the hurt they'd done to me and mine.

'You really have been keeping up,' Keever said.

'It isn't difficult. He's all over the feeds.'

'Isn't he just? The young widower bringing up his two daughters on his own, seen with a string of glamorous girlfriends. The present one a Chilean *novela* star, accompanying him at charity balls, parties, first nights at the theatre and the opera . . . Will he marry her? Will there be a fairy-tale ending? But wait,' Keever said, 'who's this? A long-lost relative. A poor little orphan working as a corrections officer in one of the work camps that contribute to the Toomy fortune. In short, you.'

There it was, like a pit opening up at my feet. I put up token resistance, pointing out I already had a part in his plan, but he hushed me, said he had plenty of people who could make sure his ride was ready and waiting in the transport pool, but only his big girl could cause the kind of commotion that would distract everyone at exactly the right moment.

'Just by talking to Alberto Toomy?'

'By confronting him. By telling him, with all the world watching, how your grandfather – Alberto's father – cheated you out of your rightful inheritance. How it drove your mother crazy. How you have nothing and he has everything. You do it right, and I know you will, it'll make quite the scene.'

By now, Keever had taken off my left sneaker and both my socks, was massaging the soles of my feet. Digging in with his knuckles. It tingled all the way up my legs to the base of my spine.

'Picture it,' he said. 'There's Honourable Deputy Alberto Toomy, with his wealth and power. And then there's you. His long-lost niece, cheated and wronged, trying to atone for some bad life choices by working as a corrections officer. And even better, you're a husky. One of the genetically polluted whose very existence is, according to Alberto's party, an affront to God. The feeds will go wild on it.'

'But they already know about my side of the family,' I said. 'It came out years and years ago, after my grandfather sold out the free ecopoets—'

Keever had knuckled a nerve in my foot, firing a sharp snap of pain up my leg and spine, straight into the base of my skull.

'Are you listening to me?' he said. 'Do I have your attention?'

'Yes. Of course.'

'Because I want you to understand what you have to do.'

His dark brown eyes. You couldn't say warm. Mr Snow didn't do warm. His barely there smile. He didn't sound angry. Apart from the times when he took off his mask, he never sounded angry. Even when he was getting in the face of the biggest con he could find, trying to goad the guy into taking a pop at him, he sounded as reasonable and patient as a surgeon explaining why it was necessary to cut you open.

'The point isn't to make news,' he said. 'The point is to cause a fuss. You'll tell him how wretched you are. You'll accuse him of stealing from you. Of causing your mother's death. You'll get in his face and make as much noise as you can, create a diversion that will pull badges away from the main population. Which means that my little show will have a better chance of succeeding. You see?'

I saw, all right.

'I'll be arrested,' I said. 'Sacked, thrown in jail—'

Keever laid a cold finger on my lips. 'I know that I'm asking a lot. But you agreed to help me and I know that I can trust you to do it. I can trust you, can't I?'

He used his malign massage *fu* to dig into that nerve again. Pain rocketed up my spine and exploded in my head like Independence Day fireworks. He was gripping my ankle so hard that if I'd been an ordinary girl the bones would have cracked.

I nodded again. I didn't dare speak.

Keever relaxed his grip, just a little. 'You get to confront your long-lost rich uncle. I get an extra diversion, space to do what I need to do. And who knows? Maybe Alberto will take pity on you. And if he doesn't, if you have to do a little jail, it isn't like you haven't done that before. And when you come out I'll set you up for life. OK?'

'OK.'

I don't have to tell you that agreeing to go along with this mad, bad plan was the last thing I wanted to do. But when Keever Bishop said jump, you pulled on your jumping gear and got to it.

'Swear you'll put on the best show for me,' he said.

I swore.

He pulled me close, told me I was his big strong girl.

'Now why don't you get out of these clothes so we can celebrate this happy turn of events?'

3

I should explain why I didn't tell Keever about you. Why I didn't tell him that I was carrying his child. After all, he made no secret of the fact that he had six children by five baby mothers – the kind of harem a true apex predator deserved. Ordinarily you and I would have been just one more example of his reproductive fitness, stowed away in an apartment in Esperanza, allowed a trickle of credit, visited now and then by his lordliness . . . But, this is the, what do you call it, the crux of the matter, there wasn't anything ordinary about the situation. First, Keever was planning to say goodbye to all that. To everything in his former life. Second, I was a husky, and taking a husky for a prison sweetheart was one thing, but maintaining her and her mixed blood kid outside the wire was something else. And while Keever didn't care that everyone in the camp knew that we were an item, it wouldn't do for a con to get a CO pregnant. The commandant had given Keever a pass on most things, but even she wouldn't have been able to ignore something like that. That was why he'd made sure that I'd been fitted with an implant, but the damn thing hadn't worked, perhaps because it was designed for mundane women rather than huskies, more likely because it was a bootleg injected into my thigh by a disgraced doctor who was serving an eight for supplying fake nanobiotics.

I'm trying to explain why, after my fone told me she had noticed changes that indicated I might possibly be pregnant, after I'd missed my second period and my breasts grew tender and the morning sickness kicked in, I decided that I couldn't keep you. It's hard, admitting that. But at the time there didn't seem to be any other way out. If I let nature, as they say, run her course, the service would come down hard on me because of who the father was. Disciplinary proceedings, a custodial sentence for me, one of the state orphanages for you . . . Worse than that, Keever would have considered it a betrayal, and I knew what happened to people who crossed him, knew that I wouldn't be safe wherever I was sent, whatever protection I was promised. Keever had a long reach, and was relentlessly unforgiving.

He liked to tell stories about how he dealt with those who had disappointed him. I remember one in particular because of its flamboyant savagery. A business associate went on the run with a slice of Keever's credit and Keever tracked her to Singapore, kidnapped her, and tortured her to death in the ruins of a flooded shopping mall. She gave up where the stolen credit was cached soon enough, but Keever refused to grant her a quick merciful release. Instead, he sliced her face and hung her upside down over a pool infested with moray eels specially trained and starved by their keeper.

Keever relished the gory detail. How his men had lowered and lifted the woman over and again so she wouldn't drown. How her blood had driven the eels into a frenzy. How they'd gone for the eyes and tongue. How they'd thrashed as they ate their way into her face and torso. The woman thrashing too, the water turning bright red. How she'd looked, raised out of the water with a garland of living ropes hanging from her.

'The thing about those eels,' Keever told me, 'they have mouthfuls of needle teeth that all point backwards. Once they bite, they lock on. The only way they can get loose is to take a big bite of flesh with them. I made a nice little movie of it. Showed it around. Anyone who saw it, I never had a spark of trouble from them afterwards.'

So I was in a tight spot. I couldn't tell my friends about you, tap them for advice, because I couldn't be certain that it wouldn't leak back to Keever. My fone was no help either. When I asked her what I should do she told me to follow my heart, which was about as profound and useful as a greeting card message. She presented as a wise older woman, my fone, with a handsome face and long grey hair and a star burning on her forehead, an image I'd got up after I'd been given my first fone at age eighteen and hadn't changed because of nostalgia or laziness (sometimes it's hard to tell one from the other). But like all AIs quickened after last century's killing sprees and net wars she wasn't much brighter than a dog, was throttled by legal and ethical constraints, answered serious, life-changing questions with platitudes. So I had to figure out what to do all by myself, and could see only one solution.

By the time I knew absolutely and definitely that I was carrying you, the ribbon-cutting ceremony was only a couple of weeks away. If Keever's escape plans worked out, he'd soon be gone. If they didn't, he'd be thrown in some high-security hole until he was extradited to Australia. Either way I'd never see him again. All I had to do, I thought, was take a couple of days off after the ceremony, travel to Esperanza and get what I thought of as my problem fixed, and never ever tell anyone what I'd done. It wouldn't even cost me anything. Thanks to a hateful bit of legislation the new government hadn't gotten around to repealing, huskies could obtain free abortions from a special clinic, a nice neat way of keeping our numbers down.

That was my plan, such as it was. Shameful as it was. And then the news about Alberto Toomy muscling in on the ribbon-cutting ceremony, and Keever's idea about having me confront him, threw a shitload of sand in the goddamn gears.

Keever had a script for that confrontation, and we rehearsed it like a play. Mike Mike playing Alberto Toomy, me playing myself, Keever stepping in whenever he thought I'd deviated from what I was supposed to say and do.

'There's only two things you need to get across,' he said. 'Number one, you and Alberto are blood relatives. Number two, his side of the family stole what should have been shared with your side. You're living proof that his fortune, everything he has, everything he's done, is founded on selfishness and injustice. The feeds will eat it up. They'll rip him apart and make you a hero.'

Mr Snow. Cool, languid, all-knowing, sitting on his bed in his blue gym shorts while Mike Mike and me went through the corny scene one more time. I had to play along, even though I knew that it didn't have anything to do with providing a diversion for Keever's escape. He already had that covered. And it didn't have anything to do with justice or revenge, either. Like I already said, my family's relationship with the Toomy clan was old news dug up by my grandfather's enemies long ago, an attempt to create a scandal that never gained any traction. Even Mama hadn't been able to revive it, and I was damn sure that Keever knew that nothing I said or did would make any difference.

No, the little drama he'd cooked up was all about tidying away a loose end. He believed I was stone in love with him, didn't want me chasing him after he escaped, and was too sentimental to deal with me in the usual way. I guess I have to give him that. I have to take that away from our relationship. Instead of having me spiked, he was going to let the service deal with me. If his little drama worked out, I'd be thrown in a hole for disobeying orders, assaulting an important visitor, so on, and when I came out after two or three years, no job, no future, I'd be no danger to him.

So there it was. If I didn't co-operate I'd be on the sharp end of Keever's displeasure. But if I did, I'd be arrested, pretty soon the evidence of my liaison with him would become undeniable, and I'd be in a worse kind of trouble.

Meanwhile, preparations for the ribbon-cutting ceremony gathered pace. Everywhere in the camp smelled of fresh paint. Cons filled potholes, shifted heaps of construction materials out of sight, washed and polished construction machinery, erected flagpoles along one side of the apron of freshly laid gravel where the VIPs' helis would land. My string was put on landscaping duty, planting the approach to the bridge with carpets of cultured mountain avens, purple saxifrage, and marguerites. The force-grown plants probably wouldn't survive a week, let alone last out the coming winter, but sue me, I felt that it was a little like ecopoet work, and while I was out in the weather, watching the cons set out swirls of flowers, I could forget for a short while the impossible knot of my troubles.

The cons were given extra rations and promised time off during the ceremony, but after spending the day supervising their strings COs had to attend security briefings and practice drill. We polished our boots and belts until they were black mirrors, cleaned every piece of our kit. Late in the evening the buzz of conversation in the mess was muted and I could pass off as exhaustion my preoccupation with Keever's plan.

By then, everyone in the camp knew that Honourable Deputy Alberto Toomy was coming to stir the shit. And my friends knew all about my connection with him because I'd told them the whole sorry story during one of those stupid bonding sessions.

Paz wondered if Alberto Toomy already knew about me. Knew that I was working there. Maybe, she said, he'd had a hand in moving me from guarding the transport pool to the VIP security detail. 'Maybe he's planning a surprise meeting. A surprise reconciliation with his long-lost niece. A terrific human interest story with a happy ending.'

It was Keever who'd swung my move, of course, but I couldn't tell Paz that. It was the eve of Independence Day, the day before the ribbon-cutting ceremony, and although there was still no sign that Alberto Toomy and his people had found out about me, I was still hoping that they would, that they'd ask the commandant to remove me from the security detail or transfer me out of the camp. Anything, so long as I didn't have to go through with Keever's plan. I'd even thought of reaching out to my uncle, telling him hey, guess who's working at Kilometre 200, wouldn't it be lovely to meet up, so on, but the risk that Keever would hear about it was too great.

I told Paz that as far as I was concerned I'd be happy if I never had to lay eyes on the Honourable Deputy. 'His side of the family have never shown any interest in mine, and it was his party that set up the pass laws, all the rest of the shit we have to put up with. Not to mention they were talking about sterilising us if they won the election. Ending the husky problem once and for all. What good could come out of meeting someone who thinks like that? Nothing, that's what.'

'Oh, I don't know,' Paz said, half teasing, half serious. 'Maybe you could persuade him to take up our cause. Enrol him in the campaign for equal rights for edited people.'

'Isn't going to happen,' Sage said.

'It's unlikely,' Paz said. 'But someone like Alberto Toomy admitting that we're fully human could change everything.'

'Isn't ever going to happen,' Sage said, with that dark stubborn frown we knew well.

We were crowded around a table in back of the mess, away from the boisterous crowd sharing the live stream of an ice hockey match in Charcot Stadium, O'Higgins. I was drinking steadily, beer with vodka chasers, scared shitless about the next day. Scared about what would happen if I did what Keever asked me to do. Scared about what would happen if I didn't.

'You could meet him yourself,' I told Paz. 'All you have to do is sign up for the security detail.'

I was only half-joking. If Paz stepped up to the Honourable Deputy, asked him to put in a good word for the husky nation, I might be spared.

'A man like him wouldn't talk to a no–account goon like me,' Paz said. 'But you're family, Stral. You could just maybe pull it off.'

The hockey fans cheered loud and long, saving me from having to reply.

'The least you can do is gouge him for some credit,' Lola said. 'Then we can hit Esperanza after this circus is over. Blow it big style. Or maybe he'll take you in. Maybe he'll give you a job, an apartment, all that good stuff you claim he stole from you. And we could come live with you.'

'Why not?' I said. 'I'll need someone to help me spend all the money you think I'll be getting.'

'We could be his bodyguards,' Lola said. 'Four huskies standing behind him in some kind of uniform, fully strapped? It would freak people's heads. I wouldn't even mind you were my boss.'

Paz said, 'Why is it, whenever people think about us, even when we think about ourselves, it's always some job involving muscle?'

'Maybe because of gym rats like you,' Sage said.

Paz clutched her chest with a mock shudder, as if she'd been shot with a taser taglet. 'Did I ever tell you that before I became a CO, I wanted to be a lawyer?'

'Only about a million times,' Lola said.

'It's funny how you keep forgetting about it,' Paz said. 'I would have been a good one too. But along came the Exempted Labour Act and huskies couldn't be lawyers any more. Just in case they were able to represent their own interests too well. Imagine the embarrassment that would have caused. So I started working as an investigator for poor old Murray Gibbs instead, and I guess even you, Lola, remember how that ended.'

We all knew how it had ended. How Paz had worked for a broke-ass attorney with whisky on his breath at nine in the morning, searching for strays and runaways, people who tried to duck out on debts or child support. How most of her assignments felt like they were grinding dirt into her soul, but sometimes she believed she might have done some good-helping kids who'd fallen into bad company, helping people in the husky community find what Murray called extra-legal solutions to disputes, so on. Then she came to work one day and the office was trashed and her boss had disappeared. There was a rumour that Murray had crossed someone in the police, but Paz knew better than to try to chase it down. Especially as one of her contacts passed on an anonymous tip that it might be best if she left town for a while. No point asking what would happen if she didn't, so she joined the prison service, and that was that.

'My point being, forget working close protection or whatever,' Paz said. 'Tell your uncle I'm up for all kinds of paralegal shit, Stral. Tell him I'd be damn good at it.'

It got us into talking about fantasy jobs. The jobs we really wanted to do, if only we could. If only we weren't what we were. Paz wanted to be a judge, why not? Sage wanted to own a fishing boat – she knew the work, she'd be her own boss, she wouldn't have to take shit from anyone any more. I thought of the Wheel, all my stupid plans and secrets, said that getting through life one day at a time was hard enough.

'What about you, Lola?' Paz said. 'What's your secret ambition, your heart's desire?'

'Maybe I'd just like an ordinary life,' Lola said, which was so sad and funny and true that we all had to drink to it.

'You probably won't get within spitting distance of old Alberto,' Lola said to me, a little later. 'But if you do, if he's in any way sympathetic, all kidding aside, I hope you'll remember to put in a good word for your friends.'

The fierceness in her look startled me.

'What I hope, he won't turn up,' I said.

4

Independence Day dawned cool and dull under a sky sheeted edge to edge with low cloud. The cons were squared away in their blocks. No work for them today. Soldiers were busy around two double-decked wagons in the freight yard, unloading gleaming black rovers that would ferry the VIPs from place to place. And I was in my dress blues, heading to the 0700 security briefing with a pounding head, a raw stomach and a shaky sense of impending doom that steepened when I saw Lola sneak into a seat in the back row.

She'd been assigned to VIP security at the last minute. She worked for Keever. And sometimes two and two make four.

I was majorly upset that Keever had sent one of my friends to dog me, angry with Lola for agreeing to do it, but for a little while busy work pushed all that to the back of my mind. I was part of the group tasked with sweeping the freight yard. Checking track-laying machines, the printers that had extruded bridge components, hopper wagons loaded with gravel and hardcore, the enormous machine that had cut a tunnel through Ferguson Ridge. And the special train waiting to be switched to the main line, a sleek silver locomotive and two silver passenger cars levitating bare centimetres above the guideway track.

Helis carrying VIPs started to come in, buzzing overhead and settling on the square apron east of the camp, its parade of flags bowing and snapping in rotor downdraughts. I could see people climbing down, see them being greeted by the commandant's staff, but it was too far away to make out who they were. One after the other they were driven off to the commandant's quarters for a celebratory lunch and a round of speeches, while us COs completed the security checks and were given coffee and crackers and cardboard cups of chowder.

We wore dark blue service dress jackets and trousers, light blue shirts. Blue caps with polished black peaks, black boots. Shock sticks holstered at our hips. The mundanes had thermal long johns under their uniforms and stamped their feet and beat their arms across their chests and complained about the cold. A few flakes of snow were fluttering down and I could smell coming flurries on the chafing wind.

I tipped my chowder away when no one was looking. I'd thrown up my breakfast, was running on caffeine and nerves.

It was 1400 now, no sign yet that the VIPs were about to stir from the cosy fug of their lunch. I wondered if Keever was waiting in his room for everything to kick off, or was he out and about with Mike Mike, making last minute tweaks to his arrangements, chivvying cons, COs, whoever else was in on the breakout? I realised that I didn't know very much about it. Nothing but the broad strokes, and the stupid script I was supposed to stick to. I spotted Lola among a little group of COs nearby and she met my gaze for a moment, eyes bright under the peak of her cap, before looking away.

At last, the bullet-nosed locomotive and its two passenger cars drew out of the loop onto the main line, halting a little way from the viewing platform. The red ribbon stretched across the tracks rippled in the breeze. The first of the bridges was small as a toy in the distance, its spotlit bow spans gleaming with unreal clarity in the fading daylight.

We made our final inspections and lined up in parade formation, two ranks, a short distance from the platform and the train. Word went around that the schedule for the ceremony had been pushed back because lunchtime speeches had overrun. It was past 1500 and a thin snow had begun to fall, little scatters of hard granules blowing on the wind, when at last a convoy of black rovers came muscling down the access road. I looked over the heads of the guards in front of me, trying and failing to spot Alberto Toomy among the people being ushered to the platform. Small drones passed and repassed high overhead, slicing through gusts of snow. A platoon of soldiers in black and white uniform struck up a medley of ancient show tunes on polished brass instruments.

An electric ball of excitement and anxiety revolved inside my ribs. Everything was running late, I had lost sight of Lola, and there was still no sign of Honourable Deputy Alberto Toomy. Maybe he hadn't come after all. Maybe he had made some kind of principled stand against attending the actual ceremony and was stirring up trouble by inspecting the blocks and asking awkward questions. And then I saw him. Saw Alberto Toomy step out of the last rover in the line, dressed in a pale yellow coat with a fur collar that flared at the back of his head, his hair sleek as a seal's pelt. He turned to help a young girl climb down, and I knew at once who she was.

Kamilah Toomy, Alberto Toomy's eldest daughter.

My cousin.

5

Once upon a time, not long after I was released from the orphanage, I set out to reconnoitre the headquarters of Pyxis, the construction company owned by the Toomy family. Riding the subway to the centre of Esperanza, I felt like the vengeful heroine of a novella, a splinter of ice in her heart, a vial of black poison concealed in her underwear. But when I entered the lobby of the city-centre skyscraper where Pyxis leased three floors hard reality displaced every trace of my silly fantasies. The space was dizzyingly tall, impossibly lux. Water sheeted down a three-storey cliff of backlit glass into a pool surrounded by tropical plants I had no names for, and giant panels displayed images of sailing ships stranded in pack ice, images of fur-clad explorers from the Heroic Age man-hauling sleds or gazing across stark white wilderness, looming above people in immaculate business gear scurrying to and fro on inscrutable errands, breezing through the security gates in front of banks of big bronze-doored elevators. They belonged there and I so didn't, and not just because I was the only husky in the place.

I retreated into the underground passages and strip malls of CORE, let my fone guide me to an escalator that carried me up to a quiet little park under a dome, with a view across a six-lane avenue to the cluster of skyscrapers driven like nails into Esperanza's heart. The air around them swarmed with signs and ads, synchronised waves of runabouts and bicycles washed along the avenue, a heli neatly touched down on the roof of a tower whose sheer sides were studded with the green blisters of pocket gardens, and I felt a kind of numb humiliation because there was nothing in that world of marvels that had anything to do with my scrappy, insignificant life.

If I'd been any kind of real heroine I would have dedicated myself there and then to finding a way of bringing down Pyxis, the Toomy family and the whole rotten system on which they had fattened. Instead, I sat on the rim of a planter and squeezed out a few self-pitying tears, thinking of Mama, our home on Deception Island, everything I'd lost, and at last, prompted more by hunger than conscious decision, headed back to the subway and Star City.

I didn't attempt to breach Pyxis's perimeter again, let alone try to find my way to the Toomy family's estate east of the city, with its manicured heathland and stands of lenga beech, its faux modernist house with levels of glass and concrete stepping down the side of a rugged cove to the sea (my fone had found a piece about it in an architecture journal). That one time was enough to show me that Mama was right. The rich inhabit a world that barely intersects ours, as hard to reach as the gold at the end of the rainbow's span.

But here were Alberto Toomy and his eldest daughter in the work camp, in my world, standing in a press of VIPs under the gull-wing canopy of the viewing platform. I couldn't look away from them. The man who had inherited the wealth my father should have shared. His daughter, who enjoyed without thought the benefits of that wealth, the privilege it bought.

She was fourteen. Slender, pale and blonde. The woman she would become just beginning to bloom. Laying a hand on her father's arm, saying something that made him smile.

The chairman of the construction consortium introduced the vice-president and the vice-president began his speech, his back turned to me and the other COs. If you want to know what he said you can look it up, but frankly it isn't worth the effort. I mean, it wasn't history in the making. It was nothing more than a blatant publicity stunt dressed up with patriotism, meant to impress the electorate and reassure the rest of the world that the new government was no less eager to exploit the peninsula's resources than its predecessor.

The speech ended in a polite ripple of applause and the vice-president was handed an oversized pair of gold-plated scissors which he used to snip the red ribbon stretched across the tracks. More applause as wind caught the cut ribbon and blew its shimmering length out into the snowy air. The army band struck up that old old sleigh-ride tune and people began to file down the steps and move towards the train that would carry them across the bridges and back again.

Alberto Toomy and his daughter were shadowed by a neat man in a black one-piece suit, no doubt personal security. The three of them briefly stopped, people moving past them on either side, and then Toomy's daughter and the bodyguard cut away from the herd and headed off towards the fan of sidings where the construction machines were parked.

It was almost 1600.

Any moment now Keever's main event would kick off.

The sergeant in charge of my squad gave the order to break ranks and go to our positions. According to Keever's script, I was supposed to bull my way through the crowd of VIPs, beard Alberto Toomy and tell him and everyone else who I was. Instead, I set off at a slant towards the girl and her bodyguard.

You could say that I was rebelling against Keever, in full knowledge of the consequences. You could say (as the prosecution did, at my trial) that I was acting on fantasies of revenge I'd cultivated for years. All I know is that I believed that Kamilah Toomy was the kind of person I could have been in another life, if our grandfather had gone down a different road, if I'd been born into the square side of the family, if I wasn't a husky. I wanted to see her close and plain. I wanted to ask her what it was like being her, wanted her to know what it was like being me. It was stronger than mere curiosity. It felt as if all of my life had been leading up to that moment. Everything else dropped away. I was floating on a saintly, righteous calm.

Then Lola caught up with me and grabbed my arm, forcing me to stop and turn to her.

'What the fuck are you doing?' she said, white around the eyes with anxiety. 'You're going the wrong way.'

'How much did Keever pay you to make sure I do what he wants?'

'I'm here to back you up is all.'

'Remember the oath we swore? One for all, all for one, so on? You want to back me up, let me do what I need to do.'

'That was just some shit Paz made up. And we don't have time for this,' Lola said, pointing towards the train. Alberto Toomy was waiting his turn to climb aboard the second carriage, chatting amiably with a woman in a red coat that appeared to have been woven from feathers.

'I hope Keever paid you up front,' I said. 'Because good luck getting it out of him after this.'

'As if you didn't get anything out of being his baby,' Lola said. 'We have a bare minute before the fucker gets on that train, so let's just do this.'

'Try and make me.'

For a moment we stood glaring at each other. I was ready to hurt Lola, she saw it and let go of my arm, and I went on towards the girl and her bodyguard, walking fast, glancing back just once to see Lola talking to the falling snow, no doubt telling Keever or Mike Mike about my defection. I didn't care. In that moment what I wanted to do counted for more than anything else. And it felt right, felt as if a hand was at my back, urging me along.

The bodyguard positioned himself in front of the girl and asked me what I wanted. I told him that I needed to know where he was going, staring straight at him rather than the girl.

'We have permission,' he said. He was in his forties, had a stern shuttered face, all angles and planes, that looked like it had been hacked from stone. Flakes of snow were settling in his hair, on the boxy shoulders of his black one-piece.

'You've strayed outside the security envelope,' I said, trying to sound cool and professional even though I was making it up as I went along.

The girl spoke up, saying, 'It's all right. My father said I could see the machines.'

Her pale face was dappled with random butterscotch patches. A white fur hat, sunshine-coloured hair spilling across the shoulders of a short white jacket buckled over a pale grey bodysuit.

'We have permission,' the bodyguard said again, and glanced past me for a moment.

I knew that Lola was coming towards us, said to the girl, 'The machine over there, the long yellow one? Do you know what it does?'

'It's a bridge girder erector. An old design, but very functional.'

'I see that you know something about them.'

'I'm going to be an engineer.'

She had the absolute confidence of someone who never had to struggle for anything she wanted. When she glanced at my ID tag I felt a prickle of caution, wondering if she'd recognise my name, but then she was looking at Lola, who was approaching at a steady trot.

Across the tracks the train sounded its horn and began to glide away towards the first bridge. The military band was playing some silly spritely tune. It was too late to confront Alberto Toomy, too late to get with Keever's script, and I didn't care.

'That one, the girder erector, I've seen it in action,' I told the girl. 'It's pretty amazing.'

We walked towards the long low-slung machine, the bodyguard and Lola following as I explained how it could pick up a section of decking and roll to the end of an unfinished bridge, supporting itself on unspanned pillars while it dropped the decking in place. I was rapidly exhausting the little knowledge I'd gleaned from a brief conversation with one of the operators, knew that I was getting deeper and deeper into trouble, but felt a fine high recklessness. I told the girl that the girder erector and the rest of the construction machinery were about to be sent down the line to work on the next stretch of the railway, asked her why she hadn't wanted to ride along with her father, and that was when the bodyguard tried to shut down the conversation, pointedly thanking me for my time and help.

'You want to shoot some pics, don't you?' he said to the girl.

Lola spoke up, startling me. 'We'll have to come along with you. All photography within the bounds of the camp requires authorisation.'

The bodyguard looked as if he was about to argue the point, but the girl said that it was fine. 'Besides, they can tell me about the machines.'

'Absolutely,' Lola said, staring at me.

The girl pointed to the tunnel borer, a gleaming cylinder thirty metres long with a gleaming bouquet of big disc cutters at one end and a spoil conveyor at the other. As we set off towards it, Lola touched my arm and leaned in, told me quietly that I was to stay cool and follow her lead.

'What do you mean?'

'See that ute?'

Off in the distance, hazed by falling snow, the little crew utility vehicle was motoring along the access road, parallel to the double fence of the camp's southern boundary.

'What are you into, Lola?'

'Keever has sent a couple of his people to collect the girl.'

'You're kidding.'

'It was supposed to go down while you were calling out her father and diverting everyone's attention. But you fucked that up, so now you're going to help me.'

'No way.'

'Keever's people will keep her some place safe, and while the state police are doing everything they can to find her, he can slip away under their radar. She'll be turned loose as soon as he's in the clear.'

'And you're all right with that?'

Lola gave me a flat frank look, no trace of warmth in it. The way she'd stare at some newb CO, looking for some weakness or peculiarity she could pounce on.

'I need the money,' she said. 'And we both know what Keever will do to us if we don't go through with this, so don't give me any more grief. When it kicks off, stick up your hands, keep quiet, let the girl be taken away.'

'The bodyguard might have something to say about that.'

'I'll put down that slick son of a bitch, no worries. And afterwards, when we raise the alarm, I'll tell you exactly what to say,' Lola said, and picked up her pace, catching up with the girl, telling her that she could take as many pictures of the tunnel borer as she liked.

I had one of those moments when you know you should say or do something but embarrassment, fear or whatever holds you back. And then the moment passed. I was still in the middle of Keever's thing, no way out, and if I didn't find some way of dealing with it I was done.

Off in the distance, the train sounded its horn as it eased across the first bridge, its lights and the floodlights on the bridge's trusses blurred by falling snow. The bodyguard tossed a little saucer-shaped drone into the air, with neat movements of her hands the girl sent it skimming down the length of the tunnel borer, and the ute cut past a string of hopper wagons and pulled up in front of us.

As two men climbed out the bodyguard stepped forward, Lola close behind, telling him it was a security check, perfectly routine. They were dressed in standard issue cold weather gear, the men, blue down jackets and black watch caps, but one had a non-regulation pigtail and the other wore a pistol at his hip. I was trying to figure out angles as they walked towards us, was wondering if the bodyguard would back me up if I rushed them, when the girl's drone dropped out of the air. A moment later sirens began to shrill amongst the blocks. The train had halted on the bridge and the floodlights had snapped off and my fone was blinking a red dot, no signal, in the corner of my vision.

One of the men had drawn his pistol and the other was brandishing a shock stick, yelling at the bodyguard to put his fucking hands in the air. The bodyguard did no such thing. Quicker than it takes to tell it, neat as a ballet dancer, he turned sideways, conjured a little black pistol into his hand, extended his arm, and with cool precision shot them. Shot the one with the pistol square in the forehead, killing him on the spot, shot the other in the knee, and swung around, raising his arm to protect himself, too late, as Lola slapped him upside the head with a rat-tailed sap. The crack of the blow echoed off the flank of the tunnel borer and the bodyguard collapsed, completely unstrung. Lola kicked the pistol out of his hand and turned to me, saw that I'd drawn my shock stick.

'Don't,' she said, just as I lunged forward.

6

I was kneeling on the small of Lola's back, securing her wrists with zipcuffs, when the man who'd been shot in the knee sat up, clasping his leg and telling me I was a damn fool or some such. I ignored him, scooped up the bodyguard's pistol, bundled the girl into the ute and scrambled in beside her. A quick glance showed me that the vehicle was set to manual and its AI and comms were borked – much later I was told that it had also been fitted with a device that spoofed its GPS, fooling surveillance systems into thinking it was somewhere else, frustrating attempts to find me. All I knew at the time was those two bravos had been flying under the radar, and that suited me just fine. I didn't want to be tracked either.

As I drove towards the camp, flooring the ute's accelerator, bucking over ramps that crossed the tracks, the girl found her voice, asked me what I thought I was doing.

There was a question.

'Taking you to a place of safety,' I said.

She attempted a commanding tone. 'You must take me to my father.'

'He'll catch up with you later.'

'What about Franco? Your friend hurt him . . .'

I guessed that Franco was the bodyguard, told the girl that he would be fine, held up a hand when she started to ask another question. 'We're in bad trouble,' I said, 'but I'm going to take care of it.'

I overtook a squad in riot gear jogging towards the camp, drove past the guard tower at the corner of the perimeter wire. Two

COs were standing at the rail up there, watching the blocks over the sights of their rifles. The roof of one of the blocks was on fire, black smoke blown flat by the snowy wind.

Keever's thing had kicked off, he had somehow cut power and comms, and was no doubt making his way through the wire to the transport pool and freedom. And I had my own plan. It had clicked into place after I zapped Lola and saw the girl standing rigid with shock. She was my golden ticket. The way off the peninsula. The way to save myself and save you. I was crazy, I admit it. But I was lucidly crazy. I knew exactly what I had to do and nothing seemed impossible. It was singing in my blood.

I cut across the parking lot where my girls and I had played basketball a couple of days before, followed the short road to the yard of the transport pool. My heart gave a little kick when I saw that the outer gate was open. Keever had been there. I was sure of it. There and gone. I briefly wondered where he was, if he was in the air or if he was being driven to the coast and a rendezvous with a fast boat. Wherever he was going, I hoped it was a good long way from the peninsula, hoped he would be too busy to think about coming after me.

The door of the transport office stood open too. I parked the ute beside it, had to use a little force to extract the girl. More or less carrying her inside, where two COs lay jackknifed on the floor, black tape over eyes and mouths, wrists bound to ankles with double zipcuffs. One a woman I didn't know, the other the grey-haired veteran, Arnie Velasquez, who'd supervised me when I'd done a stint there. Their heads coming up as the girl and I stepped inside, both of them making furious incoherent sounds.

I marched the girl past them, pushed her through the door to the visitor processing suite. It took less than a minute to find a box of prison-orange bracelets and snap one around her slender wrist. The bracelet squirmed under my fingers as it adjusted its grip. We fitted every visitor with one. They used skin conductance or some such thing to block fones and apps. I stuffed a couple of spares in my pocket and switched off my own fone – switched her off completely, because I knew that police could get inside fones supposedly offline. A swathe of icons popped up and turned red and faded, and that was it, I was on my own. A cannon working single o, as poor dead Bryan would have said.

The girl was looking left and right, up and down, no doubt hunting for vanished icons and menus. 'What have you done?' she said.

'Making sure no one can track you when comms come back on line. You really don't know who I am, do you?'

'You're one of the prison guards. Aren't you?'

'I'm also your cousin,' I said, the word like a pebble in my mouth. 'Austral Morales Ferrado. Your grandfather, Edward Toomy? He was my grandfather too. Your father, he's my uncle.'

The girl stared at me for a bare second, then raised a hand as if to tap the air, but her fone was dead, she couldn't look up the crazy mad husky looming over her, find out if I was telling the truth.

'What do you want?' she said, sounding small and scared and uncertain.

'A new life. And you're going to help me get it.'

Back in the office I opened equipment lockers, pulled out two sets of cold weather gear, a flashlight, a box of foil blankets and the tight roll of a sleeping bag. Working in a hurry, worried that someone could walk in at any second, the two bound COs squirming on the floor behind me, making noise behind their gags.

Snow boots, one large pair, one small. Ration packs, the squat black cube of a field stove. I shoved everything into a kitbag, steered the girl outside, saw three men in orange coveralls run past and disappear into the falling snow. The doors in the blocks were supposed to lock down when the power went off, but Keever must have sabotaged some or all of them so that he could reach the transport pool. Those three cons had discovered his escape route, and they wouldn't be the only ones. I wanted more than anything to get out of there, but I knew what cons would do to the COs tied up and helpless, so I locked the girl and the kitbag in the ute, ducked back into the office. Found a pair of scissors and sawed at one of Arnie Velasquez's zipcuffs, telling him that cons had broken out, he and his pal needed to find a good hiding place. The zipcuff snapped and I shoved the scissors in his hand and ran back outside.

A muscular bravo in a white vest, orange coveralls pushed down to his waist, was pulling at the ute's door. Rocking it, banging on the canopy, shouting at the girl to let him in, looking around as I stepped up behind him and zapped him with my shock stick and punched him to the ground. He was bigger than Lola but a lot less trouble. I'd zapped her three times and she'd kept trying to get up and at last I'd had to knock her out with her own sap.

Two more cons were running across the yard. I swung into the ute and took off, skidding on a patch of slush and nearly smacking sideways into the post of the outer gate, straightening up and turning north.

The girl said, 'Did you kill him?'

It took me a moment to realise what she meant. 'I put him down is all. The other COs will throw his ass back inside the wire when they find him.'

'Where are we going?'

She was pressed against the door, knees up to her chin, arms wrapped around her shins. Trying to make herself as small as possible. Trying to make herself disappear.

'You'll see.'

I hadn't worked that out yet. I was beginning to realise there were a lot of things I hadn't worked out.

There was a space of silence. The girl looked out at the snow blowing through the dark air, snow falling across mudflats and braided channels that stretched towards the sea. At last she said, 'Are you really my cousin?'

'Yes I am. Really and truly. Didn't anyone ever tell you about me? My side of the family?'

The girl looked at me, looked away. 'I know that my grandfather had a son, before he married. He didn't say he was . . . like you.'

'A husky. You can say it. I'm a husky, first generation. My father was a mundane, just like you. An ecopoet. Salix Gabriel Morales, the son of Isabella Schilling Morales and Edward Toomy. Who ran away before my father was born, and never offered us any help when we needed it.'

'Is that why you're angry?'

'I'm not angry. I'm explaining what this is about. Why I'm going to ask your father to pay what's owed.'

'I have a special number for emergencies,' the girl said. 'If you let me call it, I'll say that you rescued me. My father, his people, they'll sort out everything. Any trouble you're in, they can make it go away. There'll even be a reward. I'm certain of it. I mean, you saved my life.'

'Fones are down right now. The man who sent those two bravos to snatch you also took out the camp's comms, part of his escape plan. But don't worry, I won't let him get you.'

'If you want money for helping me, you don't even need to ask my father. I have some.'

'Do you have it here?'

'I can get it.'

'And if I want it, I suppose I'll have to unlock your fone. Give you a chance to call for help. I don't think so.'

Another space of silence. Then the girl said, 'This is the first time I've been in a vehicle that someone drove. I mean actually drove.'

'I guess it's a day of firsts.'

'You're pretty good at it.'

I wondered if she had been trained for situations like this, trained to be friendly and co-operative with kidnappers, or if it was just the kind of polite, empty conversation that fills the idle hours of the rich.

'I had a good teacher,' I said.

Way back when on Deception Island Mama had let me tootle around in an ancient jeep because the ability to drive was, according to her, one of the essential survivalist skills. I knew that I'd need everything she'd taught me in the coming days, was starting to put together what I had to do, where I had to go.

It was a little past 1700 now, growing dark, the weather settling in. A constant hail of white pellets, the kind of snow called graupel, rattled on the ute's canopy. Visibility was down to a couple of hundred metres and I was driving as fast as I dared, wondering how much time I had before the girl's disappearance was discovered. Before the bodyguard, Lola and the wounded bravo were found and questioned. Before what I'd done came out. Before the demon or whatever it was that had taken down the prison's security system was isolated, and the drones and hounds were booted and let loose on my ass. The snow and darkness would help to obscure my trail, but not by much.

I wasn't frightened, though. I was elated. I was free and I was on the move and nothing seemed impossible.

About halfway to the quarry I made a decision and turned off the road and bumped down a stony slope and headed across country, running roughly parallel to the course of the Eliason River. Years ago, Mama had made me memorise the locations of the old ecopoet refuges. There was one up on the edge of the Detroit Plateau, about twenty kilometres to the south and west. We could hole up there for the night, and when I'd worked out the necessary details I'd call the girl's father and tell him what he had to pay me if he wanted to see her again. I wasn't going to ask for much. Just enough for my fare and a new identity. And then I could leave the girl behind and make my way south to Square Bay and the people smugglers. It wasn't far. Over on the other coast, some two hundred and fifty kilometres to the south. I could drive there, or steal a damn boat. I could fucking walk if I had to.

It all seemed so simple, there at the beginning. Little did I know, et cetera.

I was driving over flat terrain cracked into big polygonal plates and lightly covered in snow. House-sized boulders, erratics dumped by retreating ice, were dotted about like a giant's game of marbles. Off to the left, a line of trees intermittently visible through gusts of snow marked the course of the river. More trees thickened ahead, and quite soon I was driving through the fringes of the forest, wallowing up and down low ridges, swerving left or right as trees smashed out of the darkness. Crooked spires no more than ten or twelve metres high, bent and warped by snow and ice and wind. I remembered hiking with Mama through a forest just like it the summer we escaped, remembered columns of dusty sunlight slanting between pine trees, moss and ferns thick on the ground. A green cathedral that seemed as old as the world, planted out by ecopoets just fifty years before.

It was almost completely dark now. I had switched to night-vision mode, a ghostly blue-and-white view patched from the ute's forward cameras. I couldn't use my fone to navigate because it might betray my position, but the ute had a simple compass and by aiming roughly south-west I soon found the river.

It was broad and shallow, trees growing right up to its edge. The ute jacked up when we hit the water and I drove slowly and steadily, the water never rising higher than the door sills. We crossed a crescent of sand and gravel on the far side, and before we re-entered the forest I glimpsed a high spur rising above the trees in the snowy dark and hoped it was Weasel Hill, one of the high rocky ridges that clawed the edge of the basin. I could see the route in my head. Cross the Pyke River, follow the contour line to the western end of the Albone Valley, find the old ecopoet road that ran alongside the remnant of a glacier to the edge of the Detroit Plateau and the refuge.

The girl sat beside me, silent and somewhat sullen. Resigned to her fate, I hoped, rather than plotting trouble.

The Pyke River ran fast and strong, white water glimmering in the dark where it broke around rocks and slalomed down rapids. I drove upstream until I found what looked like a good crossing place, bumped the ute down irregular steps of bare rock, and drove straight into the water. The sturdy little vehicle surged onto a pebble shoal and dipped down into the water on the far side, pushing a crest of white water ahead of it. I could see the far bank through the falling snow, and then the ute hit some kind of sinkhole or crevice and slewed sideways and slammed to a halt.

The girl gave a little scream. I crushed the accelerator, wrenched the yoke to and fro. No good. The ute was tilted nose down, the nearside front wheel jammed fast.

'I thought you knew what you were doing,' the girl said, which didn't help any.

'I can fix this.'

'If you'd let this thing drive itself, like you're supposed to, you wouldn't have got us stuck.'

'Shut up and let me think.'

It was getting hard to control my temper. I used to talk back, my Mama would swat me. But if I swatted the girl I'd probably break something.

'Well we can't stay here,' she said. 'And I'm not going to walk all the way to wherever.'

I switched on the headlights. They made two tunnels of light through the falling snow. One just above the surface of the running water, one a little higher. Dim shapes crowded the far bank. Trees.

'You won't have to walk,' I told the girl. 'See, this thing has a winch.'

I shucked my boots and stripped to my underwear, a struggle in the cramped space, knotted my shock stick in one sock and the pistol in the other and tied the socks together and hung them around my neck. I was still wearing my stupid cap. I took it off after I opened the door of the ute, spun it away into the night, and stepped out into the current. It washed around my waist, muscular, cold as ice. I told the girl to stay exactly where she was and sloshed around to the front of the ute, bare feet gripping slimy stones under the water. Switched the winch to free spool and pulled out the cable, hauling it behind me as I waded to the bank. I looped it around the biggest tree I could find, pulling it tight and clipping it with the hitch hook. Then waded back in, swung inside the ute, all wet and steaming beside the shivering girl, and engaged the winch motor.

'Now you'll see how it's done,' I told her.

A spray of droplets leaped from the cable when it spanged taut, shining like diamonds in the glare of the headlights. I cranked the motor in short pulls, rocking the ute to and fro until at last it jerked free and the winch was reeling it in, pulling it at a slant against the strong river current. I saw a shelf of rock looming out of the dark and yanked the yoke hard over, trying and failing to steer out of trouble. The girl gave a little scream, the ute banged

48

into the rock and scraped past, and I switched off the damn winch motor and took control, driving the ute through the shallows, bumping up onto the riverbank.

I mopped myself dry as best I could with my jacket, pulled on my clothes and boots, and climbed out of the ute and uncoupled the cable from the tree. When I came back, squinting in the dazzle of the headlights, the girl was gone.

After the first little kick of panic a cool calm rolled over me. I grabbed the flashlight I'd stuffed into the kitbag, circled around the ute and found prints in the snow leading away downstream, caught up with her in less than two minutes. She was walking steadily through the falling snow, hunched inside her little jacket, her fur hat tamped low over her eyes. When I laid a hand on her shoulder she stopped and stood there, shivering, refusing to look at me.

'You're going in the wrong direction,' I said.

'No I'm not,' she said, trying for defiance but sounding close to tears. 'If I follow the river it will take me back to the work camp.'

'You'll probably break a leg, stumbling around in the dark on your own. If the cold doesn't get you first. Or wolves.'

'There aren't any wolves. You just made that up.'

'There are wolves and things worse than wolves out here. Bad people. Crazy people.'

'As bad as you?'

'I'm the kind of bad person you want on your side. I saved you from the bravos who tried to snatch you, didn't I?'

The girl stared off into the darkness, as if taking one more look at the path she wanted to take.

'Let's get back to the ute,' I said. 'I know a place where we can rest up. We'll be there before you know it.'

7

The ute's steering was cocked to the right and a couple of its body panels were crumpled and gouged, but otherwise it appeared to have survived the river crossing relatively unscathed. We headed west, slanting towards the Albone Valley, climbing a long slope out of the forest. Trees thinning to scattered clumps, snow falling thickly now, visibility down to a few metres. I was driving at walking pace, more or less feeling my way along, when the night-vision display cut out and a ribbon of alarm icons began to stream across the canopy. A bare moment later all four wheels lost power and poisonous white smoke began to snake into the interior.

The girl and I clambered out into snow blowing on a freezing wind. As I dragged the kitbag from the ute I glimpsed a flicker of flames at the buckled edge of the battery compartment – something must have been fritzed when we hit that rock. I scooped big handfuls of snow over the fire, but there were flames inside the ute now, and with a sudden thump and blast of heat the entire vehicle caught alight.

We retreated to a safe distance and watched it burn. A chalice of flames tinting the snow falling around it blood red. Stinking smoke driven this way and that by the wind.

I was having trouble sequencing what had just happened, yet it somehow seemed inevitable that I'd end up here on this bleak hillside in a snowstorm, my plans actually going up in smoke in front of my eyes.

'Well this is great,' the girl said. 'What are we going to do now?'

She'd lost her hat – taken it off in the ute, forgotten to retrieve it when we'd scrambled out.

'We're going to walk,' I said, because in my mind we were still travelling towards the refuge and I couldn't think of any other way of getting there. Bringing up my fone, making a call, asking for rescue? It didn't even cross my mind.

I shook a heap of cold weather gear from the overstuffed kitbag, sorted out a down gilet, a pair of gloves, a windproof jacket and windproof trousers. Threw them at the girl and told her to put them on.

'My bodysuit will keep me warm,' she said.

'Then why are you shivering? It's minus ten plus wind chill, and going to get colder. Put on that gear and lose your fancy shoes,' I said, handing her the smaller pair of snow boots I'd snaffled back in the transport office.

I let her lean against me while, standing on one leg and then the other, she kicked off her silver-toed ankle grippers and stepped into the boots. I pulled windproof trousers over my uniform pants, shrugged into a windproof jacket, and wedged my feet in the other pair of snow boots and stamped around in a circle until they had adjusted to a snug fit.

The burning shell of the ute sizzled as it sank into snow melt, flames flickering, flaring in a gust of wind, dying back. I thought of the distance we had to go, thought of drones sailing high in the snowy dark, spotting the fire and swooping in to investigate.

'We have to get going,' I told the girl, and had to make some ugly threats to drive her forward.

The burning ute diminished to a dying star, lost in snow and darkness as we climbed the bare slope, slogging through drifts, picking our way by the small beam of my flashlight. The girl trudged in my footsteps, the hood of her bodysuit pulled over her head, the collar of the overlarge jacket turned up and buttoned tight so only her eyes showed. We must have looked as strange and desperate as a pair of explorers from olden times, got up in inadequate clothing, stumbling through a storm in unmapped and unforgiving territory.

I hoped that we were heading into the Albone Valley, hoped to find an overhang or crevice in the bluffs along its north side where we could shelter, but the girl was already flagging, dropping behind, floundering through the snow. At last we blundered into a small field of erratics, found two big boulders leaning together with a narrow space under the point where they kissed. I scraped a brittle lace of ice from the floor and built a snow wall in front, and the girl and I sat shoulder to shoulder in this modest shelter while I used the stove to brew tea from snow melt, stirring plenty of sugar into it. The girl drank quickly, gripping the cup in both hands, but refused to share the biscuits and jam I found in one of the ration packs.

'Food is fuel,' I said. 'You'll need it.'

She made the smallest of shrugs inside her overlarge jacket.

'The only way out of this is to stick with me and do exactly as I say.'

'Look where that got us,' she said under her breath.

I gave her a break, pretended I didn't hear that. I'd found only one sleeping bag in the lockers of the transport office, insisted that she take it. She was too tired to argue. There wasn't enough space for us to lie down, so she sat half-turned from me, head pillowed on a bulge of stone. I had been warm enough during the hike, but despite huddling close to the stove I could feel the cold settling into my bones. The reality of our plight was sinking in too. It was a very comprehensive disaster. I'd lost the ute, I wasn't certain where we were, how far we had to go, how things would play out when I tried to ransom the girl.

I thought of my friends, what they'd say. Lola, her opinion didn't count, by now she must have been arrested for the same shit I'd been caught up in. Sage would probably tell me to ditch the girl, go it alone. And Paz . . . Paz would call me every kind of fucking fool, but she knew my family's history and I believed that once she calmed down she'd be sympathetic, tell me that I was a husky, and huskies always finished what they started.

Weak sauce I know, but it was all I had. I couldn't go back. Couldn't surrender. No, I'd go on, I'd find the damn refuge and ransom the girl and in a couple of weeks I'd be in Auckland, looking across the waters of Waitematā Harbour at the carnival lights of the Wheel . . .

When I woke, my clothes were crackling with frost, my feet were frozen, there was a sliding queasiness in my gut, and the girl was gone. The sleeping bag crumpled beside me, the snow wall trodden down. I scrambled out into thin dawn light and a keen wind. It had stopped snowing. Thin strips of cloud layered above the distant ridge of Weasel Hill glowed pink ahead of the rising sun. I saw the girl standing in a knee-deep drift a little way below me, semaphoring with her arms. And heard a voice blowing on the wind and felt my heart catch.

I ran straight at her, knocked her into a drift and held her tight while the voice, a woman's voice, called her name. Called Keever's name.

Muffled against my breast, the girl said, 'They found us.'

I told her to shut up. The voice was faint and far off, coming and going. Kamilah Toomy. Kamilah Toomy. We are here to help you. We are here to help you. Keever Bishop. Keever Bishop. Surrender the girl. Surrender the girl. Kamilah Toomy. Kamilah . . .

I thought of police drones floating through Star City before a raid, warning people to get off the streets and stay in their homes until further notice. Sometimes a lockdown would last for two or three days while snatch squads went from door to door, looking for gang members or political troublemakers while monotonous threats and orders broadcast by drones echoed through the canyons between the apartment blocks. But I couldn't see anything moving in the paling sky and the voice was drifting away, fading to silence. If there had been a drone up there above us, the thing had moved on.

The girl squirmed beneath me, said she was freezing to death, couldn't breathe, and I relented and let her sit up.

'They'll come back,' she said, angrily dusting snow from her clothes. 'They won't stop looking until they find us. But if you let me go, I won't tell them about you.'

'If I let you go, you'd freeze to death in about five minutes.'

'I'm not entirely helpless. I can light a fire, they'll see the smoke . . . And when they find me, I'll tell them I don't know anything about you. I swear I won't.'

'Listen,' I said.

'What I am supposed to be listening for?' the girl said after a moment.

The snowy slope dropped away to dark forest cut by the Pyke River. Above us, cliffs rooted in cones of scree curved south and west towards the Albone Valley. Everything quiet and still in cold early light, only the whisper of wind hunting among stones and boulders and the chirp of an unseen bird, now here, now there. A hopeful sound that lifted my heart.

'Do you hear any more drones?' I said. 'Any helis, any search parties? No? That's because they aren't looking for me. They don't know where I went, where I'm going. They don't care. They think Keever Bishop kidnapped you. They're looking for him. And Keever, he probably isn't even on the peninsula any more.'

Lola must have told the state police that I'd taken the girl, but no one had seen me drive off with her. And it was no secret that I had been Keever's baby behind the wire, the police probably thought I'd gone with him . . . I was suddenly brimming with stupid optimism. I had gotten away free and clear, the blizzard had blown itself out, things could only get better. The refuge was no more than a day's walk away. We'd hole up there and I'd figure out what to do next. How to ransom the girl. How to arrange my passage off the peninsula.

The girl wanted to know who this Keever Bishop was, why the police thought he had abducted her. That was the word she used – abducted. I told her that Keever was a bad man, rich and powerful, sent down for tax evasion, more or less running the camp. Told her that he was going to be extradited to Australia, to stand trial for murder, and had worked up a plan to get out from under.

'He organised the riot, it gave him cover while he escaped. And abducting you – sounds nicer than kidnapping, doesn't it? Abducting you, that was part of his plan too.'

'How do you know all this?' the girl said. 'Wait. You were working for him, weren't you?'

'He found out that I was related to your father, told me to use that to make trouble at the opening ceremony. I thought it was to create a distraction, like the riot. I didn't know he wanted to snatch you until those two bravos turned up.'

'So you took me instead.'

'I like to think I saved you.'

I was growing uneasy about where this conversation was heading. Exactly how I was involved with Keever, how Alberto Toomy was involved with him. Why I had gone on the run. All kinds of complications I didn't need, and the girl didn't need to hear about. So when she started to ask another question I gave her a hard look and held my hand up, palm out, the way I'd shut down a con who started to get mouthy.

'You don't have to worry about Keever Bishop,' I said. 'He's long gone. It's shaping up to be a fine day, and we have some walking to do. The sooner we get to it the better. But before we set off I think we should have some breakfast.'

The touch of nausea had vanished. I was suddenly ravenous. Back inside our little cave, I brewed tea, broke open one of the ration packs. The girl ate a handful of dried fruit and nuts, nibbled half a *marraqueta* spread with apricot jam. I devoured everything else. The rest of the *marraqueta*, chicken and rice, a lump of quinoa and avocado, a chalky *leche asada*.

'It's cold, we'll be walking a fair way, so we need to load up with plenty of calories,' I told the girl, but she refused to share the *leche asada*. Sulking again.

I packed up the stove and the sleeping bag and we set off, the girl stepping in my bootprints, careful and neat as a cat. It was slow going, slogging through fresh-fallen snow, stumbling into buried sinkholes, climbing down into ravines, climbing back out. I was constantly aware that we were exposed to any eyes hanging high in the blue blue sky, that we might even be visible to a spysat, two dots moving through a powdery white landscape, but the sun was warm on our backs, the cold air scoured my lungs, feathery wisps of snow blew from the crests of ridges, sparkling in diamond sunlight, and the whole world seemed fresh and clean. Reborn. Renewed. I remembered walking with Mama on days like this and my heart lifted on a tide of bittersweet nostalgia and for a little while everything seemed possible.

We followed the curve of the cliffs into the mouth of the Albone Valley. Tongues of rocky debris mantled with snow, remnants of landslides common in glacial valleys after the disappearance of ice that had once buttressed the valley walls, plunged to a river snaking among scattered clumps of dwarf pines and big boulders washed down the valley by floods. On the far side, the cliffs of Wolseley Buttress stood against the sky, sheer black rock fretted with white snow. Ahead, the valley climbed towards the remnant of the glacier which had carved it. No sign of civilisation apart from an old mining road on a low embankment, the snow that covered it untracked, and a truss bridge thrown across the river.

And there, beyond the curve the mining road made before it crossed the bridge, was a smooth ribbon of snow cut into the slope above the river. The beginning of the ecopoet road, exactly where it should be.

We stopped for a brew of tea and a bite to eat on a gravelly runout blown clean of snow. A little way below, the ecopoet road bent around an elf stone, a finger of smooth black rock set in a kerb of white stones. One face carved with runes in a language made up by someone back in the twentieth century. I pretended to translate them, although I actually remembered the stone's name from Mama's geography lessons. *The Gate of the Ghost Wolves.*

I told the girl that my grandmother had once met a man who claimed to have met the man who made the elf stones. 'He was one of the first settlers. A geologist employed by one of the mining companies. His work took him all over the peninsula. He'd find suitable stones, lever them upright, use an automatic cutter to engrave them.'

'There's one near the harbour in O'Higgins,' the girl said.

'That's right. *The First and Last.* At the spring equinox people hang wreaths of kelp on it and wish for a good summer.'

'Do you believe in them?'

'That there are actual elves? Creatures who were living here before people came, who cause mischief if we trespass on their sacred places? They're just stories people tell. But I like the idea that there are things we don't know. City people think the back country is some kind of park. It really isn't. It's a wilderness, full of danger and mystery.'

'But it was made by your people. They designed and planted all this.'

'They quickened it. It's grown wild and strange in its own way since then.'

At first glance you might have thought that the two of us, chatting away as we sat in the warm sun, were good companions resting in the middle of a leisurely hike. But the girl's hands were crawling around each other in her lap, and every so often, when she thought that I wasn't looking, she glanced sideways at me, nervous, appraising.

She said, 'What about you?'

'What about me?'

'Do you think that your parents and the other ecopoets should have made people like you?'

'Your mother and father made you what you are,' I said. 'How is that different?'

'But they made you into something else.'

'A monster, you mean. Less than human.'

I wasn't angry. I'd heard it all a hundred times before. The ignorant, the prejudiced, the genuinely curious – they all expected me to justify my existence. They all wanted to know what it was like to live inside the skin of someone edited down to their germline, a symbol of the free ecopoets' rebellion, so on.

The girl said, 'Is that what you think you are? A monster?'

'I'm as human as you,' I told her. 'Just a little different, is all.'

Remember who you are, Mama used to tell me when I came home upset because tourists had stared at me or had made remarks or taken pictures. Remember that this is your land. You live here, it's yours by right. They are only visitors.

The girl asked if was it true I had a layer of blubber under my skin, could I close my nostrils underwater? Having fun with me now. I thought that was a good sign, it meant that she was relaxing. Letting down her guard. And if I told her about myself, who and what I was, it would help her understand why I had done what I'd done, maybe even win her sympathy.

'I'm nothing like a seal,' I said. 'Or any other kind of animal. All of my edits are based on human genes. Some Inuit, some

57

Fuegian. Storing brown fat and burning it when I need to stay warm, that's a Neanderthal trait. My elevated metabolism, higher core temperature and what's called non-shivering thermogenesis, I get that from the Kawésqar. You know who they are, the Kawésqar?'

The girl shrugged.

'They're native to Patagonia. Back in the day, they could sleep naked in primitive shelters at zero degrees. There's a story that once upon a time a group of Kawésqar visiting Esperanza were mistaken for huskies. Attacked by ignorant yahoos. Of course, we're a lot bigger than most Kawésqar. And most other people, come to that. Some say it's just a side effect of the genetic mix. Others claim it was designed in. Increasing someone's size lowers their surface area to volume ratio. Minimises loss of body heat, so on. Though if we were smaller, I guess, we wouldn't be so scary. People might pay less attention to us.'

'Isn't it what you are, how you were made, that people are really afraid of?' the girl said. She seemed genuinely interested.

'There are plenty of countries where it's legal to change the germline. Where people like your father don't discriminate against people like me.'

'I don't think he's ever talked about huskies.'

'He's a member of the party that was planning to neuter us. Hard not to take that personally. But that's not what this is about.'

'No, you want money,' the girl said flatly.

'I want a little help is all.'

'Then call him. Call my father. Get this over with.'

So much for winning her sympathy.

'I will. In a little while. When we get to where we're going.'

'You still haven't told me where that is.'

'You'll see when we get there.'

'Maybe I won't go any further.'

'Of course you will.'

As we walked on, I asked the girl whether she knew the story of how our grandfather, Edward Toomy, had met my grandmother.

'I know he ran around with ecopoets when he wasn't much older than me, he had a son he didn't know about until years later. My father's enemies tried to use it against him.' The girl glanced at me, said, 'Didn't he die, the son? Your father.'

'His fishing boat sank in a storm,' I said. 'A couple of years after that we were rounded up and exiled to Deception Island.'

I'd been three years old back then, have only vague memories of a bustle of women in the aftermath, of being scared when Mama clutched me so fiercely I thought she'd never let me go. I can't remember if she cried then. I know she didn't ever cry afterwards. She turned her grief outward, turned it into anger. I don't really remember my father, either. Little more than a looming friendly presence, rough hands scarred by hard work. I can't see see his face, can't hear his voice.

The girl said that she was sorry, and seemed to mean it.

'I'm not angry with you,' I said. 'Or trying to make you feel guilty. But we're family, and you deserve to know the true story of how Eddie and Isabella met, how they had a son together. It's a pretty good story, too. Has a little of everything. Adventure. Romance. Oh, and betrayal. We mustn't forget betrayal, because that's what led to this.'

The Ballad of
Isabella and Eddie

When Isabella Schilling Morales moved to the Antarctic Peninsula, the world was still struggling to adapt to the consequences of global warming. Climate change driven by the increase in the temperature of Earth's atmosphere and oceans had been wilder and more extreme than predicted way back at the beginning of the twenty-first century. The weather had become feral. Deranged. Heatwaves were more frequent and more intense. Rainfall was heavier and droughts were longer. Meltwater from ice sheets in Greenland and Antarctica had contributed to a rise in sea level of more than three metres and more than a billion people had been made homeless, displaced as coasts and cities were flooded, fleeing famines, water wars and civil wars. It was a comprehensive disaster.

The Antarctic Peninsula, a skinny archipelago of mountainous islands united by permanent ice sheets and curving north from the mainland like a thumb sticking out of a fist, had warmed much faster than the rest of the continent. Coastal ice shelves broke up, undermined by intrusion of warmer currents, and glaciers retreated inland, exposing land and lodes of ore which had been buried under ice for millions of years. After expiration in 2048 of the old Antarctic Treaty System, which had set aside the continent as a scientific preserve, new agreements permitted exploitation of the peninsula's mineral and petroleum resources in exchange for funding of geoengineering projects that could help to protect the icecap on the mainland. The first settlers were sponsored by governments and transnational corporations, but they were soon followed by kleptocrats seeking sanctuary from political and social instability, and despite storms and mountainous waves a good number of refugees also made it across the Drake Passage. An oil tanker crowded with Pakistani men, women and children beached on Elephant Island, for instance, half of them freezing to death before help arrived. A container ship from Mozambique limped into port at Esperanza with less than a hundred survivors among two thousand dead. One day an ancient 777X packed with more than four hundred people fleeing civil war in Uruguay, including the former Vice-President, ten cabinet ministers and three Supreme Court judges, landed at O'Higgins International Airport. So on, so on. At last, the Antarctic Authority was forced to impose a quota system. After that, the only people granted permanent residency rights were those who could afford to purchase citizenship, and key workers sponsored by the authority or by transnats.

Isabella Morales was one such worker, armed with a brand new doctorate in bioengineering from the Universidad de Chile, recruited by ecopoets who were greening tracts of coastal land. There was still an abundance of marine life on and around the shores of the peninsula, but its sparse terrestrial ecosystem had failed to adapt to post-warming conditions and human activity had introduced invasive species which flourished as the climate thawed. Rats, cockroaches, Argentinian ants. Iceland poppy, yellow bog sedge that choked new waterways, grasses that displaced meadows of native mosses. Rather than attempt the near impossible task of eradicating the invaders, there was the idea, back then, that it would be better to establish robust and diverse ecosystems that could withstand them, to guide and channel inevitable, inexorable change.

It was a version of ecopoiesis, the old technocratic dream of fabricating self-sustaining ecosystems in orbital colonies, on lifeless planets. Critics grumbled that it was nothing but hubristic greenwash, an attempt to divert attention from exploitation of the peninsula's resources, but they were outnumbered by advocates who claimed that it would be a small but significant atonement for all the wildernesses destroyed or compromised by climate change, industrialisation, deforestation and agriculture. A symbol of hope and renewal in an age when even nature could no longer be considered natural.

Building terrestrial ecosystems from scratch was less ambitious than the lost dreams of turning Venus or Mars into versions of Earth, but it was still difficult and monstrously expensive. Isabella joined a little tribe of third-generation ecopoets who worked in labs and greenhouses during the interminable winters and lived in tents and ATVs in the brief summers, moving from place to place, driving forward on a vast variety of projects. An energetic, dedicated, disputatious mix of scientists, Gaians and anarcho-primitivists, they were notionally supervised by the Antarctic Authority, but over the years had developed a considerable degree of independence, mutating into a non-hierarchical collective united by common goals, sharing resources and decision-making. As the glaciers retreated, exposing broad valleys between mountain ridges still capped with permanent ice, the ecopoets established a version of the tundra found on islands north of the peninsula. Later, with the effects of the great warming continuing apace, they began to plant out forests, and introduced the first animals. Slowly, a green stain of life spread south along the peninsula's ragged coasts.

Elsewhere, opencast mines were ripping apart landscapes untouched for millions of years, settlements were springing up along the west coast, and the former science stations of Esperanza and O'Higgins at the tip of the peninsula, had become sprawling cities. Apartment blocks. Supermarkets and fast-food joints and shopping malls. Too many people threatening to repeat the same old mistakes of industrialisation and overexploitation. So back then, before their work was declared illegal and they were harried and persecuted, the ecopoets were useful PR for the Antarctic Authority, a source of upbeat news stories and images of attractive young people planting trees along the banks of wild new rivers, spreading grass and wildflower seed on scree slopes, raising animals and releasing them into the wild.

When Isabella joined them, the ecopoets were more than forty years into their great work. An image of her from that time showed a beautiful young woman with wind-tousled waves of long black hair and a heart-shaped face, sitting cross-legged on a cushion of moss as she played with an Arctic fox cub in her lap. This was who Edward Toomy fell in love with. And Isabella fell for him. Love at first sight. Both of them struck by the lightning.

Edward, mostly called Eddie back then, had been born in Esperanza when his parents had been working for the Antarctic Authority. He grew up in New Zealand, returned to the peninsula on a two-year contract with a petroleum company, and stayed on because he had dual citizenship. He was twenty-six when he met Isabella. Blond hair, blue eyes, a swimmer's body and oodles of charm.

Interviews he gave later in life always mentioned that. His boyish charm and enthusiasm. His raffish good looks. How he'd been a diving champion at school, just missing the cut for New Zealand's Olympic team. Trouble was, he was also selfish and carelessly cruel. An unscrupulous rogue. He didn't mean to hurt people, but people got hurt by him all the same. He'd quit university after spending a year in a haze of drugs and beer, and signed up for work in Antarctica on a whim. Because he could live and work there by right of birth. Because he wanted to prove to his parents (mother a high-level civil servant, father an accountant) that he could make his own way in life. 'I like to think that if I'd been born in an earlier century I would have been an explorer,' he said in an interview much later. 'Or maybe a pirate.'

Instead, he fell in with criminals. But first he fell in love with Isabella, or at least fell in love with the idea of falling in love with her. And she fell in love with him. Early in summer, adrift after his contract with the petroleum company ended, Eddie moved in with her and enthusiastically embraced the ecopoets' work. To begin with, anyway. By the time winter had begun to grip the land he was already having second thoughts about joining a tribe of dedicated idealists who put the needs of the collective before the needs of any individual, and lived in the back country with zero concessions to comfort.

Isabella was assigned to the labs in Happy Valley, working on edited plants and ecosystem design, raising shrubs and saplings for the next season's planting in big greenhouses. Eddie Toomy, possessing no special skills, was sent off to drudge in the soil factory in Primavera, two hundred kilometres away. They saw each other maybe once a month, and Eddie spent most of the time bitching about his work and his bosses. He liked the idea of the nobility of labour, but he wasn't so keen on actually doing it.

Still, he stuck it out that winter. Perhaps he really was in love with Isabella, and believed that loading and cleaning out soil incubators was payment for his good fortune. And even in Antarctica winter wasn't forever. Late spring, he and Isabella were out and about together, helping to establish a biome in a valley left by the retreat of the Victory Glacier. They planted tough grasses, moss and shrubs on clay and gravel moraines that rippled across the valley floor, sprayed mixtures of soil and seeds across bare scree and rock slopes, and in sheltered spots began to establish a dwarf shrub heath by planting out thickets of skeleton-leaf willow, dwarf southern beech and dwarf birch, white Arctic mountain heather, crowberry, Magellan barberry.

It was said that if you ate the red berries of the Magellan barberry you would never leave the peninsula. Isabella fed a handful to Eddie as they lay in a mossy dell one balmy day in December, and he fed a handful to her. They had just made love, the moss was dry and soft as lambswool, and the sun was warm on their bare skin. They promised to stay together for ever and ever, talked about the future they wanted to share, the things they'd do, but their promises and plans barely outlasted the summer.

A couple of months later Eddie was supervising a road train, trucking in supplies to the Victory Valley crew along a route the railway would later follow. Sometimes he'd stay over for a day or two in Eyrie Bay instead of heading straight back, returning with a killer hangover and puppy-dog remorse. As the days grew shorter and the first snows fell, his absences grew ever more frequent. He had a big row about being assigned to work in the soil factory again. And then Isabella told him that she was pregnant, and soon afterwards he left on the road train and didn't come back.

He texted Isabella from the airport in O'Higgins, told her where the road train was parked, explained that he'd snagged a job in

Australia thanks to a tip from an old buddy. He needed some time away from the peninsula, he said, promised he'd be back in the spring with plenty of money, in time for the baby's birth. Maybe he believed all that. Maybe he believed that he just needed to get away for a while, get his head straight. He was as good at lying to himself as he was at lying to everyone else. Anyway, that was it, he was gone.

8

The girl claimed that Eddie Toomy hadn't known that his girl-friend was pregnant, said that he'd only found out about his son years later.

'You're trying to make out that he was selfish. But it was the other way around. Your grandmother didn't care that he left. She had already used him to get what she wanted. I'm sorry, but that's the truth.'

'The truth according to Eddie and his lawyers, back when his enemies were trying to smear him,' I said.

'And of course you know he was lying,' the girl said.

We were following the ecopoet road, which was pinched between a lake of milky meltwater and tall cliffs that leaned back against the cold blue sky. The terminal face of the Albone Glacier stood at the far end of the lake, a wall of dirty ice gashed by deep fractures and topped with ragged spires and pinnacles that reflected splinters of bright sunshine. We'd made good time so far, but I was beginning to feel a nagging urgency. There were only a few hours of daylight left, we still had a way to go before we reached the refuge, and I was incubating a faint but distinct queasiness, was beginning to wish that I hadn't eaten that tube of shrimp paste back at our rest stop.

'I know that Isabella tried to reach out to Eddie after he ran off,' I said. 'She gave up because he'd shed all his social media. Made himself hard to find. He was good at that. Leaving people, severing all ties. He did it to his parents after he quit New Zealand for the peninsula. He did it to my grandmother, his friends at Lake Macleod . . .'

'They were *criminals*,' the girl said, with the theatrical exaspera-tion of a child pointing out a fact that should have been obvious to everyone.

'So was he.'

'Not really. And only by accident. I didn't know him, he died before I was born, but I know he used to tell funny stories about it.'

'How he stole money that could have helped Isabella and their son, that sort of thing?'

'If you take something from criminals, it isn't really stealing.'

'I reckon they'd see it differently.'

I was thinking of Keever, thinking that as far as he was concerned I had stolen the girl from him. And of course I'd stolen you from him, too, although he didn't know about that. And yes, I knew that the girl's claim that Isabella hadn't told Eddie about their son spookily echoed my decision to keep you a secret. But that didn't have anything to do with selfishness. I'd chosen not to tell Keever for all the right reasons. To protect you. To save myself.

'My grandfather made good use of that money,' the girl said, grimly determined to defend the honour of the Toomy family. No doubt she'd been schooled about their fabulous achieve-ments all her life, how they deserved their fortune because every cent had been earned by superhuman talent and honest hard work. 'He built things, created jobs, gave to charity. You can't tell me the people he took it from would have done any better.'

'And while he was living the high life, he didn't ever try to get in touch with Isabella,' I said. 'Not until years later, when he betrayed her, and their son, and the rest of the free ecopoets. Did he turn that into one of his funny stories, too?'

'When two people split up,' the girl said, 'they tell different versions of what happened. They blame each other.'

I remembered her father's string of girlfriends. Remembered that, like me, she'd lost her mother. Yeah, but she hadn't been dumped in an orphanage or turned out into the world all alone. She'd been cushioned by all the advantages I'd been denied.

'What happened, our grandfather split our family into two,' I said. 'One half rich, the other poor. One half on the square, the other persecuted for their beliefs. Like in a fairy tale or a *novela*.'

'If this is a fairy tale, I suppose you think I'm the princess.'

'Why not? And I'm the monster. The ogre. The outcast.'

'Well you definitely did a bad thing,' the girl said, with a cool look.

I tried to turn that into a joke. 'And if you don't do what I say, Princess, I'll grind your bones to make my bread.'

Maybe it was the idea of bone-powder flour. Maybe it was the thought of bread, its thick yeasty odour . . . My queasiness thickened into nausea, rose past my heart, jumped into the back of my throat. I burped a shrimpy burp, barely had time to step behind a boulder before I doubled over and puked up my lunch. I coughed and spat and another spasm hit me and I puked again.

I'd looked up morning sickness when I started to lose my breakfast regularly. Apparently it could affect you any time of day in early pregnancy, and in some women it lasted all day long. I didn't have it as bad as that, but it was still a fucking inconvenience.

As I ate a mouthful of snow to get rid of the taste, the girl told me that she could call for help if I unblocked her fone.

'I'm not ill.'

'It could be food poisoning.'

'It isn't anything. We should get moving, it'll be dark soon.'

'My father will give you what you want, I swear he will. He'll make everything right.'

'I don't need his help. Or yours. Let's get going, or we'll be walking most of the rest of the way in the dark.'

A little further on the road began to climb steeply, slanting towards the terminal face of the glacier, rising above it, revealing a river of ice that, shattered by pressure ridges and tilted blocks and deep crevasses, curved away between the bare sides of the valley. Directly below, a massive blanket of snow-covered rubble spread across the glacier's surface, and after the girl and I followed the road around the belly of a bluff I realised where that rubble had come from, what had happened.

A section of the cliffs had collapsed and the glacier's slow steady flow had carried the leading edge of the debris beyond the landslip. It had left a scallop-shaped scar easily a kilometre long, and the road, the road, the road was gone.

Heartsick, I led the girl through a litter of fallen rocks to the splintered end of the road, an abrupt drop to a tumble of snow-dusted boulders and stone blocks. No way forward, no way to reach the refuge. Even if we could climb down there was no guarantee we could climb back up on the far side, and it would be impossibly difficult and dangerous to lead the girl across the churn of debris and the shattered surface of the glacier.

I howled. Actually howled. Howled and beat at a facet of broken rock with my fists, howled at the sky and howled into the echo of my howls coming back to me across the unforgiving ice. I couldn't fucking believe it. Couldn't believe my fucking luck. First the ute, now this. It was as if the entire world was conspiring against me.

The girl flinched away from me. I suppose I must have looked a sight. Wild with frustration. At the end, as they say, of my tether.

'Don't say a word,' I told her. 'Don't say one fucking word.'

I wasn't ready to surrender. I wouldn't ever surrender. It would mean giving birth to you in jail, nursing you in jail, giving you up to child services and a state orphanage, and there was no fucking way I was going to let that happen. So I had to find another route to the refuge, or at least find a place where we could hole up for the night. And I had to do it quickly because we had only a little daylight left, we were running out of time. I squashed the temptation to reboot my fone and ask her to find an alternate route – the way my luck was running that would lead the police straight to me. Then I remembered the bridge over the river, and told the girl that we were going to backtrack and make a slight detour.

She nodded tightly. She looked as if she was about to burst into tears. Which was pretty much how I felt.

The walk away from the glacier, following our tracks back down the ecopoet road as the sun sank towards the shoulder of the valley and shadows lengthened and the air grew colder, was like a retreat from a lost battle. We crossed the desolate truss bridge, edging past a gap where a chunk of decking had fallen away, the black river running fast below. Long fingers of cloud were reaching in from the west. More snow on the way. I could feel it. Way things were going it didn't surprise me in the least.

The mining road, broken by ice heave and blanketed in snow, climbed in steep winding coils towards the notch of a pass. Several times on the long ascent I had to wait while the girl stood with her head down, hands on her knees, doing nothing but breathe. Gasping, puffing out great clouds of smoke. My anger was turning inward. I was beginning to blame myself for the fiasco, was afraid that I was taxing the girl beyond her limits, knew that the way to freedom and the Wheel was going to be so very much harder than I'd first thought. But I wasn't about to give up. I was as stubborn as Mama, and far more desperate.

At last the road levelled out, cutting straight between tall bluffs. The girl and I slogged on through drifts of snow sculpted into ripples and waves, heads down against a freezing wind. We had climbed above the thousand metre contour, but the refuge was still more than twenty kilometres away, we had to find someplace to wait out the night as soon as possible, and now the girl stopped again. Sat down in the snow and said that she couldn't walk any further.

She shook her head dumbly when I told her that she would freeze to death if she stayed where she was, refused to get up even when I yelled at her, so I swept her up into my arms and set off at a jog along the road. Stamping across snow pack, ploughing through drifts. Sweating inside my windproofs and uniform, my feet frozen, my face numb. Once, I tripped on a half-buried rock and banged down on my knees. The girl half woke, tried to struggle out of the cradle of my arms, but I held her tight and pushed to my feet and went on, and at last saw a crowd of tall slim spires strung along a ridge off to my left, stark against the last of the daylight. It was an old wind farm, most of its turbines motionless, frozen stiff, a few faintly groaning, vanes turning in the pitiless frigid breeze, as I trudged past with the girl's awkward weight cradled against my chest. My legs and back ached, I was running on fumes, but was driven by a sharp pang of hope, knew that some kind of settlement must be nearby. Quite soon a short spur split off the road, curving towards a terraced amphitheatre cut into the flank of a low ridge and filled edge to edge with the bloody light of the setting sun. I followed the slant of the spur towards the floor of this open-pit mine, ducking through a broken gate, passing a tipper truck squatting on the rims of tyreless wheels taller than me. The rake of a conveyer belt. All kinds of abandoned machinery. Steep cones of tailings like a miniature mountain range. Everything still, everything shrouded in snow.

The place was deserted, long abandoned, and that was fine by me. The last thing I needed was company, and there was shelter dead ahead, a single-storey shack with snow drifted high against one wall and plastic sheeting stretched across its roof and lashed down with a web of nylon cords. I shouldered its door open, set the girl down and looked around. A barricade of old-fashioned office furniture, steel shelving packed with tools, parts for machines that would never run again, chunks of dark-veined rock, cans and plastic trays full of screws and nails and bolts, everything dusted with frost.

I was dragging a desk across the floor to the middle of the room when the girl spoke, asking what this place was. She had sat up and was hugging herself, shuddering and shivering like an engine trying and failing to start.

'Somewhere we can rest up a while,' I said, and tipped the desk on its side. 'Show me your fingers and your feet. I want to check for frostbite.'

'My suit keeps me warm,' the girl said.

'It redistributes the heat you make when you move about. But you weren't moving much for the last couple of hours because I was carrying you.'

'Whose fault was that?'

'Let me see.'

I had to pin her down, pulled off her gloves and boots, pulled down the hood of her bodysuit. No patches of dead whiteness on her fingers and toes, none on her ears. While she put on her socks and boots, glaring at me, I dragged another desk across the room, tipped it over so its legs meshed with the legs of the first, found a couple of filthy frost-stiffened blankets in a nest of rags in one corner and used them to improvise a tent. I told the girl to crawl inside and climb into her sleeping bag, and set the stove beside her and switched it on.

'It stinks in here,' she said. 'It smells like something died.'

'It's dry. And soon it'll be warm. We'll rest up tonight, head out at first light.'

'I won't walk any further. I don't care what you do to me. I won't.'

She was in a filthy mood, and like any angry teenager was channelling the tantrums of her much younger self. I told her that we'd both feel better after I'd brewed some tea, and went outside to collect clean snow.

The sun had set and the last of its light was fading towards the horizon, glowing red under clouds that covered half the sky. I followed my footprints back up the road to the broken gate at the entrance to the mine and climbed a hump of rock and looked all around, seeing nothing moving in the snowscape. Lucky, I thought. Lucky lucky lucky.

I'd been planning to stash the girl in the ecopoet refuge, but now I thought that this mine would do just as well. First thing next morning I'd call her father and negotiate the ransom. After he paid up I'd tell him where the girl was and make my escape across the Detroit Plateau. And if he called my bluff, fuck it, I'd tell him anyway.

The decision calmed me. I rehearsed what I needed to tell the girl and packed snow into a thick hard slab and carried it back to the shack. It was dark inside, a spark of light shining in the little tent I'd made between the upturned desks. When I set down the slab of snow and lifted the edge of one of the blankets, the girl, snug in her sleeping bag, looked up from the luminous rectangle she'd been studying.

Instantly furious, I tore it from her grip, flapped it in her face.

'What is this? What have you been doing?'

It was a slim, hand-sized tablet. One side sheathed in black leather, text printed on the pearlescent surface of the other.

Isander locked herself in the library and read long into the night about poisons.

'It's a book, only a book,' she said, snatching at it. I caught her wrist and in the brief struggle the makeshift tent collapsed around us. I reared up from the wreckage, holding the book out of the girl's reach, and that's when the door of the hut banged open and a shaggy creature stamped in and pointed a rifle at us and told us to put up our Christ-be-damned hands.

9

The intruder was a woman in her fifties or sixties, standing four-square and stinking in a long coat of badly cured reindeer hide, her hunting rifle jacked against her left hip. She was only a metre and a half tall but looked like she could fell an aurochs with a single blow, glaring at the girl and me with furious suspicion, demanding to know what we were doing in Young Old's place.

'Young Old?' I said.

'What I called him. Young because he wasn't much older than this girl. Old because his name was Oldin. Oldin Andersen. Young Old. Which hand do you favour?'

'The right.'

I wasn't inclined to ask the woman why she wanted to know. Her rifle was the kind that fired lead bullets kicked by percussively ignited explosive – back-country hunters claimed that they were more reliable than modern weapons, whose power packs were too quickly drained by the cold. This one had a polished wooden stock and a telescopic sight. I could have fitted my thumb into its bore.

'Why don't you use your left hand to ease out any weapons you got,' the woman said. 'Toss them on the floor.'

I dropped my pistol and shock stick at my feet, asked if Young Old was still around.

'He came here about ten years ago. Wanted to break down the old machines for scrap, but there wasn't any money in it so he left. You're one of them that escaped from the work camp on that goddamned railway. I heard all about it on the skywave.'

'*She* escaped,' the girl said. 'I'm Kamilah Toomy. My father is Alberto Toomy. Perhaps you've heard of him? The Honourable Deputy?'

The woman ignored her and said to me, 'The skywave said a bunch of you broke out. And the feds are offering a fat reward for your recapture. So the question is, can you make it worth my while not to hand you over to them?'

I told her that I actually was a fed, a corrections officer, asked for permission to open my windproof.

'Use your left hand. Do it nice and slow.'

I did it nice and slow, but the woman wasn't impressed by my uniform jacket, claimed that I could have stolen it. 'And this is the first time I've heard of a husky working for the feds.'

'Check out the photo on my ID,' I said, tapping the tag on my chest.

The woman squinted at it, said, 'Suppose I believe you. I'm not saying I do. Far from it. But if you are what you say you are, what are you doing out here with this girl?'

'I rescued her.'

'She's lying,' the girl said. 'Let me call my father—'

She shut up when the rifle dipped towards her.

'I'll get to you in a bit, pretty miss,' the woman said, and told me to say my piece.

'There was a big ceremony at the work camp yesterday,' I said. 'The official opening of the bridges we've been building. You may have seen some helis heading that way.'

The woman allowed that she might have noticed some extra sky traffic.

'The helis were bringing in VIPs. Very important people. Including this girl and her father. Who really is an honourable deputy, by the way. They came for the ceremony, and a riot kicked off right in the middle of it. Convicts broke out of their blocks, a couple of them tried to take this girl hostage, I stepped in and saved her. As for how we ended up here, well, I discovered the hard way that it isn't easy working for the service when you're a husky. I'd had enough, frankly, and decided to use the confusion of the riot to slip away. I broke my contract, but that doesn't make me a fugitive from justice.'

'Maybe you are, maybe you aren't,' the woman said. 'But here's the thing. I can't think of any good reason why you would want to bring that girl along with you.'

'It was kind of an accident,' I said.

'It was not,' the girl said.

'Didn't I tell you to wait your turn?' the woman told her.

I said, 'I've been trying to figure out how to return her to her father without getting into trouble. And I think you can help me.'

'Why should I do that?'

'If you help me, I'll make sure you get the reward for her safe return.'

'If there's any reward, I can get that myself. And I'll get a reward for handing you over, too.'

'There isn't any reward for handing me over. I'm not worth a thing to the authorities.'

'Well, I guess I'll have to ask them about that.'

'Go ahead. But as soon as they know where we are, they'll come and take us away. And when they get the money from the girl's father, do you think they'll share it with you? We're talking about feds. Who take from people like us with both hands, but don't ever give anything back.'

I watched the woman think about that. She said, 'I still don't see why I couldn't just talk to her father myself.'

'That would complicate things,' I said. 'Because I've already talked to him.'

'No she hasn't,' the girl said. 'It's another lie.'

I looked at her. 'When I went outside just now, how long was I away? Fifteen minutes? Twenty?'

The girl shrugged.

'It was a lot longer than I needed to grab some snow to make our tea. I called her father,' I told the woman. 'Let him know I had his daughter. I can arrange it so you can hand her over and collect the reward directly. A deal that doesn't involve the authorities.'

'I still don't see why I can't do that myself,' the woman said.

'First, you'll need his private number. Second, he'll think you had something to do with taking the girl. But if you let me make the arrangements, I can fix it so he'll get his daughter back and you'll get the reward.'

I know. A five-year-old could have spun a better story. But I was thinking on my feet with that damn rifle pointing at me, and it got the woman's attention.

She said, 'You'd let me keep the reward? All of it?'

'It seems a fair price for letting me go.'

'And how do I explain that you got away?'

'I'm a big strong husky. I overpowered you.'

'Try it.'

'I don't mean I could. Or that I want to. I mean that's what you'll tell the feds.'

'She's trying to trick you,' the girl said. 'If you let me call my father right now I'll make sure you get a reward. I swear I will.'

The woman said to me, 'Says on that badge your name is Austral Morales Ferrado.'

'That's because it is my name.'

'Your parents – were they ecopoets?'

'I'm a husky. What do you think?'

'You wouldn't happen to be related to Isabella Schilling Morales?'

'She was my grandmother. You know of her?'

'I know and admire her work. I was a biologist, once. A botanist. I surveyed this whole area, years back. I was working for the feds then. First and last time.'

'And you liked the place so much you decided to stay on.'

'Something like that. How well did you know her, your grandmother?'

'I've been told that I met her, but I was too young to remember it. I know some stories about her, though. Good ones.'

'I heard a rumour that she's hiding out somewhere on the mainland.'

'I've heard that story too.'

'Is it true?'

'Why don't I brew up some tea? I have a little food, too. I'll be happy to share it with you while I tell you what I know about Isabella, and discuss how to fix our little problem.'

'We'll go to my place,' the woman said. 'It'll be cosier there.'

10

Her name was Mayra Iturriaga. She told me that the mine had closed more than twenty years ago, after its shale-hosted copper deposits had been exhausted. Explained that she'd been using edited strains of bacteria to extract residual copper and tagalong metals, mostly zinc and silver, a touch of rhenium, from its spoil heaps. The mine's former owners had already processed the spoil, but her strains, developed from one my grandmother had developed to liberate phosphate from bedrock, were more efficient than anyone else's.

I played along with her claims to be my grandmother's number one fan and rightful inheritor, hoping that flattery would make her careless, but didn't tell her that the girl and I were related thanks to Isabella's relationship with Eddie Toomy – it would have made things way more complicated than they already were. Luckily the girl stayed quiet, warily watching as Mayra and I pretended to be the best of pals, not yet realising how dangerous our situation really was.

We were sitting cross-legged on a filthy carpet in one half of a square hut tucked behind the ruin of a big sectional garage and lined out with silvery insulation. There was a cot, a stove not much bigger than the one I carried, a plastic chair with a broken leg bandaged by black tape. Clothes and an assortment of tools and gadgets hung from pegs that jutted between the seams of the insulation. Much of the kit was brand new. Expensive. A hunting bow that looked as if it had been constructed from the bones of some exotic critter and probably cost more than a year's pay. A spear with a shaft shaped from a smoothed length of tree branch, a flaked stone point bound to it with rawhide laces. Three hand-sized drones. A neat little food printer that could convert almost any kind of fresh organic material into trail biscuits. A spotting scope and several pairs of field glasses. A rifle bipod. Behind the flimsy partition that divided the hut in two was a workbench, a tiny sink and a chemical toilet, and a two-seater skimmer, kept in the warmth like all back-country people's vehicles.

It was a comfortable ten degrees Celsius in the hut and smelled strongly of Mayra Iturriaga, who sat solid as Buddha in filthy much-patched wool shirt and trousers, her coarse grey hair braided into a rope that hung to the small of her back. She told me that she'd pulled all the metal that could be pulled from the spoil heaps, now worked as a hunting guide during the big game season and spent the rest of her time searching for seams of ore that mining company geologists had overlooked. She studied satellite maps and had learned how to dowse. She hadn't had much luck so far, the land hereabouts was a bitch that hid her secrets well, but it was only a matter of time . . .

Like all people who lived alone, once she got started talking about herself it was hard to stop her, and although I was vibrating with nerves I did my best to simulate interest. Mayra was playing the good back-country host, but she'd taken possession of my cutlery, her rifle rested within easy reach, and as soon as I'd seen all that gear pegged like trophies to the walls I knew that I'd let myself and the girl walk into a trap. All I could do was pretend that I was taken in by Mayra's act, drink tea with butter stirred into it, and wait for an opening, a moment of inattention or carelessness.

Now she was telling me that according to word on the skywave net most of the prisoners who'd escaped during the riot had been caught.

'For a while I was worried they might come this way. An old woman living alone, what could I do against desperate convicts? Luckily, it seems that most of them had the same thought, head north towards what they call civilisation. Which is why they were caught so easily. I expect that the rest will turn up soon.

Dead, most likely. Hard to survive out here if you don't know what you're doing.'

'Did they catch a man named Keever Bishop?'

'I didn't pay attention to names.'

'He's the man who started the riot.'

'And he's important to you,' Mayra said, and for a moment the thing she really was could be seen in her gaze.

'He's more dangerous than most. Like I said, the ringleader.'

'This is your second jailbreak, I believe. If the story that you and your mother escaped from prison is true.'

'It wasn't exactly prison. Where did you hear about it?'

'It's one of those tales people tell around campfires. I suppose they put you right back in prison after you were caught.'

'They put me in an orphanage.'

'Oh, that's right. Your mother died.'

I didn't rise to that. You can bet I wanted to punch her square in the mouth, but I knew I had to get her to drop her guard, catch her unawares.

'And then you took a job in a work camp,' she said. 'I would have thought you'd had enough of that kind of thing.'

'A person has to earn a crust somehow. And the prison service thought my previous experience would be useful.'

'I've seen how huskies are treated in the cities. I guess you hoped it would be better out here.'

No point rising to that, either.

'But it wasn't, was it?' Mayra said. 'Which is why you took off. Why you're here.'

'We're here because she kidnapped me,' the girl said, but with no real force. She had realised that this crazy woman wasn't going to help her.

'If she rescued you from that riot, sweetie, you should show more gratitude,' Mayra said.

'She's anxious to go home,' I said.

'You've picked up city habits,' Mayra said. 'Working in a prison. Helping to build that goddamned railway . . . What makes you think you could survive out here?'

'I've managed so far.'

'You know how I caught you?'

I shrugged. Pretending that it was no big deal. 'Either you tracked us, or you have some kind of alarm system.'

'I have cameras fixed up in the old wind farm. Watching the road, letting me know if any kind of trouble is on the way. And I knew exactly when to drop in on you because I have cameras inside Young Old's cabin, too. What do you think of that?'

I pretended to admire her cleverness, told her it was a neat set-up.

'I like to know about any visitors before they know about me,' she said. 'A person living out here on her own can't be too careful.'

'You seem to be getting along pretty well.'

'I like my own company and I can mostly live off the land,' Mayra said. 'Or I could, until that railway came along, and you people started shooting or scaring off most of the game here-abouts. I'm giving serious thought to moving south. There are plenty of old mines in the Eternity Range, I know I can squeeze metals out of their spoil. All kinds of opportunities out here for a person sharp enough to know how to take advantage.'

'When we came along you must have thought you'd hit the jackpot.'

'Oh, I wouldn't exactly say that.'

'I don't know what else you'd call the easy money you're going to get for returning this girl to her father.'

'Mm-hmm,' Mayra said, pretending to think about that for a couple of moments, then changing the subject. 'I see that you noticed the bow. First thing you looked at when you came in. I'd offer to sell it to you, if you had any money. Or anything to barter.'

Her tone was no longer playful and her gaze had chilled. So much for trying to lull her with flattery. I could feel what was coming like a change in the weather, said as casually as I could, 'I don't have much need for a bow. Your skimmer, though, that I could use.'

'I bet you could.'

A sly little smile lifted one corner of Mayra's mouth and I felt the full weight of her attention. I knew she was getting ready to make her move and she knew I was getting ready to make mine, but the girl surprised both of us. Bouncing to her feet, declaring that she'd had enough of our stupid games. She crossed the little space in two quick steps, grabbed the rifle. Mayra could have snatched her legs from under her, but all she did was shift very slightly, watching as the girl propped the heavy rifle on her hip and aimed it at me.

'I want you to tie her up,' she told Mayra. 'We'll wait until it's light, and then you can take us back to the work camp, and you'll get your reward.'

'Will I?'

Mayra was still smiling that damn sly smile.

'I give you my word.'

'I'm sure that's worth something where you come from, sweetie. But not out here.'

'I have your gun,' the girl said. 'So you better do as I say.'

Mayra winked at me, told the girl, 'Do you really think I'd leave a loaded rifle in reach of this mad bad husky?'

And then, just like that, she was on me. I saw the flash of a knife blade, grabbed her wrist to deflect the thrust, felt a sharp sting in my shoulder as I toppled under her weight. She was straddling my chest and my hands were locked around her wrists, the point of her knife quivering a bare centimetre from my throat as she strained to bring it down, teeth bared, gaze hot and dark and gleeful, and the girl swung the rifle like a club, striking her above the ear and sending her sprawling. I caught the rifle as it swung back at me, jerked it from the girl's grasp. Mayra was pushing to her hands and knees, blood in her grey hair. Jittery with panic, I reversed the rifle and slammed its butt into the back of her head and she fell flat on her face.

'I want to go home,' the girl said, and burst into tears.

I bound Mayra Iturriaga's wrists and ankles with cord I found in the garage space, tore a strip from a filthy towel and used it to gag her. She was beginning to come round, jerking and kicking, making muffled noises. When she tried to get to her feet I shoved her to the ground, showed her the hunting knife she'd tried to skewer me with, and told her that if she didn't sit still I'd cut off her clothes and sling her outside. She stayed put, glaring at me as I snapped an orange bracelet around her wrist.

'I don't know what fone apps you have,' I said. 'And I'm pretty sure that calling the police is the last thing you want to do. But better safe than sorry.'

The knife cut in my shoulder was shallow but bleeding freely, and Mayra's filthy talons had gouged bloody crescents in my wrists. I cleaned my wounds with handfuls of snow and tore another strip from the towel and had the girl tie it around my shoulder, telling her to make it as tight as she could.

'You think I'm a monster,' I said, as I carefully put on my jacket. 'But I'm nothing compared to our friend here. The stuff on the walls. All that expensive field gear. Where do you think she got it? How do you think she gets by? She stripped all the metals from the spoil long ago, and no one would employ her as a guide, crazy as she is. She's a hunter, all right, but not just of reindeer.'

The girl looked at the woman sat against the wall under her trophies, arms bound behind her back. 'Are you saying she killed people?'

'Some people like to hunt solo in the back country. Bow hunting, spear hunting. Tracking their prey on foot, no drones or heat sights or what have you. Every so often one of those hunters goes missing. Some of them fall into crevasses or are caught in blizzards or avalanches. But not all.'

'I don't think so,' the girl said. 'Not so close to the work camp.'

'A year ago the work camp and the railway weren't here. And I reckon our friend ranges south a fair way. Solo hunters track game in the deep back country, and she tracks them. She wouldn't be the first. Years back there was a man who snatched several ecopoets from their summer camps. If we dug around, I bet we'd find Young Old's body someplace,' I said, meeting Mayra Iturriaga's unblinking unreadable stare.

The girl said, 'What happened to the man?'

'The one who killed ecopoets? He was caught. Spent the rest of his life in prison. Back then, before independence, we didn't have the death penalty.'

'What about her?'

'What about her?'

'Shouldn't we do something, if she is what you say she is?'

'You want me to kill her, is that it? A citizen's execution style of thing?'

'Of course not. But you could tell the police where to find her. You could do it, you know, anonymously. So they wouldn't know it was you.'

'I could. Except she knows who I am, she knows who you are, and you're hoping she'll tell everything to the police. Nice try, but no deal.'

'You can't just leave her here.'

'Of course I can. She's tied up pretty good. We'll be long gone by the time she gets free.'

Mayra Iturriaga made a noise that sounded like muffled laughter.

I looked at her, said, 'Of course, it'll be a different kind of game if she tries to come after us. Not that she'll be able to catch up, because we're taking her skimmer.'

11

If I really was a monster, as some people claim, I would have killed that old woman then and there. Shot her dead or dumped her bound and gagged in the snow and let her freeze to death while I snored in the cozy fug of her hut, untroubled by any pangs of conscience. Instead, because I didn't want to spend a sleepless night keeping watch on Mayra Iturriaga and the girl in case one or the other tried something foolish, I decided it would be best to move on right away. Reach the refuge, regroup, sort out the girl's ransom.

It seemed so simple.

I powered up the skimmer and checked its systems, spent a couple of minutes ransacking the hut, looking for anything I could use. Mayra Iturriaga watching me over her gag while I ripped her trophies from the walls, rifled through tools and junk in the little workshop. I found a good all-weather sleeping bag and stuffed the food printer and all the weapons I could find inside it, made a point of breaking the hunting spear over my knee. Childish, I know, but sue me, it felt good. One of the chunks of frozen reindeer meat that hung on the butcher's gambrel outside the hut went into the sleeping bag too. Aside from tubs of dried beans, a couple of boxes of mouldy oats, a handful of withered onions, and a canister of loose tea and a gritty fist of sugar, there wasn't much else in the way of food, but I was pretty sure I'd find supplies at the refuge.

I considered putting up a message for Alberto Toomy on the skywave net, but decided to wait until I had squared his daughter away someplace safe. The police would stop chasing

Keever Bishop and start chasing me as soon as I announced that I was the one who'd taken her, and I admit that I liked to imagine Alberto pacing up and down in a handsome office high above the bustling streets of Esperanza, helplessly fretting over what Keever might be planning. I may not have been a monster, but I wasn't entirely lacking in malice.

Anyway, I stamped Mayra Iturriaga's radio into shards and splinters, told her that she might want to look for another line of work, and walked the skimmer out of the hut. Shut the door behind me and swung into the saddle and with the girl leaning against my back and clinging to my waist took off into the night.

The skimmer was fairly new and fully charged, and the refuge was no more than fifteen kilometres from Mayra Iturriaga's lair, but it took us half the night to get there. After following the mining road for a couple of klicks we turned north, heading up a long slope of ice and rock to the Detroit Plateau. The ice was wrinkled and ridged under its blanket of snow, slashed by crevasses. I stopped at the first that looked deep enough, gingerly stepped to the edge, and dumped Mayra's cutlery into the void. I regretted that later of course, but at the time it seemed to make perfect sense. I was in bad enough trouble without being caught in possession of evidence of who knew how many murders, and it felt like an offering or payment for the good luck I knew I was going to need.

On we went. It would have been sensible to let the skimmer find a way across the treacherous terrain, but I was possessed by a terrible urgency and drove as fast as I dared, using the night-vision app of a pair of goggles synched to the skimmer's controls. I'd managed to shut down the monotonous complaints of its AI, but several hazard warnings stubbornly blinked in a corner of my vision and the crevasse detector beeped with alarming frequency. I had to divert around all but the smallest fractures, so progress across the top of the plateau was a slow and erratic series of zigs and zags.

Clouds completely covered the night sky and it had begun to snow again, billows of dry pellets blown sideways by gusts some-times strong enough to rock the skimmer as it roared through the dark. Its open-sided canopy wasn't much protection from the knifing wind and I'd turned down the under-seat heating to save the batteries, in case there weren't any viable charging points at our destination. I could feel the girl shivering against my back, but there wasn't anything I could do about it. I was strung tight, worried that I might have misremembered the location of the refuge or passed way signs without spotting them, or that I'd been turned around by the endless diversions around crevasses and was heading into empty country, and I couldn't help imagining that Mayra Iturriaga was coming after us on some kind of war steed she'd hidden in the mine, teeth bared to the gale, flourishing that broken spear. But at last I saw a pyramid of loose stones standing on a bare ridge and knew that I was on the right track. Or some kind of track, anyhow.

Mama had taught me how to read the way signs that marked certain secret trails and roads. Pairs of rounded stones meant you were supposed to turn left or right, depending on the location of the smaller stone. Pyramids of stones meant you were supposed to keep straight on. So I kept straight on past that pyramid, and straight on past the next, descending broken terraces of ice cut by ridges of rock running roughly north to south. A third way sign guided me between two of the ridges and the path deepened into a ravine that meandered between rising walls, fallen rocks littering the uneven floor among drifts raked by the wind that blew at our backs.

The sign for the refuge was too obvious to miss. A column of flat blocks rising several metres out of the snow, dark rock and pale rock alternating like a stack of checker pieces. I stopped and looked all around and realised exactly where the refuge must be, realised that there was no way to get the skimmer up there.

A shallow crevice split the cliff face from top to bottom, with a near-vertical stairway of handholds and narrow steps carved inside. The girl took one look at it, said that if I thought she was going to climb up a cliff in a snowstorm I was even crazier than I looked, and started crying.

We were crowded together in the narrow chimney of the crevice, snow blowing around us, her sobbing, me telling her that she would freeze to death if she didn't do what she was told, threatening to haul her up there by her hair if I had to. I was ready to do it, too. I was dog-tired, the knife cut in my shoulder was a bone-deep ache throbbing with my heartbeat, and I was still pissed off about the crappy move she'd tried to make back in Mayra Iturriaga's hut. We were both trapped in that desperate situation, each loathing the other. As far as the girl was concerned, I was a monster who'd kidnapped her and dragged her halfway across the peninsula without caring if she lived or died. And I didn't see that she was just a kid, scared and strung out. At that moment she was an aggravating burden, something I had to prod and pry to get moving.

'There's shelter at the top,' I said. 'Food and warmth. So quit complaining and start climbing.'

I gave her the goggles so she could find her way up the stairway in darkness, climbed behind her with the flashlight clamped in my teeth and the heavy kitbag slung over my good shoulder. It was a hard scramble that topped out in a square little ledge hardly big enough for the both of us, the beginning of a narrow path that threaded along the cliff face above a sheer drop to the floor of the ravine, running out beyond the beam of my flashlight.

'No way,' the girl said. Wind-blown snow was whipping around us and she looked like she was about to start crying again.

'It isn't far now,' I said, although I had no idea. 'Just one more push. And it's a lot easier than climbing back down.'

I found a wire cable strung through eyebolts screwed into the rock, and we clutched this lifeline as we shuffled along the path, snow whirling around us, ceaseless wind plucking at our backs. We skirted a bulge of rock, edged down a steep slope to a crevice shielded by a low wall of unmortared stones. Inside, a rough gullet of stone sloped to a crawlway stoppered by a zippered sheet of black Kevlar. I squirmed through, played the beam of my flashlight over the walls of the refuge's blunt cylinder, and was seized by a weird sense of, what do you call it, *déjà vu*, remembering how Mama and I had camped out in places like it during our trek southwards. When the girl scrambled in behind me I had to turn away so she wouldn't see my foolish tears.

A pushplate lit a broken string of lights set in the seam where the grubby white walls curved together overhead, and started a fan that stirred the damp cold air. There was a kitchen niche at one end of the refuge, a shower and a chemical toilet behind plastic screens at the other. A long table and a few plastic chairs, a box of kids' toys. Eight shelf beds cut into the walls. Maybe one of the children who had once played with those toys had also drawn the naive little mural of a bright yellow sun beaming in a blue sky above a green line starred with big white flowers, a tundra or meadow where the stick figures of a man and a woman and two small children stood beside the slope-shouldered bulk of a mammoth.

Bootprints were tracked everywhere in the even layer of dust that covered the floor. Someone had found the shelter after it had been abandoned. I hoped that trespasser had left a long time ago.

A hatch at the back opened onto a kind of chapel carved into raw rock, a seemingly bottomless hole in the floor on one side, a slope of rubble that climbed up through a broken slot in the ceiling on the other. A faint draught wafting down the slope suggested that it might lead to a hidden entrance somewhere above the cliffs, the kind of escape route common to refuges like these.

A tripod had been erected over the hole and a cluster of nylon cords knotted at its apex dropped into the shaft, but when I hauled up the cords, hoping to find a cache of food frozen by the native cold of the rock, I found that they had all been cleanly cut. There was no food on the shelves of the refuge's little kitchen either, no crockery or cooking equipment except for a battered aluminium pan. But the hotplate worked and when I turned the tap there was a distant groaning and clanking and at last brown water spat into the sink and began to run in a steady thin trickle. I brewed tea with plenty of sugar, and after we drank it and shared a chocolate bar from a ration pack the girl and I unrolled our sleeping bags onto a couple of musty shelf beds and crawled into them.

When I woke, the refuge was faintly lit by bluish daylight shining through squares of plastic set in the ceiling, piped from some source set in the cliffs. The girl, sound asleep, curled inside her bag like a question mark, only her blonde hair showing. I felt a touch of shame, remembering how hard I'd pushed her the previous night, and left her there and went outside to check the weather.

It was still snowing. Squatting at the mouth of the crevice, watching torrents of white flakes whirl past, the far side of the ravine barely visible, everything fading into hazy grey, was very different from watching snow fall harmlessly outside the triple-glazed window of my cozy efficiency in Star City, knowing that ploughs and sweepers would clear the streets and public transport, and the bustle of Esperanza's underground walkways and malls would be completely untroubled by the weather. Even the fiercest blizzards were only a mild inconvenience in the city, but out in the back country you were hostage to something raw and elemental, inhumanly huge and indifferent. The blizzard wouldn't care or notice if it killed me, and realising that, submitting to it, was dismaying, thrilling, liberating. Sexual, even.

I remembered sheltering in the cabin with Mama as storms roared over Deception Island, and howled at the wind and the falling snow, howled wordlessly and happily, not caring at that moment if the blizzard didn't stop blowing until it had buried the entire peninsula and the glaciers returned and scraped away every trace of humanity and carried the debris into the sea.

It wasn't anything to do with my edits or some kind of behaviour coded in genes borrowed from archaic humans, nature asserting itself over nurture. It was just ordinary human defiance, a scream of *I am* into the void of the uncaring world. I howled until I was hoarse and the snow whirled on unchecked, and for the first time since I'd driven through the work camp's outer gate I felt truly free.

There was nothing to do but hunker down and wait for the blizzard to blow itself out. Back in the refuge, the girl was awake, telling me that she didn't think much of our new home.

'Are they all like this? Is this how your people lived?'

'This is just a kind of way station. There are much bigger places in the south, labs and dorms and so on. Hidden villages where free ecopoets lived and worked after the government ban.'

That's what Mama had told me, anyway. The places we'd stayed in had been much like this one, fitted into a crevice or dug into rock. One had been built into the blind end of a ravine, its concrete roof disguised by a litter of boulders. Basic quarters but warm and comfortable, with running water and battery packs that stored electricity produced by some combination of wind turbines, solar panels, and thermoelectric generators.

'Ecopoets were mostly nomads,' I said. 'Always on the move. You see that picture? The mammoth? The first ecopoets resurrected them from elephant stock and traits clipped from the genomes of pygmy mammoths that once lived on an island in Siberia. They were used to transport stuff from place to place. They helped with the landscaping, too. Moving rocks and such.'

I was in a good mood, brewing tea and thawing a chunk of reindeer on the hotplate for breakfast, shrugging when the girl said she didn't eat meat, telling her to break open a ration pack instead.

'Can I have a shower?'

'Why not?'

There was only a trickle of cold brown water, but the girl didn't complain. Saying, as she dried herself with a towel stiff as a scrap of cardboard, that it reminded her of an English boarding school she'd been sent to for a year. The patches that dappled her pale skin weren't just on her face, but all over. Pale cream and butterscotch.

There are two kinds of beauty. The kind that's carefully cultivated and preened, and the kind that's unforced, unadorned, worn as carelessly as good health. The girl's was the second kind. Created by a fortunate combination of genes, improved by a little careful editing. Her dappled skin didn't have anything to do with editing, though. It was a fashion trait created by a reversible spray-on retroviral treatment that enhanced her beauty, gave her an exotic lustre. As if she was of some ancient unfallen race, like the elves of the peninsula's myths.

This slender girl, my cousin. I could see a little of my father in her father's face, but nothing of me in hers, even though she shared one quarter of my genes. A little under one quarter, because of the editing which had made me what I was. If you'd seen us together I wouldn't have blamed you for thinking that we were from two different species. People are sensitive to small variations from what they consider to be the norm, and while the girl was long-legged, lithe and lovely, I was a hulking troll got up from seal leather and patches of yak fur, the cruel captor of a fair maiden I'd lured to my underground lair.

After she'd eaten, no more than jam scraped across crackers and a scant handful of dried fruit from one of the ration packs, the girl asked if she could have her book back. I'd forgotten about the damn thing, found it at the bottom of the kitbag, told her that she could have it as long as she didn't use it to call anyone, a little joke she took seriously.

'I told you. It's just a book.'

'What kind of book?'

'The kind that tells a story. It's harmless, really it is.'

'What kind of story?'

We were sitting on brittle chairs either side of the table. The girl in her bodysuit, which was imitating the dingy white of the walls, me in my uniform shirt and trousers, trapping the book under the flat of my hand. There was a map drawn in green on its black leather cover, a scatter of big and small islands I didn't recognise.

'You'll think it's stupid,' the girl said.

'Try me.'

'It's set in the future,' she said, with the weary patience that teenagers use to disguise their embarrassment. 'Right here in Antarctica, after all the ice has melted.'

'All of it? Is that possible?'

'Just because it hasn't happened yet doesn't mean it can't happen.'

It seemed that the map on the cover of the book was a map of Antarctica in this far future. The peninsula broken into a string of skinny islands, much of West Antarctica drowned and the

Transantarctic Mountains standing straight up from the sea, and the bulk of the continent broken by huge bays and inlets, with grassy plains in the east and mountains and forests in the north.

The islands and the mainland were divided into kingdoms with intricate arrays of kings and queens, princes and princesses, barons and knights. There were strange animals descended from species which had been edited in the deep past, magicians with mechanical servants and the ability to shape the weather and control animals and plants, and elves that lived in the forests, either descended from edited human stock or members of a hidden race that had emerged after the ice had gone. It was a place of courtly intrigue and wars, magic and mystery.

'"Green and fair and lovely," it says in the book,' the girl said. 'Although nights in winter are just as long and dark as they are now.'

'And does it snow at all, in winter?'

It was hard to imagine the whole continent without snow and ice. But I suppose that a hundred or two hundred years ago it would have been hard to imagine the peninsula with cities and settlements, forested valleys and fjords where glaciers had once flowed, and wolves and mammoths and elf stones.

'Ogres are supposed to live up in the mountains,' the girl said. 'Maybe that's what your people became.'

'Or maybe they became the people who live in these magic kingdoms, and your kind of people are long gone. What's it about, the story?'

'There's a princess, and a hero. At least, I think he's supposed to be a hero. They're from two rival kingdoms and they're enemies because the hero killed the princess's uncle. She wants to kill him, but instead they accidentally fall in love.'

I thought that it sounded exactly like the kind of thing silly little rich girls like her would be keen on, said that it seemed complicated.

'It's based on an old opera. I saw a performance of it a year ago, in Montevideo.'

The casual way she said that, as if it was no big deal to leave the peninsula.

I said, 'If you know the story, why do you need to read this book?'

'I know the opera. The book is different. I mean, it's the same basic story, but the details are different. And you have to make choices for the character you're following, and that changes the story.'

'Which character are you following?'

'Princess Isander.'

'A princess. Of course you are.'

'She's the daughter of King Geraine, the ruler of Esland, the biggest of the western islands. Smaller kingdoms around and about owe him allegiance and pay tribute.'

'So she's the daughter of a powerful man. Just like you.'

'Her family is powerful, but she isn't, especially. It's like in the old days, when men ruled and women served. Even princesses and queens. Isander has some dire skills, but she's basically sitting around waiting to be married off.'

'It doesn't sound very true to life. Everyone knows that women are stronger than men. And cleverer too.'

'The point of the story, if you follow it as Isander, is that you can help her overcome her circumstances by making the right choices. You can help her be true to herself, rather than be forced to become what her father and everyone else expects her to be.'

I let the girl talk. It passed the time, the silly story seemed important to her, and I was happy to watch her grow ever more confident in its telling. I'd put her through some hard adventuring – the crash and the hike, Mayra Iturriaga and the long ride through the frigid night – but she was a resilient kid, stronger than she looked. Like me, she'd lost her mother. That toughens you, for sure. It makes you grow up fast. It teaches you that the world is a hard uncertain place where nothing is forever. Anyway, we'd had our troubles on the way here but she'd pulled through, no real harm done. She was going to be OK.

She told me that the chief male actor in the story, Tantris, served in the court of King Marsche, the ruler of Palmis, the southernmost island in the chain that the peninsula might become in a dozen or a hundred centuries, with the world as warm as it had once been in the long ago when dinosaurs had stalked through the forests of the south pole. Tantris was the youngest knight of the court, a fine sailor, an expert swordsman and hunter, and an accomplished harp player. One of those unbearable people who are not only good at everything they do but also unerringly choose to do the right thing every time. In the opera, doing the right thing led to tragedy, the girl said, but she was going to make it come out differently.

'Some stories have sad endings no matter what,' I said.

'This one doesn't have to be like that,' the girl said.

The annual tribute King Marsche had to pay to Esland was collected by Mordred, the brother of King Geraine's wife, who sailed up the west coast of Palmis every midsummer with a small fleet of ironclad ships, plundering the coffers of nobility and merchants in towns along the way before he reached the capital. Mordred's ironclad steamships outclassed any in Palmis's navy, but Tantris, vowing to put an end to this piracy, got up a plan and presented it to King Marsche.

That midsummer, Mordred's little fleet of ironclads was as usual anchored in the harbour of Ryne, the most southerly of Palmis's towns and Mordred's first port of call on his way to the court of King Marsche. While Mordred and his captains were being entertained in the house of the Duke of Ryne, a crew of handpicked men and women led by Tantris crossed the harbour in rowboats with muffled oars. They swarmed aboard the smallest of the ironclads and subdued its crew, tied them up and cast them adrift in the rowboats, and set out to sea in the stolen ship.

When Mordred ordered his captains to raise anchor and give chase, two of his ships immediately ran into mines that Tantris had planted at the harbour entrance. Enraged beyond reason, Mordred told the rest to sail on without stopping to pick up survivors, and they chased the stolen ironclad towards an archipelago of small islands scattered beyond the southern tip of Palmis. Remembering how Mama and I had escaped Deception Island and sailed past Trinity Island and several smaller islands to reach the Davis Coast, I believed that I could picture the scene, although according to the girl the islands in the story were thickly wooded or covered with green meadows and bogs.

Tantris was leading Mordred into a trap, of course. He steered the stolen ironclad into a narrow strait between two islands and when Mordred's ships followed, threading one after the other between looming cliffs, cannon set along the clifftops on either side blasted them with pitiless fire ('That's what the book calls it,' the girl said). Only Mordred's flagship survived the bombardment. When it wallowed out of the strait, holed beneath the waterline, the survivors among its crew manning pumps and fighting fires below decks, the stolen ironclad cut across its bow and Tantris hailed Mordred and challenged him to a duel. Mordred accepted at once. He was a cunning and experienced swordsman, believed that he could easily defeat a callow youth. And besides, as far as he was concerned it was a matter of honour.

The duel was held on a small grassy island as flat as a table. As the summer sun circled the horizon, the two men fought from one side to the other and back again. Tantris cut Mordred's loose shirt to ribbons and inflicted a dozen superficial wounds, but when he pressed an especially fierce and close attack Mordred stabbed him in the thigh with a concealed dagger and told him that the blade was painted with a slow poison and only his sister possessed the antidote. I intend to kill you here and now, Mordred said, but in the unlikely event that you triumph I will still have my revenge, because you will suffer a slow agonising death with no hope of a cure.

His taunt was meant to sap his opponent's courage, but Tantris was infuriated by this treachery and fought on with redoubled strength and speed. The two men clashed and parted over and again, their blood sprinkling the wiry turf like dew, and when they met for the final time, at the dead centre of the island, Tantris struck Mordred with a hammer blow that killed him on the spot and left a sliver of sword blade embedded in his skull.

Tantris was feted as a hero when he returned to the court of King Marsche, but his wound would not heal and even the king's own physician could not help him. It seemed that Mordred had told the truth when he'd claimed that only his sister, Queen Isander, possessed the antidote. Tantris knew that the queen would refuse to help the man who had killed her brother, so he and a few friends set off for Esland, and near the harbour of its capital city Tantris cast himself adrift in a small boat with a little food and water, and a harp. He was found by fishermen and claimed to be a shipwrecked minstrel called Tristan, the only survivor of an attack by sea raiders. News of his skill as a harpist quickly spread through the town to the court. He was summoned to play by Queen Isander, and with the help of her daughter, who was also called Isander, she cured his poisoned wound. And that was how Isander met Tantris, the girl said, and the real story began.

'It seems more complicated than it needs to be,' I said. 'Why do mother and daughter have the same name? Why didn't Mordred's death start a war? And if this so-called hero was dying, how did he have the energy and time to pull off that trick to get the attention of the queen?'

'Because it's that kind of story, I suppose,' the girl said.

'The real world is sad enough without trying to make it sadder with silly stories,' I said. 'You read your book if you want. I'm going to check the lay of the land.'

'I thought you had a plan.'

'I know what I need to do. Don't worry about that.'

It was snowing as hard as ever. Contacting Alberto Toomy and beginning ransom negotiations would have to wait. I dozed for the rest of the day, woke as hungry as a hunter, and cooked up a mess of food. Noodles mixed with freeze-dried vegetables from a ration pack, a couple of the sprouting onions I'd taken from Mayra Iturriaga. Tomato sauce from a squeeze tube and chunks of broiled reindeer meat that the girl refused to touch – you would have thought that I had suggested she try succulent leg of baby. She also refused to eat her share of the chumbeque I cut in half for dessert.

We had just one ration pack left.

'There isn't much else,' I said. 'I can't forage in this blizzard. And anyway, nothing grows up here except for some lichens. Even the printer couldn't make anything worth eating from them.'

'I'll manage.'

'You need to eat. You don't have any fat on you.'

'I said I'll manage.'

I suppose it was a form of defiance.

When she picked up her book, I said that I'd tell her a real story that was far better than any make-believe.

'If this is about what my grandfather did in Australia, how he found that money, I know all about it,' the girl said. 'So there's no point making up more lies about him.'

'Let's see.'

Drugs, Guns and Money

So Eddie Toomy left Isabella Morales and the Antarctic Peninsula for Western Australia and Lake Macleod, where rising sea levels had washed away salt beds and flooded permanent ponds, and Big Green, one of the ecoremediation transnats, was farming fast-growing strains of kelp on thousands of hectares of rafts. Some of the harvest was processed to extract algin and biochemicals for the food and pharmaceutical industries, but most of it was packaged and sold for human consumption, or used as an additive for animal feed or fertiliser for farmlands reclaimed from the desert. There were also shrimp and shellfish farms and a thriving fishing industry, and desalinated water was pumped into a chain of freshwater lakes that irrigated the farmlands and created a more temperate microclimate.

To begin with, Eddie drove one of the road trains that trucked dirt from a soil factory and saplings from tree nurseries to the desert edge, where tens of thousands of acacias and eucalypts were being planted out in shelter belts to stabilise the boundary of the reclaimed land. Eddie's rig, BE-7-T-1, inevitably nick-named Betty, mostly ran herself, but Eddie took over whenever her AI became conflicted, supervised loading and unloading, and handled the paperwork and routine maintenance. He loved riding in Betty's high cab, keeping tabs on her indicators and watching the road and the scenery unravel. The vibrant green fields and belts of trees. The red desert. The intense turquoise of the new lakes under the hot blue sky.

It didn't occur to him to tell Isabella Morales where he was or what he was doing. He'd convinced himself that she had driven him away with her unreasonable expectation that he would dedicate the rest of his life to hard labour in the howling boonies while sharing everything with everyone else. Bugger that. He missed her now and then – a woman like that, who wouldn't? When his contract with Big Green was ended, he'd return to the peninsula flush with credit, and maybe they could work something out. But no way was he going back to being ordered about like a bloody bogan, living in communal poverty like some kind of monk. He was done with all that.

Big Green's workforce was half local and half the usual global stew, most of them under thirty. They worked hard and played hard. Eddie had to ride Betty ever further from the depot as the long ribbon of the shelter belt extended, and soon was overnighting in work camps. The commissary supplied ration packs, and the crews were adept at scrounging up extra food from farm workers. There were cases of beer, mah-jong and poker schools, pick-up games of football or volleyball, music from a guitar or two. And plenty of sex, too, especially for someone with Eddie's good looks, aw-shucks charm and polyamorous adaptability.

Quite soon, he fell into working for people who sold drugs to crews at the camps and workers in the kelp farms. It was an easy way to make money on the side, and no one got hurt. The gang which controlled the drug trade was also involved in theft of produce and goods from the farms and factories in the Lake Macleod development zone – oysters and abalone, rock lobsters, nanobiotics, high-end pharmaceuticals, so on – but the companies wrote it off as wastage and besides, it wasn't anything in the grand scheme of things. Billions of dollars flowed from governments to transnats and smaller companies, and everyone at every level was on the take, from government ministers pocketing kickbacks and suits awarding themselves excessive bonuses, to loaders who leaked inventory from warehouses, and drivers like Eddie who rendezvoused with gang members in the middle of nowhere, the logs of their road trains overwritten by a hack that seamlessly plugged the gap in travel records while cargo that wasn't on the manifest was offloaded. So everything was sweet as, until one day, about eighteen months into his stint at Lake Macleod, Eddie was asked to do a special job by his crew boss.

This was a leathery American guy, Leo Fowler, a veteran of the Rain Wars which had kicked off after a massive cloud-seeding project Texas deployed to boost rainfall had caused droughts in neighbouring Mexican states. The badge of Leo's unit, the Battling '88s, was tattooed on the back of his right hand, and his left eye was a prosthetic bedded in a web of scar tissue. He said that it was way better than the original or anything grown in a tank. It let him see in the dark and spy on shit ten kilometres away. It let him see into the souls of men and know whether they were telling the truth or talking trash.

That shiny black orb and its blue, human counterpart fixing on Eddie as the crew boss told him that he had been volunteered for a special road trip out into the countryside.

'What kind of road trip?'

'The kind where you pick up something from buddies of mine and keep your mouth shut. I know you know how it goes.'

Eddie said that he was pretty sure that he did. Leo ran the gang then ran the local drug trade.

The man squeezed his shoulder, a hard but not unfriendly grip. 'Did you really think this was going to be all about hauling booze and kick and smoke, or offloading cases of prawns? You're a smart guy, Eddie. Do right by me on this thing, I might could move you up to the next level. OK?'

'OK,' Eddie said, although he had the beginnings of a bad feeling about this road trip, and the last thing he wanted was any kind of promotion.

'Us white men have to stick together,' Leo said. 'Am I right or am I right? Now let's go check out your ride.'

Despite his bad feeling, Eddie felt a eager little kick when he saw the ride – an all-terrain Land Cruiser with three axles, one in front, two in the rear, ribbed mesh tyres and a transmission that could out-pull a pair of elephants. A rough tough muscle car that was going to be a lot of fun to drive.

He said, 'I guess we're in for a little off-roading.'

'Not me,' Leo said. 'I have better things to do than tool around in the fucking heat and bull dust. You're going out with a buddy of mine, good old boy name of Brandon Birdwell. He shipped in just a couple of days back, I don't believe you've met him yet. He's hard ass, but long as you do what he says you and him should get along just fine.'

Eddie was introduced to this Brandon Birdwell in the bar where Americans working for Big Green hung out, most of them veterans of the Rain Wars and brush-fire conflicts which had followed the breakup of the Republic. Pictures of motorcycles, military hardware, cowboys and sports stars on the walls, battle flags hanging from the ceiling, screens blasting out old-time rebel music and cut-ups of combat footage. Nostalgia for a simplified and deeply nativist version of history, a past that had never existed except in the mythologies of people, mostly male, mostly white, mostly straight, who found the modern world too complicated. Eddie tried not to be judgemental, but he always picked up a sour vibe in there, a mix of brash masculinity and thin-skinned butt hurt.

Brandon Birdwell looked right at home, a taciturn fellow in his forties wearing a white straw Stetson with a dent in its crown, shirtless under an unzipped camo jacket, a big tattoo of an eagle clutching burning brands in its talons spread across his bony chest. He was sitting at a table with two young toughs, gave Leo a complicated handshake involving knuckles and fingertips, studied Eddie dubiously as Leo explained that this was a reliable kid who could drive anything anywhere, no questions asked.

Brandon and his two sidekicks looked so exactly like the bad guys in some stupid action saga it wasn't even funny, but Eddie couldn't see any way of backing out of the job without Leo going Biblical on him. Had no choice but to turn up the next morning at zero dark thirty and, with Brandon Birdwell riding shotgun and the two sidekicks crammed in back, aim the big Land Cruiser north.

'All you need to do is drive where I tell you and keep your mouth shut,' Brandon told Eddie, and pulled a big chromed pistol from the duffel bag, stuffed tight as a punchbag, clamped between his knees. The pistol had a long barrel and a laser sight that steered its smart bullets to their target. Brandon made an elaborate display of checking it and aiming at a passing truck before jamming it under his thighs, and when Eddie asked exactly where they were going said that it was a simple pickup job, that was all he needed to know.

'Leo likes you, but we only just met. Far as I'm concerned, you're on probation,' Brandon added, and told his seat to ease back and pulled the brim of his Stetson low over his mirrored sunglasses and seemed to fall asleep.

One of the sidekicks gave Eddie directions. They drove past the pipework and tanks of the biofuel plant, cut around the northern end of Lake Macleod and joined the Minilya-Exmouth road, speeding across dusty flatlands and after a couple of hours turning onto an old highway that ran along the east edge of Exmouth Gulf. Seared bush stretching away on one side, glimpses of the blue sea on the other. It was June. Midwinter. Forty degrees in the shade. Once, one of the sidekicks buzzed down a window and took a pot-shot at a roo, and the hard crack right by his ear made Eddie brake out of instinct. Brandon stirred, told the two cowboys in back to stop fucking around, and seemed to go back to sleep again.

The road ended at the ruins of a big solar salt plant that stretched for thirty kilometres along the gulf coast. The place had once exported salt for the Chinese plastics and petrochemical industries, but rising sea levels had long ago drowned its evap-oration beds. Mangroves growing on submerged ridges outlined the rectangular patterns of flooded beds, a patchwork pattern stretching away into the mirror dance of heat haze. A few stretches of the elevated pipes which had fed seawater into the beds still stood here and there. The rusting remains of an excavator tilted nose down in muddy shallows.

Brandon directed Eddie along a rough track to the shell of a square concrete building that stood atop a low promontory. Directly below was a ruined quay with several long jetties jutting into a channel that ran towards the open waters of the gulf. Eddie and the others waited out the rest of the day there, in furnace heat and relentless sunlight. Around noon Brandon and his two mates broke open MRE packs, but Eddie passed. His stomach was too delicate. Brandon gave him the side-eye but said nothing.

The sidekicks were dressed in camo T-shirts and pants that mimicked the dirty colour of the concrete block wall they were squatting against, brushing flies off their faces and talking shit about people they worked with and actions they'd been in, people they'd fucked or were planning to fuck, so on. There were millions of these young fellas loose in the world, shaped and tempered by uprisings, rebellions, insurgencies, civil wars, resource wars, wars against other tribes or religions, wars against refugees or countries that attempted to turn back refugees . . . Those who survived, who weren't obviously crazy or crippled by PTSD, were often recruited by companies that provided security for transnats. Small private armies working at arm's length to provide their clients with a fig leaf of plausible deniability if things went sideways, guarding installations and key personnel, overseeing local workforces, augmenting the police and armed forces of compliant governments, fighting rebels enraged by the exploitation of their country, dealing with riots sparked by massacres of striking workers, industrial accidents, or wild weather that left local people homeless and starving.

Eddie gathered that the sidekicks were both from Alaska, had done gigs for the company that regulated merchant shipping in the Northwest Passage and for Big Green's Sahara Sea project before coming to Australia. He wondered about Brandon Birdwell's background, but the man seemed to be asleep again, stretched out in a patch of shade, his head pillowed on his duffel bag, hat over his face, hands knitted over the eagle tattoo on his chest. And anyway, Eddie was frankly too scared of him to ask.

The sidekicks grew restless after sunset. Checking and rechecking their weapons. Walking about the promontory. Staring out towards the open waters of the gulf, where the riding lights of tankers and supply ships were strung along the deep-water channel and the electric glow of the town of Learmouth shimmered at the remote horizon. There had been coral reefs, salt marshes and mangrove belts rich in bird life along this shore once upon a time, the whole gulf had been protected by strict environmental laws, but the reefs had been bleached and killed by thermal stress, the marshes and mangroves had been wrecked by weather bombs and drowned by rising sea levels, and the petrochemical industry had moved in to exploit offshore gas and oil fields.

At last, as a thin crescent moon rose over the gulf and the first stars blossomed in the darkening sky, Brandon stirred and made a short fone call, announced that it was on. More MREs were shared around, Eddie managing to choke down some chili and macaroni. He hung back as Brandon and the two sidekicks kept watch, scanning the dark channel and open water beyond with field glasses and night sights. Told himself that this was just some kind of test. A routine pickup of whatever clandestine shit Leo was peddling on the side. Because if this was something serious, seriously dangerous, Leo wouldn't have sent out a novice like him.

At last there was the sound of a motor out in the night. A boat making its way down the channel, barely visible by starlight and the moon's bone-white sliver.

Brandon gave Eddie a hard look from under the brim of his Stetson and told him to stay right there, he wouldn't be long.

'You're my backup,' he said. 'Keep close to your vehicle. If I come running, you better be ready to take off, show me you can outrun anything and everything. Got it?'

Eddie swallowed dryly. 'Got it.'

'Don't worry, kid. This ain't my first rodeo,' Brandon said, and swung his duffel bag onto his shoulder and led the sidekicks down the slope to the quay.

Eddie watched their dark figures move through shadows towards the jetty where the boat had tied up. Just enough moon-light reflected from the water to see three, no, four men standing there as Brandon and the two sidekicks approached. Eddie was too far away to hear anything of what was said, could barely glimpse some kind of activity around the boat.

The blink of a flashlight briefly revealed Brandon and another man examining a crate. And then someone gave a wordless shout and there was the sudden crackle and flash of gunfire, the sharp whirr of smart rounds, a stitching of tiny red explosions in the dark. Eddie threw himself flat on hot dirt. Terror was an elephant kneeling on his back and he was saying over and over, 'I've fucked up, I've fucked up.' More gunfire. Short bursts. Single shots. The boat motor started, almost immediately cut off. Silence, then two spaced shots, then nothing more.

It took Eddie a while to work up the nerve to go down there. He was half-minded to jump in the cruiser and bail, but he knew that Leo would kill him if he returned without knowing what had happened. Shit, Leo would probably kill him anyway, but he had to find out, so he crabbed down the slope in the moonlit dark and crouched behind thorn bushes at the edge of the quay, listening hard, hearing only the beating of his heart and the soft plash of waves.

Years later, he'd say that walking out into the open was the hardest thing he'd done in his life. Brandon Birdwell and the two sidekicks sprawled close to each other, Brandon on his back with his Stetson and half his face gone, his fancy pistol in his outflung hand. Blood black in the moonlight. The smell of it in the hot night.

Stepping like a catburglar towards the jetty, Eddie found three men lying in their blood near plastic crates set in a row, just about jumped out of his skin when one man started to crawl like a broke-back snake towards a pistol. When Eddie kicked the gun into the water the man subsided, blood pooling under his hips. Eddie squatted next to him, asked what had happened, but the man just stared at him and after a minute or so gave a sort of sigh or groan and his head dropped and his eyes weren't looking at anything in the world any more.

There was no sign of the fourth man, no sign of the duffel bag that Brandon had carried down there. The boat, a big inflatable, rocked to and fro on rippling waves about a hundred metres off the end of the jetty. Eddie studied its shadow for a long time, and at last pulled off his boots and dived in and swam out to it. Trying not to think about sharks and blood in the water. Trying not to think about the missing man rising up in the boat, taking aim . . .

He was curled up, the missing man, in a wash of blood and seawater at the bottom of the inflatable. Brandon Birdwell's duffel bag lay next to him. The motor had been shot up, but Eddie found a plastic paddle clipped to the side and with some effort, because the damn thing kept trying to turn in a circle, managed to row the inflatable to shore. He heaved the duffel bag onto the jetty and clambered out and lay there a while just breathing.

The bag was stuffed with blister packs and rolled strips of drug patches, blocks of thousand dollar bills sealed in plastic. US green, which despite the parlous and fractured state of the former superpower was still the best kind of cash currency. Packed in the crates, cradled in blocks of shaped foam, were SAW handguns, disruption rifles, heavy machine pistols and boxes of ammunition, recoilless missile launchers and fire-and-forget missiles the length of Eddie's arm, with black shafts and red or yellow warheads.

It wasn't the usual deal, that was for sure. And Eddie was in the middle of it, last man standing. Alone in the dark with seven dead men, a bag of drugs and money, and enough firepower to start a small war. He could head back, tell Leo what had happened, but knew that Leo would blame him, the man was liable to go off on one when things went wrong . . . Or he could take off, hope that this was all of it down to Leo and not some kind of cartel deal, hope that Leo didn't have the resources to find him.

It wasn't any kind of choice, really, so he did what he'd been doing all his life.

He ran.

He drove through the night. North to Roebourne, using some of the cash money to pay for a flight in a puddle jumper to Perth, where he caught the loop to Adelaide. He hid out in a motel room near the airport, checking news feeds ten or twenty times a day, finding nothing about a shoot-out in the old solar salt plant at Exmouth Gulf, no mention of him or of Leo Fowler. Leo would definitely be looking for him by now, but Eddie believed that if he could get out of the country he'd have a chance of surviving this.

He'd turned over his passport to the human resources depart- ment of the kelp farm when he'd started work there, and while he knew from *novelas* and such that there were people who could create new identities with your biometrics, he didn't have the faintest idea how to go about finding them. Instead, he applied to the New Zealand consulate in Adelaide for a replacement passport and sweated out the eight days it took to be issued.

He counted and recounted the cash – six hundred and fifty thousand dollars US – and spent a lot of time on the dark web, using half a dozen user names and the Wi-Fi in coffee shops and fast-food restaurants to sell the drugs for whatever he could get. He parcelled out less than half of the stash in various small deals, dumped the rest down the dunny. Trying to offload it to one of Adelaide's gangs wasn't worth the risk, and he couldn't take it where he was going.

The day after he got his new passport, he was back in New Zealand. Auckland. A year ago, he would have burned through the little fortune he'd lucked into quicker than thought. Drink and drugs, fancy hotels, fast cars, the usual high life that fools and fantasists think they deserve. But he'd had a shock, a big one. He believed that he had passed through the fire for a reason. He told himself that he had been given a second chance and vowed to make some changes to his life.

He didn't try to get in contact with his estranged family. Those bridges had been burnt long ago. And besides (he told himself), he didn't want to put them in danger. Instead, he hitched across the North Island to Napier, rented an apartment, and lay low. Nothing happened and nothing continued to happen. Slowly, he began to relax. He became friendly with someone who was trying to start up a crab farming business, something he'd learned a little bit about while working at Lake Macleod, and invested a serious chunk of his money in the venture.

The crab business prospered, but after helping to set it up Eddie became a sleeping partner. He bought a ten-metre sailboat, though truth be told he spent more time hanging out in the harbour bars and cafés than on the water. A tanned man in his early thirties, sunbleached blond hair, sometimes with a beard, sometimes clean-shaven, bare-chested in red cycling shorts and sandals, a straw hat or a snapback cap. A familiar figure about the town. There were girlfriends and boyfriends, no one steady. If Eddie wasn't dating someone he'd picked up in one of the tourist spots he'd maybe spend a couple of hours at the crab farm, talking to his partner about ways to expand the old business, helping to make up orders to keep his hand in. More often than not, though, he'd cycle over to the harbour, the new one built on the drowned bones of the original, and shoot the breeze with his mates over a few cold ones.

Life was good. Life was easy. Six years passed, and one day the service that Eddie paid to track certain key words in news sites and feeds forwarded a brief item – it seemed that a guy called Leo Fowler had been shot to death by police in the aftermath of a botched holdup in Levelland, Texas. Eddie hired a local investigator to dig up more details, learned that the Leo Fowler who had been shot was definitely his Leo Fowler, returned to Texas three years back, fired from a position with a security firm, involved with the local chapter of a motorcycle gang . . . It looked like old Leo had quit Big Green and fallen on bad times, and now he was dead and Eddie no longer had to look over his shoulder.

About a year later, New Zealand's biggest aquaculture company made an offer on the crab farm business. It wasn't so much about the farm itself, actually, as the expertise of Eddie's business partner, Charlie Knowles, and the novel hatchery system he had devised, but it was still a tidy sum. Charlie, a rangy easy-going guy, was eager to go for it.

'It isn't just the money,' he told Eddie. 'Although the money is nice. It's getting out from under the daily grind of running the place, and getting down to some real development work.'

'I should have helped out more,' Eddie said, happy to acknowledge his shortcomings now that he could cash in his share of the business.

'Believing I could make a go of it, kicking in the seed money, that was more than enough,' Charlie said. 'So, what will you do now?'

'I don't know. Buy a bigger boat, maybe. I could explore the coast, find a good place to build a house . . .'

'Why not?' Charlie said, even though both of them knew it was unlikely Eddie would settle down any time soon.

The paperwork on the deal was still being processed when Eddie's father died. Felled by a massive heart attack while he was doing volunteer work on the neighbourhood flood-control walls. Eddie went back to Auckland for the funeral and had a strange stiff reunion with his mother and his two brothers and their wives, saw his nephews and nieces for the first time, and met up with a bunch of old mates, most of them married too. One, recently returned from the Antarctic Peninsula, told Eddie that Esperanza and O'Higgins were boom towns where anyone with a bit of grit and know-how could make a fortune. After decades of instability, an uptick in the global economy was driving demand for the untapped resources of the peninsula. Transnats were investing in new mining and construction projects, there was talk of gaining independence from the Antarctic Authority, declaring statehood . . .

'You have citizenship, don't you? If you ever thought of going back,' Eddie's friend said, 'now's the time to do it.'

When he returned to Napier, Eddie realised that there was nothing to keep him there. He was still living in his rented flat, and he'd lately noticed that the women and men he hooked up with were all at least ten years younger than him. For the first time in a long while he thought of Isabella Morales and the life he could have shared with her. Except, let's face it, he wasn't cut out to be an ecopoet. He couldn't go back to that, but maybe he could check in with her. Show her he'd made something of himself.

One night, he'd had a few drinks, he called his friend, asked about contacts on the peninsula. A month later he was aboard a clipper ship, sailing south. Just to see how the place had changed. If he didn't like it, if his friend's contacts didn't play out, he could always move on. But he never did, and never got around to looking up his old honeyboo, either. He told himself that he really was done with all that. As usual, he was wrong.

12

'Bad people were forcing grandfather to help them steal from the company,' the girl said. 'That much is true. But there weren't any drugs, and there wasn't a shoot-out either. What happened, he was driving through the desert one day and saw scraps of paper blowing across the road. One of them stuck to the windscreen of his truck, he saw it was a hundred dollar bill, so he stopped and followed the paper trail to a crashed drone stuffed with cash. He saw his chance to get away, and that's what he did. He ran all the way to New Zealand because he guessed the drone and the cash had something to do with the bad people, he knew they would find him if he stayed in Australia.'

'Maybe that's the cleaned up version Eddie Toomy gave to his family and friends,' I said. 'But when he met with my grandmother, years later, he told her the truth. He wanted to make full confession. Wanted to apologise for abandoning her and their son. '

'I bet you can't prove any of that foolishness really happened.'

'And I bet you can't prove it didn't.'

The girl thought for a moment, the fingers of her right hand picking at the orange bracelet around her left wrist, even though she knew by now she couldn't get it off, it had bonded to her skin.

She said, 'Would your father's life have been different if my grandfather had got to know him?'

'What are you trying to say?'

'Your grandmother was an ecopoet. And so was your father. Because that's how he was raised.'

'In the tradition.'

'In the tradition. But what if my grandfather had stayed in touch? What if your father had lived with him some of the time?'

'Salix.'

'Excuse me?'

'My father's name. Salix.'

'OK. So would things have been any different if Salix had visited with grandfather now and then?'

'You mean, would Salix have become like your father, the Honourable Deputy? I don't think so.'

'So no matter what my grandfather did, Salix would have become an ecopoet. He would have married your mother and they would have had you, exactly as you are now.'

'A husky. You can say it.'

'You'd still be a husky. And your parents would still have been arrested, because they were ecopoets who broke the law and refused to accept the amnesty.'

'I don't see your point.'

'The point being,' the girl said, 'why are you punishing me for something my family couldn't prevent?'

'Of course they could have prevented it. Eddie Toomy had friends in high places. Political influence. He could have campaigned for the rights of ecopoets. He could have stopped that stupid law being passed. Or he could at least have helped my parents after they were arrested. And Salix would still be alive, and I wouldn't have spent half my childhood in a fucking orphanage, packing trays of printed chicken steaks to earn my keep.'

The girl flinched. I'd been shouting. After a short silence, she said, 'I know I have advantages.'

'You don't know the half of it.'

'But I can't help being who I am. Unless you want to blame me for being born.'

'I don't blame you for anything,' I said.

But I did. Of course I did. I was my mother's daughter, and Mama had taught me all about the unfairness of the world. It isn't just that the rich have more money than us. It's all the rest. All the social privilege that so-called ordinary people lack. The life chances that privilege opens up. The sense of belonging, of being part of a storied lineage. The rich know exactly where they come from, who they are. The rest of us inherit only fragments of lives memorialised in hand-me-down stories whose details are exaggerated and altered with every telling, or glimpsed in corrupted files from dead media. Footage of the long-lost wearing antique clothes, capering on holiday, posing at long-forgotten weddings and christenings. And yes, I know that this is one such story. But I'm trying to tell it as true as I can, even though conversations like the one I'm recounting here are patched from scraps of memory, from what I think we talked about, from what I think we should have talked about. And isn't that what all stories turn into, in the end? Even the histories of the rich eventually turn into myth. Nothing recedes into the vanishing point of time's rear-view faster than the truth.

I asked the girl if she wanted to hear the rest of the true history of our family. How Eddie and Isabella finally met again. What happened afterwards.

'If it's about how he did all kinds of bad stuff to your family, not really. I'm still awfully tired from yesterday. If you don't mind, I think I'll go back to bed,' the girl said, and stretched and yawned as unselfconsciously as a child half her age.

'No problem, I'll tell you all about it later,' I said, because, truth be told, I was talked out. 'I'll tell you everything before this is over.'

I went outside to check the weather again. The short day was almost done and it was still snowing hard. I cursed my stupid luck. If we were still socked in tomorrow we'd just about be out of food and I'd be forced to go ahead with my plan. Leave the girl in the refuge and head out into the blizzard a ways so that my fone signal couldn't be traced back to where I'd hidden her, call Alberto Toomy and tell him to pay the ransom into my offshore account right away. No police or funny stuff if he wanted to see her alive. Just a straightforward business transaction.

It wasn't much of a plan, and if the weather didn't ease up all kinds of things could go wrong. I could get lost in the blizzard's white-out. I could fall into a crevasse. The rescue party might not be able to find the refuge. And if Alberto Toomy called my bluff and refused to pay I knew I'd have to give up the girl's location anyway. Or tell the police. Let them know that Honourable Deputy Alberto Toomy had refused to save the life of his daughter, hope to cause some kind of scandal . . .

Every part of the wretched enterprise was chancy, but there was no going back. Somehow or other I would have to make it work. I fell asleep rehearsing what I needed to do, woke with my stomach full of slimy snakes writhing over and around each other, made it to the toilet just in time. When I was done, the girl was still asleep. Or was pretending to be. She didn't stir when I pulled on my boots and coat and went out.

We'd slept late. It was ten in the morning. First light. It was still snowing, but hardly at all. A light curtain of small flakes twirling through windless air. So quiet that I could hear my heart beating. The whisper of air in my lungs.

It was minus fifteen degrees Celsius and I was bareheaded and wasn't wearing any survival gear, but I wasn't especially cold. I remembered winters on Deception Island, playing in the snow with the other husky kids in the floodlit yard of the little school – the exiled ecopoets hadn't been allowed to build a children's house, kids lived with their parents and went to school instead, part of what our jailers called the renormalisation programme. Anyway, I remembered Mama waiting at the gate, a worn-down woman bulked out by layers under her windproof jacket, the other parents likewise swaddled while us kids were dressed in little more than T-shirts and sweaters and trousers. No scarves or gloves, no hats or the little neckpieces the adults wore, chinking every possible gap against the cold. Sometimes, when the wind wasn't blowing too hard, I'd strip off my sweater because I was burning like a furnace.

I was a skinny young thing, believe it or not. Tall, awkward, knock-kneed. And always hungry. Mama refused to work in the research station because it would be an act of collaboration, giving aid to the enemy, and she likewise refused to work as a guide for tourists. Her only income was from the charity of the other ecopoets and occasional work on one of the fishing boats, and she often found it hard to satisfy her daughter's enormous appetite. At mealtimes she would sometimes declare that she'd eaten enough and push her plate towards me. And I would devour every scrap, only realising years later how much she had sacrificed to raise me.

I once read about a kind of bird that parasitises other birds by laying its egg in their nest. The hatchling parasite, burly and aggressive, pushes out its nest-mates one by one so that it can monopolise the food brought by the harried parents . . .

Faintly, far off, something was making a high-pitched whine. I felt a prickling stir of alarm and stepped out into the thin snowfall. Only a narrow section of the ravine floor was visible between the cliff walls. White snow. Black rocks. Nothing moving. But somewhere down below the unmistakable sound of motors was echoing off rock walls, coming closer.

'There are six of them,' I told the girl. 'Six people on four skimmers. And one of them is Mayra Iturriaga. I got a good look at her when they parked up. I think she's been here before. Maybe she was the one who stripped the place. Took everything except a box of kids' toys, because she didn't have any use for them. She guessed that we'd hole up here during the blizzard. As soon as it stopped blowing she rounded up some of her back-country friends and they headed out to catch themselves a nice little prize.'

'Or she called the police,' the girl said.

She was watching me stuff gear into my kitbag. Hope contesting with anxiety in her expression.

'She isn't the kind of person who'd ask the police for help. We don't have any time,' I said, snatching up the tight roll of the girl's sleeping bag, 'to talk this through. Grab your shit. Right now. You leave anything behind, you won't be coming back for it.'

I hustled her through the hatch in back of the refuge into the dim little rock chapel, told her to start climbing the rubble slope.

'What's up there?'

She was standing on one foot, pulling a boot onto the other. Her cold weather gear dumped on the floor.

'These places, they all have a back door,' I said. 'Get going. You can finish dressing later.'

I didn't tell her that I hadn't bothered to check if there really was a back door, where it led to. Or that Mayra Iturriaga and her pals probably knew about it, could have posted guards. All I knew, it was our only chance.

It was a hard scramble on hands and knees to the top of the slope, right under the belly of the ceiling, then a squeeze through a pipe lined with slick plastic to a narrow kettle carved out of the rock. Snow underfoot, a rim of light above, a ladder bolted to the wall. I climbed up, put my good shoulder against the flat lid at the top, heaved. It didn't budge. I tried again, muscles straining, the ladder flexing and creaking. Nothing.

Below me, the girl said, 'I've found some sort of lever.'

It was set inside a slot carved into the rock, gave a scant centimetre when I hauled on it. Something cracked like a pistol shot, a sifting of snow fell, and I jacked a leg against the wall and hauled again. The lever jerked down by degrees and above us a hatch creaked up, shedding more snow and revealing a crescent of milky daylight.

I scrambled through first, pistol out, heart racing in anticipation. I was in the middle of a circle of standing stones, all of them leaning inwards like the teeth of a moray eel. Nothing moving but a soft sifting of snowflakes. Beyond a gap in the stones, the ground slanted to an abrupt drop. That's where the girl ran after she climbed out, and I chased her through knee-deep snow to the edge of the ravine.

The girl was shouting and waving her windproof jacket like a flag, trying to attract the attention of the people below. She gave a little scream when something sparked off one of the boulders and whanged away, and I broadsided her and knocked her into the snow and told her that she was a fucking fool.

'They shot at me!' She was lying on her back and looking up at me, snowflakes starring her eyelashes.

'Didn't I tell you they were the bad guys? Are you all right?'

'I think you may have broken my tail bone. And you're sort of crushing me.'

'Stay right there.'

There were three boulders lined up along the edge of the drop, flattened ovals like waterworn pebbles, each about a metre long.

Two half-buried in the fresh-fallen snow, the third standing proud on a pedestal stone. I knelt beside them, peeked over the edge. I was directly above the narrow ledge that led to the refuge, and realised why the boulders had been balanced there.

Voices floated up, faint but clear. Someone telling someone else to start fucking climbing. A third party saying that there was no sign of the beast woman. Who, I realised after a moment, must be me. I glimpsed a brief flurry of movement, Mayra Iturriaga clambering up the steep stair hacked into the ravine wall. In a couple of minutes she and her friends would be in the refuge. A couple of minutes after that they'd be crawling out of the back door.

I jumped up and linked my hands under the tail of the nearest boulder and heaved. It rocked very slightly on its pedestal stone and I heaved again, putting all my weight behind it, the knife wound in my shoulder waking up. Ice cracked, the boulder tilted forward, flipped over the edge so abruptly that I very nearly went with it. The girl grabbed the back of my jacket, steadying me, and someone shouted out below, a brief cry of anger that was cut off when the boulder struck the ledge with a tremendous bang and bounded away into the ravine.

The girl and I didn't wait to see what happened next. We scrambled up the slope and ran straight through the circle of stones and kept running, out into the blank white landscape beyond.

13

We'd gone hardly any distance when our headlong flight was checked by a deep drift of powder snow. After we'd floundered out of the far side I told the girl to put on the rest of her cold weather gear and extracted a couple of snowshoe packs from my kitbag and tossed one to her. They unfolded with neat precision when we stepped onto them, extruding straps around our boots, gripping our ankles, and we set off again, heading along the contour line towards the pale silhouette of a saw-toothed ridge.

The girl soon fell behind, a small figure in baggy windproofs sinking up to her shins, her knees, as she ploughed through the snow, head cowled by the hood of her bodysuit. I burned with impatience while I waited for her to catch up, knowing that we had only a little time before our pursuers regrouped, knowing that she lacked my traits and fieldcraft. She was as tender and vulnerable as an unshelled hermit crab, and somehow I had to keep her safe and whole.

'You're trying to skate,' I told her, when at last she reached me. 'You need to use your ankles less and your knees more. Lift those snowshoes up with each step. Plant them firmly. Watch how I do.'

The girl soon got the idea, telling me as we slogged along that I'd never be able to catch her on skis.

'Maybe we'll find some at the next refuge,' I said. 'Then we'll see who can catch who.'

'Another hole in the ground? Where is it?'

'Too far to reach today. See that ridge up ahead? We'll find a sheltered spot and lay low, hide from Mayra Iturriaga and her friends. It's only a couple of kilometres, but we need to get there soon as we can. So less talking and more walking.'

I was tempted to bring up my fone, ask for detailed maps and the best route to a safe place, ask about the weather, what the feeds were saying about the girl's kidnapping, whether the police still believed Keever had taken her, where they were searching for him, if they'd caught him. But the risk of being tracked was too great, and my so-called deprived childhood on Deception Island meant that I hadn't been hooked on instant access to everything and everywhere since birth. I could navigate life without assistance and constant reassurance. I had the skills Mama had taught me and I was a rough tough husky, built for cold and hardship. It wasn't much of an edge against a gang of armed bravos riding skimmers, but I hoped that it would be enough.

'This isn't the first time I've been out in the wilderness,' the girl said. 'We have a cabin on Joinville Island. I ski there all the time. Cross-country, slalom. Can you ski?'

'I'm pretty sure I haven't forgotten how.'

Mama and I had skied part of the way across country when we'd made our bid for freedom. I had a sudden clear memory of her standing on a pure white slope as she waited for me to catch up, leaning on her sticks, ski tips veed together. She'd taught me how to skate ski. Pushing from one ski to the other. Nose over knees over toes. 'Elbows in close,' she kept saying, until I'd got the hang of it. 'Stop flailing.' Hard on the thighs and shoulders, especially when you were aching from the exertions of the day before, but I'd never been happier.

The girl was talking about a skiing holiday in New Zealand, a place called Treble Cone on the South Island. I felt a sting of jealousy, thinking of the Wheel. Of sitting at the panoramic window of one of its restaurants with you, watching the harbour fall away as we rose into a warm evening sky. A future that seemed as distant as the moon.

'They have to use snow machines most years,' the girl said. 'And the runs aren't anywhere as long as they used to be. But there are some real whooshy ones.'

She was breathless, babbling, high on adrenaline and the animal exhilaration of the chase. She told me about the runs she liked best, comparing their merits. She told me that she wanted to go wild skiing on Cordillera Darwin in Tierra del Fuego, explained that you were deposited on a mountain slope by heli, skied to a pick-up point, and were ferried back to a cosy cabin.

'Daddy says he won't let me go. But I swear that it will be my present to myself on my eighteenth birthday.'

I remembered how her mother and brother had died, caught in an avalanche while skiing in the back country. Wondered if the girl wanted to prove something to herself.

'Daddy thinks it's a waste of time,' she said. 'Because I'm not good enough to win competitions or make the national team or whatever. He doesn't see the point of doing anything for fun.'

She'd hardly ever mentioned her father, I realised, except to make a threat or to appeal to my better nature.

She said, 'See, that's the downside of being who I am. The expectations I have to live up to. My father's ambitions for me.'

'Poor little rich girl,' I said.

It was a cheap shot, but she took it seriously. 'I know how it sounds. But it isn't always as easy as you might think. And I definitely don't always get to do what I want.'

'Yeah, you only get to ski in New Zealand.'

'I'm supposed to take charge of our business one day. Because I'm the oldest. As if that's a qualification for anything. As if Essie – my little sister, Esmeralda? As if she couldn't do it just as well. If not better. I'm not interested in business. Or politics. I want to be an engineer. Daddy thinks it's a phase. He indulges me. Like I'm still a little kid. But it isn't a phase. It's really what I want to do. It's my passion,' the girl said, with a breathless imitation of the melodramatic delivery of *novela* stars. An imitation, maybe, of her daddy's glamorous girlfriend.

'You like big machines,' I said. 'Which is how we met.'

The girl ignored the jibe, saying seriously, 'I want to get into geoengineering, as a matter of fact.'

'They tried that last century. It didn't work out so well.'

'There was nothing wrong with the ideas. Or the engineering. The engineering was sound. And it worked, sort of. All the different projects, they cut about two degrees off the rise in global temperature. But the world is still broken, it's still getting warmer. It still needs to be fixed.'

'Or all the ice will melt, like in your story.'

'We can still stop that. It isn't too late, and we know what to do. But it will be hard work. And it will take centuries.'

'You sound just like an ecopoet.'

I was amused by her earnest idealism, so pure, so untainted by experience.

'I have to live in the future,' she said. 'So why wouldn't I want to make it a better place?'

We walked on. Stomping through drifts of powder snow, shuffling over hardpack firn. Light flurries blowing from the white sky. The white land rising and falling in long low waves, crevasses cutting through the troughs between. Small crevasses, cracks no more than a hand's breadth across, were buried in fresh-fallen snow and a couple of times the snow gave way and I fell to my hands and knees or barked my shins on a rim of hard ice. Larger crevasses were meandering paths bridged by snow that packed them as they widened, and the girl and I had to stop at each one and probe the surface to make sure it would take our weight before we could cross. And some had grown so large that the snow bridges had collapsed, revealing blue depths floored with tumbled ice blocks, and we had to cut east or west to get around them.

All of this meant that we were making far less progress than I liked. And the girl was beginning to flag, we had to keep stopping so she could get her wind back.

At every halt I turned and studied the horizon for signs of pursuit. The girl kept looking backwards too, maybe still hoping for some kind of rescue, a platoon of state police skimmers slamming over a rise or a heli cruising towards us under the lid of low cloud, and she was the one who spotted the drone. Calling out, pointing to the sky off to our left where a small steady speck hung under the low clouds. I fumbled out the goggles I'd taken from Mayra Iturriaga, but even with their field-glasses app it was hard to make out much.

'It's one of theirs, isn't it?' the girl said. 'The bad guys.'

'It could be anyone's. The police, a hunter looking for elk or reindeer . . .'

I turned a full circle, saw nothing but snow hummocking away in every direction.

'They must have seen us,' the girl said.

'Won't do them any good if they can't catch up with us. We're getting close to the ridge and it'll be dark soon, we can give them the slip then.'

But it was impossible to ignore the drone as we went on, hard not to look back at it, and the ice began to slope downward and broken pressure ridges cut across our path, so at last we had to turn south, away from the ridge and the hope of safety. This was where the icy dome of the plateau ran up against the flank of half-buried mountains, pushing through here and there to feed glacier stubs that had once flowed all the way down to the west coast. The girl and I were following a broad hummock of blue ice mostly blown clear of snow, trying to find a way around a chaos of tilted ice slabs and crevasses, when I saw a glint of movement off to the west. It was another drone, this one maybe a kilometre away, skimming along the slope above us, hunting this way and that in short jagged bursts. The first drone was as motionless as ever, a dim speck nailed in the sky's pale dome.

The girl and I crouched in a trough between two low ridges. I pulled out a couple of foil blankets, told the girl to wrap herself in one and wrapped myself in the other, and we lay on our bellies, shoulder to shoulder, and watched the drones. One high, one low.

'It won't spot us as long as we keep still,' I said, although I knew there wasn't much hope. The blankets insulated us somewhat, but in infrared we must have looked like a couple of fallen stars burning on the frigid ice.

'If the bad guys are running the first drone, who is running the second?'

'They could be running both of them. The first could be a spotter, the other one armed in some way.'

The second drone was still moving erratically, as if tracking our footprints. Losing the trail when it crossed bare ice, searching to and fro before picking it up again. Coming closer, hunting back and forth above a tumble of ice blocks. I unshipped my pistol, dialled it to explosive taglets, tried to track the little machine as it zigged and zagged. And something swooped out of the sky, falling so fast that I glimpsed it only as a kind of after-image. It was the first drone, racing straight at the second, firing something, a net that struck and folded around its prey. I jumped up, shading my eyes, watching as it rose in a long arc, towing the captured drone behind it, dwindling southwards.

'That was my father,' the girl said. She was standing too, clutching her foil blanket around herself as she stared at the blank sky, grinning like the fox that knows where the mouse lives. 'My father and his people. They're watching us. They're protecting us. They know where we are.'

'Whoever it was, we can't stay here,' I said. 'We need to find shelter before you freeze to death. And if the bad guys were running that drone, the one that got snatched, they're probably right behind us.'

She tried to argue, of course. She believed that help was close at hand, tried to stand her ground. I had to threaten to sling her over my shoulder to get her moving again.

'You don't want to face the fact that you've lost,' she said.

'I'll give in when your father walks up and puts a pistol to my head,' I said. 'Until then, you're going to do exactly what I tell you.'

The stretch of bare ice grew narrower, gave way to snow. Below us, slumps of ice and rakes of bare rock slanted towards the frozen ridges and ripples of a glacier. The sky was darkening and it was steadily growing colder. We'd have to find somewhere to rest up soon, even if it was no more than a snow hole. I was searching for a way to reach an island of rock directly below us, thinking that there might be some small chance of shelter in its lee, when I heard the faint buzz of a motor, saw a speck moving across the long slope. A skimmer, no more than two kilometres away and leaning in a wide curve, heading straight for us.

'Stand up straight,' I told the girl. 'Let them come to you.'

'Suppose they're the bad guys.'

'I'm going to take care of them. Just stand there, you'll be fine.'

We were on top of an ice ridge, its edges cut by steep snow-packed crevices. I redialled my pistol and slid down one of those crevices, burrowing into the snow and lying quiet and still, a trickle of icy water worming under the collar of my uniform jacket. I couldn't see the skimmer but I could hear it, the buzz of its motors and the crunch of snow under its skis and drive track. A vibration shivered through my body as it went past, and I sort of swam up through the snow and saw that it had stopped a little way in front of the girl.

She stood tall and slender against the darkening sky. Unflinching. Maybe she was hoping that the skimmer's riders were her father's people come to rescue her, or maybe she had some sand in her after all.

The pillion passenger climbed off the skimmer, a big man in a hooded red jacket, clutching a pistol in his gloved fist. The girl raised her hands as he walked towards her, and I jacked up, shedding a cocoon of snow, and fired a burst of taser taglets. As the man fell down, I ran flat out at the skimmer and smashed into the driver. We tumbled over the far side and I straddled him and slammed his head against hard ice until he stopped moving. Rolled off him and aimed my pistol at the passenger as he pushed to his hands and knees, and told him to stay exactly where he was if he wanted to live.

14

I disarmed the passenger and the unconscious driver and threw their cutlery out into the chaos of ice. Cuffed the passenger with loops of memory plastic I found on his belt, snapped a fone blocker around his wrist, and squatted in front of him and told him how things would go.

'If you answer my questions, I'll leave your friend untied, so when he comes round he can cut you free. Otherwise, I'll truss him up just like I've trussed you, and leave the pair of you to freeze to death.'

I'd pushed back his hood, pulled off his goggles and scarf. He squinted at me, sullen and defiant, frozen snot crusting his beard.

'To start with,' I said, 'you can tell me how you hooked up with Mayra Iturriaga.'

'You don't have to worry about the old woman,' the passenger said. 'After that stunt you pulled back at the refuge? She's gone.'

'You're saying what? That rock killed her?'

'She fell off the cliff, smashed both her legs. Broken legs, out here? She was dead weight. So we put her out of her misery.'

Sue me and send me to hell, but I was glad to hear that the crazy old woman had taken a cold nap, and I haven't changed my mind since. Two bodies were found buried in the spoil heaps at the mine after all this was over, one of them Oldin Andersen's, the other a woman missing presumed dead after she didn't return from a hunting trip. The police reckon that Mayra Iturriaga was responsible for them, that she killed at least six more people out in the back country. Not to mention that she tried to kill me, too. No, the way I look at it, she most definitely got what she deserved.

'It's my friends you have to worry about,' the passenger said, told me that none of them had been hurt bad when I'd dropped that boulder on their heads. A busted wrist, a sprained ankle, some bruises, nothing that would keep them from the hunt. The boulder had taken out one of their skimmers, but they'd found the one I'd taken from the old woman, so call it even. 'They know we spotted you, they know exactly where you are, and they're gonna be along any minute.'

'And who are they, these friends of yours? What do they want?'

'Sit tight and you'll find out soon enough.'

'You aren't police, that's for sure. And you aren't back-country people, either. Not with that fancy gear you're wearing. So I guess you're working for Keever Bishop.'

'You think you're pretty smart.'

'I'm not the one tied up.'

'You got lucky is what it is.'

'Is Keever part of this little hunting party?'

'Like I said, wait and see.'

The driver stirred a little when I yanked his arms up behind his back, mumbling a liquid string of nonsense into his fur-trimmed hood. I brandished a loop of plastic, smiled at the passenger. I'd torn the knife wound in my shoulder during the struggle with the driver, it was throbbing something fierce and I could feel a trickle of blood creeping down my flank. That, and the fear that the rest of the crew could be heading towards us, had considerably shortened my temper.

'It's minus fifteen right now,' I said. 'And going to get a lot colder when it gets dark. No problem for me. I'm a husky. The ice is my home. But if I leave both of you tied up, strip off your cold weather gear, do you think you'll survive until your friends find you?'

The passenger told me to go fuck myself and looked away when I repeated the question. I had to slap him around to get him into a civil frame of mind, and the girl turned and walked off a little way, too genteel and weak-stomached to witness what was necessary for our survival. The bravo snorted blood from his nose, told me that Keever wasn't in on the hunt, but he was taking a very personal interest in bringing me down, very much wanted to make me pay for having inconvenienced him. I was asking if the passenger's friends were the only ones chasing us, asking where they were supposed to take us after they caught us, when the girl spoke up, telling me that the skimmer had started talking.

It was a man's voice, a voice I recognised. Squawking from a little skywave handset hung by a loop from the yoke of the skimmer.

'Mike Mike,' I said. 'What's up?'

'As if you don't know,' Mike Mike said. 'I suppose you took down those two fools.'

'Don't be too hard on them. They're out of their depth.'

'I could say the same about you, Stral. How's the girl? Have you been taking good care of her?'

'She's fine,' I said, looking at her.

'Glad to hear it. You know how this is going to play out, don't you? You know you can't outrun us.'

'I know I'm about to steal a skimmer and try my best.'

'Your best won't be good enough, I promise you that.'

'What's this all about, Mike Mike? Why are you risking your life and liberty with this kidnapping nonsense?'

'Keever had something going with the girl's father,' Mike Mike said. 'She was supposed to be collateral. You know, to make sure the Honourable Deputy behaved himself. Keever's pissed at you because you didn't stick with the script and fucked up his plans. But if you give up the girl right now, he might go easy on you.'

I thought of Keever finding out about you, said, 'You know he won't.'

'All right. Maybe he won't. But you know he won't stop looking for you. And how long do you think you can keep the girl alive out here?'

'I've done all right so far. Where is Keever right now? Is he still on the peninsula?'

Mike Mike ignored that. 'I can't promise that you'll be able to walk away from this, Stral. But if you don't give me any more trouble I'll make sure Keever doesn't take it out on the girl. You try to run, though, there won't be a pretty ending.'

'That doesn't sound like much of a deal.'

'It's the best I can offer. Wait there, OK? I'll be along shortly.'

'See you around, Mike Mike,' I said, and threw the handset out onto the ice.

I should have crippled or killed those two bravos, but I didn't. I've said it before and I'll say it again – I never was the kind of monster some make me out to be. No, I left them to be rescued by Mike Mike and took off on the skimmer, the girl riding behind me. I'd shut it down and rebooted it in safe mode, disabling sat-nav and comms and pretty much everything but the manual controls, knew that it might be carrying some kind of hidden tracking device but had to take the risk because I needed to make some distance as quickly as possible.

We cut west and south in a wide arc, climbing back up to the top of the plateau where the going was easier. My blood was singing with exhilaration. We were still being hunted, but for the moment I had the advantage.

I swung the skimmer around crevasses, jolted over ridges and fields of broken ice, smashed through drifts. At last, with no sign of any pursuit, twilight beginning to stretch out across the land, I stopped and built a snow wall against the light wind and brewed tea. That was when I realised that in the scramble to escape when Mike Mike's crew pitched up at the refuge I had forgotten to pack the reindeer meat, which I'd left outside so it would stay frozen.

The girl and I shared half the last ration pack and I stripped off my windproof and my uniform jacket to inspect my shoulder. Blood stuck my shirt to my skin, black on the blue cloth, and when I peeled it off the knife cut started bleeding again. I scrubbed it with snow as best I could, held the lips of the wound closed while the girl smoothed on a fresh bandage, and then we set off again.

It was fully dark, I was wearing Mayra Iturriaga's goggles, using their night-vision app, when at last I spotted a way sign set on a solitary flat-topped outcrop. A path descended in tight loops between tumbles of ice and rakes of rock, passed between two rugged bluffs and emerged at the head of a semicircular valley. Another way sign pointed towards raw cliffs looming at the valley's southern edge. I took a sighting and drove up a gravel slope into a narrow defile.

The refuge was at the end of a steep path choked with tumbled rocks. It wasn't much. A crescent of stones sprayed with insulation foam that walled off a low ledge, a poured resin floor, a few old traps and cooking utensils hung from hooks screwed into one wall. I set the stove in the centre and brewed up more tea, and the girl and I ate what was left of the ration pack. And that was that. The two bravos who'd come chasing after us hadn't been carrying any supplies because they were the kind of fools who didn't realise that you could get into serious trouble when you went off road in the back country. Apart from a few packets of condiments we were all out of food.

I told the girl that it wasn't a problem, I could forage in the valley come daylight. Told her that the bad guys wouldn't find us because they wouldn't know about a little place like this, and in any case they'd expect us to take the easy and direct route straight across the top of the plateau instead of diverting into the dead end of a hanging valley.

She sat quiet for a couple of minutes, knees drawn up to her chin, arms wrapped around her shins, brooding on that. She'd shucked the hood of her bodysuit and her blonde hair shone dull gold in the single sparklight I'd stuck to the low ceiling. The ride had reddened her cheeks, left her lips white and cracked.

At last, she said, 'The people chasing us, are they really working for Keever Bishop?'

'We've had a long and difficult day. Right now we should get some rest. And if you want, we can talk about it in the morning.'

'You said I didn't have to worry about him.'

'And I was wrong. I admit it. But we got away, and that's all that matters.'

'That man on the radio. He said my father was involved with him.'

'Did he ever mention Keever? Your father.'

'If he did, would I be asking you about it now?' the girl said, with a sharp edge to her voice.

'I guess not. Well, it doesn't really matter.'

Keever had mentioned something about settling business with Alberto Toomy, back at Kilometre 200, but as far as I was concerned it was a complication I didn't need.

'You could use it to blackmail him,' the girl said.

'I don't need to. I have you.'

'You could cause him some real trouble. Get back at him for what our family did to yours.'

'That kind of thing never works out,' I said, thinking of how Mama had tried and failed to cause trouble for Eddie Toomy. 'And besides, I don't want anything from your family but the price of a ticket off the peninsula.'

The girl was quiet for a moment, looking past me as she examined something in her head. 'He left in the middle of the lunch,' she said.

'The lunch before the ribbon-cutting ceremony?'

'He was gone for about an hour. When he came back, he told me that he had been talking with some of the guards about conditions in the camp. He said that the convicts had it too easy, said that he could create a nice little scandal about it. But it might be, mightn't it, that that was when he met with your friend Keever Bishop.'

'I guess.'

I was bone-tired and really truly wasn't interested in any connivance between Keever and Alberto Toomy, but the girl insisted on following her train of thought to the end.

'Do you think,' she said, 'that Daddy was supposed to help with the escape, and he refused?'

'All I know is that Keever Bishop wanted me to confront your father. To get in his face and cause a fuss. But I didn't want to play, I got in the middle of that attempt to snatch you, and here we are. Now, enough with the questions and pointless speculation. You need to go outside, shit or take a piss? No? Then get to fucking sleep already.'

We rolled out our sleeping bags either side of the stove. I drifted off while thinking about what had happened and what to do next, where to go, and when I woke it was eight in the morning, about an hour before sunrise. The girl was fast asleep and didn't stir when I ducked outside, planning to check the weather and forage for food.

It had stopped snowing. The strip of sky above the high rock walls of the defile was a deep pure blue several shades darker than my uniform, and there was just enough light to make out a small shape lying on the shawl of fresh-fallen snow.

The corpse of a hare clad in its white winter coat, a bright splash of blood on its muzzle.

15

'If it's a gift,' the girl said, 'who left it there?'

'I don't know. Elves, maybe.'

'Seriously.'

'Seriously, I really don't know.'

'It could be the owner of that drone,' the girl said. 'The one that snatched the other drone out of the sky?'

I'd been wondering the same thing. And I'd also been wondering if that predator drone could have come from the work camp, if Paz and Sage had hijacked it and were using it to keep watch over the girl and me. I mean, I knew it wasn't very likely, but it wasn't very likely that some random stranger would take pity on me either, and the idea that Paz and Sage had knocked out Mike Mike's drone, that the gift of the hare was another sign that they were trying to help me in any way they could, all for one, one for all kind of thing, had revived my hope that I'd somehow make this mess come good. But I wasn't about to tell the girl about my friends, so I said that it was just as likely that the hare had been left by a passing trapper who'd seen our plight, or by a hermit who lived somewhere round about.

The girl glanced at the entrance of the shelter, as if she expected, what's the word, an apparition wearing furs and necklaces of teeth to stoop through. 'Why would they leave it and sneak away? Wouldn't they want to at least say hello?'

'People who live out here don't have much use for other people,' I said. 'That's why they live out here. Now pay attention while I butcher this fine animal. It's the kind of thing you need to know how to do if you're going to survive in the back country.'

The hare's limp body was stretched on the floor between us, patches of grey on its belly where its winter colouring hadn't fully come in and now never would. I used Mayra Iturriaga's knife to slice circles in the skin around its forelimbs and its throat, and the girl made a choked little noise when I stripped off its fur and skin like a bloody jacket, looked away when I slit open its belly.

'I'm not going to eat any of that,' she said. 'I won't.'

'Think of it as fuel. Fuel to keep you warm against the cold. Fuel to keep you going.'

'I'll manage.'

She had a stubborn look that was becoming all too familiar.

'There's no point sticking to a principle if it could hurt you,' I said.

'There's no point giving up a principle because it's the easy thing to do.'

It wasn't a bad retort, but I wasn't going to tell her that.

'Put on your gear,' I said. 'We'll go look for grass and leaves.'

It was cold and still. No footprints in the snow except our own, no tracks but those left by our skimmer. Low clouds sagging in the sky. Nothing moving up there. Nothing I could see, anyway. But I hoped, how I hoped, that someone, Paz and Sage or a kindly stranger, was watching over us.

Kicking snow and truffling around, I found a patch of spongy grey lichen, what some call reindeer moss. Back in the shelter I stuffed a couple of handfuls into the little food printer and finished butchering the hare. I ate its heart and liver raw, amused by the girl's disgust, and seared strips of meat and the hind legs on the stove. The sizzle of cooking flesh filled the little shelter with blue grease smoke and a smell that sprang saliva in my mouth. While the girl doggedly chewed wafers the colour and texture of wet cardboard that had been spat out by the printer, I wolfed down hare meat and cracked long bones to get at the marrow, and believed that I could feel my cells plumping up with fat and protein.

Stupidly cheerful, I changed the bandage on my shoulder, packed up camp, and chivvied the girl onto the back of the skimmer. I couldn't leave her in the shelter because it was too rudimentary and too exposed, and there was the very real risk that Keever's people would follow our tracks across the plateau into the valley. No, we had to keep moving until we found a place of safety, and we weren't that far, now, from a little town name of Charlotte Bay where Mama and I had rested up during our trek. One of my grandmother's friends – Alicia Whangapirita, I believe I've mentioned her before – had helped us out back then, and I was wondering if she might help me now. Might even help me ransom the girl. And if she wouldn't or couldn't, I'd steal supplies, maybe even steal a boat, and find a place somewhere along the coast where I could ransom the girl before heading south to the people smugglers.

First, though, we had to trek across the Cayley Valley and Blériot Basin and make a short traverse across the Herbert Plateau before descending to the west coast, following the path Mama and I had taken after we'd escaped Deception Island. Fifty or sixty kilometres. Two days on the skimmer. No more than three. Most of the way was through forest, we could stay hidden, live off the land, and maybe our mystery benefactor would help us again . . .

With a full belly, good weather and a solid plan, anything seemed possible.

The valley, scooped out by a secondary ice flow, ended in a steep drop to the pitted remnant of what had to be, by my reckoning, Lilienthal Glacier. A couple of way signs led to a path cut into the sheer cliffs above the glacier. Barely wide enough for the skimmer, which had retracted its skis and dropped two front wheels to negotiate the buckled and potholed surface, the path descended in a long slant that swayed around the bellying curves of the cliffs with no barrier to prevent us going over the edge, sometimes running under overhangs, sometimes through short tunnels. Another feat of ecopoet engineering, carved by drills and picks and explosives, part of their semi-secret network of trails and roads.

The jolting ride set off a familiar queasiness. Pretty soon I had to stop the skimmer, clambering off a bare moment before I lost my breakfast. The girl watched as I stood doubled over the puddle of puke, hands on knees, teary-eyed, spitting, wiping a string of mucus from my mouth with the back of my hand.

'You've been sick every day,' she said.

'I'm fine. It isn't anything.'

But I could see her adding one and one together and getting two.

'My cousin was sick every morning when she was pregnant,' she said.

'I'm not your cousin.'

'You kind of are,' she said, with a bold knowing look I didn't like. 'How far along are you?'

I told her to get back on the skimmer, we had a long way to go.

'Two months? Three?'

'It's none of your business.'

'If it's why you ran away from the camp, I think it is.'

'Shut up and get on the fucking skimmer.'

She shut up. She got on the fucking skimmer. But I knew that wouldn't be the end of it.

The road levelled out beyond the face of the glacier, following a shoulder of rock and gravel that slanted down to a narrow meltwater lake. Mama and I had camped on the shore of a similar lake in a valley closer to the coast, fishing for char and whitefish, catching little black crayfish in the shallows, but the girl and I lacked lines and hooks, and most of all we lacked time. Mike Mike and his crew were hunting us, if they tracked us to the refuge they'd soon enough find the ecopoet road we needed to get on.

We drove past the far end of the lake, followed an outflow river that meandered between shoals of snow-capped gravel and scattered stands of weather-bent trees. Skiing through snowy meadows, bumping across frozen streams that ran down the steep valley side towards the river, skirting piles of rocks.

Quite soon the trees thickened into forest. A rugged snow-capped mountain, Baldwin Peak, rose above sheer slopes off to our left, the walls of the valley fell back on either side, and we turned south and left the river behind. As we detoured around a string of small kettle lakes I glimpsed a group of giant elk and slowed and stopped, and the girl and I watched as the bull, tall and knock-kneed, antlers shaped like ragged bat-wings and two metres wide, unhurriedly led his harem of cows and their calves off through a grove of dwarf cypress, disappearing into the deep shadows of the forest.

The girl asked if my people had made them.

'Ecopoets resurrected mammoths, but not giant elk. They were the work of a bunch of rich people who wanted to hunt them. As if the reindeer we introduced weren't enough,' I said, knowing that I was channelling Mama's scorn.

'They look as if they belong here, even so.'

'The head of that bull will probably end up as a trophy in some city fool's house.'

'I thought we'd see more animals than this.'

'Most of them have the good sense to keep away from people.'

I waited to see what else the girl wanted to say, whether she'd bring up my condition again. But she fell silent, staring off into the shadows under the trees, and I restarted the skimmer and we drove on.

Somewhat past noon we encountered a second river, running broad and shallow over a bed of white pebbles, faintly smoking in the frigid air. We crossed it easily and parked up on the far side and brewed tea, black with the last of the sugar stirred into it, and ate a scant lunch of shrivelled bearberries picked along the river's edge. Sunlight sparkled on the water and on the far bank a Siberian larch clothed in flame-red leaves flared in the sombre shade of conifers. The sheltering hush of the forest was broken only by the rippling rush of the river and the creak of trees pinched by cold and the occasional soft slide of snow from an overloaded bough. It was as if we were the first or last people in the world.

The piercing sweetness of the bearberries unlocked a tumble of vivid memories. The exiled huskies had a small co-op farm on Deception Island, and all the fish they could catch, but also planted secret gardens of bearberry, Eskimo potato and other edible wild plants to keep in touch with their traditions, a link to the way of life from which they'd been torn, which they vowed to somehow keep alive until the blessed day they could return to it.

For Mama and the rest of the adults, the island was a prison, but for most of us kids it was the only home we knew. We hiked up to remnant glaciers that clung around the peaks of Mount Pond and Goddard Hill, stole eggs from the rookeries of chinstrap penguins at Baily Head, swam in Alburfera Lagoon, camped out in summer at Crater Lake, played on black sand beaches and among the ruins of the old science station and the old whaling station in Whalers Bay.

There was a little cemetery above the beach there, excavated from ash that had buried it in the last eruption. Crosses and headstones carved with antique names, all of them men. Back then, our schoolteacher Dr Herrara told us, the only permanent inhabitants of Antarctica were the dead, lying in cold and lonely graves far from home. We liked to frighten each other with tales of ghosts hungry for warm blood, and the demonic Mr Bones who, with long talons and eyes burning red in his skull face, stalked and snatched unwary children and boiled them to fat and bones in an old try-pot.

Deception Island is a volcanic caldera that's been breached and flooded by the sea, creating a natural harbour some seven kilometres across inside a horseshoe of high ridges and peaks. There's a single narrow entrance, Neptune's Bellows – an artificial channel actually, because the original was stopped up by mudflows and rock slides triggered by a big eruption at the end of the last century. So the bay inside, Port Foster, is nicely sheltered and the interior of the island has its own microclimate. Even before global warming changed everything, meadows of mosses and liverworts grew on its stony slopes. Volcanic heat percolates up through the sand of the beach at Whalers Bay and in a tradition more than a century old us kids liked to dig natural spa pools where we'd lounge and splash all day like so many seals.

I remember lying with the others in one of those pools, water steaming in the crisp night air, the lights of the research station glimmering on the far side of the bay and the stars and the luminous wash of the Milky Way spread overhead. I remember watching the great tall curtains of the Southern Lights shimmering and flickering green and white and violet above Mount Pond, remember being gripped by the banal yet profound enlighten-ment which at some point occurs to every kid. Amazement at being who I was, alive at that particular time in that particular place out of the mind-breaking infinity of times and places in the whole wide universe. Feeling special and small at the same time. Wondering if someone like me was somewhere out there, looking up at a sky where our sun was only another star.

The island's harbour was a stopover for cruise ships from Chile, Argentina and New Zealand, and visitors came over from the peninsula too, to hike the trails, explore the ruins, and gawk at the wildlife. Especially the killer whales – the so-called killer whales, as Mama called them, because they were actually edited dolphins about half the size of actual orcas, and after four or five generations were still being tweaked to more closely resemble the real thing. There were virtual tourists, too, and some of the adults and kids (but never Mama, never me) acted as their guides, wearing spex so the tourists could see what they saw and tell them what to look at and where to go.

Many tourists believed that our village was one of the attractions, wanted to go poking around in our homes as if we were some kind of, you know, anthropological curiosity. The last of the wild humans. Mama usually chased them off, but when she was in one of her good moods she sometimes liked to buttonhole the intruders, actual or virtual, and lecture them on the stupidity and unfairness that was still ruining the world, and the righteousness of the free ecopoets' cause.

My mother. Aury Vergara Ferrado. I haven't really told you much about her, have I? She was a firebrand back in the day, a political activist born into an ordinary middle-class family in Santiago. She quit school at the age of sixteen and went off to join a tree-planting project, one of the attempts to stop the spread of the Atacama Desert, knocked around in the so-called green underground for a couple of years, and quit Chile when she heard that the police were planning to round up her and a crew of activists who'd been campaigning against the construction of mansions and ranches by wealthy climate change refugees in Tierra del Fuego.

By then, the peninsula's government had outlawed ecopoets and their work. Most had accepted the terms of the amnesty, but a few held out, disappearing into the back country. Aury helped to organise supply routes to refuges and holdfasts below the Antarctic Circle, eventually used her contacts to get herself smuggled to the peninsula, where she joined the rebels.

She hooked up with my father in a summer camp for a crew planting out alpine meadows on the steep hillsides above Sölch Fjord. It wasn't love at first sight, like with Isabella and Eddie. Aury and Salix already knew each other because Aury had spent the previous winter in the refuge where my grandmother had set up her new lab. She told me that she was first attracted to Salix by his work ethic, but knowing Mama as I do, I reckon there was an element of political calculation too. Although Salix hadn't inherited Isabella's aptitude for science, was a general pool labourer in summer and supervised the refuge's water recycling system in winter, he was his mother's son and had a certain standing among the free ecopoets.

But love or something like it blossomed, as they say, in the long days of hard work and the gatherings around campfires in the white nights of midsummer. Aury and Salix were married the next winter, and a couple of years later I was born. Another political act. Mama swore it had been a joint decision to engineer me, make me a husky, but I'm pretty sure my father didn't have much choice in the matter.

And listen. Mama may have been stubborn and obsessive, bitter and wounded, given to sudden rages and days of brooding black silence, but she was an indefatigable soldier in the struggle for environmental reparations and social justice, and she was dead right about one thing. Us huskies are something new in the world. So new we haven't yet learned how to define ourselves, which is why, after Mama died, I too often measured my worth by the standards of mundanes, when like Paz I should have accepted who I was and flaunted my difference.

After the escape from the island and everything else, too many people told me I was a monster. Some of them kids in the orphanage who didn't know better, but plenty of adults too. So that's what I became. That was the shell I grew. The mask I wore. My secret superpower. I was a thief, a convict, and an institutional thug, and then I snatched an innocent girl and took her into the deep dark forests of the back country.

I did it only because I wanted to escape my past. Because I wanted to start over. Because I thought that I could find a place where what I was, what I'd been made to be, wouldn't matter. Even to myself. And I did it for you. I did it for us. For the future we deserved to share. I took you with me just as Mama took me with her when we escaped from the island, and I was determined to succeed where Mama had failed. I don't care if it sounds like magical thinking or self-justification. I know the truth. I did what I did to save you from a world that hated and feared people like us.

16

Close to the end of the day the girl and I drove up out of the forest and crossed the broad snow-covered saddle between the Cayley Valley and Blériot Basin. A solitary peak stood off to the north, hard pinkish light glowing on its flanks, and the wind blew cold and clean and the last of the sunlight turned the snow crust's icy lace into a carpet of diamonds.

We're simple creatures. A change in the weather or a glimpse of a distant panorama can transform our mood in an instant. Looking across snowy ridges towards that mountain peak I was struck head to toe by a tingling charge of exhilaration. We had escaped, I was about to take up the path Mama and I had once followed, and this time it would all come right.

But as we descended between stark bluffs towards Blériot Basin I saw that much of the forest through which Mama had led me all those years ago had been replaced by square regiments of dark green conifers and a loose grid of access roads. A rocky hill rose from these plantations like a besieged castle. Further off, the lights of a cluster of greenhouse domes shone small and distinct at the mouth of the Blériot River, and a dab of white smoke feathered from the tall chimneys of some kind of processing plant.

I quickly disabused the girl when she pointed to the settlement and asked if that was where we were going. My brief euphoria had been displaced by nervy apprehension. When I spotted something glinting high in the darkening sky, heading north above the basin, I thought for a moment it might be a police heli or some kind of military craft, then realised that it was one of the cargo drones which transported fresh seafood from the coastal fishing villages to the cities. Still, I felt horribly exposed as we drove on in blue twilight, over stony slopes and through threadbare meadows at the eastern edge of the basin. There was entirely too much civilisation here for my liking, a good chance that we might run into a crew of foresters, a security patrol, a stray hiker . . .

We stopped for the night in the cover of a patch of trees growing alongside a swift little stream. I constructed a half-circle of loose stones and the girl helped me pack the chinks with snow and roof it with cut branches. While she warmed herself in front of the fire I'd lit in front of our little shelter, I foraged along the bank of the stream, finding patches of trampled snow where reindeer had snouted for moss and lichen, no sign of any other life except for a small bird that, scared up from a clump of dead grass, whirred away above the water and was quickly lost in the twilight.

I picked leaves from low tangles of box-leaf barberry and dwarf willow and winter's bark, dug up willow roots, set out the wire loop traps I'd taken from the refuge. When I returned to the shelter the girl was sitting by the fire in her sleeping bag, reading her book. I stuffed the leaves into the printer and chopped the willow roots into a pan of melted snow water, and it was while we were waiting for this to boil that we heard the wolves.

A pack calling each to each somewhere far off in the dark, the alpha male baying his long rising note, the rest pitching in with a chorus of howls and yips. A spooky lonesome carol that threaded a silver wire in my blood, the girl looking at me as it broke into scattered barks and fell silent.

'They'll be following elk and reindeer migrating north for the winter,' I told her. 'They won't be interested in us.'

I'd seen wolves hunting, once upon a time. Mama and I had been traversing a ridge when we'd spotted them in the snowy valley below, circling a small group of reindeer, charging at them and cutting away until the reindeer panicked and broke into a run. The wolves raced alongside them, looking for any weakness, and at last one chased down a calf which had become separated from its mother, grabbing a hind leg in its jaws and holding on as the calf kicked a circle in the snow. The other wolves swarmed in, one tore out the calf's throat, and that was that.

Remembering something Mama had said back then, I told the girl, 'If they do come at us, stand your ground and spread your arms. As long as you look much bigger than them, look like you mean to do them some hurt, they'll think twice about attacking.'

'I thought you said wolves didn't attack people,' she said.

She was sitting very still, looking across the little fire towards the trees on the other side of the stream, dark against the dark sky. The night was quiet again, but now that we knew what was out there the quality of that silence had changed.

'It's good advice in general,' I said.

As we ate a bare supper of tasteless printer biscuits and boiled willow roots, I tried to take the girl's mind off her predicament, asked her how the book's story was going, whether the prince and princess had married yet.

'If you're going to make fun of it there isn't much point telling you any more.'

'We're sitting in front of a campfire in a dark wood. Exactly the kind of place where people tell each other stories. And you won't get another chance. Tomorrow we'll get to somewhere safe, and I'll fone your father and arrange to get you back to him.'

'Where you're going to ransom me, in other words.'

'Think of it as my reward for saving you. Like this prince saving the princess in your story.'

'Tantris isn't a prince. And it isn't that kind of story either.'

'He was being treated for a poisoned wound, last I knew. By a queen who was the sister of the man who poisoned him, the man he killed. The queen and her daughter, Isander. So far, it's all been about him, hasn't it? I thought it was supposed to be about her.'

'It's a long story. This is just the prologue.'

'So do they fall in love, Tantris and Isander, while she's looking after him?'

'That comes later,' the girl said. 'First, Tantris has to kill a dragon.'

*

During his convalescence, Tantris was charmed by the beauty and kindness of the princess, the younger Isander. Any ordinary man would have schemed to win her heart, but because he was a hero and unswervingly loyal to his monarch Tantris returned to Palmis as soon as he was well enough, and told King Marsche about her. The king was still in mourning for his wife, who had died two years before. Tantris believed that if he married Isander he would find happiness again, Palmis and Esland would become allies, peace would reign, so on. You could say that Tantris was being noble, giving up the opportunity of courting Isander for the greater good, except that he wasn't in love with Isander. As far as he was concerned she was no more than a minor piece in the great game of politics and courtly intrigue.

The major obstacle to this union was the death of Mordred and the sinking of most of his ironclads, but Tantris had a plan to fix that. A dragon was terrorising the west coast of Esland. He would slay it, take its head to King Geraine, and say that he had acted on the orders of his king. Geraine would forgive the death of Mordred and agree to the marriage of his daughter to King Marsche, and all would turn from the bitter past to the sweet future.

Although it could fly and breathe fire, the dragon wasn't an actual fairy tale dragon, but a mechanical monster got up by a wizard, grown feral and cruel after its creator died. Tantris sailed to Esland in Mordred's ironclad, drove the dragon out of its mountain lair by bombarding it with the ship's naval cannon, and faced it alone, armed only with his sword, because in stories like this heroes have to kill monsters up close and personal. After a fierce battle that lasted three days, he pinned the dragon's tail with a silver nail, climbed onto its back while it shrieked and twisted, and sawed off its head.

But he'd been badly hurt in the fight, raked by the dragon's claws, scorched by its fire, poisoned by its breath. He was taken to a hospice in a nearby town, and a company of King Geraine's men sent to investigate news of the dragon's death found him there, and took him and his trophy to the capital of Esland.

Tantris hadn't counted on being wounded, or that once again he would be treated by Queen Isander and her daughter. Still, he stuck to his plan and explained that he was the loyal servant of the king of Palmis, whose idea it had been to slay the dragon, and when he asked King Geraine if he would give his daughter's hand in marriage to King Marsche, Geraine quickly gave his assent.

But Princess Isander had seen that a notch in Tantris's sword exactly matched the splinter she'd found in Mordred's skull when she and her mother had prepared his body for burial, and she also discovered that her uncle's ironclad had been sighted off the coast of Esland before Tantris's epic fight with the dragon. When she confronted Tantris and accused him of murdering Mordred and stealing his ship, the young knight explained that he'd killed him fairly in a duel, and Isander's mother took his side. Like all good queens, she was a skilful diplomat, and knew that the marriage would benefit her family and their kingdom. Tantris enjoyed the king's protection, she told Isander, and now that she was betrothed to King Marsche it was not her place to demand the execution of one of his knights.

Isander had no say in who she married, the girl told me. It was that kind of story. She also told me that she had been able to choose what Isander did next, which was to give Tantris a drink laced with one of her mother's subtle poisons.

'I thought that if the king's champion died, the marriage would be called off. And maybe something more interesting would happen. Instead, the queen recognised the symptoms of the poison and gave Tantris the antidote. The book cheated. It gave me a choice, but the choice didn't make any difference to the story. Isander still ends up sailing towards Palmis and an arranged marriage, escorted by a man she hates because he murdered her uncle. I'm beginning to think that Daddy gave me this book because it's another way of teaching me that a person can't escape her duty. We argue about that all the time. I want to study geo-engineering, but he says that there's no point because I'm going to end up running the family business. The only way you can change things, according to him, is to make a lot of money first.'

'Maybe he's right.'

'Except our business doesn't have anything to do with making the world a better place. We don't even build much, any more. It's mostly about using money to make more money. Perhaps your people had the right idea when they tried to find another way of doing things.'

'It didn't do them any good in the end. Turns out that capitalism is unkillable because it kills every other system first.'

It was the kind of thing the adults on Deception Island liked to say during their endless meetings and discussion circles. Maybe that was why capitalism always won out. There might be better alternatives, co-ops, syndicates, commons, so on, but while their members argued about ethics and the fine print of their charters and procedures, capitalism just got on with doing what it did, and gobbled them up.

The girl was enjoying a moment of self-pity, saying, 'People who don't know any better think that rich people's kids can do anything they want. But we can't. We have to do what's expected of us.'

'You could always run away and become an engineer,' I said. 'Or anything else you want to be.'

'You don't know my father,' the girl said. 'When you try to talk to him about what you want, he turns it around to what you should do. About the responsibility of wealth and your obligations to the family and the family business. And you can't argue with him, because according to him he's always right. Even when he isn't.'

'Let me tell you a story,' I said, tired of her poor-little-rich-girl act. I mean, try being actually poor. Try being an edited orphan everyone calls a monster.

'If this is more made-up stuff about my grandfather doing terrible things,' she said, 'I don't want to know.'

'It's also about Isabella. What happened after Eddie left her.'

'Nothing good, I suppose.'

'Exactly the opposite, in fact. At first, anyway.'

Eddie Pulls A Fast One

Isabella Schilling Morales was pregnant, the father of her child had run off to who knew where and hadn't responded to any of her attempts to make contact, but she had her work, she had the support of the ecopoet community, and when her child was born she felt a kind of completion. Felt that a new and better part of her life was beginning. She no longer gave Eddie Toomy much thought, didn't try to reach out one more time to tell him they had a son. As far as she was concerned, Eddie had defaulted on his parental rights. The baby was hers and that was that.

She named him Salix, after the tough dwarf willows that were a vital part of heaths planted during the first stages of greening glacial till. Salix Gabriel Morales. From age three, he passed the long winters in the children's house in Happy Valley, where Isabella had her lab and was also in charge of the greenhouses, now. Salix spent most of his time with his peers and teachers, a system of child-raising based on the old kibbutz model, but Isabella visited him for an hour or two every evening, sharing supper and his latest enthusiasms, putting him to bed and reading to him until he fell asleep. Summers, when she was working in the back country, he mostly lived in one of the children's camps. A sturdy practical diligent boy who played with other kids his age and took his lessons outdoors in sunshine, rain or sleet, helping to make wildflower gardens, acquiring the basics of arithmetic by practical lessons, learning how the land had been shaped, words for every kind of snow and ice, the names of plants and insects and animals, so on.

The ecopoets had proved that the world's warming did not necessarily mean devastation and destruction. By helping life establish itself in new regions, encouraging it to spread and leaving it to develop as it would, they had created biomes with a total economic value estimated at more than thirty trillion dollars. But although their work was far from finished, although the ice was still retreating, still exposing tracts of virgin territory, their political and financial support was dwindling. Most of the peninsula's population lived in Esperanza and O'Higgins and had little interest in the back country, transnats hit by the latest global recession had cut funding, and the Antarctic Authority, likewise strapped for cash, claimed that the peninsula's forests, heaths and alpine meadows had become self-sustaining and could colonise freshly exposed areas without human intervention.

Despite the cutbacks, many ecopoets refused to quit the peninsula after their visas and contracts expired. They believed that they were the first true natives of the biomes they had quickened. They rebelled against the Authority's attempts to restrict their work, there was talk of self-determination and living off the land, and a vocal minority wanted to give prospective parents the chance to edit their children with a package of traits that would adapt them to the harsh climate of the new lands of the south.

Isabella had strong sympathies with these self-styled free ecopoets. As far as she was concerned, too much of her time was taken up with writing up proposals and dealing with administrative duties and committee work instead of working in the field. Every project was constrained by a thousand petty regulations and the Antarctic Authority's nit-picking tick-box bureaucracy, and in the ecopoet community debates about ongoing work and future projects were too often stalled by emotion and ideology, the tyranny of special interest groups, and the innate conservatism of the old guard.

In the past ten years, for instance, only two proposals to introduce new bird species had been approved – burrowing owls, to control numbers of grassland shrews, voles and mice, and Magellanic woodpeckers, to deal with infestations of wood-boring beetles which were spreading through the forests. Isabella supported a plan to introduce species of songbird into the peninsula's songless forests, salt marshes and meadows, had helped to design an edit that would allow small birds to survive freezing during the long winters. A similar edit, based on traits possessed by Arctic woolly bear caterpillars, which spent most of their lives deep frozen, briefly thawing in summer to feed before freezing again, repeating this cycle for six or seven years until they had grown large enough to pupate and transform into adult moths, had been used in several species of butterflies introduced to alpine meadows, but after several interminable debates the oversight committee rejected Isabella's plan to trial it in a small number of South Georgia pipits. No use pointing out that songbirds would contribute to ecosystem diversity and create new niches, or arguing about their aesthetic qualities. The committee ruled that it was a frivolous exercise that would divert scarce resources from conservation of native birds, and told Isabella that in fifty or a hundred years birds from Tierra del Fuego, Islas Malvinas and South Georgia and the South Sandwich Islands would almost certainly begin to colonise the peninsula, there was no need to interfere with a perfectly natural process.

Steering new projects through the reefs and hazards of ecopoet politics and Antarctic Authority bureaucracy, managing ongoing projects, chairing meetings that settled disputes and smoothed snags in the daily running of settlements, so on, took up most of Isabella's time. She knew that she wasn't seeing her son as often as she should, and to make up for it she took Salix with her when she returned to Chile for the first and last time since she'd left for the peninsula.

Like the rising generation of ecopoets, many of the younger citizens of the peninsula chafed under the rule of the Antarctic Authority. A new political movement, the Independent Democratic Alliance, won control of municipal councils in Esperanza and O'Higgins and with the tacit support of Argentina and Chile began to campaign for independence from the rule of the Antarctic Authority. The majority of the peninsula's permanent inhabitants were originally from Argentina and Chile, their first language was Spanish and their culture was largely Hispanic, and the two countries were the principal investors in the peninsula's mining and fishing industries. An end to exploitation of the south by the old countries of the north! The south for the peoples of the south!

Isabella was a member of the delegation that represented the ecopoets in talks about the peninsula's independence, a process that had been ongoing for two years, no end in sight. Despite an endless round of committee meetings, presentations, discussion groups and press events, she found time to visit the laboratories of scientists who'd worked with her on various projects, to take Salix on excursions to one of the reconstructed beaches, the Preservar la Vida Silvestre Nacional, with its famous collection of rare and resurrected species, the Parque Metropolitano and the summit of Cerro San Cristóbal, and to spend a long weekend with her parents.

Salix found the visit confusing and tiresome. There were too many people and too many buildings, it was too green, too warm, too wet, and he had little in common with his grandparents, aunts and uncles and cousins. The lingua franca of the ecopoets was English, the lingua franca of science. Salix had difficulty following his cousins' machine-gun Spanish, and couldn't understand why different members of the same family lived in separate houses and apartments, why they didn't share their stuff, why they had so much of it. It was as if he had landed on an alien planet with completely different customs and climate, and after eight years' absence Isabella felt much the same. She had lived most of her adult life on the peninsula. It was her home, now and forever.

Two months after Isabella and Salix returned from Chile, the talks broke down and the peninsula made a unilateral declaration of independence. Within a week, the offices of the Antarctic Authority had been shut down and the pro tem government of the Republic of Antarctica had been established. Argentina and Chile signed treaties with the new nation and loaned warships and troops to defend its borders, but neither the other member countries of the Antarctic Authority nor the UN made any serious objections, and most of the transnats with interests in the peninsula were swayed by promises to relax controls over mining, oil and gas extraction, and fishing. The Independent Democratic Alliance won a sweeping majority in elections for a new government, the transition to self-rule was smooth and mostly trouble-free, capped by a week of fireworks, parades and concerts in the peninsula's two cities, and the focus of the global media moved on.

Although they had given the independence movement unqualified support, the ecopoets quickly realised that the new regime had little love for them or their work. According to the new government, the peninsula was no longer a frontier land, was making the transition to a mature democracy. The ecopoets had done much useful work in the past but had become an unaccountable elite that believed themselves above the law, wanted to control access to land that belonged to everyone, were tinkering with plants and animals without proper oversight, and even had plans to alter the genomes of their children. It was time to open up the back country for everyone, to take direct control of greening the land and begin a programme to integrate the ecopoet community into the mainstream of society.

Within a year, the government passed a Land Act that created four national parks and required every ecopoet to register with a new agency and comply with its regulations. Most ecopoets co-operated, believing that they could negotiate some kind of agreement that would allow them to continue their work, but Isabella and a significant minority of the rising generation believed the Land Act was only the overture of a plan to shut them down, confiscate everything they had created, and turn the land over to the same kind of short-term interests which had driven uncontrolled industrialisation, plundering of mineral and biological resources, burning of fossil fuels, and all the other venalities and stupidities which had contributed to global warming and climate change.

While Isabella and her comrades were making plans to defy the government and continue their work in any way they could, carpetbaggers like Eddie Toomy were moving into the cities of the north. Back in the twentieth century, Esperanza had been one of the first civilian settlements in Antarctica, a key element in Argentina's efforts to claim sovereignty. Women and children had lived there all year round and it was the birthplace of Emilio Marcos Palma, the first person born on the continent. Part of the original site is underwater now, flooded by the sea-level rise. The rest, including two of the original red-painted buildings, a grotto dedicated to the Virgin of Lujan and a stele commemorating the deaths of early explorers, has been relocated to a little heritage park behind the Paseo, a seawall topped with an esplanade and a four-lane highway.

When Emilio Palma was born (there's a statue of him on the esplanade, his heel rubbed smooth by couples hoping for a baby), there were only fifty permanent inhabitants in Esperanza. Now there were close to a hundred thousand, and more were arriving every day. Eddie Toomy set up brassplate companies fronting for outside interests, used the fees and the money from the sale of the crab farm to buy rental apartments, then got into building them himself. Within a year, he was employing two dozen people. He was still a hustler with little interest in the niceties of accountancy or planning law, but he was smart enough to realise that he needed to diversify. The peninsula was dependent on food imports from Chile, Argentina and New Zealand, and the government was giving tax breaks to local producers to promote self-sufficiency. Eddie purchased a controlling interest in a small greenhouse farm, then moved into aquaculture, taking advantage of a relaxation in the licensing regime to set up fish and kelp farms along the east and west coasts, winning contracts to supply new factories and mining towns.

Soon, he was a millionaire many times over, married with two kids, Alberto and Amalia. He donated money to several of Esperanza's schools, helped to found one of its hospitals, was an early supporter of the up-and-coming National Unity Party and a regular guest on news feed panels. A plain-speaking self-made bloke who preferred common sense to the opinions of experts, one of the peninsula's success stories.

He liked to tour his fish farms at least once a year, travelling in a small plane he piloted himself. A rich man's indulgence. One summer's day he was flying with two passengers towards a kelp farm on the Oscar II Coast when his plane was hit by a storm that blew in from the Weddell Sea. He couldn't fly above it, didn't have time to fly around it. The little plane plunged through rain, hail and furious crosswinds, was slammed towards the ground by a wild downdraught, then caught in the wind shear of a tailwind that abruptly reduced the lift generated by its wings. Eddie fought to regain control all the way down, crash-landed on a pan of gravelly till close to a river south of Cape Disappointment. The plane's cabin exploded with thousands of inflated balls to cushion the impact, but one of the passengers was killed outright, the other was badly injured, and Eddie broke a wrist and three ribs and was knocked unconscious.

When he came to, the storm's crashing rain had thinned to a mild drizzle and a rainbow spanned the seaward end of the river valley. Eddie helped the surviving passenger, his chief accountant, out of the wreckage and settled her as best he could under the stub of a torn-off wing. The plane's comms had been knocked out, there was no fone signal, and it had come down in the middle of an unpeopled stretch of the coast. There was no sign of a settlement or even a road, but as Eddie was considering his options three mammoths appeared on top of the ridge on the far side of the river, each carrying a rider and bundles of cargo.

Ten years before, a new act passed by the government had finally and absolutely outlawed the ecopoets. Some had moved into the cities and settlements during the so-called amnesty, or had quit the peninsula altogether. Some had been arrested. And some, like Isabella and Salix, and the three rovers who rescued Eddie, were still living in the back country. They'd set up caches and refuges, moved along hidden trails, and lived off the land as much as possible, assisted by supplies from sympathisers on the peninsula and supporters in Chile and Argentina who dispatched cargo drones across the Drake Passage.

For a while, the government chose to ignore these self-styled free ecopoets. It had other, far more pressing problems to deal with. Establishing diplomatic and trade links with the other nations of the world, fixing an economy leaking below the water-line because productivity and earnings were far lower than wildly optimistic pre-independence forecasts, setting up a task force to police fishing grounds, negotiating with transnats over exploitation of the peninsula's mineral and petrochemical resources. Public utilities and much of the infrastructure of Esperanza and O'Higgins had been sold off piecemeal to finance independence, subsequent problems with power and food supplies had triggered widespread civil unrest, and the cities had been placed under martial law for three of the first five years after the Republic of Antarctica's declaration of independence. The people of the South Shetland Islands announced that they wanted to secede so that they could benefit from the sale of rights to oil and gas reserves under the seabed . . .

So a few hundred mostly peaceable free ecopoets living out of sight in the back country, causing little trouble and doing useful work, were very low on the list of the government's priorities. But then the Independent Democratic Alliance lost an election to the neoconservative National Unity Party, which immediately set about making good a pledge to deal with what they called the rebel scofflaws. Over a hundred free ecopoets were captured during raids on refuges in the north and more than twice that number of sympathisers were rounded up in Esperanza, O'Higgins and various coastal settlements. A carefully curated media campaign culminated in show trials, and warrants were issued for the arrest of the leaders of the movement, including Isabella Schilling Morales.

The free ecopoets had mostly moved south, below the Antarctic Circle, but the trio which found Eddie Toomy after his plane crash were returning from stripping out equipment from a number of old refuges, and one of them recognised Eddie because they had both worked in the soil factory back in the day. There was his infernal luck again.

The ecopoets gave Eddie and his injured companion such first aid as they could and called in the accident on the skywave net, an open system that bounced shortwave radio signals off the ionosphere. The woman who knew him from the old days told him that his former girlfriend and her son were both living free in the back country, and Eddie realised that the boy, born eight months after he'd left the peninsula for Australia, must be his.

'Isabella should have told me,' he said, forgetting that he'd burned all his social media when he'd left, hadn't told her where he was going.

'Well I suppose that was her choice,' the woman said. 'You didn't ever try to get in touch?'

'I feel bad about that. I do. But there were complications in my life, time passed . . . What's his name? The boy?'

'Salix. Salix Gabriel Morales. He looks a bit like you, I guess,' the woman said grudgingly. 'Same blond hair. And he isn't a boy any more. He married just recently, and has a daughter. A fine husky girl born just two months ago.'

Eddie pretended that his shock was entirely about discovering that he was a father and a grandfather. 'At my age!' he said. 'Imagine!'

The woman shrugged. She'd never much liked Eddie, who'd always preferred to complain about work rather than actually getting down to it, and she believed that she had said too much. Still, when Eddie asked her if she would tell Isabella that he'd like a chance to meet with his son and his granddaughter, she promised that she would pass on the message, adding that it might take a while for Isabella to receive it. Ecopoets used the skywave net sparingly, and because she had a price on her head Isabella took more precautions than most. She could be here, she could be there. It might take a year for her to receive the message, another year for Eddie to receive her reply. If she wanted to reply.

Eddie said that he understood, said that he would be patient. He also said that he would repay the ecopoets for saving his life, claimed that his close brush with death had given him a new perspective. He wanted to atone for past mistakes, and most of all he wanted to meet Isabella and his son and ask for forgiveness.

It was almost entirely bullshit, of course. The last thing that Eddie had thought before the plane smacked down was that it was so fucking unfair. But he had long ago mastered the knack of faking sincerity, and even managed to squeeze out a couple of tears. It helped that, despite the so-called painkillers he'd been patched with, his ribs were giving him hell.

Soon after the ecopoets and their mammoths had disappeared over the ridge on the far side of the valley, a heli from Barilari Bay touched down next to the crashed plane. The chief accountant had lapsed into a coma by then, died the next day in Barilari Bay's clinic without recovering consciousness. And Eddie returned to Esperanza and set about making good on his promise, donating to a charity that helped former ecopoets who had fallen on hard times after accepting the amnesty, establishing contacts among senior members of the community, and setting up a small operation that used drones to drop caches of freeze-dried rations, drugs and medical equipment in likely spots below the 67th parallel. Caches which reported that they had been opened were renewed, establishing several locations where free ecopoets could reliably find supplies.

One day, almost exactly a year after the plane crash, one of the people Eddie employed to manage this little project forwarded a message sent via the skywave link of one of the caches. Isabella Schilling Morales had agreed to meet with him. A month later, he was on the west coast some fifty kilometres south of the Antarctic Circle. Waiting alone on a slanting shelf of fractured sandstone above the strand line at Bagnold Point. Summer, an armada of white clouds sailing the blue sky on a brisk west wind, patches of sunlight sparkling on the blue sea, Liard Island shimmering at the hazy horizon on the far side of Hanusse Bay. Eventually, an hour past the appointed time, two young men, both of them huskies, materialised from the rocks above him. They patted Eddie down and led him up a trail that climbed along the ridge and dropped to the rocky shore of a shallow bay on the far side. And there, by a tall slab of blood-red stone that had been levered upright and carved with elvish runes, he was reunited with his former lover and promptly betrayed her.

Eddie counted several of the National Unity Party's honourable deputies as his friends. One was the godmother of his eldest son, Alberto. Another often stayed at his holiday home on Joinville Island. It would be a tremendous scandal if it was revealed that Eddie had an outlaw son who'd edited his daughter, turned her into a monster. And if the bloody woman who had helped him after the crash knew about it, the rest of the so-called free ecopoets must know about it too. No way could it be kept secret for ever. It wasn't just the personal embarrassment, although that would be pretty fucking bad. Opponents of the National Unity Party would certainly make use of the scandal, Eddie's pet politicians would cut him off, and because every aspect of his business depended on his reputation, his contacts and his political influence, he'd be shamed and ruined.

It was as if Isabella and Salix had been conspiring to damage him in the worst possible way. But they hadn't counted on his cunning, because he'd seen at once how to turn it around by pulling one of his famous fast ones, a bold clever devious dodge that would neutralise any hint of scandal, strike a blow for law and order, and help the government to clear up an infestation of dangerous criminals. That was how he'd sold it to a friendly minister, and through her won the support of the police. Maybe he believed his own PR, his image of a buccaneering but essentially good-hearted rogue. 'Life should be an adventure,' he liked to say, 'because otherwise what's the point?'

But he was also the same careless selfish man who'd quit the ecopoets and left his lover out of nothing more than boredom, not once thinking of the hurt it would cause her, and like all selfish men everywhere he believed that he had an absolute right to see the child he'd fathered. Confronting the boy and his mother was most definitely part of his plan, so imagine the anger he had to suppress when Isabella told him that Salix had decided that he would rather not meet him.

Eddie pretended to be magnanimous. He said that although he was disappointed he completely understood why Salix might not want to meet the father who had never been part of his life, said that it must have been tough growing up on the run, hiding out in the wilderness without a proper home or education.

'He had exactly the kind of education he wanted and needed,' Isabella said. 'While you, as I recall, quit university. Or were you thrown out? I can't quite remember.'

Eddie had given several versions of the story. Basically, he'd been sent down after he'd dropped classes because surfing and partying were more his idea of fun, hadn't bothered to tell his parents about it. He hadn't bothered to tell them when he'd headed off to the peninsula, either.

'I turned out all right in the end I reckon,' he said.

'So did Salix,' Isabella said.

The implication being, no thanks to Eddie. Well he supposed that he deserved that little dig.

Isabella wasn't exactly forthcoming about their kid or her life, so Eddie found himself doing most of the talking, telling her about his business interests, his brilliant success. He even told her the true story about how he'd gotten hold of the seed money for the crab farm back in New Zealand, something he'd never told anyone else, apart from a woman he'd picked up in Buenos Aires one night a few years back, when he'd been up there on business. Oh, and that drunken night with an old mate in Auckland, after his father's funeral . . . But those didn't really count because his mate and the woman, he'd forgotten her name, had even forgotten what she looked like, both of them had thought it was just another of his tall tales. Hadn't realised what it meant. Isabella, though, he could see that she understood, and it felt good to make a clean breast of it, to unstopper the secret he'd kept from everyone he knew, even his wife and kids. Isabella had known him back then, she knew what he'd been like, knew how he could have fallen into bad company by mistake. And besides, he could tell her what he liked and it didn't matter, because when this was over no one would believe her if she repeated it, they'd just think she was trying to get back at him. It was, he thought, a tasty bit of revenge for not being allowed to meet his son and his granddaughter.

'It turns out that the amount I've spent supporting your people is about equal to the cash money I found in that old duffel bag,' he said. 'So I suppose you could call it atonement for the whole stupid episode.'

Actually, he'd blown more than three times that on this bloody operation, but why let the truth get in the way of a nice little embellishment?

Isabella said that the ecopoets were grateful for his aid packages, but he didn't have to help them just because he felt guilty. The two of them sitting on a rock together, or maybe walking on a moss lawn. The ecopoets had edited several species of moss that grew quickly, spreading in lush emerald carpets, breaking rock down into soil. Imagine Eddie and Isabella walking on such a carpet in bright cold summer sunlight, half a dozen ecopoets watching and waiting by the sea's edge, where several small fast boats were drawn up among the rocks. Eddie dressed in brand new hiking gear, Isabella in a long coat woven from blond mammoth hair. His old honeyboo. She had aged more than he had expected, and she had an edge to her that he didn't remember. She'd always been pragmatic when it came to her work, but it had been softened by a kind of romantic idealism. A touching innocence. No sign of that now. She was all business, briskly astringent, more than a little cynical. Life had toughened up both of them. It had a way of doing that.

'If you really want to help us,' she said, 'there's something that would count more than a few crates of food and medicine. You're a supporter of the ruling party. You have contacts in government. You have influence.'

'A little, I guess. Not as much as some people say. But a little. Have you been researching me, Iz? I suppose I should be flattered.'

He was wondering, actually, just how long she'd known about him and his brilliant career. After all, he hadn't exactly been keeping a low profile. She could have told him about their son years ago.

'The point is that what you have to say counts for something,' Isabella said. 'It has weight. You could use that to do some real good. You could have a private word with your friends in government. You could start up a public campaign. I'm sure you have contacts in the feeds, too. I'm sure they'd want to hear what you have to say.'

'And what exactly would I have to say?'

'Your friends in the National Unity Party have passed a great deal of iniquitous legislation against huskies. Free clinics that encourage husky women to abort their children. Pass laws and the ban on huskies travelling outside the peninsula. The ban on huskies joining the police and the armed services, tacit encouragement of all kinds of petty discrimination . . . Speaking out about that would be hard, I know, but it would also be incredibly useful.'

She talked for quite a while, lecturing him on the unfairness of the world, telling him what he should do about it. As if it was his fault. As if fixing it was that simple. Good old Isabella. She might come on as a canny weather-beaten rebel, but underneath it she was still a soft-hearted idealist. Telling him that if nothing else he should support husky rights for the sake of his granddaughter. The little girl who'd been turned into a monster because of her parents' stupid beliefs. A monster whose mere existence might have derailed his career, if he hadn't been smart enough to figure out how to deal with it.

Eddie tried to make the right noises, expressed doubt that he could do very much. 'It's not really about the politicians, Iz. They're only reflecting public opinion. As for persuading ordinary people to change their minds about ecopoets . . . Given what you've been getting up to, it would be a pretty tall order. Even for someone as influential as you seem to think I am.'

He was having a little fun, but at last, growing impatient, wanting to wrap this up, he promised that he would see what he could do, said that he hoped they would be able to talk again. And after they parted, the stealthed drones that had been watching over him, military kit, no way they could be spotted by civilian equipment, followed Isabella and her retinue as they made their way south in their fast boats, cutting through the strait between the Arrowsmith Plateau and Adelaide Island before splitting up and taking separate paths among the little islands beyond to separate refuges. Six of them, along with their families and associates, were arrested a few days later. The first of a chain of mass arrests that included the capture of Salix Gabriel Morales, his wife, and their young daughter. But Isabella Schilling Morales escaped, and although the police chased down every rumour and alleged sighting, once sending a team to China after someone claimed they'd seen her working on a project to rewild the upper reaches of the Yangtze River, they never caught up with her.

Aside from that, Eddie's scheme had been a terrific success, but he soon discovered that his tame politicians had become much cooler towards him. They no longer returned his calls, meetings were suddenly difficult to set up, deals stalled or evaporated. He'd done his bit, he was the hero of the hour, the man who'd put an end to the free ecopoet problem, but his so-called friends thought him an embarrassment and a liability.

'Some believe that if you can betray your own people, you could just as easily betray them if you thought it might be useful,' one of the few who'd stuck by him said.

'The ecopoets never were my people,' Eddie said. 'And that bloody woman never told me I got her pregnant, never gave me the chance to meet our son, or his daughter. As for what I did, it was my duty as a citizen, but I guess I shouldn't be surprised that someone like me isn't trusted by the so-called elite.'

He liked to believe that he was an outsider who'd made good, a larrikin who used his God-given cunning and guile to get one over on people who didn't care for his rough and ready ways, thought they were better than him. But although he pretended to be indifferent to what he called the establishment, said that it was bloody typical of them to cut him loose after all the hard work he'd put in and the personal risks he'd taken, he was wounded by the chilly gulf that had opened up between himself and those he'd considered close personal friends. He vowed that he would make sure that his sons had all the benefits he lacked, and the rest of his life was consumed by wheeling and dealing. Making money was his way of proving to himself that he'd been in the right all along.

He rode out the so-called scandal manufactured by enemies who revealed that he not only had an illegitimate son who was a big wheel in the free ecopoet movement, but also a granddaughter who'd been illegally edited, turned into a so-called husky. Made no public comment after Salix was lost at sea when a freak storm sank his fishing boat. A few years later the sea also claimed Eddie. He was a passenger on a jet-wing that while en route to Buenos Aires vanished somewhere over the Drake Passage, and his body was never recovered.

17

I had just turned eight when my grandfather died in that jet-wing crash, vividly remember Mama's frustration and anger when she gave me the news. She'd dearly wanted to punish Eddie Toomy. For refusing to help his son – my father, her husband – and for betraying the ecopoets, which as far as she was concerned had killed Salix, who wouldn't have drowned in that storm off Deception Island if Eddie hadn't pulled his fast one. But now Eddie had put himself beyond her reach, and she was angrier with him dead than when he'd been alive.

The girl, of course, refused to believe any of it. According to her, according to the Toomy family version of the story, the government had forced Eddie to become a double agent, threatening to reveal that he had a son who was a criminal fugitive if he didn't co-operate with them.

'And anyway, it wasn't as if he did anything wrong,' she said. 'I mean, he helped to round up people who had rebelled against the rule of law. He was a hero, if you ask me. And talking of betrayal? After he helped the government, after he did everything he was asked, someone leaked the information about his links with the ecopoets to his enemies.'

She'd been indoctrinated with this spin all her life, truly believed that her grandfather had been an upright citizen blackmailed by the state and double-crossed by politicians. I couldn't persuade her that, like the rest of Eddie's stories, it was a pack of self-serving lies invented to justify his folly and selfishness.

'It doesn't matter anyway,' she said, stubborn to the last. 'He's dead. Everyone involved in that sad story is dead.'

She was young. She didn't yet understand that the past is never past.

'It should matter to you,' I told her. 'It's how we ended up here. When you get home, ask Alberto to tell you what really happened in the campaign against the ecopoets. And if he can't or won't, a girl smart as you should be able to dig out the truth from police records, so forth.'

The girl held up her left wrist, the one with the orange fone-blocking bracelet locked around it. 'If you take this off, I can ask my father right now.'

'In all the excitement when we left the camp, I kind of forgot to bring along the gizmo that makes those things let go,' I said. 'And you should quit trying to pry it loose. You'll only hurt yourself.'

'You call him then.'

'Right now he'd tell me anything I wanted to hear. Say anything to get his precious darling daughter back. And afterwards he'd change his story, claim I put the words in his mouth. Come to think of it,' I said, 'I bet he's already changed those records. That's what people like him do. Rewrite history to suit themselves, bury the bodies of people they wronged . . .'

There was a silence. I snapped branches and tossed the pieces on the fire. A galaxy of sparks whirled up into the dark and winked out. After a little while, the girl asked about my grandmother, if I knew where she'd gone, if she was still alive.

Mama believed that Isabella had gone further south. To Palmer Land, or even the mainland. That's where we'd been heading after we escaped. Trying to find a Shangri-La that probably didn't exist. But I don't know anyone who saw or met Isabella after the police broke up the last of the free ecopoets, she didn't ever try to get in touch with my parents after they were arrested, and although I guess there's some small chance that she's living like a hermit in some remote refuge, dressed in a sealskin coat and handstitched mukluks, cooking seal steaks or a butterflied penguin over a blubber fire, she most likely died years back. Frozen at the bottom of a crevasse, maybe, or buried by her fellow refugees in a remote and secret grave. I like to think that grave has a view of a sea where bergs still sail, that in the brief summer thaw it's

163

covered with wild flowers. I like to think that it's a far better resting place than the trench in the potter's field where Mama was dumped in a cardboard coffin.

I told the girl all that, told her that we both knew who was responsible. I knew it wasn't her fault, but I couldn't help blaming her. Like wading in the shallows of a lake and kicking up stinking black mud, talking about the past had stirred all kinds of bad memories and feelings.

She shook her head very slightly. Looking at the fire, not at me. She'd withdrawn, become unreachable. The way Mama sometimes did.

'We should get some sleep,' I said. 'Tomorrow's another day, and all the rest of that shit.'

We lay back to back in the crude little shelter and I fell asleep thinking of everything that could go wrong on the way to Charlotte Bay, everything that could go wrong when I got there. I thought of the woman who'd helped Mama and me. Alicia Whangapirita. A kindly grey-haired woman who'd worn lots of necklaces – she'd given one of them to me when Mama and I had stayed with her. Black stone beads on a waxed cotton thread. The police confiscated it when I was arrested, and although they told me I'd get it back of course I never did. She had worked in my grandmother's lab back in the day, and although she'd chosen to come in out of the cold during the government amnesty she'd remained sympathetic to the free ecopoet cause, had helped to smuggle supplies, so on.

Would she be happy to see me again? Probably not. The girl's kidnap must be all over the feeds, no way would anyone with any sense want to have anything to do with me. But I couldn't stay out here, not with Mike Mike and his bravos looking for me, and all I needed was a place to hole up, somewhere I could stash the girl while I set up her ransom . . .

When I woke, dull light was filtering through the shelter's pine-bough roof. The fire was out and the girl was foraging along the edge of the stream, coming back with a couple of fistfuls of twigs and leaves, saying there'd been no gift this morning from elves or whatever and she couldn't find any berries either, so she was going to make biscuits. Could I eat biscuits?

She was anxious. Conciliatory. Perhaps she was beginning to believe the truth about Eddie Toomy, or was at least beginning to understand my point of view. More likely she was trying to appease the crazy monster holding her prisoner in this God-forsaken wolf-haunted wilderness, who yawned and scratched at her wounded shoulder, and told her that she better not have disturbed any of the fucking traps.

I found a collared lemming strangled in one of the wire snares, a little puffball in its white winter coat. They'd been edited, lemmings, could freeze solid in winter and thaw out and be ready to go in spring. Sometimes, when the snow started to melt in spring, so many of them appeared all at once it was if they'd fallen from the sky.

The girl was pretending to be very interested in watching the food printer hum and chuckle to itself as it digested her offering. I built a small fire in the previous night's ashes, put on a pot of snow to melt and boil. Used my knife, thumb close to the point, to shuck the lemming's fur suit, gutted it with my little finger, popped it into my mouth. Nutty flesh, crunchy little bones. Another taste of my childhood. Someone had introduced a species of subarctic mice to Deception Island and in winter they would come into our one-room house, looking for shelter. If we don't eat them we'll be overrun, Mama used to say. We're part of the ecosystem's regulatory mechanism.

The girl gave me a frank look of disgust. I told her that she'd eat lemmings if she didn't have any other food. That she'd eat a boiled shoe if she was hungry enough.

'A person can survive on these biscuits,' she said primly, pulling a ragged wafer from the printer's slot. 'They contain all the essential nutrients.'

'That's fine, until that little gadget breaks down. As machines tend to do, out here. Also, you know why reindeer never get anything done? It's because they have to spend all day eating grass and lichen to stay alive.'

I would have loved, right then, to have been able to run down a deer and bite out its throat, like the monster the girl so obviously thought I was. But the idea of a gush of hot salty blood triggered a wire to my belly and it tried to turn itself inside out and I leaned sideways and threw up the mashed lemming. I made a joke about having eaten too quickly, staring hard at the girl, daring her to say something, anything, about my condition, about you, and boiled up willow bark tea to ease the cramp in my stomach, the tender ache in my shoulder. I was sipping tea and cautiously nibbling at a biscuit and thinking of you when the girl suddenly stood up.

'Listen,' she said.

I didn't hear anything at first. Then a faint bugling, like a trumpet blown flat. It wasn't wolves this time. It was a mammoth, calling in distress somewhere on the slope above us.

18

The mammoth stood at bay above a bend of the stream, backed into a clump of boulders while three wolves prowled up and down in front of it. The wolves turning to look at the skimmer when I braked a few hundred metres away, but standing their ground. They were long and lean and raggedy, probably young males who'd split off from the main pack. Mostly grey and white. Touches of auburn on their ears and muzzles. Yellow eyes. You wouldn't ever mistake one for any breed of dog.

'We have to do something,' the girl said.

'This is kind of between the mammoth and the wolves,' I said.

'They want to kill it.'

'That's what they do,' I said, and explained that wolves generally didn't attack frontally, they were trying to force the mammoth into making a run for it so they could give chase and bring it down. 'If it has any sense it'll stay where it is until they lose interest. But if it panics, then that's that. Either way, there's nothing we can do to help, and we have places to go, things to do.'

The wolves had decided that we weren't a threat and had turned their attention back to the mammoth. One of them, the biggest, made a quick feint towards the boulders, pranced away in a flurry of snow when the mammoth hooked low with its curled tusks. It was about a metre and a half tall at the shoulder, with a sloping back and a barrel belly and a thick coat of coarse strawberry blond hair that hung in a kind of matted skirt around the solid pillars of its legs. It was favouring one of its hind legs and there were vivid spatters of blood on the apron of trampled snow around it.

'It's hurt,' the girl said, and, I still can't believe it, jumped down into calf-deep snow and stepped forward, shouting and clapping her hands.

The wolves turned to stare at her, heads low, haunches high. I drew my pistol and swung off the skimmer and spread my arms and stamped my feet. In the stretching moment of silence I could feel my pulse butterflying in my throat. Then the biggest wolf turned with a smooth flowing motion and the others followed, all three running flat out across the snow, vanishing around a rake of black rock.

The mammoth watched the girl sidelong as she stepped towards it, its eye small and brown under the bulge of its forehead. Eyelashes to die for. It was emitting a kind of rumbling snore. I could feel it in the soles of my feet.

The girl jumped when I laid a hand on her shoulder. 'It's a wild animal,' I said. 'Dangerous as any wolf.'

She shrugged away from me and took another step, holding out her hand. The mammoth's trunk quested towards her snakewise, snatched something from her open palm, fed it to its mouth.

'I was saving a biscuit,' the girl told me with a silly smile.

'This is absolutely none of our business.'

The girl ignored me. The flexible tip of the mammoth's trunk was snuffling her palm, the pockets of her windproof jacket.

'Look at its ear,' she said. 'Isn't that some kind of tag? It must belong to someone.'

It was a thick oblong of plastic clipped about where a person would wear an earring. Someone owned the fucking beast all right. And would almost certainly be looking for it.

'They should have taken better care of it,' I said, and grabbed the girl's wrist, told her when she tried to pull away that if she didn't get back on the skimmer I'd leave her for the wolves.

'They might be the people who took out the drone and gave you that hare,' the girl said. 'It might lead us to them.'

I should have ignored her. I should have tied her up and slung her across the saddle of the skimmer, left the mammoth to the tender mercy of the wolves. But I was hungry and tired, I wasn't thinking straight, and although I doubted that the mammoth had anything to do with our mysterious benefactors (I still favoured Paz and Sage), I reckoned that its owners would most definitely owe us a favour if we stepped in. I mean, how was I to know that it would get us into so much trouble?

'Let's say we rescue it,' I said. 'And let's say we find the people it belongs to. I have to be sure that you won't say anything about how we came to be out here.'

'I mustn't tell them that you kidnapped me, you mean.'

'I'm serious. I want you to give me your word that you'll behave. If you won't, that's it, we're going to leave your little friend behind.'

After a moment, she nodded.

'I need a bit more than that,' I said, and pulled the glove from my right hand and spat on my palm and stuck it out. 'You do the same, we shake, it seals the deal. In the city, you sign a contract. This is how we do it out here.'

I'd just made it up, but like Paz said, we were a new thing, and that gave us the right to invent our own traditions.

The girl, her gaze locked with mine, pulled off her glove and spat, dry and delicate as a cat sneezing, and we shook hands.

'So this is what's going to happen,' I said. 'If we can get your new friend to follow us, we'll lead it up out of the basin and cut across the Herbert Plateau. There's an old tree nursery on a road that cuts down from the west side of the plateau to the coast. If we haven't found the mammoth's owners by the time we get there, that's where we'll leave it. OK?'

'OK.'

She didn't look very happy, but it wasn't as if she had a choice.

'Good. Now let's get going before the damn wolves change their minds.'

We hadn't gone much more than a kilometre when the wolves came back. I told the girl to hang on, made a sharp U-turn, and cut past the mammoth and drove straight at them. All three immediately turned as one and plunged away downhill, vanishing into a thin line of trees.

'They won't go far,' I said, as we drove back to where the mammoth had stopped, its wounded hind leg crooked up. 'They'll keep following us, hoping we'll make a mistake or get tired. It's what they do.'

'They're clever.'

'They're ruthless. They have to be.'

The three wolves returned to the chase a couple of kilometres further on. Rather, they'd been there all along, but had grown bold enough to show themselves again.

I stopped the skimmer and aimed my pistol at their leader, hoping to bring him down with a taser taglet. But he was canny enough to stay out of range, so in the end I shot a tree instead. Shot it with two explosive taglets and set it on fire. It burned quickly, snow on its branches hissing to steam as flames wrapped it from base to crown, sending up a spire of white smoke that was a perfect sign for anyone looking for us.

The wolves scattered but soon returned again, trailing us with canny persistence, never getting close enough to shoot. No sign of the mammoth's owners, no sign of any help from the sky. Maybe the owners of that predator drone had lost track of us in the forest. Maybe we were finally out of range. Whatever, we were on our own, the damn wolves weren't ever going to give up, the mammoth was limping badly, and every time it stopped to rest its wounded leg the wolves stopped too, watching with intense concentration until, after some chivvying from the girl, it started walking again.

In this fashion we travelled six kilometres in as many hours. Mounting the long slope of Blériot Basin's southern flank as the grey sky darkened, the mammoth limping, halting, limping on. The girl and I driving alongside it on the skimmer, the wolves following some way behind. A grim little procession climbing above the treeline, plodding through wind-sculpted snow, across bare slopes of scree, until at last, just after sunset, I cut towards an outcrop of boulders that stood on a flat setback below the crest of a ridge.

That's where we made camp. I helped the girl herd the mammoth into the lee of the boulders and parked the skimmer in front of it, and we were more or less back where we had started. We couldn't build a fire because there weren't any trees on the bare slope, and we didn't have any food either, not even lichen or grass we could turn into cardboard biscuits. I used the stove, by then down to a quarter of its full charge, to melt a pan of snow and brew tea. The wolves sprawled together in a hollow some way down the slope, hard to see in the twilight. The basin spread beyond, the lights of those greenhouses twinkling at the horizon. We really hadn't come very far.

'Maybe they'll give up in the night,' the girl said.

'Maybe.'

'But you don't think they will.'

'If they come close enough I can zap their leader, put a good scare into them.'

But we both knew that wasn't very likely.

I took first watch. The moon was a dim smudge behind the cloud cover, barely enough light to make out the shape of the land, so I used the night-vision app of the goggles to keep track of the wolves. Three bright phantoms just out of range of my pistol, watching me watch them. It was almost companionable, like the camps of two groups of travellers heading towards the same destination.

A cold wind blew out of the west, feathering snow off the knife-edged ridge. I walked up and down to keep warm, trampling a narrow slot in the snow. When the girl volunteered to take over I told her she could stand watch for just an hour, warned her about frostbite. 'Stay close. Wake me if anything happens.'

'What if they, you know, decide to charge at us?'

We were two shadows on the pale slope, looking out into the darkness towards the spot where the wolves were laid up.

'They probably won't,' I said. 'But if they do, scream as loud as you can.'

'You could give me the pistol.'

'I don't think so.'

'I know how to use it. I was trained on a counter-kidnapping course.'

'When you get home you should ask for your money back.'

I handed over the goggles and wriggled into my sleeping bag and sat with my back against a boulder, listening to the wind and the uneasy movements of the mammoth. If the damn thing panicked it could trample me, knock the skimmer over and send it rolling down the slope . . .

I jerked awake when the mammoth bugled a shrill call. Stood in a flare of hasty panic, thinking that the wolves had finally chosen their moment, tangled my feet in my sleeping bag and fell flat on my face. As I pushed to my knees, groping for my pistol, the mammoth bugled again and the girl materialised out of the faint moonlight, pointing past me, past the clump of boulders. On top of the ridge, dark forms were moving against the dark sky. Two mammoths, each carrying a rider, turning one after the other down the slope towards us.

19

The mammoth riders, Alya Ross Zappia and Archie Meabe Diez, were husband and wife, employees of a company that managed the forests below the west side of the Herbert Plateau. The two of them grey-haired and weather-beaten, dressed in long leather and fur riding coats over cold weather gear, armed with hunting rifles and accompanied by a pair of elkhounds. Alya, a practical broad-beamed woman, set to examining the injured mammoth while the girl told Archie how we had rescued it from the wolves.

'You won't have to worry about them any more,' Archie said, making a show of studying the dark slope through the scope of his rifle. But the wolves had slunk away. They knew when they were outnumbered. They knew better than me, it turned out.

Mama would have called Alya and Archie half-and-halfs. People who were neither one thing nor the other, spending some of their time in the back country, the rest in a settlement or town. The mammoths they rode and the mammoth we'd saved from the wolves, a three-year-old female named Marguerite, were part of a small herd that carried people and supplies where machines couldn't go, dragged out felled and dead trees, so on. Alya fed Marguerite with a swatch of compressed hay and treated her wounded leg with nanobiotics and spray bandage, while Archie explained that a small crew of troublemakers had stopped by their settlement yesterday. Asking all kinds of questions, swiping supplies, turning the mammoths loose out of sheer bloody mischief before they left.

'They were looking for a husky woman and a young girl,' Archie said. Under the fur brim of his hat his shrewd dark eyes reflected sparks of light from the lantern his wife had set on top of a boulder. 'I can't help wondering if you might know them.'

I shot a look at the girl, who so far had kept her word, hadn't said anything about our circumstances. 'Was one of them a big man called Mike Mike? Shaved head, neat little chin beard?'

'That's the fellow,' Archie said.

'I know his boss slightly,' I said. 'Where did he and his friends head off to, when they left your settlement?'

'Down towards the coast. Maybe Charlotte Bay. They didn't say and we didn't ask.'

Archie sketched a rough map in the snow. It seemed that Mike Mike and his crew had circled around the Cayley Valley and Blériot Basin, cutting through Catwalk Pass to the Herbert Plateau and taking the road to the coast. That's where the foresters' settlement was located, according to Archie, not far from the old ecopoet tree nursery.

It made sense. Mike Mike must have figured out that we'd be heading towards Charlotte Bay, the only town on this stretch of the west coast, was planning to get there before we did.

'City folk,' Archie said. 'If they wanted hospitality and help all they had to do was ask, like any civilised human being.'

According to him, the foresters had had a time of it, rounding up their mammoths. 'Marguerite is the last. She always was skittish. Bolted out across the plateau, then wandered north instead of coming back home. Bad luck she ran into wolves, but good luck she ran into you.'

'Good luck for her, at least,' I said.

I was wary and suspicious, wondering whether the two foresters had recognised us from police alerts or news feeds, wondering what Mike Mike might have told them. But they seemed friendly enough, didn't ask where we'd come from or where we were going, what kind of trouble we were in. At the time, fool that I was, I thought that it was no more than backcountry courtesy.

Archie broke out supplies and heated up a mushroom stew sharpened with juniper berries and pine needles, and he and his wife sat with the two dogs, watching benevolently as the girl and

I ate most of the food, and telling us a little about their work. It wasn't so different from the work of ecopoets – growing and planting out saplings, thinning new growth and cutting brush, removing trees that showed signs of disease, keeping watch for fires sparked by summer lightning storms, so on. They raised quail, ring-necked pheasants and grey partridge, so that people from the city could shoot them and think they'd bagged wild birds, and in winter worked as guides for sports hunters. They hunted for their larder, too. Their dogs, alert muscular beasts with black and white coats and tightly rolled tails, had been bred to track big game like elk and reindeer, wolves even, and hold them at bay until their owners arrived.

The girl dozed off while we talked and Alya and Archie turned in soon afterwards, sleeping under a heap of furs close beside their mammoths, but I stayed awake. Drinking tea, walking up and down in the dark. I didn't entirely trust the foresters, but figured that it couldn't hurt to ride along with them and score supplies at their settlement. Heading to Charlotte Bay was out of the question now, we'd have to travel further south. To Neko Harbour, say. Or maybe I could find another refuge, hide the girl there while I negotiated with her father. It didn't seem impossible.

At first light, we breakfasted on a mess of porridge Archie boiled up, laced with plenty of butter and gritty brown sugar, broke camp, and headed on up towards the Herbert Plateau. The girl and I riding the skimmer, Alya and Archie perched on shaped seats strapped to the shoulders of their mammoths, the stray, Marguerite, trotting between them and the two elkhounds loping along on either side. No sign of the wolves, no sign of anything moving anywhere on the snowy slopes.

The mammoths and their riders set a good pace, leading us into a steephead valley, climbing past a chute of broken ice at the far end and topping out and heading across the plateau. About an hour into the journey the lump of porridge in my stomach began to revolve and I got the sweats and dry heaves and had to stop the skimmer. After I'd purged, I told the foresters it was probably something I'd eaten yesterday, no reflection on their hospitality. They made no comment, but when I returned to the skimmer the girl volunteered to drive.

'I know how. And if you aren't feeling well . . .'

'It isn't an illness,' I said, with a glare that shut her up, and we went on, picking up an ice road that cut through dunes of blown snow and corrugated fields of sastrugi, skirting the blue eye of a shallow meltwater lake and turning south, running parallel to broken ridges of snow-streaked rock off to the west.

Towards noon the road climbed to the top of a low rise and I saw a chip of green in the distance and stopped to give it the once-over. The zoom app of the goggles revealed a big faceted structure looming over a scatter of tumbledown outbuildings on a flat-topped hill – the girl told me that it was one of the radar stations built by the Argentine military when the cold war over the continent's resources had heated up back in the last quarter of the previous century. There was a station just like this one south of O'Higgins, she said, she'd visited it last year.

'They kept watch on three-hundred-and-sixty degrees of sky, could detect incoming aircraft or missiles hundreds of kilometres away. After the crisis passed, they were used to track satellites and orbital debris.'

'Does anyone have a use for them now?'

'I don't know about that one,' the girl said. 'But the station I visited had been abandoned a long time ago.'

'Doesn't much look like any kind of place where forestry workers would live, does it?'

I had an uneasy feeling. I didn't remember seeing anything like that installation on the journey with Mama, which meant that we'd gone past the road that descended towards the coast.

Alya and Archie were waiting for us a little way ahead. When we caught up with them Alya looked down from her seat and asked if everything was all right. Her mammoth was dark-haired and hump-shouldered. The curls of its tusks were tipped with caps of wood stained black and fretted with patterns intricate as snowflakes.

'What's that place ahead?' I said. 'Who lives there?'

My left hand was in the pocket of my jacket, gripping the pistol.

'Just some people we know. We can rest up there. You can find supplies.'

'I thought I could find supplies at your settlement. But we passed the turn-off for that, didn't we?'

'After those troublemakers came through and took what they wanted, we're low on what you might need. But you can buy all kinds of stuff up ahead.'

Alya's face was, what's the word? Impassive. Like stone. Impossible to read. Frost stars glittered in her eyelashes, the crown of her fur hat.

I said, 'Why am I just now learning this?'

'We thought you wouldn't want to take the same route as the people looking for you. You come with us, it's OK.'

I thought that things were very far from being OK. Had the sick feeling that I'd been led astray by these so-called foresters, that maybe they weren't who they claimed to be, weren't from that settlement on the coast road – if it even existed.

'If it's all right with you, we'll head on past,' I said.

Alya shrugged as if it was no concern of hers. 'You go where you want. But it's a long way to anywhere you can get food. And there's plenty of food right there at the stopping place.'

'We'll manage,' I said, still trying to figure out how to play this, and that's when the girl jumped off the skimmer and ran across the road.

'This woman kidnapped me,' she said to Alya, speaking quickly, breathlessly, as I came up behind her. 'I'm the daughter of an important man, he'll pay a reward for my safe return.'

She tried to duck away when I gripped her shoulder. I turned her around, gave her a little shove towards the skimmer. 'We had a deal,' I said.

'I only agreed because there was no choice. And anyway, you're a criminal. So it doesn't matter what I promised. It doesn't count.'

'You gave your word. Of course it counts.'

The girl looked at the foresters sitting on their mounts, watching our little show. 'Please,' she said. 'Please please please take me with you.'

I pulled out my pistol, holding it by my side, telling Alya and Archie, 'I saved your mammoth and you shared your food, so I reckon we're square. You go your way, I'll go mine, and that'll be that. But first, you'll have to give up your rifles. You know, just for insurance. I'll leave them a couple of kilometres down the way. When I'm gone you can double back and collect them.'

'Is that how you want it?' Alya said.

No change in her expression, her calm gaze. Archie sat still and watchful beside her, the flaps of his fur hat tied under his chin, the long barrel of his hunting rifle sticking up behind.

'It's how it has to be,' I said.

'You're making a mistake,' Archie said.

'Keep quiet, Archie,' Alya said, without moving her gaze from me.

'We can take the girl, let you go free,' he said.

'Didn't I tell you to keep quiet?'

'I made a mistake when I thought you could help us,' I said. 'Now, how about you hand over your rifles. You first, Alya. By the barrel, if you please.'

Neither Alya nor Archie spoke or gave any sign I could see, but the damn dogs leaped up and ran under the belly of Alya's mammoth, ran straight at me. I managed to jerk up my pistol and shoot one with a taser taglet, and as it yelped and writhed the other slammed into me and bit down on my arm, clamping its jaws just below my elbow. I guess the idea was to make me let go of the pistol, but I pushed against the dog's weight instead, the claws of its hind legs scratching on the surface of the road as it tried and failed to keep its balance, and as its head was forced up I chopped its throat with the edge of my free hand. It yelped and let go of my arm, and I grabbed it by its collar and hind legs and tossed it straight at Alya.

She had unshipped her hunting rifle, was aiming it at me, but it slewed sideways when the dog slammed into her and in that bare moment I fired my pistol again. Not at Alya or Archie, but at the eye of Alya's mammoth. The taglet must have hurt worse than any hornet's sting. The animal bellowed and reared up, toppling Alya from her perch, and took off down the road. The other mammoths followed, Archie yelling and gripping the horn of his seat like a rodeo rider, the stray, Marguerite, bringing up the rear.

Alya lay on her back, dazed by her fall, barely stirring when I kicked the sole of her boot. The dogs growled, but flinched back when I flourished the pistol at them. The bites in my arm were beginning to hurt. Under my weatherproof, the sleeve of my uniform jacket was wet with blood.

'Don't hurt her,' the girl said.

'Get on the skimmer before you cause more trouble,' I said. 'Go on now.'

The girl looked at the green building, far away on its flat-topped hill.

'There's nothing for you there,' I said. 'Nothing you want, anyway. Get on the damn skimmer.'

'Where are we going?'

'Down to the coast. As fast as we can.'

'They were helping us.'

'They tricked us and led us here is what they did. And now I'm going to do my best to get away.'

I turned back the way we'd come, preferring to face Mike Mike rather than the unknown. But I hadn't gone very far when the girl cried out and thumped an urgent tattoo on my back. I glanced around, saw skimmers shooting away from the old radar station, and immediately swerved off the ice road. I was hoping to find a hiding place or a way off the plateau between the half-buried hills, but the pursuers were faster, and knew the terrain. As they gained on me a fat little orange cylinder capped with two pairs of props spun down out of the air, effortlessly matching my speeding skimmer. A voice blared from it, telling me to give up, it would go easy if I did, and when I aimed my pistol at the damn thing it fired something that smacked into my shoulder, a sticky ball exploding in a tangle of cords lively as snakes. Whipping around me, tightening, pinning my arms to my sides, yanking my hands from the skimmer's yoke.

The skimmer slewed sideways and the girl and I tumbled off, rolling apart in a flurry of snow. By the time I'd struggled to my feet the girl was running towards our pursuers. Tripping on an ice ridge, jumping up, running on, no doubt believing that she was being rescued. I shouted after her, but it was no good. People were climbing off the skimmers. Two walked past the girl, heading towards me.

I struggled against the cords that bound my arms and braced for a fight I knew I couldn't win.

20

The inside of the radar station was as tall and hollow as a decommissioned cathedral. Shafts of light lanced through rips in its walls, splashing on and around a circle of tents and vehicles. Six, seven mammoths staked out along a high line. Dirty snow patching the poured concrete floor, trash scattered everywhere.

A couple of dozen people, half of them children, turned out to watch as the girl and I were marched into this filthy little camp. One was a husky, a burly boy maybe the girl's age or a little younger. Our gazes met for a moment as I was hustled past. I was bruised and bleeding, arms bound to my sides by a tangle of cords, leashed by a leather strap looped around my neck and tugged along by one of my captors like a prize animal. Which I guess I kind of was.

I'd managed to get in a few good kicks when the two bravos had tried to subdue me out on the ice, headbutting one before the other shot me with a beanbag round. When I came back to my senses they'd taken away my cutlery and fastened a bracelet – not one of mine, this one was black rather than prison orange – around one of my wrists, blocking access to my fone. I had a bad feeling that they'd done this kind of thing before, and then I saw that one of the vehicles in the camp, an ancient sno-crawler, was painted with a big mural of an angry skua, wings flared and hooked beak gaping, and knew who they were, knew that I was in serious bad trouble.

The girl and I were pushed through the flaps of a yurt, the onlookers crowding in behind us. It was warm and close in there, easily twenty degrees Celsius, dimly lit by random sparklights floating under slanting roof poles. The floor was lapped with a deep puddle of dark brown cultured fur, and an old woman sat on a low stool in front of a curtained bed, the hem of her suede skirt brushing the toes of her sturdy mukluks.

The man holding the leash – he was the bravo I'd headbutted – deftly tripped me, and when I fell to my knees jerked my head up and around so that I was facing the woman. I could have knocked him down easily enough, but then what? So I stayed where I was, kneeling on soft fur with the knot of the leash digging into the angle of my jaw, meeting the woman's gaze, asking her why she and her friends were interfering with an officer of the law.

'Show respect to Judge Boudou,' the bravo holding the girl said.

'I'd like you to show some respect for my uniform,' I said.

'The laws and offices of the government you work for mean nothing out here,' the woman, Judge Boudou, said. 'And you resisted arrest after assaulting two of our people.'

'I'm under arrest, am I? By whose authority?'

'By the people's authority,' Judge Boudou said. 'Which I represent.'

She had leaned forward to study me, blue-veined hands knitted under her chin. Her white hair pulled back in a thick pigtail from a face severe as midwinter, her fingers knuckly with rings carved from bone and wood, faded tattoos on her forehead and cheeks. The kind of tattoos which had sleeved Mama's right arm, patterns of dots and lines which if you knew how to read them told the story of a life's work. Places seeded with life, refuges and roads constructed, plants and animals edited.

The girl spoke up, introducing herself, asking Judge Boudou if she was in charge of this place.

'This is a democracy governed by the people for the people,' the woman said. She spoke quietly but purposefully, giving each word equal weight. 'I am merely its voice.'

'My father is Honourable Deputy Alberto Toomy,' the girl said. 'If you can, please, could you call him, tell him I'm safe and well. Tell him where I am.'

There was a tremor in her voice but she stood straight-backed and was doing her best to ignore the bravo who gripped her arm, and I have to admit that I admired her salt.

'We know who you are, and we know that this woman is accused of kidnapping you,' the judge said. 'We'll decide the truth of that, and what needs to be done about it, in good time.'

The girl started to tell her about the reward, but had the good sense to shut up when the judge raised her hand and turned to me. 'You've caused us a great deal of trouble. The police have been here, looking for you. So have a gang of city folk. Both parties making threats and demands. Telling us what you did. Asking if we had seen you. Ordering us to turn you over to them if we did.'

'You were an ecopoet, once upon a time,' I said. 'Going by those tattoos. And as you can see my parents were also ecopoets. My names is Austral Morales Ferrado. My mother was Aury Vergara Ferrado, my father Salix Gabriel Morales. Maybe you've heard of them. And maybe you've also heard of my grandmother, Isabella Schilling Morales.'

It sounded good. A pedigree I hoped would count for more than the political prestige of the girl's father, her family's wealth.

'I spent five years planting trees in Cayley Valley and Blériot Basin, twenty more establishing a salt marsh at the mouth of the Cayley River,' the judge said. 'From installing pioneer communities to developing permanent coverage, my crew did it all. I was the one who edited pendant grass, boosting its growth rate and increasing the depth to which its roots penetrated, so that it could better stabilise mud banks. In short, there isn't anyone who's done more to spread the green than me, so don't try to impress me with your family history. And besides, none of that matters now. The ecopoets may have quickened the back country, but they also abandoned it. They surrendered.'

'Not all of them,' I said.

'If you mean the free ecopoets,' the judge said, 'their resistance didn't last long. We're the custodians of the land now. We safeguard the rights of free people and true citizens. This is our territory, you've come here with a girl you may have kidnapped, and we must decide what to do about that.'

'She really did kidnap me,' the girl said, with forthright indignation. 'She took me from a labour camp on the east coast, dragged me halfway across the peninsula—'

The judge raised her hand again, said to me, 'Because we live here, because we use it and care for it, this land is ours by right of adverse possession. And we have established our own code of law, our own way of settling disputes.'

Behind me, several onlookers voiced assent.

'We like to think we're fair and reasonable,' the judge said. 'We don't convict anyone without due process and consideration of evidence. So if you have an explanation for what you did and why you did it, we'll be happy to hear what you have to say for yourself.'

I knew that there wasn't any point in trying to convince this so-called judge and her kangaroo court that I had saved the girl from a worse fate, or that I had a good reason for wanting to ransom her, so I flatly said that my business was no business of theirs. The bravo I'd smacked in the face with my forehead seemed to take that personally, cuffed me about the ears and told me to respect the people's authority, but the judge intervened, said it was my choice to talk or condemn myself by silence, and invited the girl to say her piece. So I knelt there, bound and leashed, stubbornly close-mouthed, while the girl explained who she was, what I'd done and what I was planning to do, told the judge about the reward her father would be willing to pay for her safe return and repeated her request that the judge call him right away.

'It isn't my decision,' the judge said. 'Everything we do here is determined by discussion and democratic vote. We've heard both sides of the story, and now we'll discuss it. When we have decided what to do, we'll talk to you again.'

As I was led out of the yurt I spotted Alya and Archie among the onlookers and called out to them, told them that I admired the way they had played me.

'You brought this on yourself,' Alya said. Her dreadlocks were bushed above a bandage wrapped around her forehead and the two dogs sat either side of her, watching me narrowly, bristling tails cocked at their spines.

'Maybe I did, but you brought me here,' I said, and was dragged away before I could say more. I'd like to be able to tell you that those two scunners were caught up in what happened later at

Charlotte Bay, I'd like to be able to explain exactly how they got what was coming to them, but the flat truth is that I never saw or heard of them again. Pick up the world and turn it over, as Mama liked to say, and you won't find *fair* written anywhere on it.

A little way outside camp I was forced to sit with my back against the stub of a girder rooted in the concrete floor. A pair of legcuffs were fastened to the girder by a short length of steel chain. The bravo half-strangled me with the leash, jamming the pistol he'd taken off me against the back of my head for good measure, and the woman who'd helped him take me down aimed her beanbag shotgun at my face while another woman locked the legcuffs around my ankles, then looped a cord around my wrists, sliced through the cords that bound my arms to my sides, and pulled the loop tight, fastening my hands together prayerwise.

After the leash was whipped away from my neck, I asked why the girl hadn't been tied up with me. Was it because they had a thing against huskies?

'Behave like a beast, we treat you like one,' the bravo said, lifting the hem of his weatherproof jacket so he could tuck his pistol – my pistol – into the waistband of his trousers.

'Looks like I didn't break your nose,' I said. 'But those eyes are swelling nicely. Getting a good colour to them, too.'

'Keep that up, I'll break your fucking head,' the bravo said. He was about my age, his pale freckled face flushed with anger.

'If you want to go at it one on one,' I said, 'I'm up for that. You can even leave my hands tied.'

For a moment, I thought he might try to take a pop at me, that I might be able to grab him in a clinch and get hold of my pistol, but the woman with the shotgun spoke up. 'Any more smart talk, we'll gag you. Just sit there nice and quiet while we decide what to do about you and the poor little girl you kidnapped.'

Dumb and angry as I was, I couldn't resist a parting shot. Calling out to the bravo as he and his friends walked away, telling him that I'd be waiting right there in case he changed his mind. But the scunner didn't even look back.

21

While Judge Boudou and her people sat in a talking circle in that yurt or around a cosy campfire or whatever, the husky boy I'd spotted earlier came out to keep watch on me. Squatting on a stool a little way off, ignoring me when I told him he could come closer, I wouldn't bite. Shrugging when I asked why he wasn't with the others, discussing what they should do with me and the girl.

'I know how it is,' I said. 'Being treated like we're not really people because of who we are. What we are.'

'I'm not really supposed to talk to you,' the kid said.

He was no more than thirteen or fourteen, but already as big as me, dressed in a filthy old windbreaker patched with duct tape, fleece trousers with ragged cuffs hanging several centimetres shy of his ankles. Dark skin, a big flat nose, a lot of curly black hair squashed under a wool cap.

I told him that from my experience of talking circles I reckoned that we'd be stuck with each other a fair old time, so there was no harm in getting to know each other. 'You already know my name. Austral Morales Ferrado. But I didn't catch yours.'

'Levi,' the kid said, glancing at me, glancing away.

'I guess you heard me tell Judge Boudou that my parents were ecopoets back in the day. And I know, what with you being a husky, that your parents must have been ecopoets too.'

'If you think it means we have something in common, it doesn't,' the kid, Levi, said.

'I'm just curious as to how you ended up here, where you and your parents came from. Me, I grew up on Deception Island. My parents were free ecopoets, they were sent there after they were arrested. And then, after the eruption – do you know about that, the eruption, how some of the free ecopoets escaped?'

Levi shrugged, as if he wasn't especially interested.

'I escaped with my mother. Aury Vergara Ferrado. I mentioned her name to the judge, in case they knew each other. My mother was a mover and shaker back in the day. Anyway, we escaped from the island and we reached the mainland and we headed south. Got a fair way along, too, but didn't make it all the way. My mother fell ill and she died, and the police caught up with me.'

I waited for Levi to say something, but he looked away towards the line of tethered mammoths. He was just a kid, didn't know how to respond to that.

'To cut a long story short,' I said, 'I ended up in a state orphanage in Esperanza. So I know what it's like, growing up among people who aren't anything like you.'

'The judge took me in and raised me,' Levi said. 'I'm part of her family, and these are my people.'

'You're loyal to them is what you're saying. Even though they make you sit out here, guarding me, instead of being part of their talking circle.'

'I'll be allowed a say when I'm old enough, just like everyone else,' Levi said. 'And I'll be the judge's bodyguard and enforcer, too.'

'You're definitely big enough for the job. But if the judge took you in, Levi, what happened to your parents? Are they still alive, what?'

Levi looked away again, looked back. 'I know my mother isn't.'

'I'm sorry to hear that. Something else we have in common.'

'I told you. We don't have anything in common.'

'Did your mother know the judge? Did they work together?'

It took a little while to tease the story out of him. It seemed that he'd been found by two of Judge Boudou's people while they'd been doing forestry work, a baby lying next to a dead woman. Rather than trying to locate his family the judge had sort of adopted him. Nothing official. He didn't have a fone, lacked any kind of ID. He didn't even know his real name or the name of his mother, who'd been buried on the spot. I also learned that the man and woman who'd taken me down were the judge's son and daughter, Noah and Emzara, and got a quick smile from Levi when I said that Noah had taken a definite dislike to me after I blacked his eyes.

'The city folk who passed through here, looking for me,' I said, ever so casually. 'Have any of them ever been here before?'

'I can't talk about that.'

'One of them, Mike Mike – tall, has a little beard? He's the right-hand man of Keever Bishop. Also known as Mr Snow. I was wondering, have your people ever done any business with him?'

'I can't say.'

'I understand. But why I ask, Mike Mike and his crew are looking for us because I rescued the girl when Keever Bishop tried to have her kidnapped. They nearly caught us, too, but we had some unexpected help,' I said, and told Levi about the gift of the hare, and the predator drone which had snatched from midair the drone run by Mike Mike's crew.

'This was after I stayed at one of the old ecopoet refuges,' I said. 'It isn't much of a stretch to believe that there might be people like us living out here. Huskies who are keeping an eye on those refuges. Who maybe install cameras so they can see who uses them, so they can find huskies who have gone on the run. What do you think? Tell me it isn't just a pretty story I've made up to comfort myself.'

I'd got it up to win his sympathy, of course, it being no more and no less believable than Paz and Sage appointing themselves my guardian angels.

Levi shrugged. There was a complicated, what's it called, nuance to his shrugs I couldn't quite grasp, but I believed that one meant that I might be right, I might be wrong, it wasn't for him to say.

I said, 'You've never heard talk of huskies living out in the wild? The judge and her people, have they ever done business with anyone like that?'

'If there are people like us out there, if they helped you, why haven't they ever tried to help me?'

The kid wasn't stupid. It gave me a little hope.

'Maybe they don't know about you,' I said. 'Or maybe, if they were friends of your mother's, they think that you're dead. But somebody out there likes me. That's a plain fact. If you help me escape, we can go look for them together. And who knows, we just might find your family. Or people who know where your family is.'

'I have a family.'

'I mean your real family.'

'The judge took me in, she raised me as one of her own. You expect me to turn my back on that, just because of some fairy story?'

'It's real enough. Go ask the girl about the drone. Ask her about the hare.'

The boy shrugged again. 'This is my family. This is my home. And you made trouble for us, coming here.'

'You don't have to come with me if you don't want to. All you have to do is find the key for these legcuffs. I'll do the rest. And if I run into the people who helped me, I promise I'll tell them about you.'

'I think you should shut up now.'

'The judge and the rest, they aren't talking about whether or not they should give me back to Keever Bishop. They know they have no choice about that. No, they're talking about how to do it. Where and when. How much they should be paid. After they hand me over, you know, Keever will hurt me bad nasty for saving the girl from him. For meddling in his business. And when he's had his fun, torturing me in ways you can't begin to imagine, he'll kill me.'

Levi shrugged.

'And that's not the worst of it,' I said. 'This is something I haven't told anyone else. Something you could use against me, but I'm going to tell you anyway. Because I think you're a good kid. Because I think you'll want to do the right thing. What it is, I'm pregnant.'

Levi glanced at my belly, blushed when he saw that I'd seen him look.

'I don't have a bump yet,' I said. 'But I really am. A couple of months along. So if you help me, you won't just be saving me from Keever Bishop. You'll also be saving my child.'

A moment of silence stretched. I felt as if I'd jumped off a bridge. I'd hadn't planned to tell the kid about you, but I was desperate and scared. Remember that story about Keever's revenge on the woman who crossed him? That flooded shopping mall? Those eels? Thoughts about that, about the grotesque things Keever might do to me, had jangled at the edge of my mind ever since I'd driven out of the work camp with the girl. He was the Mr Bones of my imagination. I was certain that Judge Boudou and her people were going to give me up to him, and was equally certain that Levi was my last best hope.

He said, 'How can I be sure that you're telling the truth? That this isn't just another of your stories?'

'The same way you can be sure that I'm telling the truth about the drone and the hare. By asking the girl. She's seen me being sick every morning, has guessed why. And she isn't exactly my friend, so you can be sure, too, that this isn't something we've cooked up together.'

I was watching the kid think about that when, my rotten luck, voices rang out in the chill air, and there were Judge Boudou and her son and daughter walking out past the sno-crawler painted with that damn skua, walking towards us.

First thing the judge wanted to know, of course, was what Levi and I had been talking about.

'You looked very friendly, the two of you.'

'I was the one trying to be friendly,' I said. 'The kid was just being polite, but only up to the point when I told him he should do the right thing by me.'

'And what would that be?'

The judge, swathed in a patchwork sealskin longcoat and leaning on a walking stick shod with a steel ferrule, was giving the boy a look that could have frozen the sea.

'I asked him to unlock my legcuffs,' I said. 'He wouldn't, the little fucker. So much for blood loyalty.'

'He wasn't supposed to speak to you at all,' Judge Boudou said, and lashed out at Levi with her steel-tipped stick.

He took the blow on one muscular shoulder with unflinching stoicism, and in that moment I saw his life entire. Growing up in the rootless rag-tag tribe, an unloved stepchild bullied by the other kids for being different, forced to do every kind of menial work and normalising it the way kids do, the way I'd normalised life in exile on Deception Island.

'I'm too easy on you,' the judge told him, 'and you take advantage of my kindness. Get along now, we'll talk about this later.'

Levi glanced at me before he turned and walked away, and a kind of acknowledgement passed between us. I like to think that was the moment he decided to help me.

'As for you,' Judge Boudou said to me, 'the people have come to an agreement.'

'You're going to get what you deserve,' said the bravo I'd head-butted, Noah. His black eyes had developed nicely in the short while since I'd last seen him. One was swollen shut, shiny purple as a ripe plum.

'We're going to take you to Charlotte Bay,' Judge Boudou said. 'And hand you and the girl over to the police.'

'Why take me to them when they could fly straight here?'

'We won't have them trespassing on our territory,' Judge Boudou said smoothly. 'The handover will take place on neutral ground.'

It was impossible to read anything in her wintery expression, and her daughter, Emzara, had a pretty good poker face too, but the truth was plain to see in Noah's stupid smile. If they really were planning to take me to Charlotte Bay, it wasn't to meet the police or anyone else in authority. I had already guessed what would be coming, but it was still a plunging shock.

'What about the girl?' I said.

'If all goes well, she will soon be reunited with her father,' Judge Boudou said.

'And you'll get the reward,' I said.

'We'll get paid, don't you worry,' Noah said.

But not, I thought, by Honourable Deputy Alberto Toomy. I was scared and angry but stepped on the urge to call them on their lie, tell them that I knew what they were really planning to do. If I pretended to believe them, maybe they'd relax around me, grow careless, give me a window of opportunity

But I couldn't resist a little jab, saying, 'You took an awful long time debating what to do with me, when any right-thinking person would have known at once.'

'Listen to the mouth on her,' Noah said. 'We should maybe sew it shut.'

Judge Boudou ignored him, telling me, 'It was not the decision of any one person, but of us all. And before we made it, every different opinion had to be heard and debated. That's how democracy works.'

'I was brought up by ecopoets,' I said. 'I know all about democracy. And what I see here, it isn't anything like it.'

The judge ignored that, too. 'I hope that you'll accept the punishment you deserve with the dignity and discipline that befits your uniform,' she said. 'We're leaving tomorrow. I suggest that you spend the time between now and then reflecting on your sins.'

One of the bravos stayed behind to keep watch. I did my best to ignore her and paced around the stub of girder for a while, clockwise for three turns until the chain wound tight, then three turns anticlockwise to unwind it. Thinking of what I was facing, thinking of all the paths I should have taken instead of the one which had led me here. The dog bite had mostly stopped bleeding, but was throbbing with an unpleasant heat. I reckoned that I needed medical treatment the judge and her people weren't about to give me, but that was the least of my worries.

Night quickly fell inside and outside the shell of the radar station. Windowlights came on in the little camp, the woman keeping watch was replaced by a man, and a little later two people walked out of the circle of vehicles towards me. Levi and the judge's daughter, Emzara. Her beanbag shotgun was slung over her shoulder and she carried a flashlight, shining it in my face, telling me to sit still or else, telling the kid to give me my bedding and my supper.

Levi dropped a couple of blankets at my feet, then set down a plastic canister of water and a mug, saying quietly, 'It's yellow bean soup. Be careful. It's hot.'

'I told you not to speak to her,' Emzara said, and cuffed him on the back of the head. He didn't so much as blink, staring at me with a careful blank expression.

As they turned to go, I called after him. 'Hey, Levi? I hope you find out your real name one day.'

That was the last I saw of him. I don't know if he stayed on with what survived of Judge Boudou's little gang, if he was arrested and ended up in Star City or if he lit out into the back country. But I dearly hope to see him again one day, because I want to thank him for what I found at the bottom of that mug of soup.

22

Early morning, grey light infiltrating the spacey interior of the radar station and the camp beginning to stir, the girl brought me breakfast and an apology. She was escorted by a man who, while she set down a flask of tea and a bowl of cornmeal porridge in front of me, chatted with the bravo who had been guarding me in the last watch of the night.

It was piercingly cold in the draughty ruin, so cold I'd had trouble sleeping. Frost crackled on the blankets I'd wrapped around myself, and the bare centimetre of water left in the plastic canister had frozen solid. It was only a small consolation that my guard, swaddled in seal fur, boots resting on a stove's cube, looked as miserable as I felt.

As I warmed my bound hands on the flask, the girl asked if I was OK.

'As you see,' I said.

'You should drink that tea while it's still hot.'

She was squatting on her heels in front of me. Her blonde hair was brushed and shining and there was a shine in her face too. A hopeful eager shine that I didn't like at all.

'I'll save it for later,' I said. I'd thrown up the soup in the night, wasn't sure if my empty stomach could deal with a bowl of steaming mush.

'I'm sorry it ended up like this,' the girl said. 'I asked Judge Boudou to let you go. I really did. I told her that you didn't mean to harm me, that the gang chasing us were the real bad guys. But she said it was up to the police to decide that, and she's going to take us to this town later today. Hand us over to the authorities there. I'll put in a good word, I swear I will. And I'm sure my father won't be too angry with you after I tell him what happened, why you had to get away. I mean, you're family, sort of.'

'You're too sweet for this world,' I said. I was trying to tamp down my anger at this foolishness, but it wasn't easy. 'Too sweet and too trusting. You think these people are going to help you, don't you? You think they are law-abiding citizens. I bet you even think that Judge Boudou is some kind of judge.'

'I know she isn't a real judge. But she represents the law out here.'

I glanced at my guard and the girl's escort, lowered my voice. 'I'll tell you exactly what she is. What her people are. See the sno-crawler over there? The one with the picture of the angry bird splashed across it? We had people in the work camp with tattoos like that. They call themselves True Citizens. They believe that they are upholding the old Antarctic Treaty. That it supersedes any laws made since then, that they are the true custodians of the land.'

'They sound like ecopoets.'

'Ecopoets didn't believe that they were better than anyone else. And they did useful work. But the True Citizens, they're just a bunch of malcontents who think they have the right to steal land from the government. They don't call it stealing, of course. They call it adverse possession. They have a network of self-appointed judges who make rulings that have no meaning outside of their stupid fantasies. Judge Boudou, she's one of them. And her people, these True Citizens, they aren't in any way custodians of the land. They're criminals, plain and simple.'

'I'm not stupid,' the girl said. 'I know Judge Boudou and her people are probably doing this for the reward money. But as long as they do the right thing it doesn't matter, does it?'

'Wake up, Princess. Look around you. Think it through. Did you sit in on that debate of theirs? Did you hear them agree to give us up to the police? Did the judge let you talk to your father? She didn't, did she? Because she doesn't want him to know where you are.'

'She said it would all be sorted out by the police.'

'She flat out lied is what she did. She and her people, they may work as foresters and such in summer, but in winter they turn to shadier kinds of business. Such as using the ice roads to move contraband. And one of the things Keever Bishop does, he runs a network that smuggles all kinds of shit up and down the west coast. Judge Boudou and her merry band of True Citizens probably don't work for him directly – if they did, we'd have been handed over to him straight away. But they do business with him. They know him, they know that he wants you, and they know what he does to people who cross or cheat him. Mike Mike gave them a taste of that when he passed through, looking for us. So what they're planning doesn't have anything to do with turning us in to the police and claiming your father's reward. No, they're going to do what's in their best interest, and sell us out to Keever.'

'You're the one who is lying,' the girl said indignantly. 'If the judge and her people are as bad as you say, if they mean to do me harm, they would have chained me up like they chained you up.'

'They chained me up because I'm a big bad husky, and they know I know what they really are. But you aren't any kind of threat, Princess, and where would you go if you ran away, how long would you last? Now listen,' I said, when the girl started to object. 'Listen hard and listen good. There's an easy way to discover who's telling the truth. All you have to do is go find a skywave radio. I bet just about every vehicle in the camp is equipped with one, it's how these people stay in touch with each other when they're working different places in summer. Find a radio, switch it on, start talking. Put out a message to the police. Tell them who you are. Tell them we're up on the west side of the Herbert Plateau, at the old radar station. And tell them to come quick, before we set out for Charlotte Bay.'

'I know what you're trying to do.'

'I'm trying to save you.'

The girl shook her head. 'You're hoping to cause some kind of trouble so you can escape.'

'We're already in trouble. We've been in trouble ever since we stopped to help that damn mammoth.'

But I couldn't make her see the truth. Judge Boudou had told her what she wanted to hear, and that was that. It ended up with me calling her a fool and her calling me a liar and flouncing off, with her escort trailing behind.

With nothing else to do, I drank the tea and ate the porridge, spilling half of it because it wasn't easy, eating with my wrists bound together. I'd barely finished when four of them came for me. Noah, Emzara and two other bravos, a drone floating along-side them, the guard standing up and joining the party.

I'd been planning to co-operate, all meek and mild, hoping they'd go easy on me and maybe make a careless mistake I could exploit, but even as she walked towards me Emzara shot me with that damn beanbag gun. The round hammered into my chest and knocked me on my ass, and while I lay there, struggling to breathe, one of the bravos stepped up quickly and lightly and slapped a patch on the side of my neck.

Things went all woozy and loose after that. Blurred lights, distant voices. Shadows looming and receding. For a little while it seemed that I was back on the boat with Mama, pitching on the sea's relentless swell as we fled Deception Island, but when I came to my senses, such as they were, I found myself lying inside a box or crate narrow as a coffin and printed from dirty grey plastic.

The lid was locked down tight, just a little light filtering around its edges. The unpadded floor jolted under my back. There was a rushing swaying sense of movement. My head ached, my chest ached, my whole body ached. My wrists were still tied together but they hadn't bothered to bind my legs, and I pried at the heel of my left boot with the toe of the right and managed to lever it off and used my knee to trap it against the side of the crate. Wriggling back and forth, I worked it up onto my chest, caught it in my bound hands and shook it until Levi's gift tumbled out of the slit in the lining where I'd hidden it.

It was a little knife about the length of my thumb – a sturdy sliver of glass with an edge flaked to razor sharpness, fabric wrapped around one end to make a handle. The kind of *puñal* cons make to protect themselves or settle a score. One like this, sometimes called a wolf claw, you make a fist and jam it between two fingers, use it to slash the face of your enemy or punch her in the throat or eye.

I caught it between my teeth and commenced to saw at the cord around my wrists. It took a long time. The vehicle was jolting down a steep gradient, taking sharp turns that banged me around inside the crate. I cut my lips a couple of times, swallowed blood, kept sawing. Sliced my wrists, the meat at the base of the joint of my thumb. At last I was through to the cord's plastic core. I carefully nicked it, spat out the knife and managed to stick it under the flap of my jacket's breast pocket, and captured my loose boot and worked it back onto my foot.

After that, I had nothing to do but brace myself against the rattling ride. The light prying at the edges of the crate's lid grew ever dimmer. By the time the ride smoothed out and the vehicle picked up speed it was about as dark as midnight. I was certain that we were either in or were approaching a town, and it had to be Charlotte Bay because there weren't any other settlements with paved roads within a day's drive of the plateau.

At last the vehicle stopped. I heard muffled voices. Someone laughing. I lay still and quiet, trying and failing to make out the conversation. After a little while the crate slid out and down, dropped to the ground with a bone-rattling bump. The lid cracked open, hinged aside. Cold air and lamp-lit twilight, Noah looming above me, stepping back, telling me to get out.

He aimed a pistol at me as I stood up, a pair of bravos and the girl at his back. She was hunched in her windproofs, pinched and miserable, glancing at me and glancing away. I had to resist the urge to tell her I told you so.

My crate had been dragged out of the back of a battered old land cruiser. A harbour partly lit by industrial arc lights stretched into darkness. Strange to see a place with no trace of snow. The bracing smell of the sea filling the air, the faint musical clatter of wires and stays of boats rocking at anchor, a sprinkling of lights defining the contours of a steep hillside. It was Charlotte Bay all right, but there was no sign of the police. Instead, Noah helpfully pointed out a bunch of vehicles parked up by a low square building at the far end of the harbour. According to him, that was where Judge Boudou was handling the final negotiations for the exchange.

'I didn't want you to miss what's going down,' Noah said. 'Oh, but your fone doesn't work any more. That's OK. Take a look right here.'

He stuck a hand-sized scrap of screenpaper on the flank of the land cruiser. It showed an unsteady feed from someone's eyecam, Judge Boudou talking with a big man in a long quilted coat, its fur collar turned up around his shaved head.

Mike Mike. It was a shock to see him in civilian clothes, in the open air. Several men and women were ranged behind him, dressed in hooded red jackets, machine-pistols and shotguns slung on their shoulders.

'They'll come and get you and the girl as soon as they've transferred the credit,' Noah said. 'Won't be long now.'

I pretended to be interested in what the scrap of paper was showing. 'So your mother and sister are fronting the deal. Doing the important work while you babysit me. It must be hard, *pendejo*, knowing your sister is smarter than you. Knowing you'll never be worth much of anything.'

Noah tried to laugh this off, asking the others to imagine how scared this she-whelephant must be, running off her mouth like this.

And yes, I was scared, but I was also trying to channel Lola, who always had a good line in insults and trash talk. I was trying to get under Noah's skin, to provoke him the way seasoned cons provoked new arrivals, getting in their faces and disrespecting them, forcing them to fight or forever be labelled a weak-ass punk.

'Listen and learn,' I said, 'because it's plain to see none of you know what you're doing. You should have held me some place safe until you got paid, then told the other party where to find me. Instead, I'm out here in the open, where they can snatch me any time they want. A basic amateur mistake. But that's exactly what you are, isn't it? A bunch of amateurs.'

Noah glared at me with his one good eye, saying, 'As if you know anything about it.'

'Why we're here, I'm in the kidnapping business too. Does your mother have false teeth?'

'I think you should shut up now,' Noah said.

'Because I don't see any negotiations there,' I said. 'I see an old woman about to go down on her knees in front of that big guy. She has false teeth, she can spit them out and really get to work.'

He came at me then, roaring, aiming to pistol-whip me to my knees, and I jerked my wrists apart and snapped the nicked cord that bound them and spun him into a neck lock. He was a big man, but I was bigger, I was stronger and, this was what really counted, I was pretty damn desperate. As he bucked against me, one of his bravos tried to put me down with a beanbag round, but I saw the gun come up and wrenched Noah in front of me and the round hit him in the face with a sound a cabbage makes when it hits the floor of a farm stack from twenty stories up. He went limp and I grabbed his pistol and shot the man who'd shot him. Hit him in the leg with a ballistic tag. He sat down hard and I put the pistol on the other bravo, who took a step backwards and raised his hands.

I disarmed them, locked them in the land cruiser. As we hurried towards the water's edge, the girl, breathless and close to tears, wanted to know why we hadn't just driven away.

'Because there's only one road in or out of this town, and knowing Mike Mike he'll have posted someone to watch it. But it's OK. I have a plan.'

She wrenched free. 'I won't go with you. I won't.'

'You can't stay here,' I said. 'And you aren't able to look after yourself.'

I could hear a crackle of shots in the distance, guessed that the two parties had realised we were escaping and each was blaming the other. I grabbed the girl's arm, something in the distance caught fire and lofted a plume of orange flame into the night, and we were running towards a couple of fishing boats. We were halfway there when a spotlight swung down the length of the harbour. Its beam lit up the cruiser, tracked sideways. I pulled the girl down, covering her with my body as it swung past. It splashed on a row of shipping containers, paused, then swung back and fixed on us. A man shouted something in the dark beyond the glare and I pulled the girl up and we were running again.

We'd almost reached the boats when she gasped, stumbled, and sprawled full length, the back of her windproof shedding a little flurry of insulation. Something small and angry cracked past, I realised that someone was shooting at us, realised that the girl had been hit, and scooped her up and ran headlong, jumping down into the nearest boat, breaking the lock of the wheelhouse with a kick, setting the girl down inside, telling her to stay put.

The boat was tied up with two hawsers, fore and aft. I had to scramble back onto the quay to free the hawser loops from their bollards, saw figures running towards me through the slant of the spotlight's beam. Shouts. Shots. I scrambled back into the wheelhouse, punched the starter button. White water churned astern and I hauled the wheel hard over and aimed Noah's pistol through the open door of the wheelhouse and shot up the other boat with explosive tags. It was burning in half a dozen places as I turned my stolen craft in a long curve, heading towards the entrance of the harbour and the open sea beyond.

The Happiest Days of My Life

Although Deception Island's volcanic caldera is flooded by the sea, it's still active, squatting as it does over a weak spot in the Earth's skin where fingers of molten rock ooze up from deep pockets and chambers, breaking the surrounding rock, finding a way to the surface. I've already told you about digging spa pools in the warm sands of the island's black beaches, how the ruins of the old whaling station and a couple of science stations were partly buried by mud flows and ash from a big eruption at the end of the last century, so on. Now I want to tell you how another eruption helped Mama and me escape. I want to tell you about the happiest days of my life.

In the years of our exile, cinder cones clustered on the east side of the island sometimes breathed out puffs of steam, and there were dozens of minor earthquakes that did no more than rattle the crockery. Little reminders that we were living on the slopes of a volcano, but nothing especially alarming until the water in Fumarole Bay began to steam and roil. A new vent had opened underwater, pumping out lava, pushing up a lumpy little island. A couple of days later, a big tremor shook everything on the island. There was a landslide on the western slopes of Stonethrow Ridge, a second vent cracked open on the flank of Mount Pond, throwing a plume of smoke and ash high into the sky, and after consulting with the authorities on the mainland the governor ordered an immediate evacuation of the island's entire population.

By the time the ferry arrived ash was snowing everywhere on the island and the air was filled with an acrid haze of volcanic smog. Like the rest of the ecopoets, I wore goggles and had tied a folded triangle of cloth, wetted with milk to absorb the worst of the air's smarting sting, over my mouth and nose. We'd been put to work at the research station in Whalers Bay, packing valuable equipment and rounding up the so-called killer whales, supervised by short-tempered mainland police armed with pistols and shock sticks and dressed in black coveralls and helmets, face masks with oval visors over snouty filters. One of us kids called them space pigs, and we took to making oinking noises whenever we passed one.

As far as we were concerned, the disaster was huge fun. A festival of cheerful anarchy, ecopoets mingling with lab staff and island security, all rules suspended. The killer whales were loaded one by one into padded transport slings and swung through the air onto the ferry's rear deck, where they were wetted down with seawater sprays. It was midsummer and we worked all through the long evening, the sun glowering low in the hazy sky like a sore and inflamed eye. Slabs of sea mist hung above the bay and to the north and east the tall plume from the vent on Mount Pond leaned eastward, the root of a great thundercloud expanding across the ocean. A constant deep rumble thrummed in the air, the ground. You could feel it through the soles of your shoes.

In the middle of all this, a rumour spread that the governor's residence was on fire. I saw a squad of police form up and march off, and a few moments later Mama emerged from the busy swirl of people and took my hand and told me to follow her.

As we slipped away from the research station, hurrying through the steady fall of ash, she told me what was going down. Told me that she was part of a crew of a couple of dozen ecopoets who were planning to escape, had set the fire as a diversion. We met up with the others at Fildes Point and under cover of the sea mist and general confusion scuttled half the fishing boats anchored there, climbed aboard the rest, and headed out through the channel at Neptune's Bellows into the open sea. The only home I'd ever known soon disappeared below the horizon, but I was too excited to feel any pangs of sentiment or loss.

Mama and her friends had hacked limiters built into the navigation systems of the boats to prevent them from sailing more than ten kilometres from the island. They'd also sabotaged the comms of the ferry, the radio tower on Roland Hill, and the terminal of the undersea cable that linked the island with the mainland. The authorities didn't learn about our escape until the ferry and its cargo of evacuees reached Livingston Island early the next morning, and by then our little fleet had scattered east and south in the brief night, each taking leave of the others as they ploughed their different courses.

Our stolen boat drove more or less due south, passing the sheer cliffs of Trinity Island and their swirling clouds of seabirds, heading towards landfall near Cape Herschel. There were seven of us aboard. Mama and me, Roxana Sanchez Jara and Laura Vega Garramuño, and their daughters, Astrid, Nelly and Conny. All three girls, like me, like most free ecopoet children born before arrest and exile, were huskies. Astrid was twelve, almost exactly my age. The twins, Nelly and Conny, were three years older. Sleepless and excited, we took turns standing at the bow in sea spray and cutting wind, keeping watch for ships, aircraft and drones. Once, we saw a pod of hourglass dolphins leaping above the waves with unchained exuberance. Once, a big white bird with sooty wings glided alongside our boat, matching its speed and course. A black-browed albatross according to Astrid, who knew all about birds. It accompanied us for several minutes before veering away towards some destination of its own, and I felt that the spirit of my father had briefly visited and blessed us.

Meanwhile, Mama, Roxana and Laura crowded in the little wheelhouse, steering the boat and discussing their plans, talking endlessly and reasonably as grown-ups did. Mama was possessed by determined purpose, telling me that it was our duty to evade capture and make our way south and find a place where we could start afresh. Our boat didn't have enough charge to make it all the way down the length of the peninsula and it would be too easily spotted once news of our escape spread, so we would make landfall as soon as we could and hike the rest of the way. After lots were drawn it was decided that Mama and I would be put off first, and the others would travel a little further down the coast. Splitting up was the best way of evading the authorities, and we promised each other that we would meet up again below the Antarctic Circle.

I had spent most of my life on an island just twelve kilometres across. I had no real understanding of the world beyond, the hundreds of kilometres of trackless terrain we would have to cross on foot, how long it would take, how hard and dangerous it would be. All I knew was that nothing would ever be the same again, and I was filled to bursting with giddy eager anticipation. Like every child I sometimes liked to imagine that I was the heroine of a *novela* in which everyone else was a supporting player, and now I had been thrown into exactly that kind of grand adventure.

Mama and I waded ashore in a little cove west of the mouth of the Blériot River, and in the blue twilight of a midsummer midnight we hiked south and east through a Sitka spruce plantation. Orderly rows of dark green conical trees all the same size pressed close together above carpets of brown needles, nothing growing in their deep shade but frills of pale fungus on fallen branches. Mama grew ever more angry as we walked. The land uncovered by the retreat of the ice had been a chance to quicken new oases of life and watch them grow wild and strange, she said. From the first seeds of ecopoiesis to a complex web that discovered its own checks and balances as it was pushed and pulled by fluctuations in climate and the activity of keystone species. A great work of time that couldn't be quantified in terms of profit, utility or any other human measure except, maybe, beauty. But the government had dispersed or exiled the land's custodians, promises and vows made a century before had been broken, and commercial interests were displacing the new ecosystem's emergent complexity with sterile industrial monocultures. A filthy craven betrayal of the ideals of a new country and its people, so on, Mama ranting in fine form, calling down curses on those responsible for this obscenity.

We stopped now and then to uproot saplings planted in transparent protective tubes, or to ring-bark older trees. Mama showing me how to strip away bands of living bark, cutting off

205

the flow of water and mineral nutrients upwards and the flow of sugars downwards, so that the tops of the trees would die of thirst and the roots would die of starvation. These token acts of sabotage gave her a grim satisfaction. If we could kill the entire plantation, she said, the forest would grow over the scar in a few decades, the little unmakers, wood-boring beetles, saprophytic fungi and all the rest, would remove every last trace of the corpses of these alien intruders, and all would be as it should be once again.

We hid in a ditch when the mechanised brontosaurus of a tractor rig roared past, then rose up and went on, leaving the plantation behind and plunging into scrub that straggled among marsh and strings of little lakes and streams that less than two decades later would be gone, the streams diverted, the marshes drained, the lakes filled in, the scrub bulldozed and ploughed under and replaced by ordered squares of edited trees. Our little act of defiance leaving no trace except in my memory.

But back then most of Blériot Basin was still a wilderness growing according to its own logic, and after we climbed slopes still raw with the scrape marks of lost ice I saw for the first time an actual forest. There had been a windbreak of stunted Guaitecas cypress around the garden of the governor's residence on Deception Island, and clumps of dwarf birch and willow huddled in spots sheltered from the salt-laden gales that over-swept the island for more than half the year, but here were trees growing wild for as far as I could see.

Mama named each species, told me about their individual virtues, explained how seedlings had been raised in nurseries and planted out by hand. A person could plant between five hundred and two thousand seedlings every day, she said, carrying them in sacks slung over their shoulders, using a spade to pry at the stony ground and inserting each one with a sprinkling of enriched soil from the soil factory. She told me that everything growing there, every tree, every bush and blade of grass, was rooted in the work of generations of ecopoets, and almost all of the animals, from worms to reindeer and wolves, likewise owed their existence to people who had designed and quickened intricate webs of species and left them to find their own balance. She talked about life in the bush camps, the songs and the stories and the camaraderie of common purpose, seemed happier than she'd been for a long long time.

I'd become used to her long silences and unpredictable sudden bursts of anger, the way she had of turning from me, becoming remote and unreachable even when we were jammed together in our little house by bad weather. I didn't understand then that she was too often caught in the jaws of depression's black dog. She had lost her freedom and her husband, was raising a child whose future was uncertain, who would be persecuted everywhere outside the island community. The bitter taste of failure, the lash of self-blame, self-hatred – she shed all of that in the first days as we walked south. It was like watching a flower open to the sun. Although she was only thirty-two when we escaped she had always seemed much older. Careworn. But in those first days of freedom she began to look her true age. Smiling easily, laughing, full of energy.

She was happy and so was I. Alive to every moment, greedily absorbing novelty as only a child can.

Mama believed that we might find free ecopoets living in the far south, told me that we might even find my grandmother, told me every detail of the shelter we would build. There was plenty of work to do, she said. The ice was still melting, exposing land that could be seeded with new life. There would be new species to be edited and introduced. Campaigns against atrocities like the spruce plantation to be organised and executed. She and her friends had made all kinds of plans during the long years of exile. Now she could begin to think about making them come true.

So we headed out across Blériot Basin, climbing a steep slope to the permanent ice and snow of the Herbert Plateau, cutting west and descending through a pass where a white-water river rushed in wild spate around huge boulders. Making our way through wooded slopes to Charlotte Bay, where we were given supplies and the gift of a short hop to Flandres Bay. And we skied up long slopes from Flandres Bay and crossed the Forbidden Plateau to the wild, sparsely populated east coast and hiked south, making our way across a series of parallel valleys and mountainous ridges and at last turning towards the west coast again.

Days of endless light. The sun briefly dipping below the horizon after midnight and almost immediately rising again. It was warm enough to sleep out in the open – when we needed to sleep. The long days and brief white nights confounded our internal clocks and we often walked until two or three in the morning. It was the same with everyone else. Our first night after leaving the boat, in the scrub forest of Blériot Basin, we were woken by the distant crackle of gunshots, and the next day found the decapitated carcass of a giant elk, its head and great spread of antlers taken as a trophy by some wealthy hunter. In Charlotte Bay kids played outside way after midnight, and cafés and bars never seemed to close. Up on the Forbidden Plateau we saw three skimmers chase each other across the snow in midnight's spectral twilight. Everywhere on the peninsula people were making the most of the brief summer.

We walked every day. Ten kilometres, twenty. Stopping now and then to pick berries or dig for tubers, to nap for a couple of hours in some sunny spot before moving on. I was young and strong and sturdy, and despite her new energy and purpose Mama sometimes struggled to keep up with me. She taught me how to choose a good site to make camp, how to find the runs that small animals used in the undergrowth, and make wire-loop traps and set them just so. She taught me how to light fires with a fire plough, a bow and drill, with a lens shaped from clear ice. How to build a shelter by notching a young tree's trunk and bending and staking it to form a ridge pole and weaving walls on either side from cut branches. Now and then we'd sleep in one of the old ecopoet refuges. I've already told you about the one tucked into a ravine, its flat roof covered in boulders. There was another hidden behind a waterfall, and one cut into a ledge high on a slope with views down the length of Andvord Fjord, steep slopes crowded with trees rising on either side of a crooked sleeve of vivid blue water, sparkling waterfalls unravelling past cliffs, and a little cluster of black roofs, the fishing village of Puerto Constitución, gleaming at the shore near the fjord's mouth.

There was a sadness to those old refuges. An echo of lives lived and long lost. Like the abandoned winter station we found in Green Valley, where volunteer saplings grew among raised vegetable beds in smashed greenhouses, army graffiti was scrawled on the walls of wrecked labs, and the broken foundations of a cluster of cabins long ago burnt to the ground were smothered in drifts of blue-berried honeysuckle. We spent a day there while Mama picked over the ruins, possessed by the ghost of her black dog, and I thoughtlessly gorged on raspberries growing wild in a walled garden and fell asleep on a cracked slab of concrete in the warm sunlight.

There were old gardens scattered throughout the coastal forests. Some bounded by rough stone walls overgrown with moss and ferns, others squares or rectangles scratched into stony earth on slopes that faced south-east and caught the most sunlight, or patchworked around huts built of earth-chinked stones and roofed with plastic sheeting weighted down with rocks and wired to rotted batteries that had once stored electricity generated by solar paint. Most of these plots were overgrown with weeds, only a few edible plants remaining, but occasionally we came across fields that had been cleared and replanted with neat rows of crops. White lupins, blueberries and lingonberries, sea kale, the inevitable Eskimo potato.

Once, we came across several square fields of dwarf barley etched on a hillside. Wire fences to keep out reindeer, a gravel road wandering down into the forest. Mama froze at the sight of them, said that while the replanted fields were mostly likely cultivated by half-and-halfs, these were something else. Some kind of experiment left to grow over summer. Like the spruce plantation it was a stupid waste of land, a reversion to the bad old days of the oil age when agriculture had been dominated by monocultures that used more energy, in the form of fertiliser and fuel for machines, than was harvested. People never learned, Mama said. Especially the rich, who made fetishes of things that other people couldn't afford. That barley would probably be used to make bread sold for silly amounts of money, or to brew rare expensive beer drunk by the same kind of people who used ice ten thousand years old, brought up from deep cores in glaciers on the mainland, to chill their drinks.

Like those barley fields, Mama said, every biome quickened after the retreat of the ice – salt marshes fringing the mouths of meltwater rivers, forests spread across valleys, alpine meadows on high rocky slopes, moss lawns in cirques which had once been tamped full of snow and ice a hundred metres deep – were human artifacts. But they weren't parks or gardens, ever the same like so many pictures. They didn't evolve in a linear predictable manner towards some stable end point, but were in a constant state of dynamic disequilibrium. It was not possible to completely describe the state of a biome at any particular moment, nor was it possible to predict future states, but you could sketch the broad limits of possibility, and because they weren't as rich as natural ecosystems and changes driven by global warming were still ongoing, the biomes of the peninsula required a certain level of protection and management. Exactly how much protection, how much management, had been endlessly debated by ecopoets in their heyday, most favouring a light touch and the gradual introduction of new species to increase diversity and robustness. But after their caretakers had surrendered or had been rounded up, most of the biomes had been left to grow as they would, and it was a tribute to the clever designs of their initial states that they had survived as well as they had in the past couple of decades.

Anyway, Mama and I skirted those fields, wary of drones or cameras that might be watching over them, and hurried on into the forest on the far side. We were ragged and sunburnt and lean. We lived on what we could forage and catch. We avoided other people, made long detours around villages and settlements. I swam several times in the sea, in churning surf, among slicks of bull kelp, once among penguins that shot past me like torpedoes, trailing long wakes of silvery bubbles. Mama swam too, but never for very long – the water was too cold for her. We saw fish eagles play fighting above a fjord, locking claws and plunging towards the water and breaking apart at the last minute, over and again. And on our traverse of the Forbidden Plateau we descended into a crevasse and clambered over blocks fallen from ice bridges that curved overhead and found at its far end a cathedral vault and a tumble of ice descending into depths we did not dare to investigate, everything lit by a glow as blue and holy as radioactivity.

The days and days of walking blur together. It's hard, now, to sort dreams from actual memories. I remember climbing to Mapple Valley's high southern crest and seeing a panorama of parallel razorback ridges bare as the moon stretching away under the cloudless sky. I remember a circle of upright stones in a mossy chapel in the forest below the Forbidden Plateau, lit by a beam of sunlight slanting between the trees. The glass and concrete slab of some plutocrat's back-country house cantilevered out from cliffs overlooking Wilhelmina Bay. The broken castle of an orphaned iceberg grounded on a rocky shore, with freshets of sparkling meltwater cascading down its fluted sides and a thick band of green algae tinting its wave-washed base. But did we really see, in the pass between Starbuck and Stubb Fjords, an albino reindeer poised near the thin spire of an elf stone named *The Endless Song of the Air*? Did we glimpse a pyramid set on a remote bastion of bare rock in the ice and snow of the Bruce Plateau? I've looked long and hard, but I've never been able to find it on maps or in satellite images. And did we really see people dancing naked in a circle around a huge bonfire in a forest glade near Tashtego Point? I can't be certain that it wasn't one of my dreams, but whether it was real or imaginary the memory of it still wakes the pulse of drums in my blood.

I'm trying to tell you how happy we were, Mama and me. Not only in those few moments indelibly fixed in memory, but also during the uneventful hours of walking through the forest and crossing meadows and hiking up long slopes of scree or snow, or when we rested beside a little campfire, taking turns to braid each other's hair or simply sitting in companionable silence. The times we picked berries together in some sunny clearing or among the sliding stones of a mountainside, or spear-fished in icy rivers, or gathered sea moss and limpets from the salt-wet stones of the seashore.

Some old-time writer once claimed that happy families are all alike, while unhappy families are each unhappy in their own way.

If that's true, then happiness can be earned only by sacrificing or suppressing some part of whatever it is that makes us different, by unselfishly giving up our wants and desires and submitting to something larger than ourselves. Family. Society. God. But in those long summer days, walking south with Mama, it seemed to me that happiness was a gift that fell on us as lightly and freely as sunlight. It was as simple as lying on wiry turf with the sun warm and red on my closed eyes, or the heart-stopping shock of jumping into a meltwater pool. It was a gift the world gave you if you gave yourself to the world.

The people who'd planted those regimented rows of spruce trees, built that house on an almost unaccessible cliff, harrowed and fertilised and planted those barley fields, constructed deer-proof fences around them, sprayed them with weedkiller – their version of civilisation was a constant struggle to impose order on a world that worked otherwise. Our version, the ecopoets' version, was as meandering as a river following the contours of the landscape. It was not about getting but about letting go. Surrendering not to God or the artificial constraints of society, but to nature. That was the most important lesson Mama taught me. As we walked south I learned how to live in the world while taking the least from it and leaving only the faintest of footsteps, and I was so very happy.

We had begun our long hike at midsummer, and now summer was beginning to fade. We didn't know it at the time, but all the other escapees had been recaptured. Roxana, Laura and their daughters had been caught by a police patrol three days after they had beached the stolen fishing boat in an inlet south of Portal Point. The rest had been picked up here and there. Two had gotten as far as Square Bay, where they'd been promptly betrayed by a police informant.

As for Mama and me, we turned west and cut across the Bruce Plateau, where a knifing wind blew sheets of ice crystals across undulating snow that stretched away in every direction and the horizon vanished in a glittering haze and the sun glimmered in a halo or temple of light with bright but heatless sundogs burning on either side. And under that spectral triple sun we came across the site of an ancient airplane crash. Most of the debris field was buried under a century of snow, but there was a long curve of aluminium fuselage polished by the wind, and a row of five seats standing on a hummock of ice as if planted there, blue fabric sunfaded, a tattered length of safety webbing flapping in the ceaseless wind. We passed the drum of an engine nacelle half-buried in ice, and looming beyond was the shattered tail, its fin upright as a tombstone and painted blue with a white star.

I felt a weird chill as we walked through the shadow of that forbidding marker, as if sensing the presence of the ghosts of passengers and aircrew, lingering traces of the sudden violence of their last ends. It clung to me long after the wreck had vanished into the haze of wind-blown ice crystals, and Mama felt it too. She couldn't stop shivering when we made camp at the end of the day, even after I opened my coat and hugged her to my body's heat. By the time we were coming down off the plateau, making our way through a narrow defile between blocks of wind-carved ice, the chill had sunk into her bones. That night, as we lay between two big erratics, it ignited into full-blown fever.

She forced herself to walk a few kilometres the next day, and the day after that. We were following the course of a shallow river that wound through boulder fields and a scrub of dwarf willow and black spruce when, in a stony clearing by a bend in the river, she sat down and couldn't get up again. She hunched with a blanket shawled around her shoulders as waves of cold and heat passed through her. I brewed willow-bark tea and bathed her forehead with a towel soaked in icy river water, but nothing helped and soon she was in fever's full grip.

I sat with her, sleepless and miserable and afraid. The unpeopled wilderness stretching all around, as uncaring as the stars spread across the clear dark sky.

Mama was quieter and weaker the next day, wrapped in both our blankets and lying on a bower of dry moss inside the low arc of a windbreak I'd built from loose stones. I tried and failed to get her to eat, fed her sips of willow-bark tea laced with the last of our sugar. In a moment of lucidity, she told me that there was a settlement just a few kilometres away, where the river ran into a little bay, told me what she needed.

Late in the afternoon I built up the campfire and left a bottle of water and sticks of rabbit jerky within reach, kissed her, and set off downstream. Scrambling past a ladder of waterfalls, cutting through a scrubby forest of trees scarcely taller than me, I reached Holtedahl Bay shortly before sunset.

I waited until the brief night fell. The settlement's clinic was a small white building, dark and quiet. I broke a window and climbed inside, forced open the dispensary cabinet and took all the painkillers, antipyretics and nanobiotics I could find. But as I slipped away through the settlement, moving from shadow to shadow, I was spotted by a sleepless man sitting on his porch, the alarm was raised, and after a brief frantic chase the settlement's two police deputies caught up with me on the far side of the scrub forest. A search party set out to look for Mama after one of the deputies, a kindly woman with three kids of her own, had calmed me down and persuaded me to tell my story, but by then it was too late.

I like to think now that Mama had willed it. That she had sent me on a futile mission so that she could die alone in the wild back country she loved rather than be recaptured and spend the rest of her life in prison. But at the time I believed that I had failed her.

Soon enough the state police arrived, and I was flown to Esperanza along with Mama's body. The eruption that had caused the evacuation was still rumbling along. Much of Deception Island was covered in ash and gashed by rock falls and mudslides, and the exiled ecopoets had been scattered among settlements on the South Shetland Islands. Although my lawyer argued that I should to be returned to my community, although three families volunteered to take me in, I was made a ward of the court and transferred from juvenile prison to the state orphanage in Esperanza. And that's where I became a monster.

I told my friends in Kilometre 200 about it once, during one of our vodka-fuelled bonding sessions.

'My first night in the dormitory, everyone stared at me but no one stepped forward to help or say hello. I was the only husky, rumour was I was some sort of criminal, and I was also the new fish. They were all waiting to see how I'd measure up to the girl who'd appointed herself alpha bitch. Pilar Guzman. She was a mundane, three years older than me, ten centimetres taller, twenty, twenty-five kilos heavier. A hefty girl. Not too bright, but used to getting her own way. So just before lights out, I was getting ready for bed and found someone had pissed on my sheets. Pilar and her crew of acolytes were watching. Making comments. Making sure I knew who'd done it. Because, of course, they wanted to see what I'd do.'

'They weren't exactly endowed with imagination, were they?' Lola said.

'Bullies have their traditions, like everyone else,' Sage said.

'So what did you do?' Paz said.

'Stripped the bed and flipped the mattress. Went to sleep.'

'You didn't stand up to this Pilar creature,' Lola said. 'So I know that wasn't the end of it.'

'Of course it wasn't. The next day, Pilar and three of her toadies cornered me after the evening meal. The toadies braced me while Pilar slapped me around, told me I was going to do her share of the chores, run errands for her, so on. And when I got back to the dormitory I found that they'd soaked my bed in piss again. Both sides of the mattress this time.'

'So then you beat her up,' Lola said.

'I slept on the floor. And the next morning, in the bathroom, I waited until Pilar went into one of the stalls to do her business. They had doors on the toilet stalls, but they didn't meet the ground. I reached underneath and grabbed her legs and pulled. Pulled her all the way out of there. She was knocked silly when her head hit the toilet bowl. Bleeding from a scalp wound, a lot of blood on the white tile floor. Everyone watching, no one trying to interfere.'

'You showed them who you were,' Lola said.

'I didn't have the sense to stop there,' I said. 'After I pulled Pilar out, I kicked open the door and grabbed her by the neck and stuffed her head in the toilet bowl. She was still struggling, but not so much any more, when two orderlies banged in. They had to use their shock sticks before they could pull me off her. I got thirty days solitary for that.'

'Tell me this has a happy ending,' Paz said. 'Tell me that when you came out no one bothered you again.'

'They called me a monster. All the usual names. The other girls, even some of the guards. But yeah, no one much bothered me. I didn't mind at first, and by the time I realised that it was kind of lonely, I'd sort of grown into the role.'

'We've all been there,' Sage said. 'We've all been called a monster or a freak by people who should have known better.'

'You didn't get your own crew?' Lola said. 'A reputation like that, you could have ruled the place.'

'I wasn't into that kind of thing,' I said. 'The pecking order, whatever. I was outside all that. I'd become . . . What's the word when you quietly put up with shit?'

'Stupid,' Lola said.

'Stoical,' Sage said.

'Yeah, that,' I said. 'I was stoical.'

'But you're not that little girl any more,' Paz said. 'And you're with friends now. One for all, all for one, right?'

We drank to that, clinking glasses, knocking back scorching shots. And yes, I was happy then, among people like me, sharing our stories. For the longest time after Mama died I was gripped by the bottomless ache of that loss, by guilt, by my very own black dog. Poor Mama. Poor me. I thought that I deserved the state orphanage. That working in its stacks, in the termite colonies that turned waste paper and wood into protein, packing printed chicken steaks, so on, was a kind of penance. I thought that I deserved a life filled edge to edge with misery, like that plantation crammed with spruce trees, no other life possible in the darkness underneath.

Those six years in the orphanage weren't all bad, after I was let out I had some high old times hanging out in Star City, working with Bryan, and life was pretty fine after I became a CO. Before I got mixed up with Keever, anyway. But nothing was ever as good as walking through the forests and meadows of the back country, Mama telling me stories about their creation, the hand-to-mouth fugitive existence we shared. Those were the happiest days of my life, and the point of this, what I'm trying to tell you, is that above and beyond wanting to escape the silly trap I'd made of my life, I did what I did because I wanted the two of us to share something like that. Because I had the stupid idea that somehow I could find my way back to that summer, those wild gardens, those days overflowing with the unqualified bliss of being alive and free in the land our people had quickened.

23

The girl, dazed and groggy, didn't seem to be particularly upset when I told her what had happened. Told her she'd been shot. I was steering the stolen boat through the dark sea and she was sitting on the pitching floor of the wheelhouse, poking a finger in the hole in the back of her windproof jacket, telling me that she remembered running, remembered bright light all around. 'And then I tripped, and you were carrying me . . .'

There was a hole in the back of the short white jacket she wore under the windproof, too, and a hand-sized dark spot, like a bruise, in the smooth pale grey material of her bodysuit, but no sign of a penetration wound, no blood.

'A stray round knocked you down. I think it only grazed you, or maybe ricocheted off the ground, gave you a little love tap. I picked you up and carried you the rest of the way. Saved your ass again, but no need to thank me,' I said, trying to turn it into a joke, trying to make out it was nothing while thinking about how much worse it could have been. She'd been in my care and I'd failed her in the worst possible way.

When I'd switched on the overhead light so that I could look her over, I'd been confronted by my reflection in the dark mirror of the wheelhouse's wraparound window. Ashen skin and a bristling cap of jet-black hair. The crag of my brow overshadowing my bruised eyes, the squashed bulb of my snout. I was strung-out, sleepless, crashing after an adrenaline high. I looked like a mugshot of my own ghost.

The girl winced as she probed her back. 'My bodysuit is supposed to be bulletproof,' she said. 'It must have saved me.'

'Does it hurt?'

'A little. When I breathe in.'

'I'll check you out properly when I'm sure we aren't being followed,' I said, and switched off the light. The boat would show up on the radar and sonar of anyone tracking us, but no sense in making things too easy for them.

The girl said, 'Where are you taking me?'

'Someplace safe. Just hang in there.'

Behind us, the lights of Charlotte Bay dwindled into the vast night. No sign of pursuit. No searchlights stabbing out of the dark, no drones swooping down, blaring threats and commands. Maybe the True Citizens and Mike Mike's crew had shot each other to pieces. Or maybe the firefight had attracted the attention of the local police, the survivors were either in custody or on the run . . .

I heaved to off Portal Point and after a brief search found a first aid kit in the crew cabin. Apart from a spectacular bruise developing across the small of her back, the girl seemed unhurt. The kit's diagnostic wand told me in a prissy voice that it could not detect any internal bleeding, but recommended that the patient should be properly examined by a suitably qualified person.

'Did you hear that?' the girl said. 'You have to take me to a hospital.'

She was sitting on the edge of a bunk, braced against the boat's rocking sway with one hand, fastening her bodysuit with the other. Her fingers moving slowly. Trembling. Butterscotch dapples sharp-edged on her bloodless face. Shock finally settling in.

I told her that it wasn't anything that rest couldn't mend, patched her with painkillers and fed her a sleeping tablet. She didn't protest or resist when I tucked a blanket around her, and I left her to sleep it off and fired up the boat's engine and aimed due west.

I'd switched off comms and radar and satnav, everything that might be used to track us, was plotting a course by compass and dead reckoning. Sweating through a bad couple of hours as the boat wallowed through the choppy ink-black sea against a fierce headwind. At last the solid shadow of Brabant Island rose against the night and I turned south, running parallel to the coast. By the time I had negotiated a way around the southern end of the island first light was seeping into the sky, and soon afterwards I motored into a cove in the north side of Duperré Bay, dropped anchor under the dripping belly of a cliff.

The girl was asleep, blonde hair tangled on the filthy pillow, an arm dangling over the edge of the bunk. I rearranged the blanket around her and sat and watched her breathe for a while, hearing a faint catch, like the beginning of a hiccup or a sob, at each inbreath. Her temperature was slightly elevated but her pulse seemed steady. I knew that I should take her to a clinic, knew that I wasn't going to. I told myself that I had saved her from the True Citizens and Keever Bishop. I told myself that I was back on track.

I brewed a mug of tea in the filthy little galley, plenty of sugar and half a stick of butter dissolved in it, and shucked my jacket and shirt and examined my dog-bitten arm. After I washed away a crust of dried blood the crescents of raw punctures on either side of the muscle below my elbow began to weep straw-coloured liquid, and the skin around them was blackly bruised, hot and tender, but all I could do was douse everything with nanobiotics and cover it up with bandage spray and hope for the best. My arm was throbbing like a malignant engine but I decided against painkillers. I needed to stay sharp.

The True People's fone-blocker had welded itself to my wrist. When I pried at it with the point of the scissors I succeeded only in cutting myself, told myself it didn't matter. I was hoping to get some help with setting up negotiations with the girl's father, and if that didn't work out I could use the boat's comms, move from place to place so I couldn't be tracked down . . .

There was enough light now to take in the sweep of the stony shore of the cove. Along the strand line a small crowd of gentoo penguins stood watching the sea with inscrutable patience, as if waiting for the appearance of their penguin messiah. Beyond, a line of bare hills faded into the grey overcast. A bleak primordial place seemingly untouched by ecopoiesis or civilisation. And then I saw, tucked under a low rise at the far end of the beach, a small black hut.

My first reaction was to haul up the anchor and hightail it out of there. But anyone living in that hut would have seen the boat come in, if they'd already called the police I wouldn't get far on the open sea, and if they hadn't it was possible that they'd help me out. I wasn't so dumb that I'd forgotten my last run-in with a back-country hermit, but I reckoned that I was due some good luck, and bolted the hatch to the crew cabin and pulled a salt-crusted windproof over my uniform jacket and heaved the boat's life-raft canister over the side. As soon as it hit the water the yellow raft unfolded and inflated with a tremendous hiss, and I hauled it close by its painter line and climbed down and paddled through the low waves to the shore.

I hadn't gone far, walking past a straggling fringe of indifferent penguins, stones crunching underfoot, strands of bull kelp rising and falling on the rippling wash of the tide, the stench of penguin shit heavy in the cold air, when I felt a familiar clench in my stomach and bent over, hands clutching knees, and threw up the tea. Nerves, I told myself as I rinsed the taste of spoiled butter from my mouth with a palmful of seawater. Nerves and exhaustion. I hadn't slept properly for three days. I'd been stabbed and bitten and beaten up, the girl had gotten herself shot . . . It was a wonder I was still standing.

The little hut, clinker-built and tarred black, its curved roof shaped from a single sheet of plastic, stood in the shadow of the cliff among a kind of garden of sculptures got up from metal rods, wire, feathers and penguin bones. A rowboat rested upside down on blocks among a scatter of crab pots. No sign that anyone was home.

The door was propped open with a lump of granite. When I stepped inside I disturbed a couple of penguins, and as I shooed them out one gave me a vicious peck on my shin, dodged the kick I aimed at it and hopped out the door, cackling. Damn thing had taken a good chunk out of me, the wound was bleeding freely, and I sat on the narrow cot and bandaged myself with a strip of cloth torn from a mouldy sheet before taking stock.

The place clearly had been abandoned for a long time. Its plank floor was crusted with dried guano. On one shelf a row of old paper books had swollen with damp into a single mass. On another, rusted cans had shed their labels like autumn leaves. But it wasn't entirely cheerless. The walls were painted bright red and shingled with charcoal sketches of penguins and the profile of the mountain in different weathers, and oil paintings on scraps of wood were jigsawed over the cot. Views of the sea, portraits of icebergs, cloudscapes, apocalyptic sunsets . . .

I found a grave on the far side of the hut, a mound of stones with a flat piece of rock for a headstone, a name painstakingly scratched into it. Agustyn Dos Santos Pistario. I imagined a small shaggy man (that cot wasn't anywhere near big enough for me) sitting on the doorstep of his hut, dressed in patched clothes, stitching holes in a net or shaping the scaffolding of one of his funny little sculptures. A hermit who'd turned his back on the rest of the world, eking out a bare living by fishing and poaching penguin eggs, capturing the beauty of the place he loved in charcoal and oil paint. And after he died someone had found his body and had buried him, had left the door of his hut open so that his spirit could rove freely.

I sat by his grave, with its view of the open sea beyond the cove's headlands, and went over my plan one more time. It wasn't much, relying as it did on the help of someone I hadn't met for a dozen years, someone who might have moved away, might be dead, might turn me in to the police, but it was all I had. Thoughts of sailing the little fishing boat north to Chile or south and west to New Zealand were impossible fantasies. Back in the day, a band of tough old explorers had navigated from the mainland to South Georgia across winter seas in a leaking rowboat, landing on the uninhabited south side of the island and hiking across hard terrain in impossible weather to find help at the whaling station on the north shore. An amazing feat of endurance. But I wasn't anywhere near as salty or confident as those heroes, I'd almost certainly be spotted and intercepted if I made for the open ocean, and in any case the damn boat didn't have enough charge to go more than a couple of hundred kilometres.

I dozed off, jerked awake. Maybe I could send the girl back across the strait after making her promise not to tell anyone where I was, and just stay here. Clean out Agustyn Dos Santos

Pistario's hut, break down his cot and rebuild it to fit me, use his nets and crab pots to catch toothfish and king crabs. I pictured myself tramping, swollen with pregnancy, across twenty kilometres of rough terrain to the island's only settlement in Buls Bay. Giving birth to you in the clinic there, bringing you home. The two of us making gardens in the bare hills, greening the island as my parents and the other ecopoets had greened the fringes of the mainland. Another fantasy, an idle daydream of the kind of life Mama had wanted to find in the far south, but it was lovely and enticing and I fell asleep while playing with it, woke an hour later, stiff and cold, and walked back along the shore towards the boat.

Often, when we try to weigh up the whys and wherefores, we discover that we've already made our decision. Everything else is justification.

After I climbed aboard, the girl started to bang on the hatch set in the floor of the wheelhouse. I ignored the racket, fired up the skywave radio and put out my request for a one-to-one conversation and sat down and waited. The girl soon gave up on her protest, but started up again when I received a call-back.

'Are you still living in Charlotte Bay?' I said.

'Where else would I be? Who is this?'

I wanted to confess everything, wanted to know if she could help me, but this was the skywave net, anyone could be listening in, so I cut the connection without replying. The rest of my questions, the favour I needed to ask, would have to wait until I could arrange a face-to-face meeting.

When I unbolted the hatch, the girl swarmed up the steps like a hornet escaping from a bottle, angry and upset, demanding to know where we were and what I thought I was doing, locking her up like that. She'd been scared that I'd abandoned her or had wandered off and had some kind of accident, said that for all I cared she could have died down there, so on.

'You were asleep when I left you,' I said. 'And you seem perky enough now.'

'It hurts to breathe, and that gadget said I needed hospital treatment. And your dog bite, you should get that looked at too. That kind of thing can get badly infected. You could lose your arm.'

'I've dealt with it. And quit looking so hopeful. I'm not about to keel over.'

'I don't want you to die and leave me stranded out here. Wherever this is.'

The girl was looking out of the window of the wheelhouse. Penguins clumped along the stony shore. Bare hills squatting under low grey cloud.

'Brabant Island,' I said. 'And no one is going to strand you here. In a day, two days at the most, you'll be back with your father.'

'You keep saying that.'

'This time I really mean it. Cross my cold black monster's heart.'

'If you're planning to turn yourself in to the police, you could do that right away,' the girl said hopefully. 'I mean, this boat must have some kind of fone.'

'Why don't you go below and fix breakfast? There's food in the galley. Some of it may even be the kind you can eat.'

We stayed on the boat for the rest of the short day. I was certain that it had been reported missing, that the police must have realised that it had something to do with the ruckus at the harbour. Perhaps they'd arrested the True Citizens and Mike Mike's crew. Perhaps they knew by now that I wasn't part of Keever Bishop's gang, that I was the one who had taken the girl. I imagined a fountain of little drones spraying into the sky above Charlotte Bay, scattering in every direction, searching along the coast, patrolling in fixed patterns above the open sea. Nothing I could do about that except sit tight under the dubious cover of the cliff and the low clouds and hope that the police would assume I'd head south, wouldn't think to check out the islands on the far side of the Gerlache Strait.

Rain briefly rattled on the wheelhouse window. Clouds rifted apart and sunlight shone on the hills to the north, the snowy flanks of the Solvay Mountains. And then the clouds closed up again and the rain came back, turned to sleet blowing slantwise across the cove.

The girl lay on the bunk in the crew cabin, reading her book, and I dozed in the wheelhouse, stretched out on a sleeping bag that smelt strongly of a stranger's sweat. As light faded from the sky, I hauled the life raft onto the foredeck and the girl and I ate a kind of porridge she'd boiled up from two kinds of beans. She took her portion plain. I crumbled dried fish into mine, sprinkled it with plenty of hot sauce, drank a big mug of sweet tea. The dog bite was still throbbing and my pecked shin sharply ached, but I was rested and ready to go.

In the wheelhouse, with the anchor wound up and the motor churning water astern as I backed the boat away from the cliff, the girl reminded me that I still hadn't told her where I was taking her.

'I'm going to meet an old friend,' I said. 'In the last place the police and Mike Mike will think of looking for us.'

24

As our little boat ploughed through the sea's dark swell towards the mainland I tried to jolly the girl along, telling her that we'd had a bit of an adventure all told, but we were almost at the end of it. Maybe things hadn't gone exactly the way I'd hoped, there'd definitely been some setbacks, but it was all coming together at last. I'd get what I was due, she'd get back with her family, we'd never have to see each other again. I was stupidly cheerful, and like most stupid, cheerful people thought it would be easy to buck up those who weren't.

'Tell me about that book of yours,' I said. 'What's happening there?'

'As if you care,' the girl said.

She was still sulking about being locked in the crew cabin, was fretting about my plan, didn't believe that it had any chance of working, said that it was desperate and ridiculous. Kid had serious trust issues.

'After that thing with the poison,' I said, 'I do kind of want to know how it worked out. Also, the princess and the hero were on a boat, heading back to the court of the hero's king. Doesn't that sound familiar? Maybe I can learn something that will help me.'

'I doubt it.'

'Why not?'

'Because the two of them accidentally fall in love. And then there's a shipwreck.'

'Oho. Now you really do have my attention. You're going to have to tell me the rest, because I won't shut up until you do.'

I had to dig it out of her in bits and pieces to begin with, but she gradually relaxed, started to get into the story. Explaining that as far as Princess Isander was concerned she was a prisoner on the ship that Tantris had stolen from her murdered uncle, sailing towards an arranged marriage to a man she'd never met, in a country she scarcely knew. She'd already tried and failed to poison Tantris while he had been recovering from the fight with the dragon. Now she tried again, ordering her body servant, Barbara, to add a drop of venom distilled from the slime of a certain kind of frog to Tantris's wine. But Barbara, scared of what would happen to her if the murder plot was discovered, doped the wine with a love potion instead, hoping that once Tantris was besotted he would agree to take Isander wherever she wanted. Anywhere but the court of King Marsche.

Isander insisted on sharing the wine. She wanted to poison Tantris, and she also wanted to kill herself rather than endure a forced marriage. So they both drank, and each saw the other afresh, and in a fever of mutual desire they fell into each other's arms, kissing and rekissing. Isander guessed at once what had happened, but it didn't matter. She had to be with Tantris. Ached for him. And Tantris knew that he was breaking his oath of loyalty to his king by sleeping with Isander, but he didn't care. Nothing mattered but their hunger for each other.

They thought that they would have only a few days of bliss before they reached their destination and preparations for the wedding began. But a storm blew up as the ironclad was making its way along the eastern coast of Palmis, driving it a long way off course. For a day and a night it pitched among mountainous waves, hail rattling like shot on its hull and decks, lightning playing about its masts, and as the storm began to die back on the morning of the second day a dragon stooped out of the clouds and breathed fire down the length of the ship and with its lashing tail broke the masts and smashed and swept away the smokestacks.

It was a relative of the dragon that Tantris had killed to gain favour in the court of Isander's father – some say that it was the dragon's daughter, grown more monstrous and more powerful than her mother. The ironclad's guns couldn't drive her off. She made pass after pass, and soon the ship was on fire from bow to stern and beginning to sink, its rudder gone and its hull badly holed. All hands took to the lifeboats. Most were lost as the dragon picked off the boats one after the other, but Isander and Tantris managed to make landfall, and escaped into the forest that ran down to the shore.

And that's where they lived together for three years, the girl told me. They built a cabin in a clearing where a grandmother tree had recently fallen. Tantris hunted in the forest and fished in a nearby river. Isander tended her garden and collected wild herbs. One day, while searching for a certain rare plant in the forest, she heard horses approaching and managed to hide just before a company of soldiers rode past, carrying shields with the armorial bearings of King Marsche. She tracked them through the trees, and when she reached the edge of the clearing saw that Tantris had already surrendered and was deep in conversation with their captain.

That was as far as she had read, the girl said. Before she could go any further she had to decide what Isander had to do next.

'She should kill the soldiers,' I said. 'Free Tantris and escape with him deeper into the forest.'

'There are too many soldiers. And they are armed and she isn't.'

'But she has an advantage. Think about it.'

'You mean her potions.'

'Exactly. She could surrender to the soldiers, invite them to eat before they return, and poison their food.'

'But then she would have killed innocent people for a selfish reason,' the girl said. 'And in this kind of story something like that always comes back to hurt you.'

'So what do you suggest, Princess?'

'In the opera I told you about? All of this happens before Isander and Tantris arrive at the court of King Marsche and the story really begins. Well, not the part where the dragon attacks the ship, or the part about living in the forest. Instead, Isander marries the king and sneaks around with Tantris behind the king's back. The courtiers keep trying to catch them out, and eventually their tricks drive Tantris mad and he flees to his castle. The king sends a messenger to tell him that he's forgiven, but Tantris thinks the messenger has come to kill him. They fight, and Tantris is badly wounded. Isander comes to heal him, but she's too late. He dies of his wounds, and she dies of grief.'

'So it doesn't really work out.'

'The point is, it's the story of a great romance. A love that survives impossible odds. That survives death, even.'

'I guess you think that Isander should surrender. Go to the court of this king, let fate take its course.'

'And I suppose you have a better idea.'

'If Tantris really loved her, he would have fought those soldiers. Instead, because he surrenders without a fight, she realises that the potion must have worn off. That he really loves the king more than he loves her.'

'That's not bad,' the girl said. 'But what does she do about it?'

'She also realises that if Tantris's love for her is false, then her love for him must also be false. I can tell you why, too.'

'All right. Why?'

'Before those soldiers turned up, Isander and Tantris had been living together for three years. They'd built a home and settled down. They had an idyllic little life. But they didn't have any children.'

'It isn't that kind of story,' the girl said.

'It isn't the story that doesn't allow them to have children. It's Isander. She knows all about medicine and herbs. She knows how to cook up a potion that will prevent her from becoming pregnant, and that's just what she did. Because, deep down, she knows that the love she and Tantris have for each other isn't real . . . Why are you looking at me like that?'

The girl's smile glimmered in the dim light of the wheelhouse. 'Nothing. Just a passing thought. It doesn't matter.'

'What happened between Keever Bishop and me, it wasn't anything like your story. And I definitely didn't intend to get pregnant. It was a stupid mistake. An accident.'

'Is that why you ran away? Because you didn't want him to find out?'

'If I told you that was why we ended up here, would you feel better about it? Would you be sympathetic?'

'I don't think you want anyone's sympathy.'

'I'll tell you one thing I have in common with the princess in your story. Both of us know that we don't need a man. Isander must have learnt about hunting and fishing from Tantris. And she knows how to grow plants for food, and how to find useful plants in the forest. She can look after herself. So instead of surrendering to those soldiers or rescuing Tantris, she takes off on her own. You told me that in the future, where this story happens, all the ice in Antarctica has melted. That there are new lands, all kinds of strange animals and people. Dragons, wizards, monsters. So why can't Isander have adventures of her own, instead of doing what men want her to do? And in the end, when everyone knows that she's a hero, maybe she can win back Tantris. She frees him from the dungeon where the king has been keeping him, and takes him off into the world so that they can have more adventures.'

The girl thought about that while the little boat heaved and rolled and plunged and spray shot out of the dark and smacked against the window of the wheelhouse. The engine vibrated under the floor. The deck. My bad shoulder and my bad arm hurt from wrestling with the wheel, but there was no way I was going to let the boat drive itself. Mike Mike or the police might hack it, steer it straight to where they were waiting for us.

Eventually, she said, 'That's what you want, isn't it? To escape everything. To have adventures.'

'It's hard to believe, I know, but I'm really the kind of girl who wants a little cottage and a garden. Somewhere quiet and peaceful, far from every sign of people,' I said.

I was still nursing my foolish hopes. If I'd known then what was coming I would have turned the damn boat around and driven it back to Brabant Island and Agustyn Dos Santos Pistario's little hut. Or given it its head, and let it take me where it would. Or found the fucking police and surrendered. But right there and then, sailing through the nightblack sea, I believed that I was doing the right thing.

When the shadow of the mainland appeared ahead of us I realised that I didn't know how to find my way along the coast in the dark, had to briefly switch on the navigation system to get my bearings. Even then, the girl still didn't get where we were going. At last, as we passed the little light shining at Portal Point, I gave in and told her.

'I don't believe you,' she said.

'I told you that we were going to the one place the police wouldn't think of looking for us.'

I didn't put into the harbour below the town. That would have been a recklessly stupid move, even for me. Instead, I headed across the mouth of the bay to the old docks south of Meusnier Point, edging past the foundered hulk of a bulk carrier ship, anchoring in the lee of the wreckage of a huge boom conveyor that reared out of the water like the backbone of a vanquished dragon.

The girl, when I told her that she had to wait below while I made arrangements to get in touch with her father, asked if she could come with me, promised that she'd keep quiet and cause no trouble.

'You know why you can't. It won't take long. A couple of hours at most.'

'Are you really going to talk to him?'

'One way or another, Princess, I'm going to set you free. That's why I came back here instead of heading south.'

It seemed to satisfy her. She gave me the number I could use to contact Alberto Toomy, clambered down into the crew cabin without any fuss. I bolted the hatch and set a couple of net weights on top of it for good measure before I paddled ashore in the life raft. I guess you could say that I had trust issues too.

25

The gash in my leg jabbed me at every other step as I hiked along the shoreside service road, the dog bite on my arm and the knife cut in my shoulder throbbed at different rhythms, but otherwise I felt pretty good. It was a cold clear night, the air zesty with the salt spray of waves slapping the breakwater, the moon's skinny crescent tilted above the high ridge that curved around the bay, painting blue shadows on snowy crests. After a little while, I caught myself whistling some old childhood tune. Why not? I'd escaped from the True Citizens and Mike Mike's crew, there were no signs of police drones or patrols, and I was on my way to ask an old family friend for a little help.

Quite soon, the wreckage of one of the big geoengineering projects from the last century loomed out of the moonlit dark. A tank farm, concrete bunkers, a bouquet of radar dishes, and three colossal rail-guided launch tracks aimed out to sea, concrete blast pads reared up behind them like the gravestones of giants. A little further on, I saw that the launch control tower had burned down and one end of the payload assembly building had collapsed, presumably wrecked by storms in the years since Mama and I had passed through Charlotte Bay.

I remembered sitting at a window in the apartment where we'd been stashed by our host, looking out at these ruins while Mama told me that the project hadn't failed because its science and engineering were unsound, but because it was too big and expensive, had been started too late, and had taken too long to show any results. The people who'd designed it had been thinking in terms of a century or more, she said, but the politicians who'd had to approve the enormous costs couldn't see any further than the next election cycle. If the planet had been run by a world government able to ruthlessly mobilise people and resources, global warming and climate change might have been reversed. Instead, efforts to fix them had been doomed by the same short-sightedness and competing national interests and jealousies which had delayed attempts to cut the amounts of carbon dioxide and other greenhouse gases pumped into the atmosphere, the same compromises and half-measures which had shut down the work of ecopoets and driven them into exile. We're going to leave all of that behind, Mama had told me. We're going to find a better way of living.

It wasn't Mama's fault that her plans had turned out to be as futile as any of those old geoengineering projects. I mean, we'd almost made it. It was just rotten bad luck she'd fallen ill on the last stretch. As I walked through those ruins I believed things would be different this time. That I still had a good chance of reaching New Zealand and making a new life there, with you.

The service road joined a two-lane highway that ran past the town's seafood processing plant, its loading bays lit up, white steam feathering from a tall aluminium chimney. Beyond it, the lights of Charlotte Bay sprawled across the slope rising above the harbour. I climbed a steep street, passing shuttered industrial units, empty lots colonised by fireweed, blighted half-empty or abandoned apartment buildings. The place hadn't much changed since Mama and I had briefly stayed there, but back then I'd been a kid who'd grown up on an island where there were no build-ings with a third storey, and I'd thought that Charlotte Bay was a glittering metropolis.

The bar where Mama and I had first met up with her friend was further back from the harbour than I remembered, tucked into the ground floor of a low-rise apartment block. No sign, just a frontage of ribbed black resin under the overhang of a walkway, the small red light over the door barely bright enough to read the liquor licence posted there.

It was a little after midnight, but the joint was still busy. It was a little like walking into a den of shaved, beautifully ugly bears, because everyone in the place – the bartender, people watching a screen showing horse racing in Christchurch, a scattering of singletons and couples, including two young guys who were getting into some serious personal pornography in a dark corner – was a husky. It was strange, being among my people again. It almost felt like coming home.

I'd like to say that the brief hush that fell when I entered was down to my notoriety or commanding presence, but most likely it was because I was a stranger in a town short on strangers, a vagrant dressed in a filthy uniform and salt-stained windproof. Doing my best to ignore a variety of stares and comments, I went up to the bar, with its heavy mesh screen and slot where drinks were served, and told the guy behind it I wanted to talk to Alicia Whangapirita.

'I don't know her.'

'I think you do – her name's on the liquor licence. Tell her that Aury's daughter wants to meet up. I'll take a glass of tea, black, plenty of sugar, while I'm waiting for her. And what are you serving by way of food?'

I was working my way through a big plate of fried squid doused in vinegar when a young woman and a pair of young men, all three of them huskies in civilian clothes, banged through the door. They crossed the bar in a flanking move, the two bravos moving either side of my table and the woman standing just out of reach, telling me that I was coming with her.

I looked her up and down, taking my time, trying to seem cool and unflustered. I knew that she and her friends weren't plain-clothes state police because the state police didn't employ huskies, but it was possible that Alicia had ratted me out to some kind of local militia.

'And why should I do anything you ask?' I said.

'For one thing, I run this place,' the woman said.

She was about my age and my height, as seriously muscled as Paz. Dusty brown skin, ebony hair in glistening ringlets. A crude black-ink tattoo, a skull with roses sprawling from its eye sockets was half-hidden by the collar of her sealskin jacket.

'I came here to talk with the owner, not her hireling,' I said.

'And I want you to come with me,' the woman said. 'Do I have to tell you there are two ways we can do this?'

After the bar's cosy fug, the freezing black air was like a dash of water in my face. I was hustled to a runabout, told to spreadeagle against it. The woman patted me down quickly and thoroughly, taking Noah's pistol, finding Levi's little glass knife tucked in my jacket pocket, then locked a bracelet around my wrist to block the fone that had already been blocked. When I pointed this out, the woman shrugged and told me to get in the runabout.

'This isn't exactly the kind of reception I had in mind,' I said, 'when I decided to pay a visit to an old friend.'

'What makes you think you have any friends here?' the woman said. 'Just get in the damn car.'

I got in the damn car. The four of us made a close fit. As it drove us across town, I asked the bravos if any of them remembered me.

'Last time I was here, I hung out with a gang of kids about my age. They showed me the secret places they had in the ruins of that old project, their hideouts and such. We had some fine fun.'

The woman, jammed beside me in the rear seat, said it must have been before her time.

'Twelve years ago, give or take. The town hasn't changed that much, from what I can see. Though it seems smaller, somehow.'

'It isn't like Esperanza, if that's what you mean.'

'Did Alicia tell you I used to live in Esperanza? How is she, by the way?'

'We aren't here to answer questions,' the woman said. 'We're here to keep you from causing any more trouble.'

The runabout pulled up outside a ruined apartment building at the north-western edge of town, part of a cluster of long low blocks built more than seventy years before to house people working on the old climate engineering project. Its face was covered in a mesh of scaffolding and the windows of its apartments were black and empty, but its lobby was lit up like Christmas. It was exactly the kind of place where small-town vigilantes dealt out summary justice to troublesome strangers, and I confess that I felt a scrape of apprehension as I was hustled towards it.

Clean orange and yellow walls inside, the smell of fresh paint thick in the warm air, and Alicia Whangapirita, imagine my relief when I saw her, sitting on a stool among folded drop cloths and paint cartons. An honour guard of cheap plastic droids stood motionless on tripod legs behind her, painting wands aimed at the floor.

She ignored my attempt at a breezy greeting, long time no see, so on, saying, 'The state police are looking for you after that gunfight down at the harbour. You and the girl you kidnapped.'

She was a tall woman with a square handsome face, her hair cut a lot shorter than I remembered, and turned snow-white. A dozen or more necklaces, stone beads, glass beads, woven wire, fine silver chains, overlapped on the breast of her pale blue sweater. Gifts from the kids she'd helped out over the years.

When I started to explain that it wasn't exactly what you could call a kidnapping she gave me a severe look that reminded me of the times I'd been called up in front of the orphanage's manager. 'You stole one of Sunny Pang's boats. And burned the other to the waterline.'

'The one I borrowed, I brought it back. The other, that was down to the people who were trying to catch me.'

I know, I know. It wasn't exactly true. But if they hadn't been chasing me, I wouldn't have had to set fire to the other boat. And how I was thinking, Mr Pang would have a better chance of winning compensation from Keever Bishop than from me.

'A day later,' Alicia said implacably, 'you put out a call for me on the skywave net. Which the police could have overheard. Which could have put me right in the middle of your hot mess.'

'I couldn't think how else to find out if you were still living here.'

'And then you came back here, and put yourself on display in my bar.'

'Because I thought I might find you there. And I kind of did,' I said, with a smile that Alicia didn't return.

'This town is home to more than two thousand decent, hard-working people,' she said. 'Many of them former ecopoets. We were dumped here after the amnesty and we've done our best to make a go of it. We built up the fishing industry. We take in husky children who have nowhere else to go. We just won a grant to renovate disused buildings and generally spruce up the place. And your criminal foolishness could undo all of it.'

'If I made a mistake coming here, let me go on my way. You won't hear from me again.'

'Do you know why I decided to have this conversation?' Alicia said. 'It doesn't have anything to do with you, or the help I gave your mother that one time, or my friendship with your grand-mother. It's about making sure that you do the right thing, right now, and let that girl go.'

'Well, that's partly why I came here. Because I really do want to get her back to her father.'

'You don't need my help with that. All you have to do is surrender to the police.'

'If you let me explain how it all happened, you'll see that it isn't quite that simple.'

Alicia gave me another hard look, then said, 'I'll give you five minutes. For the memory of your mother.'

It took a little longer than that to explain about Keever Bishop, his escape plans and his involvement with Alberto Toomy. How Alberto may have been planning to welch on their so-called busi-ness arrangement, which was why Keever wanted to kidnap his daughter, why I'd been ordered to embarrass him at the ribbon-cutting ceremony.

'Keever knew there was bad blood between my family and the Toomys,' I said. 'He wanted me to confront Alberto and cause some kind of diversion. But I didn't do what I was told. I didn't go anywhere near Alberto because I was too busy rescuing his daughter from Keever's bravos.'

'You didn't rescue her,' Alicia said. 'You kidnapped her.'

'It didn't start out that way, but I guess that's what it turned into. I got the idea that I could get money to buy passage off the peninsula. Not even very much money, as far as Alberto Toomy is concerned.'

'And you thought I would help you with this mad scheme?' Alicia said. 'Because I once helped you and your mother? Child, you're either terribly naive or seriously deluded.'

'Here's why you should,' I said. 'You have two sons, both of them huskies. I remember playing with them when I was last here. Your bar, everyone in there was a husky. And you told me that you've been taking in husky kids, too. Some of them, I bet, from state orphanages. The woman standing behind me, I know she's done time in one. That tattoo on her neck, the skull with roses growing out of its eye sockets? Some of the older kids in the state orphanage I was sent to after my mother died, they gave each other tattoos like that. They used squid ink they stole from the aquaculture stacks.'

There was a small silence. The leather jacket of the woman at my back creaked as she shifted her stance.

Alicia said, 'I tried to help you after your mother died. I made an application to foster you, but it was refused. As were my requests to visit you. I tried again to reach out to you when you left the orphanage, but you never replied.'

'I know I shouldn't have ignored you,' I said, 'but I was young and stupid. I thought that I could look after myself.'

'But here you are now,' Alicia said.

'The point I'm trying to make, it isn't about me,' I said, although I had been hoping to work the guilt angle, win Alicia's sympathy by reminding her of my sad, bad childhood. 'It's that there are plenty of huskies living here, and I don't suppose they're treated like second-class citizens. But thanks to people like Alberto Toomy, it isn't like that everywhere else. He's one of the National Unity Party's honourable deputies. One of the scunners who voted against lifting travel restrictions for us. Voted for compulsory sterilisation, too. But if you can find a way of letting the world know what I told you, that he was tight with a major criminal, it will do serious damage to his reputation and his party. And that will definitely help the husky community.'

'Do you have any proof of this?' Alicia said.

'There must be evidence of that meeting at Kilometre 200. Witnesses, surveillance footage. And if you let me talk to Alberto, negotiate terms about giving his daughter back, I'm pretty sure I can get him to tell me about it.'

The woman in the leather jacket said, 'I was in the state orphanage in O'Higgins for a couple of years. You got that right.

But you know what? I didn't become a criminal. Most of us didn't. But you, kidnapping that poor girl, coming here making excuses for yourself, implying that it was your rotten childhood made you do it, claiming you can use it, somehow, to improve the lot of huskies? *Dio mios*! Don't you know what the haters are saying about you? They're using it as proof that they were right all along. That we're low-life freaks. Monsters. You've become the poster girl for every kind of intolerance and prejudice. And you talk about helping our community?'

'I made some mistakes,' I said. 'I admit that. Absolutely. I made some bad choices. But I came here to make it right.'

'You want to make it right? All you have to do is turn yourself in to the police,' the woman said. 'Shit, I'll take you there myself.'

Alicia said, 'It doesn't matter what Alberto Toomy may or may not have done. The best way we can help you, the only way, is by ending this foolishness and making sure that his daughter is safely returned to him.'

'If you won't co-operate,' leather-jacket woman said, 'I'll go find the girl. She can't be far away. Still on that stolen boat, most likely.'

I couldn't meet their gazes. I knew that they had it right about the girl, but I also felt cornered, felt that no one wanted to hear my side of the story. And so, for exactly the same reason I'd told Levi, driven to it by the same hopeless desperation, I played my last card.

'There's something else you should know,' I said. 'The reason I had to run off from the work camp, my job, everything else, I'm pregnant. And Keever Bishop is the father.'

Alicia had one of the young men fetch tea, asked the other to bring me a chair. The atmosphere had changed. I was no longer a prisoner, up before a kangaroo court. I was a guest, although not exactly a welcome one.

Trying to ignore the scornful stare of leather-jacket woman, I told Alicia about you, why I was certain that Keever was your father, why I didn't ever want him to know about you, why I'd be in bad trouble if the prison authorities found out, where I wanted to go.

At the end, Alicia set down her teacup and gave me a serious look. 'You still have to do the right thing by the girl.'

'As soon as her father pays what I'm owed.'

'I'm not convinced that he owes you anything,' Alicia said. 'And if he refuses to pay the ransom, if he refuses to even talk to you, you'll still have to let her go. Agree to that right now or you'll leave me no choice, I'll have to hand you over to the police.'

'I swear I'm not going to harm her, whatever happens. But I think he'll pay. Not just because of the girl, but because he'll want to buy my silence, too.'

'Because of his supposed connection with Keever Bishop.'

'I don't want much from him. Just enough to pay people smugglers to get me to New Zealand. Pocket money, as far as he's concerned. And I don't want much from you either. Just a little help to get me to Square Bay.'

'And how will I do that?'

'Remember the lift you gave my mother and me all those years ago?'

26

Alicia and I were working on our second brew of tea when a teenage girl delivered a handful of brand-new disposable fones, the kind I'd smuggled across the wire for Keever. Before she let me use one, Alicia made me promise all over again that I would never ever mention that she'd helped me. Leather-jacket woman said my word was useless, I'd start squealing the moment I was arrested, which was bound to happen sooner rather than later, but I ignored her, swore on Mama's grave that as far as I was concerned I'd never met Alicia, let alone talked to her, swore that one way or another the girl would be set free by the end of the day.

'If she isn't,' Alicia said, 'we'll call the police ourselves.'

'If this crashes and burns, the girl will still get back with her father,' I said. 'But if it comes right, he'll be taken down for aiding and abetting a notorious criminal. And then everything else he's involved in will come out.'

'As if people like him are ever punished for what they do,' leather-jacket woman said.

She had a point, but I wasn't about to tell her that.

'I'm going to give the girl back to her daddy,' I said to Alicia, 'and give her daddy to the cops. And you'll never see or hear from me again.'

'All I ask is that you don't try to be clever,' Alicia said, and handed me one of the fones.

I made a voice-only call to the number the girl had given me and a woman answered at once, saying that she was very glad that I had decided to do the right thing and make contact, telling me that her name was Sabrina Maxwell Bullrich, she was here to help.

'We're very concerned about you and Kamilah, Austral. Especially after that unpleasantness at Charlotte Bay.'

'There's no need to worry about the girl,' I said. 'The girl is fine.'

'May I speak with her?'

'Maybe you could tell me who you are first.'

'Kamilah's father has an insurance policy that covers situations like this. I've been hired by the insurance company to speak with you on his behalf.'

'So you aren't police.'

'I have nothing to do with law enforcement, Austral. I'm a crisis negotiator, pure and simple. I'm here to help you in any way I can.'

'What about Alberto Toomy? Is he with you?'

'He has been notified that you have made contact, but he isn't a party to our conversation. Nor is anyone else. This is just between you and me.'

'You know what you sound like? Some kind of AI. Not even a very good one.'

I was as twitchy as hell, was already beginning to lose my temper. It felt as if I was being strung along while Sabrina Maxwell Bullrich tracked my fone signal and dispatched a crew to deal with me and rescue the girl.

'Actually, I'm a husky, like you,' the negotiator said. 'Born in the south, raised in Star City.'

'Then you know Five Points. What it is.'

I can't remember if I already told you, that's the name of the bar where I used to hang out with Bryan.

'I know I spent too many nights drinking too much in there when I was a lot younger,' the negotiator said.

'And you know who owns it.'

'Keever Bishop, once upon a time. But he doesn't own it any more. It was confiscated when he was convicted. Could I speak to Kamilah, Austral? It won't take but a moment.'

'I told you. The girl is safe and well.'

'I'm sure she is. But listen – and this is just a silly formality, something to satisfy my bosses. If it isn't possible for me to speak to Kamilah for whatever reason, could you please ask her to give you her safe words.'

'Her safe words?'

'Before we can proceed any further, before I can help you get what you want, I need what's known as proof of life.'

'Is this some kind of trick?'

I was acutely aware that Alicia and the others were watching me, was trying not to show my nerves.

Sabrina Maxwell Bullrich said, 'I'll be frank with you, Austral. The Charlotte Bay police showed us security footage of the shootout. We reviewed it very carefully, and we are concerned that Kamilah may have been injured.'

'I told you. She's okay.'

'We're concerned, Austral, because something appeared to knock her to the ground.'

'It was hardly anything,' I said. 'She was hit by what I think was a ricochet, but her bodysuit protected her. She has a little bruising is all. Apart from that, she's completely fine.'

Alicia looked like a fox that had just spotted a lemming. Very quiet, very still.

I smiled at her, told Sabrina Maxwell Bullrich, 'You can thank me any time you want for saving her from the bad guys.'

'I can arrange medical attention for Kamilah. Whatever you think she needs.'

'I checked her out and like I already told you she's fine,' I said, still smiling at Alicia, ready to make a move if leather-jacket woman tried to snatch the fone.

'Then all I need are her safe words,' the negotiator said. 'It really is no more than a formality. But a necessary one.'

'I'm not trying to scam you, if that's what you think.'

'I don't think anything of the sort. Is Kamilah nearby?'

'I'm not going to tell you where she is.'

'I don't expect you to. Just ask Kamilah to give you her safe words. She'll understand,' Sabrina Maxwell Bullrich said, and hung up.

Alicia immediately wanted to know what was wrong.

'I have to talk to the girl,' I said.

27

When I got back to the boat the girl wanted to know if I'd talked to her father, had we come to an agreement, was I going to let her go, so on, so on.

'Your father is employing some kind of negotiator,' I said, when she'd run out of breath. 'Works for an insurance company. Before I get into the business of returning you to your family, she needs proof that you're alive.'

We were down in the crew cabin, where it was safe to switch on a light or two. Sitting on the edge of bunks facing each other across the narrow aisle as the boat gently rocked on the incoming tide. The air damp, as chilly as the water pressing against the hull. It was five in the morning and I felt grainy and stretched thin, was finding it hard to think straight. The girl, though, was wide awake, saying, 'If that's the only problem, I can speak to her right now. How do we do it? On the radio? Or do you have a fone?'

'What I need are your safe words.'

'My safe words?'

'You better be able to remember them, because if you can't the deal's off. You'll be stuck with me.'

'Of course I remember them,' the girl said.

'And?'

She closed her eyes. Took a breath. 'Foreign penitent periodic beauty.'

'That's it?'

'That's it.'

'This is a crucial part of the deal. So don't even think of trying to spoof me.'

'What good would that do me? Just say the words. Or let me say them. Wouldn't it be better if this woman heard my voice?'

The girl was watching me unwrap a disposable fone. Alicia had insisted on destroying the first in case some kind of trace had been stuck into its tiny mind during my conversation with Sabrina Maxwell Bullrich.

'Best thing you can do is keep your mouth zipped,' I told her. 'I mean it. One word out of turn, I'll lock you down here, have this conversation in the wheelhouse.'

The girl pressed a finger to her lips. There was a shine to her gaze. A hopeful excitement.

'Everything goes right, you'll soon be on your way home,' I said, faking a confidence I didn't feel.

Sabrina Maxwell Bullrich answered at once, asking how I was, was everything all right.

'Don't ever cut me off like that again,' I said.

'I hope it gave you time to gather your thoughts, Austral. Do you have what we need to move forward?'

'If you mean "foreign penitent periodic beauty", then yeah, I do.'

'Good,' Sabrina Maxwell Bullrich said. 'Very good.'

'Now we've got that out of the way, let me talk to Alberto.'

'That wouldn't be a good idea. For all kinds of reasons.'

'His daughter wants to talk to him too,' I said, looking at the girl. 'I know he's listening in. I can practically hear him breathing.'

'As a matter of fact, he isn't. We insist that the client allows us complete autonomy. Now, are you ready to tell me what you want to do?'

'What are you saying?'

'I'm saying, Austral, that you're the one in charge. Not me. Not Kamilah's father. Not anyone else. Only you. So I need to know what you want from us.'

It took me a moment to realise what she meant. I'd been expecting this to play out over an hour or two of back and forth.

I said, 'You mean you're ready to pay the ransom?'

'Of course. In situations like this, we always pay.'

'Just like that.'

'My one and only job is to ensure the safe return of my client's daughter. The best way to do that is to help you get what you want.'

'First, a sum of money. Transferred to an offshore account.'

'If you tell me how much you need, and the details of your account, I'll see what I can do.'

I told her, and Sabrina said at once that she didn't think that it would be a problem.

'Your account will be credited in less than half an hour,' she said. 'Then you can tell us where Kamilah is. You can let her go. We'll do the rest.'

'And tell the police they can start looking for me. I don't think so. Paying the ransom is the first part of the deal. The second part, when you come to collect the girl, I want you to bring Honourable Deputy Alberto Toomy with you. No police, no tricks. Just you and him. We'll meet him, we'll talk, and then I'll take you to his daughter.'

There was some to and fro. Sabrina told me that I was being unreasonable, that Alberto Toomy couldn't possibly agree to my demands, but I refused to give any ground, assured her that the Honourable Deputy wouldn't be in any danger, suggested that she let me speak to him directly, let me ask him was he willing to collect his daughter in person. At last she said that she was going to hang up so that she could discuss my proposal with him, she'd call back in ten minutes.

'It had better be no more than that,' I said, but I was speaking to dead air.

'He won't agree,' the girl said, after I'd told her how it had gone down. 'He doesn't like being told what to do.'

'The negotiator has a honey tongue. She'll convince him. And besides, he'll want to do right by you, and he'll also be wondering if he'll get a chance at being on the spot when the police take me down. Thinking about how it would play on the feeds.'

But the girl wasn't convinced and I caught a little of her anxiety, began to imagine that Sabrina had traced the call and had contacted Charlotte Bay's police, told them to bug out for Meusnier Point. I actually climbed onto the roof of the boat's wheelhouse to look for cruisers and drones, maybe a speedboat racing towards us. The crescent moon was sinking towards the mouth of the bay. Splinters of silvery light gleamed on the dark sweep of water beyond the old docks. Nothing moving out there and nothing moving along the service road either, the ruins stretching quiet and still towards the lights of the town. I must have dozed off for a moment, because I almost dropped the damn fone when Sabrina called back, telling me that Alberto Toomy had agreed to meet me, telling me that the ransom had been transferred.

This time I was the one who rang off, because I needed to check my offshore account. Botching the security checks twice because I was all nerves, going through them very slowly the third time, scared I'd lock myself out. And there it was. The cost of my ticket off the peninsula, no more, no less. I wondered why I didn't feel anything. Maybe it was because the numbers on the fone's screen were just numbers. Maybe I wouldn't feel good about this until it was over, and I was drinking a cocktail (one of those virgin deals, of course, because I'd still be incubating you) in the Wheel's revolving bar.

I called Sabrina, told her where I wanted to meet Alberto Toomy.

'Be there in exactly three hours. That should give you just enough time to get here from Esperanza. If that's where you're calling from.'

'We'll keep our part of the agreement, Austral. And I know you'll keep to yours, but let's stay in touch. If there's anything else you need—'

'Three hours,' I said, and snapped the fone in half and skimmed the pieces over the side of the boat. I broke out another fone and texted Alicia to tell her the deal was on, deep-sixed that one too, and climbed down from the roof of the wheelhouse and told the girl it was time to go.

She hunched into herself on the floor of the life raft as I paddled us ashore, shivering from more than the chill of the water, and when we climbed up to the quayside and she saw the runabout waiting there she stopped dead, demanded to know where I was taking her.

'Not far,' I said. 'Long as you do exactly what I tell you to do, you'll be back in Esperanza before the day is out.'

'Like all your other plans worked out.'

'I got us this far, didn't I?'

'You got us into bad trouble we're still not out of,' the girl said, but began to perk up as the runabout drove us past the moonlit ruins, saying that she knew where we were, this was part of Project LUCI, the Large Unconventional Cooling Initiative.

'I studied it for a school assignment. This was one of the places that shot reusable rocket planes into the stratosphere, where they dumped payloads of diamond dust. There's a boundary between the stratosphere and the lower atmosphere – the place where we live, where weather happens? So the idea was, the dust would stay up there, create a thin layer wrapped around the world. It was supposed to reflect some of the sun's light and heat back into space, like dust from big volcanic eruptions . . . I'm talking too much, aren't I?'

'It sounds like a neat idea. Shame it wasn't given a proper chance. Science rarely survives contact with politics, so on.'

Something Mama had liked to say. Without science and hard work, idealism is just words on the wind – that was another one of hers. Not to mention her all-time classic, reality is all we have.

'It must have been amazing, working on something like this,' the girl said. 'Seeing those rocket planes go up.'

'So what kind of thing will you build when you become an engineer?'

'I don't know yet. I mean, I'm only fourteen.'

'And bright with it. So I'm sure you have some idea.'

She watched the shadowy skeletons of those big launch tracks swing past. 'I think I could learn a lot from the way your people engineered ecosystems from the bottom up. It was another crazy mad big deal like Project LUCI or the Sahara Sea or whatever, but it was cheap, it used intensive labour instead of machines, and it was also about a way of living. I mean, look at you.'

'Being a husky, it isn't a lifestyle.'

When the girl blushed, the dapples on her skin grew darker. 'What I'm trying to say, you weren't ever part of the greening work, but it's still a big chunk of who you are.'

'It runs in the family. My side of the family. For all the good it did.'

'There's all this dead tech,' the girl said. 'And there are the forests we walked through. Which has lasted?'

She said that the ecopoet refuges were really a single settlement distributed down the length of the peninsula. She talked about clusters of connected villages. She talked about low impact cities that blended into the landscape. Managed wildernesses, submerged infrastructure, so on. She was nervous but she was also happy. She knew that she was close to the end of her ordeal. She knew that she was going home.

As for me, if I was lucky, if things worked out, I'd get to live like a fugitive for the rest of my natural born. It was what Mama had been aiming at when we escaped from Deception Island, our long walk towards it had been the highlight of my dumb little life, but I wasn't a kid any more. I knew how hard it was going to be. And then there was you.

And then there was you.

You know how you know you've grown up? When you begin to worry about the future, because you know things will be different there. That isn't one of Mama's, by the way. It's all mine.

The runabout followed the road past the seafood processing plant and trundled uphill and halted outside one of the derelict apartment blocks. I took the girl's arm in a gentle grip and led her into the ruined foyer and up a flight of stairs to a dismal corridor lit by stark strip lights, and a stuffy overheated two-room apartment like the one Mama and I had stayed in, back when.

The girl didn't like the droid that stood outside the door like a CO outside a cell. And didn't like it when I told her that I was going to leave her in the apartment until I'd had my little talk with her father.

'You think you've won, don't you?' she said. 'You think you'll get away. But you won't. People like you never do.'

Then her little flare of anger winked out as suddenly as it had appeared and she apologised and said that she didn't mean it.

'Of course you did,' I said. 'Remember what I said about the princess? Did you try pushing the story in that direction?'

She nodded. 'While I was waiting for you to come back.'

'How's it working out?'

'Isander found some people on the far side of the forest. They weren't friendly at first, but then she cured a sick child.'

'It's the beginning of a glorious adventure. You'll see.'

'What about you?'

'What about me?'

'Will you be all right?'

'I'm a monster, remember? Monsters can take care of themselves.'

'Until they run into a hero.'

'If I see anyone looking even the faintest bit heroic coming towards me you can bet I'll hightail it in the other direction.'

'So this is what? Goodbye?'

'You'll be back with your father in a couple of hours and I have places to go, people to meet. So yeah, this is goodbye. You take care, Kamilah. Build those cities. Do good. Don't make any of the dumb choices I've made, or I swear I'll come back to haunt you.'

I wanted to hug her, but she had started to cry, and turned away from me because she was ashamed of her tears. So I hardened my heart, told her that there was no point trying to escape and locked the door behind me and went up to the roof, where it was just possible to make out the dim shape of a cargo drone squatting on the other side of a fenced children's playground. Alicia had kept her word. Until that moment I hadn't been sure that she would.

It was the smallest model of cargo drone. Truck-sized, pods shaped like old-fashioned bullets bookending the slot of its empty cargo bay, two pairs of tilt rotors on stubby wings. It sort of reminded me of a pair of mating dragonflies locked together tail to tail, and looked about as fragile.

After I squeezed into the cramped windowless passenger pod and dogged the hatch, the drone shivered itself awake and took off vertically. I unrolled the last of the disposable fones and synched it to the drone's external cameras and watched the shadows of the apartment building and the ruins of Project LUCI fall away into the night. Then the view swung around, the hum of the drone's rotors deepened, and its nose pitched down and it drove south, towards Square Bay.

28

A little over an hour into the flight the fone flashed an alert – a live feed showing a two-seater heli squatting in grey pre-dawn light near the wreck of Project LUCI's payload assembly building. I zoomed in as a man in a blond full-length fur coat climbed out of one side of the heli's bubble cabin and a husky woman, she had to be the negotiator, Sabrina Maxwell Bullrich, climbed out of the other. Dressed in cold weather gear overstrapped with equipment, she headed towards the runabout parked nearby, walking around it, raising one of its doors and bending to look inside.

The feed came from the droid I'd parked under a slant of fallen roofing. I told the machine to start walking, aiming it towards the heli and its passengers. They were dumb and cheap, the droids. Alicia's work crews donated to the community any which began to throw glitches, and kids used them to stage terminator duels. You can guess the kind of mayhem. Alicia called it acting out, said it was better that they smashed up a few disposable machines than each other.

Anyway, the droid I was steering was one of Alicia's rejects. One of her people had talked me through the steps to link it to the fone, so that if I was caught I could explain how I'd stolen it from the town's sports centre. It had a bad limp and had lost gross motor control in both arms, but its cameras and voice-link were working fine, and that was all I needed.

'Did you really think I'd surrender to you?' I said, hearing the tinny echo of my words as the droid relayed them.

Alberto Toomy was on it in three strides, his face filling its field of vision like an angry moon. 'Where is she? Where is my daughter?'

'I'll lead you to her after we've had our little chat.'

'Talk then,' Alberto said. 'Try to justify what you've done.'

'There's no way I can,' I said. 'And that isn't what this is about.'

I was lying in that cramped throbbing compartment some-where high above the Bruce Plateau, squinting at the fone's dinky screen, and I was confronting my uncle face to face, and both were equally real.

Alberto Toomy stepped back and I saw that Sabrina Maxwell Bullrich had come up behind him. She said, 'Honourable Deputy Toomy has done everything you asked, Austral. Now it's your turn.'

'Kamilah is hurt,' Alberto Toomy said. 'She needs medical atten-tion. She needs to come home. I'll listen to whatever you have to say to me. If you have a grievance I'll do my best to help. But please, for my daughter's sake, let's wind up this conversation as quickly as possible.'

He stood stern and straight-backed in his long honey-coloured coat, arms folded across his chest, sleek black hair artfully dis-ordered. The very picture of a distressed and exhausted father bravely challenging his daughter's kidnapper. He knew that I would be recording this, and I had no doubt that he was recording it too.

'What it's about,' I said, 'is Keever Bishop.'

Alberto Toomy pretended to think for a moment. 'Your accom-plice. The man who organised the escape from the work camp.'

'Who also sent three people to kidnap your daughter during the ribbon-cutting ceremony. Her bodyguard managed to shoot two of them before the third, Lola Contreras, knocked him out. She would have taken Kamilah, but I stopped her. But I bet you know all about that, don't you? Lola must have confessed every-thing to the authorities, and they would have told you.'

'You're claiming that you rescued my daughter?'

'From Keever Bishop,' I said. 'Who had a very particular reason for wanting to get hold of her.'

Alberto ignored that, saying, 'But you didn't rescue Kamilah, did you? You were also working for this Keever Bishop. Lola Contreras and several other correctional officers have given sworn statements that not only were you smuggling contraband into the work camp for him, but you were also his lover.'

253

'I quit working for him the moment I realised he wanted to snatch your daughter,' I said. 'I stepped in and saved her from his bravos. And after that, yeah, I took off from the work camp and brought her along with me. I had to get as far away from Keever Bishop as possible, and I thought that I could use her to get the price of a ticket off the peninsula.'

'Then you admit that you kidnapped her,' Alberto said, and Sabrina put a hand on his arm. Warning him, perhaps, that he was going off script.

'I don't deny it. It should have been a simple trade, but things blew up when a crew working for Keever tried to take her back. Up on the Detroit Plateau the first time, and then in Charlotte Bay. I believe you met one of them when you visited Keever in the work camp,' I said, working around to what I wanted to get out in the open. 'A man called Mike Mike. That's his jail handle. In the world he's Michael Michelakis.'

'I don't know anyone by either of those names.'

'But he knows you. And he knows about your business relationship with Keever Bishop. He told me all about it after I took down two of his bravos.'

Alberto Toomy raised his eyebrows in a theatrical display of bafflement. 'I don't have the faintest idea what you're talking about.'

Neither did I, exactly. Although Mike Mike had mentioned that Keever had something going with Alberto Toomy, he hadn't given any details. But there was nothing to stop me taking a big fucking guess, and that's what I did, putting it out there, hoping to needle my uncle into revealing something, hoping that maybe, just maybe, the police, the news feeds or anyone else who saw the recording of this conversation would follow it up. I wasn't doing it for myself, for revenge or whatever. Really I wasn't. I wanted to pay off my debt to Alicia by causing trouble for one of the enemies of the husky people.

I said, 'You were supposed to help Keever Bishop avoid extradition to Australia. And when that fell through, you were supposed to help with his escape from the work camp. Mike Mike told me that Keever was planning to use your daughter as leverage. To make sure that you wouldn't try to wriggle out of the deal.'

Like I said, I didn't have much in the way of proof, but you have to admit that it was a nice little story. And as luck would have it, it turned out to be mostly true, although at the time there was no way of telling from Alberto's stony expression that I'd hit close to the mark.

'If you believe anything some no-account career criminal told you,' he said, 'you're a bigger fool than I thought.'

'It isn't just Mike Mike. Your daughter told me that you talked to Keever a couple of hours before he escaped from the work camp.'

'How could she know such a thing?'

'Oh, that's right. You left her at the lunch in the commandant's quarters while you and Keever discussed your mutual business interests.'

'There was no meeting. I inspected one of the blocks. I talked to a number of prisoners. If you're trying to get me in trouble, I'm afraid that these wild ravings won't do it.'

'Because no one will believe a husky?'

'Because you're a criminal.'

'I'm also your niece. And crime runs in the family, doesn't it? Your father was involved with drug dealers, gun runners. He started his business empire with money he stole from them.'

'It isn't a secret that we are related. And it's well known that my father liked to tell colourful tales that had only a glancing relation to the truth.'

'Did he tell colourful tales about how he betrayed my grandmother and their son? His firstborn child. My father. My mother tried to talk to you about it, but you refused to listen. And you refused to help her, too.'

'I'm afraid that you have that the wrong way round. Your mother didn't try to talk to me. I tried to talk to her. I reached out to her several times, but she refused to accept my offers of help.'

'You're lying.'

'I have copies of our correspondence, such as it is. And the authorities will have copies too, because they monitored all communications to the ecopoets exiled on Deception Island. I'm sorry, Austral. I truly am. Because if this is about trying to get some kind of revenge because you blame me for how your life turned out, you should know that your mother made it very clear that she didn't want to have anything to do with me, and didn't want me to have anything to do with you, either. And if she told you differently, well, I'm sure she had her reasons.'

You could have rendered down Alberto Toomy's oleaginous smile and deep-fried a whale in it.

'I was in a state orphanage for six years,' I said. 'Why didn't you help me then?'

'Perhaps I should have reached out to you. I admit that. But your mother had consistently refused my help, I was starting out in politics and your side of the family had already caused me embarrassment, and I confess that I took bad advice. But now I have to wonder,' Alberto Toomy said, 'why you didn't reach out to me. Was it because of the stories your mother told about my father? The resentment and anger she felt towards him, which you obviously feel as well? All I ask now is that you don't make Kamilah suffer for it. Whatever bad blood there is between us, let it end here.'

I didn't believe a word of it, but it was a devilishly cunning piece of spin.

'Your daughter's a fine brave kid.' I said. 'Her father may be a rotten excuse for a politician, but she's on the square.'

'I'm not a criminal, Austral. And I don't associate with criminals.'

'Keever Bishop would disagree.'

There was that smile again. 'Mr Bishop appears to have escaped from the peninsula. I doubt that we'll be hearing from him any time soon.'

'And I guess you think that no one will believe anything someone like him says about someone like you. An honourable deputy. The Shadow Minister of Justice. Heir to a fortune, so on. But if you think you're going to get away with this, think again. Keever prefers a hands-on approach when he's dealing with people who've upset him. And because he isn't the kind of man who forgives or forgets, he's going to catch up with you sooner or later.'

'Now you're threatening me.'

'Did Keever ever tell you the story about the moray eels? You should give serious thought to beefing up your security, Uncle.'

'Fortunately, I have done nothing that needs to be forgiven. Apart, perhaps, from failing to reach out to you after your mother died. And now we've had our little conversation, it's time you honoured our agreement and told me where Kamilah is.'

Well, he was right about that. I'd put everything I knew about my uncle's involvement with Keever Bishop on the record, for all the good it would do, and now I had to do the right thing by the girl.

I told Alberto Toomy and Sabrina Maxwell Bullrich to get in the runabout, and it drove them through the ruins of Project LUCI to the abandoned apartment building. A second droid was waiting on the steps to the entrance, and I used its rear-facing camera to watch them follow it through the ruin of the lobby.

There's this saying, ghosts in the staircase kind of thing, about coming up with a killer exit line too late, when you're already walking away from some kind of humiliation. This sort of felt like that, except I hadn't walked away from it yet, was trying and failing to come up with something cute while steering the droid that was leading them up the stairs, and now down the dingy hall.

'In my experience? Things catch up with people sooner or later,' I said. 'I don't just mean Keever Bishop. There's our family history, too. All the miseries our parents and grandparents handed down. I plan to get away from all that and start over. And I hope that Kamilah finds a way of getting out too. But you, Uncle, it made you what you are. You can't ever escape it.'

Alberto Toomy didn't reply to that, simply gave the droid a patient, weary look. As far as he was concerned this was almost over, so anything I said was irrelevant. And then Kamilah, she must have heard us coming, was shouting behind the closed door, and her father pushed past the droid and rattled the door, kicked it, calling her name.

Sabrina turned to the droid. 'You have to unlock it, Austral.'

But the damn key was in my pocket and I was flying south inside the cargo drone, so all I could do was watch as Sabrina told Kamilah to stand well back from the door, squaring up to it and rearing back and kicking it under the lock. It slammed open and Kamilah was there.

Her father reached for her and she slapped him hard and burst into tears, and that was all I saw, because Sabrina shut the damn droid down.

29

So there I was, free and clear and all alone, riding in a cargo drone above the icy spine of the peninsula. I was fried by sleep lack, the compartment was freezing cold and too small to stretch out in, and the stupid gash in my leg had begun to bleed again, but it was only a minor wound, I was built for the cold, it wasn't a problem, and I was too jacked to sleep. I made myself as comfortable as possible, curled up on thin padding, brooding on Alberto Toomy's claim that he'd tried to help Mama and me back when we'd been exiled on Deception Island.

After looking at it from every direction I couldn't see how it wasn't a lie. Mama had blamed the Toomys for our family's misfortunes, and if any one of them had tried to give her charity she would have told me all about it, used her refusal as a lesson. Don't give in to them, Austral. Remember who you are. So on. As for Alberto Toomy's suggestion that I should have asked him for help when Mama died . . . Fuck that noise. I had been twelve years old back then, hurt and confused and lost. Even if I'd wanted to, I wouldn't have known how to reach out to anyone. Especially to people who had shown in the worst way that they couldn't be trusted.

The more I thought about it, the angrier I became. At Alberto Toomy. And at myself, for not realising exactly what kind of a slippery son-of-a-bitch he was, for not realising that people like him would know how to deflect every kind of accusation, pull jujitsu moves that put the blame on their accusers. Then, like a fire burning to ashes, my anger turned to self-pity. It was obvious, I thought bitterly, that Alberto Toomy hadn't been in any way interested in my stupid little life. He hadn't even known that I was working as a CO at the work camp. Or if he had, he hadn't given me a moment's thought. And then there was all the rest, dismissal of my rescue of Kamilah, accusations about how I'd treated her . . .

I hoped that some of the shit I'd thrown at him would stick. And if it didn't, I told myself, it wouldn't matter. I was leaving all that behind. All the bad history. All the bitterness. I was going to start over, and you were my shot at redemption. I would give you the kind of life Mama and I had been hoping to make for ourselves after we escaped from Deception Island. That dream had skipped a generation, was all. Meanwhile, I had to let my anger and self-hate go. Leave it all behind, Austral. Watch the damn view and look to the future.

I was already further south than I'd ever been before. The sun was coming up and the Bruce Plateau was unreeling below, a rumpled expanse of ice dotted with blue meltwater lakes, dark shadows of glacial valleys scooped into its western flank. A snowy mountain top drifted past. Slessor Peak, still half-buried in ice despite the great melting. Soon afterwards I crossed the Antarctic Circle and was flying above the Avery Plateau, and at last the drone made a wide circle, the camera feed flaring with dawn light, and began to descend towards Square Bay and my rendezvous with the people smugglers.

It was the site of another old failed ecoengineering project. Once upon a time, kelp had been harvested from farms in the bay and nearby fjords and processed into hectares of tough thermally reflective material that was flown south to the mainland and spread across glaciers that flowed into the Western Antarctic Ice Sheet. More than half of that ice sheet had been lost by then, undermined by warming sea currents. Wrapping the glaciers had been part of a desperate attempt to minimise and manage the retreat of what was left. The project had been abandoned after much of the ice had been lost in a series of catastrophic collapses, but there were still kelp farms in Square Bay. Smart fabrics spun from their biomass were exported all over the world, and fish caught off the coast were flown to Esperanza and O'Higgins.

The cargo drone skimmed above ridges of bare rock. I saw rugged islands scattered across blue sea off to the west, an industrial park, and the huge airfield which had serviced the old project. And then the drone was dropping towards a corner of the airfield, kissing the ground with delicate precision, the roar of its rotors winding down to silence.

When I cracked the hatch a frigid blast of air washed over me. Minus twenty-five degrees Celsius, clean and heady as a shot of aquavit. Hectares of white concrete, glass and steel administration buildings on one side, hangars and several big airships in blue and white livery and ranks of cargo drones on the other. A distant view of slopes of black rock striped with snow. Everything pin-sharp in the new light of the new day, realer than real, heightened by my eager anticipation. Extracting myself from the cramped compartment, taking my first tentative footsteps in this clean cold fresh world, was like a rebirth.

First thing I wanted to do was find a café or diner, celebrate my freedom with the biggest breakfast I could buy. I started to walk towards the distant glitter of the administration buildings and a vehicle cut away from one of the hangars, a boxy all-terrain tractor painted shocking orange, beetling towards me on two pairs of triangular tracks, big windows darkly tinted so I couldn't see if there was anyone inside. I watched, uncertain and afraid, as it drew up in front of me, hoping it didn't have anything to do with police or airport security. A moment of stillness, and then doors slid back and Keever Bishop and Mike Mike and two bravos swung out.

I was too amazed to move. Keever was on me in three strides, slapping my face, left and right and left again, hard blows that blinded me with blood-red shock and knocked me to my knees.

30

The two bravos hauled me to my feet and pinned my arms while Mike Mike patted me down, finding the disposable fone and a little blunt-tipped folding knife I'd filched from the life raft's emergency pack, nothing else – Alicia had refused to return the pistol and Levi's wolf claw. Keever watched with an expression of wry amusement, immaculate in a white parka with a fur-trimmed hood. Mr Snow. Always in control. Always wearing some kind of mask. Stepping forward when Mike Mike was done with me, starting in about Kamilah.

'She was shot, according to the police. Is that true? Did she die? Did you say a prayer over her body and give her a burial at sea? Have you run all the way here because you're scared about what her daddy will do to you when he finds out? Well, you don't have to worry about him any more. He claims to be an important man, an influential man, but you know what? He's actually a hollow man. A man without principles. A shonky wuss who makes promises he can't keep, who doesn't have anything like the power and influence he likes to boast about. Oh, maybe he's something in the city. But out here he's nothing. Out here, the only person you should fear is me.'

I'd learned long ago that you didn't interrupt one of Keever's monologues. When I was sure he'd finished, I said, 'The girl is alive and well and out of your reach. Back with her father, as a matter of fact.'

'You let her go?'

'I ransomed her.'

'Really. And how much did you get?'

262

'A meeting with the Honourable Deputy and the price of a ticket out of here.'

'And we thought we were dealing with some kind of criminal mastermind,' Keever told Mike Mike.

'I guess she doesn't know,' Mike Mike said.

'Of course she doesn't know,' Keever said.

His malicious delight – that wasn't a mask. That was all too real.

'Poor Austral,' he said. 'You'd been planning to escape for quite some time. Working for me, grovelling for kickbacks, saving pennies in that offshore account you thought I didn't know about. Dreaming about getting out, running all the way to New Zealand. But you didn't know that I have a piece of the people-smuggling biz, did you? You didn't know that I knew all along what you so badly wanted. That after you escaped at Charlotte Bay I knew you would be coming here. And here you are, and here I am. And I have to ask, do you think it was worth it?'

I flinched when a departing cargo drone roared low overhead, but Keever's gaze didn't waver. Fixed on me. Feeding.

'I saved Kamilah Toomy from kidnap,' I said. 'That has to count for something.'

'Don't flatter yourself. Snatching that silly little girl was only ever a sideshow to the main event.'

'Still, you went to a lot of trouble, trying to get her back after I rescued her. I guess you were planning to use her to force her father to do something for you,' I said. 'Something he didn't want to do. Something you really needed.'

I know, I know. Provoking Keever was a dumb thing to do. But at that moment I figured I didn't have anything to lose, thought that I deserved to know what had kicked off the mess I was in. And as much as I could read him, he seemed to be amused by my sass.

'When you gave up his daughter for that piddling ransom,' he said, 'didn't you think to ask the Honourable Deputy about his connection with me?'

'I told him that I knew he was involved with you. He didn't like that.'

'I bet he didn't. We had a mutually beneficial business relationship, but like his kind always do, he got too greedy. I paid him a handsome fee to stop that extradition order, and after he took the money he didn't do a thing except make all kinds of bullshit excuses about why he couldn't swing it. And then he had the barefaced audacity to try to squeeze more out of me, claiming he had worked out a new angle and this time he could definitely make the extradition go away. Thinking that I'd be so desperate I'd agree to any price. By then I'd made other plans, but I reckoned I could turn his little scam around. Have some fun with him, cause him some grief. So I said that I'd be happy to consider his offer, but he'd have to come meet me, he could use the ribbon-cutting ceremony as cover. And when the arrogant son-of-a-bitch told me he was bringing his precious darling daughter along, she would provide extra distraction for his visit, I knew I could use her to show him who was in charge. And that, my big girl, is what you fucked up.'

'What did you want him to do?'

'Do? I didn't want him to do anything. I was going to punish him for trying to fuck with me. Nobody does that and gets away with it. As you're about to find out.'

I thought of moray eels and cold pierced me through and through. Keever saw it, smiled his narrow knife-blade smile.

'You could have come with me when I got out,' he said. 'We would have had such fine fun together. But no, you had to go and fuck it up. I always wondered if you were good at anything. Now I know. Fucking things up – that's your special talent.'

Another cargo drone roared overhead, its shadow flickering over the orange tractor, over our little tableau. I didn't look up this time. I was too angry to be distracted.

'You never wanted me to come with you,' I said. 'You wanted me to confront Alberto Toomy at the ceremony. You wanted me to get into trouble so you wouldn't have to bother with me any more. You wanted to use me as a diversion while your bravos snatched that poor girl.'

'Listen to this,' Keever said to Mike Mike, still smiling that damn smile of his. 'Sounds like someone finally woke up.'

'Woke up too late,' Mike Mike said.

'I definitely see things differently now,' I told Keever. 'I see what you really are. And I also see that I was a silly little fool to get involved with you. To think we had some kind of relationship. To think it made me special.'

'The only kind of relationship we had was strictly business, and you know it,' Keever said calmly. He might as well have been talking about the weather in some other country. 'It provided me with a little amusement, and you were trying, in your clumsy way, to hustle me. You didn't manage it of course, you had to squeeze the money for your ticket out of the deadbeat Honourable Deputy instead, but as far as you were concerned that's all our little thing was about. So don't you try to make out you're any better than me. I mean, you didn't really rescue the girl, did you? You kidnapped her. You ransomed her. You used her, just like I was planning to use her.'

That stung, as the truth always does when you hear it from someone you have good reason to despise.

'What you wanted to do to her was cold, even for you,' I said. 'I've done some questionable things. Some bad things. But at least I never wanted to kidnap and kill someone's daughter because they tried to fuck me over. I mean, people have been calling me a monster all my life, because of what I am, how I was edited. But you're the real monster. Something heartless and cruel and calculating walking around in a human skin suit.'

'Haul her up,' Keever told the two bravos on either side of me. 'Hold her straight.'

They pulled me up by my arms, crucifixion style. The knife cut in my shoulder stabbed me afresh.

'Let me give you an idea of what you've got coming to you,' Keever said, and hit me in the gut with the iron heel of his palm. A hard jolting blow under my ribs, knocking all the wind from me. I was dry-heaving but air wouldn't come. If those two bravos hadn't been holding me up I would have fallen to my knees.

Keever studied me as I gasped and choked. I could barely see him because my eyes were full of freezing tears. When at last I got my breath back, I said, 'You shouldn't have done that.'

'Done what?'

All innocence now. Framed by the fur hood of his parka, his face was as blank as a skim of snow over a cold blue empty chasm.

'Shouldn't have hit me.' I coughed half a litre of snot and spit down the front of my windproof. Everything was haloed with rings of light. 'Not there. Not in the belly.'

'Strictly speaking, it was the solar plexus. And didn't I have good reason?' Keever said, appealing to Mike Mike and the pair of bravos. 'Haven't I been grievously provoked?'

I told him why not. I told him about you.

He didn't believe me at first. He said to Mike Mike, 'Can you believe this?' He said to me, 'That's a new low, even for you. Did you think I'd forgotten about the implant I bought you?'

'It didn't work.'

'You can't lie your way out of this.'

'Get me a diagnostic stick. I'll spit on it and then we'll see who's lying.'

'Maybe we should get going, boss,' Mike Mike said. 'Find some-where safe and quiet where we can sort this out.'

'Don't I pay the fuckers who run this place to look the other way?' Keever said, and studied me for a moment. After that quick moment of anger he was Mr Snow again, coolly calculating angles, saying, 'My big girl. If this is true, why didn't you tell me?'

'I didn't want you to know.'

'I suppose you were afraid I'd throw a wobbly.'

He thought that being afraid of him was a compliment.

'Who do you think it will look like?' he said. 'You or me?'

I knew then he wasn't going to kill me. Not straight away. Not until he was certain that I was pregnant. Not until after you were born. It should have been a relief, but it wasn't. I was already regretting telling him about you, didn't like to think about how it would be, growing huge with you in Keever's tender care. What he would do when you were born. To me. To you.

Maybe he saw something of that in my face, because his smile deepened. 'I was beginning to wonder if it was worth it, waiting to see if you'd manage it to make it here. Turns out I was right to hang on. Bring her along, boys. Time we were off.'

They stuffed me on the bench seat in the back of the tractor, the two bravos either side of me, Keever and Mike Mike sitting up front. As the tractor drew a wide arc away from the drone and headed out across the runway Keever told me that we would be catching a ride on a ship the next day, first to Hong Kong, and then to South Africa.

'Do you reckon South Africa will be too hot for a hairy old whelephant like you?' he said, and something roared low overhead and a shipping container slammed down a dozen metres to the left of the tractor. A tremendous noise, fragments of concrete spraying out of an expanding dust cloud, something smacking into the windscreen. The glass sagged in a shattered web and Mike Mike grabbed the yoke and pulled a hard right and we shot through the rolling dust and the container was behind us.

Keever peered through the smashed windscreen, looking up at the sky, telling Mike Mike he better get a wriggle on, the fucking thing was circling back. The tractor accelerated and swerved left, Keever turned in his seat and told me that if this was anything to do with me I was fucking dead, and another container dropped out of the sky and hit the concrete right in front of us.

We crashed into it a bare second later. The impact threw me forward and I shoulder-slammed Keever and broke his neck. Later, the prison authorities inserted a bionic spine into his brain so that he could control his wheelchair with his thoughts. When they don't switch it off and leave him helpless after he kicks off about something, that is, which apparently is a lot of the time.

Silence inside the wreck of the tractor. Sunlight slicing through settling dust. Crash bags deflating. The doors were buckled and the windows had blown out. Keever slumped in his seat, chin on his shoulder. Mike Mike was bleeding from ears and nose, gargling blood. The bravo on my left was stone cold unconscious, but the one on my right stirred when I started to scramble over him, caught at my legs, at one of my feet. I kicked out but he wouldn't let go, and when I tumbled through the window I left a boot behind.

I stood up and staggered a few steps. My shoulder was broken and my left arm hung uselessly. The tractor was crumpled against the container's black cylinder, which leaned at an angle in shattered concrete like an elf stone that had erupted from the ground. It had split along its seams and rainbow banners of spilled fabric flapped and flared in the cold wind.

As I limped past it, Mike Mike fell out of the tractor and picked himself up and started after me. Both of us hobbling along in slow motion, bleeding from various injuries. I ducked away when Mike Mike made a grab at me, and when he tried again I punched him square on his silly goatee and his legs buckled and he sat down.

'Fucking whelephant,' he said thickly, his eyes wide and white in a mask of blood.

'Yes, I am. And I kept Kamilah Toomy from you, so what does that make you?' I said, and aimed a kick at him and missed and fell over, almost passed out from the pain of my broken shoulder.

I was trying to push to my feet when a little galaxy of red stars blossomed on me, on Mike Mike, on the concrete around us. A very loud voice was saying something about surrendering. Mike Mike laced his hands on top of his head. Drones were hovering above us, silvery stars hung at different heights against the blue sky, a heli was racing low above the runway, and vehicles were pounding towards us from three different directions. My shoulder hurt like hell, something grated inside my chest with every breath, and even if I could have gotten back on my feet I was all out of road. So I sat where I was and waited for the circus to arrive.

31

Kamilah Toomy was the chief prosecution witness at my trial, but consistently refused to agree that I had ever meant her any harm. I don't know what her father made of that. He gave his evidence and answered cross-examination questions without once looking at me, and when he left most of the stringers in the courtroom followed him, but not because they wanted to ask him about the trial. He had troubles of his own. Most of the sympathy he'd gained during the kidnapping of his eldest daughter had evaporated when Keever, quadriplegic, still facing extradition to Australia, had decided to hurt his former business associate as much as possible. There wasn't enough hard evidence of their dealings – smoothing out snags in property deals, leaking confidential information about local development plans, so on – to prosecute Alberto Toomy. He'd been careful about that. But Keever's testimony, underscored by my own small contribution, destroyed his reputation. He quit as an honourable deputy after he was fired from his Shadow Cabinet post, but the scandal tainted the National Unity Party. Their candidate lost the special election to replace him, and at the next general election they were roundly defeated, reduced to a powerless rump.

There was, everyone said, change in the air.

As for me, I was sentenced to fourteen years hard labour, spent the first three in a work camp at Cape Worsley. I was working on the Trans-Antarctic Railway again, but this time I was part of the convict labour force. It wasn't so bad. I was assigned to one of the landscaping strings, the kind of work ecopoets had once done, the kind of work I had been born to do. Then the government put an end to the camps, and I did the rest of my jail time in a minimum security facility on the outskirts of O'Higgins, earning my keep in a print shop that made runabout shells. As far as I was concerned, it wasn't any kind of improvement.

The police found the body of that crazy old woman, Mayra Iturriaga, buried in a snowdrift near the refuge south of Wolseley Buttress. She had been shot in the back of the head, and Mike Mike and the surviving members of his crew each had twenty years added to their sentences for that. Lola Contreras was given five years hard time for her part in Keever Bishop's plot to kidnap Kamilah Toomy, reduced to just six months because she turned state witness against him. What happened to her after she was released I neither know nor care.

My friends Paz Sandoval and Sage Ibarra were also arrested, and although they were released without charge they were promptly cashiered from the prison service. Paz wrote me several times after I was sentenced. She'd lost contact with Sage after Sage signed up as a deckhand on a North Korean deep sea trawler, and after trying and failing to make a go of a private detective business in Esperanza moved to Argentina – by then, travel restrictions for huskies had been lifted. Last I heard, she was a park ranger in the Staten Island Reserve, had married a husky woman name of Reya, and had two kids, both of them healthy husky girls.

On her eighteenth birthday, Kamilah Toomy inherited a trust fund set up by her mother. She studied architecture in Chile and returned to the peninsula and set up her own practice. I don't know if she followed that story of hers to the end, don't know what happened to Princess Isander and Tantris. In one of the versions of the old tale on which it was based, Tantris married another woman and went to live in the duchy of his wife's family, on the west coast of Palmis. Some years later he was mortally wounded in a battle with sea raiders, and he dispatched a messenger on a swift ship, asking Isander to come and tend to him. The ship was supposed to rig a white sail if Isander was on board when it returned, and a black sail if she wasn't, but when it appeared at the horizon with a white sail, Tantris's jealous wife told him the opposite. He died just before Isander made landfall, and soon afterwards she died too, of heartbreak. The jealous wife buried her outside the wall of the graveyard where Tantris was interred, but according to the story a white rose grew from Isander's grave and from Tantris's a green briar, and they met above the graveyard wall and twined in a true lovers' knot, the white rose and the briar.

It's a nice enough ending, I guess, even though the two of them had to die before they could find peace together. I don't yet know how my story will end, but I don't suppose it'll be anything like as neat as that.

A month ago, seven years into my sentence, I was told that I was being released on account of good behaviour and successful completion of my rehabilitation programme. Also, I suspect, because of more kind words from Kamilah Toomy. After I had absorbed the news, I began to make this story in memory of you.

I lost you when you were barely three months old. A miscarriage while I was recovering from my injuries in prison hospital. A routine check-up showed that there was no fetal heartbeat. Two days later a small operation removed you from my body.

The doctors wouldn't tell me if your death had been caused by a fatal incompatibility between husky and mundane genes, or by trauma from the crash of the tractor, the hardship of the trek, Keever's sucker punch. Miscarriages are still quite common was all they said. And, don't think of it as losing a child, it was just an embryo that failed to progress. But I know that you were female, that you would have been a girl child. A daughter.

I also know that had you lived I would have been judged unfit to be a mother on account of serving a major stretch, and the authorities would have taken you from me and raised you in an orphanage or with a foster family, would have forbidden me to have any contact with you. Call me selfish, but I think that knowing you were alive but never having any news of you, knowing that it was impossible to ever meet or see you but always hoping that one day it might be otherwise, would have been a crueller punishment. The sting of a death recedes into the past, but hope claws us afresh each and every day. Even so, I like to believe that for your sake I could have endured it.

As it is, when I lost you I felt that I'd also lost every chance of a better, brighter future. One of the nurses, meaning well, told me that it was my job to live on. And I have, hard though it often has been. I passed through the usual stations of grief, had to correct several scunners who called me out over you, was twice thrown in the hole for it and once was beaten so severely I ended up back in hospital. And believed that I deserved every moment of punishment.

One day, it was about eighteen months later, a cold spring day early in November, I was riding back to camp on a flatbed truck with the rest of my string, all of us chained together, sprawling or sitting among our gear, when we passed the local elf stone. It was a skinny pillar high on the prow of a steep-sided ridge, standing small and sharp against the darkening sky, overlooking the wide curve the railway and the service road makes there.

Everyone on the peninsula knows that elf stones were created by some old geezer back in the early days of settlement, a mad art project or some kind of elaborate prank. And everyone knows that the stories about elves and their stones were borrowed from Icelandic folklore about the Huldufólk. The hidden people. But none of that matters. Those stones, those stories, help to humanise our tough bleak land, help us believe that it's possible to make our lives here, and that's why we respect them, why the railway bent around that ridge.

There was nothing special about that particular day. We'd spent the shift spraying grass seed and fertiliser across a long stretch of geotextile slope protection, I was bone-tired, sticky with gunk that had blown back on the constant wind, had passed the spot where the elf stone stood (it's called *The Place Where The Wind Sings Itself To Sleep*) a dozen times before. But in that moment it struck me that the way the railway bent around that damn stone was exactly like the way you had shaped my life. And it was then that I knew that you always would be a part of what I was, a hard fact I couldn't shift or erase, and I felt, I don't know what to call it, it wasn't exactly relief or comfort, but maybe it was a kind of acceptance. And maybe that moment was the seed from which this account grew. This story of how you came into the world and left it so early, as true as I could make it, as true as I remember. The memorial I wasn't able to give you when you passed. A confession made without hope or expectation of forgiveness.

As for me, I've long ago given up my stupid idea of finding some kind of nirvana on the Wheel. When they hand me my papers and the prison gate slams shut behind me I'm heading south again.

Alicia Whangapirita was interrogated by the police after I was arrested, but she stuck to the story that I'd stolen the cargo drone and hacked the runabout and the droids, and they didn't have enough evidence to charge her with aiding and abetting. She also claimed that she didn't have anything to do with hijacking the cargo drone which had dropped its load with pinpoint precision, saving me from Keever. I reckon she was telling the truth. Someone else had been watching over me. The same person who'd taken down Mike Mike's drone and left that hare outside the shelter.

One day, maybe, I'll find out who it was. Like I've already said, I believe that my grandmother died soon after she escaped the government's attempt to round up the free ecopoets, if only because it's too cruel to think that she survived but never ever tried to reach out to her son, or to Mama, or to me. But it's possible that her legacy somehow endures.

I've thought a lot about the story I told Levi. How his mother might have been part of a group of ecopoets living wild and free in the far south, growing crops in greenhouses buried under the ice, catching fish, hunting seals, pretending to be half-and-halfs when they visit the settlements and towns of the north, monitoring the old places they were forced to abandon, keeping watch for stray huskies they could recruit. How someone like that might have decided to help me after I'd been spotted sheltering in that refuge, so on. I can't see why it can't be true, still wonder if Levi ever got up the courage to leave the True Citizens and set out to search for his real family.

Call me a crazy old romantic, but I'm heading south to look for him, for them. If I fail, if I can't find any free ecopoets out there, maybe I'll end up like Agustyn Dos Santos Pistario, living out the rest of my life in splendid solitude on some cold and otherwise uninhabited shore, but however it pans out I think I'll be content. I was made for the south, after all. And as someone else in some other story once said, there's too much civilisation around here for my taste.

One last story. One last last story. This one from the time when Mama and me were travelling south after our escape from Deception Island. A nation of two, living free and easy in the forests and meadows of Antarctica.

Perhaps you remember that after we had been given a ride to Flandres Bay we crossed from the west coast to the east. Skiing over the white breast of the Forbidden Plateau, descending towards Crane Bay. It was while we were making that descent that I came across a small bird lying under a crackling sheet of frost. Frozen hard. Eyes white stones. I wanted to bury it, but my mother took it from me and briefly studied it, said that it was a rufous-collared sparrow and told me to stow it in the inside pocket of my insulated jacket.

'You'll see,' she said, when I asked why. 'A little bit of ecopoet magic.'

So I carried the bird as she asked, and as we went on a cold star of meltwater grew at my breast and warmed and dried. The sun circled behind us, dipping towards the horizon, and we unclipped our skis and hiked down a steep defile beside a tumble of ice, leaving the high country behind, making camp in a hanging valley where a cushion heath spread among stones dappled with yellow lichen. Mama was stirring soup over a little fire when I felt something twitch at my breast. It was as if a second heart had started to beat, quicker and lighter than my own.

The bird had woken up. As I cupped it in my hand, Mama told me that this small magic was my grandmother's doing. Years back Isabella had edited several species of songbirds so that they could survive freezing, released them into the wild to live and flourish as best they could. This one had probably lost its way and fallen and frozen through and through, but the warmth of my body had revived it.

The dry crispness of its feathers, the scratch of its tiny claws on my skin, its bright black eyes. White bars on wings that fluttered ever more strongly against my fingers.

Mama didn't need to tell me what I had to do.

We walked up a slant of stone, Mama and me, and at the lip, high above the milky eye of a meltwater lake, I opened my hands. The bird stood on my palm for a moment, then gathered itself and launched into the air, and with a swift eager bobbing flight dwindled away into the luminous sky of austral summer's midnight.

Acknowledgements

Some novels have especially long periods of inception before they begin to grow and flower. The seed for this one was planted way back in May 1997, at a seminar about science and science fiction held in the Abisko research station above the Arctic Circle in Sweden, and particularly during a train ride that descended from the snow-bound Arctic plateau through forested fjords to the Norwegian coast. My thanks to John L. Casti and Anders Karlqvist for inviting me to participate, and the Swedish Council for Planning and Coordination of Research for financial support.

Oliver Morton coined Project LUCI's name in a tweet; I'm grateful for his permission to use it here. His book *The Planet Remade: How Geoengineering Could Change the World* hugely informed my thinking about the geopolitics of big fixes for the planet's climate.

Thanks also to my agent Simon Kavanagh for firefighting and help in giving *Austral* shape and form, and to Marcus Gipps and Craig Leyenaar for editorial support. Stephen Baxter read an early draft of the book and made many useful suggestions, and he and Alastair Reynolds read the final draft and flagged up further crucial fixes. My gratitude to them both for their timely help. Thanks also to Pat Cadigan, Judith and John Clute, Jo Fletcher, Barry and Judith Forshaw, William Gibson, Josephine Hawtrey-Woore, Simon Hawtrey-Woore, Stephen Jones, Sherif Mehmet, Kim Newman, Josette Reynolds, Russell Schechter, Jack Womack, and to the staff of the Marie Curie Hospice, Hampstead.

ABOUT GOLLANCZ

Gollancz is the oldest SF publishing imprint in the world. Since being founded in 1927 Gollancz has continued to publish a focused selection of bestselling and award-winning authors. The front-list includes **Ben Aaronovitch**, **Joe Abercrombie**, **Charlaine Harris**, **Joanne Harris**, **Joe Hill**, **Alastair Reynolds**, **Patrick Rothfuss**, **Nalini Singh** and **Brandon Sanderson**.

As one of the largest Science Fiction and Fantasy imprints in the UK it is no surprise we have one of the most extensive backlists in the world. Find high-quality SF on Gateway written by such authors as **Philip K. Dick**, **Ursula Le Guin**, **Connie Willis**, **Sir Arthur C. Clarke**, **Pat Cadigan**, **Michael Moorcock** and **George R.R. Martin**.

We also have a strand of publishing in translation, which includes French, Polish and Russian authors. Gollancz is home to more award-winning authors than any other imprint, with names including **Aliette de Bodard**, **M. John Harrison**, **Paul McAuley**, **Sarah Pinborough**, **Pierre Pevel**, **Justina Robson** and many more.

The SF Gateway
More than 3,000 classic, rare and previously
out-of-print SF novels at your fingertips.
www.sfgateway.com

The Gollancz Blog
Bringing you news from our worlds to yours. Stories,
interviews, articles and exclusive extracts just for you!
www.gollancz.co.uk

GOLLANCZ
LONDON